GLORY'S WAR

Tor books by Alfred Coppel

Glory
Glory's War

GLORY'S WAR

BOOK TWO OF THE GOLDENWING CYCLE

ALFRED COPPEL

A TOM DOHERTY ASSOCIATES BOOK
NEW YORK

TOR

GLORY'S WAR

Copyright © 1995 by Alfred Coppel

All rights reserved, including the right to reproduce this book, or portions thereof, in any form.

Edited by David G. Hartwell

This book is printed on acid-free paper.

A Tor Book
Published by Tom Doherty Associates, Inc.
175 Fifth Avenue
New York, N.Y. 10010

Tor® is a registered trademark of Tom Doherty Associates, Inc.

ISBN: 0-312-85471-4

First edition: April 1995

Printed in the United States of America

0 9 8 6 5 4 3 2 1

For Liz: Thanks for "the willing suspension of disbelief."

BOOK ONE

1

BRONI

Descending at an acute angle to the ecliptic plane of Ross 248, the Goldenwing *Gloria Coelis* sails with courses and skys'ls backed to the near sun's light, slowing and dropping delta-V. Within a month of ship's time, *Glory* will assume orbit around the Accursed Twin—known to Wired Starmen as Ross 248 Beta. *Glory* is traveling at eighteen percent of the speed of light, the energy imparted to her by the pressure of tachyons on her hectares of skylar dissipating. On Christa McAuliffe, *Glory*'s last port of call, 6.9 years have passed since *Glory*'s departure. The red shift behind her and the blue shift ahead are scarcely discernible after a voyage of eight months uptime.

In a ship's day *Glory* will begin encountering the edge of the Rings. These are the multiple asteroid belts that contain most of the mass in the Ross 248 system.

In addition to the Rings, there is a double planet system consisting of a pair of terrequivalent worlds, R248 Alpha and R248 Beta, These orbit a point 160,000,000 kilometers from Ross 248. Together, Alpha and Beta orbit the primary once each 1.33 Earth standard years.

Since Goldenwing syndics seldom feel themselves bound by the protocols of the Survey Service, the Ross twins were christened Nineveh and Nimrud by the quixotic Starmen of the colonizing Goldenwing, *Nostromo,* nine hundred Earth standard years ago. Alpha is sometimes listed in the starcharts as Blessed, Beta as Accursed.

Glory's business is with the Accursed Twin.

*

Broni Ehrengraf has the watch. She is junior syndic aboard *Glory*, an astroprogrammer in training. This is her first experience conning the ship in a deepening gravity well and she imagines that she is unsupervised. She is not. From his quarters, and Wired to *Glory*'s mainframe, Duncan Kr, the Master and Commander, is aware of every move Broni makes. He is pleased with her performance.

Dietr Krieg, *Glory*'s Cybersurgeon and the man who gave Broni her artificial heart as well as her Starman's drogue socket, is also monitoring her from the medical terminal in his quarters, a kilometer and a half from the bridge.

Both Captain and Cybersurgeon are connected by drogues to the ship's computer. As Broni receives her gigabits of information from the sensors scattered throughout the vast sailplan, Duncan and Dietr receive them too. The girl is a talented addition to *Glory*'s crew, but space is an unforgiving environment and Duncan and Dietr have been in space for more uptime years than Broni has been alive.

Their ship is huge and fragile. It almost seems to have been built on the skeleton of a vast bird or insect. Its body is a tubular construct a kilometer broad and twenty kilometers long. The hull walls and all the interior partitions of a Goldenwing are made of monomolecular filament woven into a silvery green cloth of enormous strength. Nine masts carry her vast spread of golden sails. As she catches the light of the Ross sun, her sails flash and reflect the M6 star she is approaching. Her rigging, spun of polyethylene line as thin as a human hair and stronger than steel, glitters with St. Elmo's fire and the crackling release of static charges built up in the maze by *Glory*'s swift passage through the interstellar medium.

Broni has been aboard *Glory* for almost a standard year. Though she came from a backward planet, her skills are exceptional. Her empathic abilities are of a quality to make her a superb syndic. Planet Voerster, Broni's homeworld, was rich in Talent, Duncan thinks sadly, remembering.

Broni has eagerly accepted the rather outré (she thinks) ways of the Wired Starmen. She lies naked in the gel within her pod. The thick cable from the drogue socketed in her skull to the interface panel floats in the near-zero gravity. Golden hair forms a halo around Broni's pretty face.

While Wired to the ship's mainframe a syndic very nearly *becomes* the ship, and Broni can feel the tingling impact of the tachyons that penetrate everything but skylar. Each subatomic particle had its origin in the White Hole at the galaxy's center and has been traveling for millennia to reach the space surrounding Ross 248. When she is Wired, Broni feels each particle as it penetrates her naked body. The sensation is sublime, electric.

The ship, with her steep orientation to the plane of R248's ecliptic, is dropping like a stooping hawk. Or like the Glory of Heaven for which she is named, thinks Broni. The girl, a Voertrekker from Planet Voerster, has had much religious training. Like much aimed at the young, religion has not been particularly effective with Broni. She is the product of the aristocracy of a backward planet. Her birth insulated her from religious dogmas, her planetary heritage has limited her scientific knowledge. The latter is being corrected by her fellow syndics. Ironically, the former has no advocate aboard the *Gloria Coelis*.

I am like Mira, Broni thinks with childish satisfaction. An animal in my proper habitat—space. Mira is the eldest of a family of cats who have been ''enhanced'' by Dietr Krieg as an experimental amusement. They roam the ship, connected to the mainframe's signals by the hair-thin antennae that protrude from their small, furry skulls. The most sensitive Talents aboard, Duncan and Anya Amaya, can almost exchange thoughts with them.

Right now Broni can sense Mira as she leaps easily from bulkhead to bulkhead in the near-zero gravity. She is seeking Duncan, as she often does. She has imprinted on the commander. ''How female,'' the Cybersurgeon says. But the Master and Commander has that effect on the female gender.

Broni can also receive low-level thought impressions from the sail monkeys who live on deck and in the rig. The monkeys are cyborgs made long ago on the Mother World. Their purpose is to aid men in sailing ships whose sailplans spread across kilometers of space. Their agility is enormous, their sailing skills invaluable. Without them there would be no controlling the vast skylar wings of *Glory* and her sisters.

But soon the rig will be clear of monkeys. It is standard procedure aboard *Glory* to retire them to the Monkey House for feeding, refitting and recharging while in a gravity well. The near presence of a star disorients them. No one has yet discovered why.

Broni's untrained empathic Talent detects the emotional sendings of her shipmates, all save Duncan, who is difficult to read.

Anya Amaya, the Sailing Master, and Damon Ng, the young Rigger, are making love in Anya's quarters. Broni allows her attention to dwell on them longer than strictly necessary. Broni is seventeen Earth Standard and the product of a sexually repressed society. The uninhibited ways of the Goldenwing syndics sometimes astonish and embarrass her. But they fascinate her as well.

Anya, who enjoys Wired sex, detects her attention and idly suggests that she seek elsewhere for amusement. Broni flushes. The Wired tingle of tachyons on her nubile breasts makes her nipples rise. She senses that Anya Amaya is laughing at her.

Broni directs her attention outward from the ship. Duncan is in the background, and she relishes his presence. Impressions come through the drogue in a torrent. In this sector of the Orion Spiral Arm the stars are widely spaced, but hot and bright. Broni can feel the heat of their nuclear fires. *Glory* senses them and brings them to the bridge for Broni to experience. She conns the ship, feels the fires, hears what her cousin, the Astronomer Select of Voerster, called the Music of the Spheres.

Duncan is smiling at that. He has opened himself to Broni, allowed her a glimpse of his shadowy, enigmatic, melancholy depths.

In confusion, Broni withdraws from the depth of the man, unsure of her feelings for him. *Glory* brings her instead Dietr Krieg, the oldest, and most self-absorbed, of the syndics. He is, as it so often happens, immersed in one of his thousands of cybersurgical programs. Broni senses blood and life pulses. She even detects a suggestion of the program she underwent when her damaged heart was replaced by Dietr while *Glory* was still in orbit around Planet Voerster.

On Voerster she was dying. Aboard the Goldenwing she can live— Forever? Of course, not that long. It is only the planetbound who think Wired Starmen immortal. Einsteinian time dilation informs the syndic that they live only a normal span of years, but they live much of it at near the speed of light.

On Voerster, the family she knew are now ancestors. It gives the girl a strange, uneasy feeling. But Amaya has explained that these emotional anomalies are a way of life among the men and women who crew Goldenwings.

Broni knows that she has chosen a life of adventure, far from the limitations of life on a colonial world. Her choice brought pain and loss to herself and to her mother, the fabulous Eliana. Broni Ehrengraf Voerster has abandoned all that she knew. But as she turns her attention outward, far beyond the ship, to the stars, she knows that adventure is her immortality. And her perceptions will grow as her skills increase.

She senses the trilling of *Glory*'s family of cats, Mira's clones and offspring. They are trailing after Mira as she makes her way through the fabric plena that connect the myriad sections of *Glory*'s hull. Broni becomes aware that Buele, the idiot savant who came aboard with her, is following the kittens. Buele's Talent, according to the older syndics, is enormous. Buele is an empathic prodigy. Broni smiles vacantly within the pod. Who could have guessed that Buele was so grand while he was still potboy to her old cousin Osbertus, the Astronomer Select of Voerster?

But Buele, like everyone else, has his failures. For weeks he has been trying to communicate telepathically with the cats. He is trying now. And failing. The cats receive him but are simply not interested.

Duncan's command to Buele comes through *Glory*'s computer loud and clear: "Let them be, Buele."

Broni senses the sending that prompted Duncan's admonition. It came from Mira and she wants her kittens left alone, untroubled by human curiosity. Duncan's sending discloses his location. He is in the uppermost covered deck, called the carapace, a large open space enclosed with a curving transparency abaft a foremast. It is a favorite place to Duncan. He often spends hours floating in the nearly null gravity, watching the changing patterns of *Glory*'s rig and the distant stars beyond.

Broni turns and quivers in the gel. Confused images impinge upon her vulnerable mind. Her breasts feel tight, her vagina moist. It is a blatantly sexual response to the force of the Master and Commander's personality, powerfully enhanced by the computer link.

She experiences his deep melancholy and longs to comfort him. But she cannot. Duncan is grieving. He is remembering Eliana Ehrengraf Voerster, Broni's mother, whom neither she nor he will ever see again.

Broni suppresses her adolescent longing for the captain. As from a great distance, Anya Amaya sends approval. Syndics have peculiar moral codes. Broni is learning that whatever might endanger *Glory* is tabu. The *only* tabu.

With no help whatever from the computer Broni can hear—and feel—the soft susurration of her prosthetic heart. It is powered by a nuclear microdot. If she stays in the microgravity aboard the ship, the heart can keep her alive indefinitely. Gravity can kill her.

Enhanced, she can hear the blood pumping through her body, the oily sounds of her movements within the gel. Her soft golden hair makes a living sound as it haloes her face.

But most of all Broni hears the ship. The Goldenwing sings as she sails the tachyon trades spiraling out from the unimaginably distant galactic center. It is a song that has enraptured Broni Ehrengraf from the first moment she was Wired.

There is a saying among Starmen: "Who has heard a Goldenwing's music never wearies of it."

Each standard century there are fewer Goldenwings in the

sky. There is a silent race afoot throughout the Near Stars. The colonial worlds are straining to build faster-than-light starships before the last Goldenwing is lost.

It may happen. But it is far from certain.

2

A MINOR BATTLE IN AN UNIMPORTANT PLACE

On R5/1557, a planetesimal classified by Intelligence as "lightly held," the Task Commander of Operation Skybolt lay pinned down and wounded under the wreckage of a Nimmie main battle tank.

Andrey Alexandrovich Volkov, a Starshiy Leytenant in the Territorial Guard of Ararat, was bitterly angry at the poor quality of the intelligence he had been given. Most of the unit Andrey led was native to Ullah's Vista, the Volkov estate in southern Ararat. Andrey, himself, had left the estate only to attend University in Nostromograd and for military training in Kiev. His soldiers were all young people he knew well, and because the Ephors of Nineveh were arrogant fools, they were all—himself included—going to die on this worthless rock.

Andrey had not been overjoyed at the necessity of becoming a soldier, but each generation of Ninevite landholders had taken the military path for four hundred years. Every new decade seemed to bring another Recurrence—the Ninevite way of referring to the war against the Accursed Twin. For Andrey Volkov and his people it appeared that this Recurrence would be the last.

They had been landed by shuttle from the battle cruiser *Potemkin* with instructions to clear the Nimrudites from R5/1557 and stand by to be retrieved.

But in the basaltic ravine where his company had first deployed, the unit had been ambushed by a company of armored crawlers supported by a pair of battle tanks. No soldier of the Territorial Guard had ever encountered a main battle tank, and Andrey had been assured by the Assault Officer aboard *Potemkin* that the Nimmies were incapable of deploying such formidable vehicles on the tiny planetesimals of the Rings. The Assault Officer had been wrong.

The battle—a skirmish, actually—had lasted only half an hour. Eighteen of Andrey's thirty soldiers had been killed in the first ten minutes. Andrey had been wounded and the survivors of the Task Group had been scattered. Communication was difficult. Ninevite frequencies were jammed.

The fight had been lost almost before it had begun. Andrey Volkov's Slavic fatalism was deeply engaged, but the terrible waste of it all lingered like a bitter taste in his mouth.

In the last Nimmie attack, the company medic, a boy named Pavel Borovik, who had once dreamed of becoming a Sharia priest, had been cooked by a laser fired at close range by one of the main battle tanks. Andrey, dismayed and enraged, and at great risk to himself, had placed a satchel charge under the armored behemoth and detonated it. Moist air and vaporized blood had exploded into space as the tank ground to a halt. But there was still another on the ridge, and Andrey's own wounds were draining away his strength.

There were six wounded troopers sheltering behind basalt boulders within a dozen meters of Andrey and the tank he had destroyed. Like all the Ninevite breed, the boys and girls from Ullah's Vista were brave and stoic. *And stupid,* Andrey thought bitterly. *Why have we been doing this for the last four hundred years?*

The troopers were doing their best to die quietly, in the disciplined manner recommended by homebound urban apparatchiks, who did *their* military service by marching in parades in Saint Petersburg.

Despite the minus 184 degree Celsius temperature on the surface of the planetesimal, Andrey was bathed in sweat. Ninevite armor was infamous for poor moisture management. In training this was an inconvenience. In combat it was deadly.

His helmet-visor had fogged and the computer in the backpack had misinterpreted the low light level as a sign of planetary nightfall, causing the shoulder lights to turn on. This had drawn a veritable rain of missiles and laze bolts from the Nimrudites on the high ground. In desperation, Andrey had powered-down the computer, making the fighting devices attached to his armor useless. But it was too late. The mishap had resulted in the deaths of Leytenant Orgonev, Troopers Rokossovsky and Temko, and Electronic Specialist Greshkin, a young man Andrey's age whom he had known all his life.

Andrey had smashed the shoulder lights with the pommel of his pistol and now had only the strong zodiacal light of the Rings to see by. Everyone fought bravely, as befitted men and women of the First Aliyah, but bravely or not, they were dead or dying and they would never return to the grasslands of green Ararat.

The Nimmie tank seemed light for its bulk. *Which meant,* Andrey thought, *that still again Nineveh had begun the Recurrence with inadequate technology and faulty intelligence.* The academicians of Saint Petersburg had assured the military Ephors that the people of the Accursed Twin were still years from discovering the super-secret techniques of nullgrav technology. But Andrey could move the monstrous wreck under which he sheltered with one hand. Another supposed military monopoly had turned out to be no monopoly at all. In fact, the assumed superiority of Ninevite science was now gravely in doubt. No spacecraft on Nineveh had ever been able to lift into space a machine as massive as the tank under which Andrey lay sweating and bleeding.

The attack had been a fiasco from the outset. Intelligence had assured the Assault Officer on *Potemkin* that the planetesimal was held by a single understrength infantry platoon. No heavy armor or artillery. Light vehicles only.

Potemkin had landed Operation Skybolt with no attempt at concealment. *Like an exercise on the shores of Ararat,* Andrey thought. *Like a war game in which the dead rise and hold critiques of tactics.*

Actually the skirmish had been lost before *Potemkin* disappeared sunward. Now, two hours later, most of the assault force lay burned, broken and desiccating on the frozen mare beyond the near horizon.

The objective, a laser artillery projector beyond the saw-tooth ridge just ahead, was unattainable now. Had always been unattainable given the power deployed. The Task Force, Andrey Volkov's first independent command, was finished. Andrey Volkov accepted the unpleasant fact that he and his soldiers were going to end their lives here on this lump of rock in the Fifth Ring.

Andrey was a young man, and the idea of an untimely death made him sick to his stomach. Oleg Yurieyev, the senior noncom of the troop, had also been with Andrey since Classification Training. Andrey had watched him die in agony, his blood boiling away inside his superheated armor. *That was not supposed to happen,* Andrey thought. The force had been assured that the stories about obsolete equipment and weapons was Nimrudite propaganda. It now appeared it was not.

Enemy technology was conceded to be advanced. But among the Territorials, everyone was sure that one soldier from South Ararat was worth five Ninevites from the North. And one Ninevite from anywhere was worth ten of the ancient enemy. In every Recurrence of the war, it had been so. But no longer. The Nimmies were learning to fight.

A man needed more than propaganda out here in the Rings, Andrey thought bitterly. The damned Board of Ephors need not have deceived us quite so completely.

He moved a cramped leg and set the battle tank rocking. If the damage he had inflicted finally disabled the nullgrav generator in the wreckage above, the tank would sink and crush him. *Not a pleasant prospect,* Andrey thought. So much for heroics. He inched closer to the space between an unseated tread and the rock overhang that barely sheltered the remnant of his force.

Somewhere on the ridge a motion sensor pinged and a concussion rocket blazed down from above, soundlessly spewing fire and sparks as it struck the rocks a dozen meters from where Andrey sheltered. Wonder of wonders, it failed to explode. Instead it spun off like a child's pinwheel against the black sky filled with jagged points of reflected sunlight. The warhead detonated soundlessly fifty meters behind and above the Ninevites with the usual deadly sketch of a null-gravity explosion. Particles of metal clattered against Andrey's armor.

He pressed his tongue against the communicator switch inside his helmet. "Task group report," he breathed.

It was fully fifteen seconds before anyone responded. The replies, when they came, were not reassuring. Only five troopers checked in. Five left out of a company strength of thirty. The mission had turned into a catastrophe.

The last to call in was Maida Ulanova, the peasant girl from north of Nostromograd. She sounded faint and distant.

"What is your condition, Maida?" he asked.

"I have been hit, Your Honor."

"How badly?"

"It doesn't matter, Your Honor."

Andrey suspected that Maida's response was the result of the conditioning the medical staff insisted on giving the enlisted ranks along with the G-resistant drugs.

As each generation of Ninevites faced its own reprise of the War of the Twin Planets, the ruling bodies relied more and more on behavior modification to keep troops in the field. One result of the conditioning was a reinforcement of the natural stoicism of the Russian peasant stock from which most of the population of Nineveh was descended. The country folk had a saying on Nineveh: "Life is hard, but soon you die." The First Aliyah did not produce complainers.

The response came from far back along the genetic line, from the lands between the Caspian and the Black seas of the Mother World. The Jihad had killed millions there in its time. Fatalism had been the only response. And fleeing the slaughter, the colonists of the Goldenwing *Nostromo* had brought their fatalism with them.

"Damn it, tell me, how badly are you hit, Maida?" Andrey demanded.

"I am going to die, Your Honor. Pray for me."

"Maida." But what should he tell her? She might be lying

out there on the flank with an arm or a leg burned away. His own sister, Ekaterina, had been out here once, but Kat was no peasant girl. She was *boyar*. She knew how to fight. How to survive.

"Tell my family, Your Honor. Please."

"I will. Go gently, *dvayurni brat*." The Old Russian for "cousin" was a term of endearment among the people of South Ararat.

Silence.

Four troopers left. Pinned down on this Godforsaken piece of stone fifty million kilometers from the second Volga, ten light-years from the first.

So very far from the beloved grasslands of Ararat, from the gemlike golden dome of Mornay Mosque. From the blue waters of the Sea of Aralsk. So far from home.

Andrey raised his eyes to the starry sky. One could actually see the relative motions of the nearby planetesimals and cosmic debris. The red sun was hidden from view by the bulk of the tiny world on which the troop was dying.

Andrey felt a great anger and frustration. His troop had been landed here with orders to occupy and pacify the planetesimal. No explanation about why the place was of value, or even of interest. The Nimmies had it. That was reason enough to fight and die for it.

The enemy had been present *in force*. Andrey suspected battalion strength at least. The Ninevite force had never had a chance. The Nimmies had lain quietly as the *Potemkin* dropped the assault force in nullgrav harnesses and veered away in the direction of the next target body in the Ring. That was *Potemkin*'s mission. Find and attack Nimrudite bases in the Fifth Ring, which the Ephors considered Ninevite territory.

"Troopers," Andrey said into his radio. "Form on me." *The fact is,* he thought bitterly, *that I am not a soldier.* A half year of training at the Officer School and some stirring speeches by the Military Ephors did not convert a wheat farmer into a soldier. The people of the Accursed Twin appeared to have learned to handle things more efficiently. Were they actually about to win the long war? It did not seem possible. The thought of Nimrudites overrunning and claiming the grass-lands of South Ararat was almost more than he could bear.

Firing flashed on his left. Molten droplets of basaltic rock scattered from the pits burned into the ground by the enemy lasers. Andrey lowered his night vision glasses to inspect the ridge ahead. Heat radiated from at least four armored crawlers. *One for each of us,* he thought. He had not expected quite so neat a balance of forces.

"Get ready," he said.

Through the hiss of enemy jamming, he heard his people respond with clicks as they had been taught.

We must not only be fatalistic, he thought. *We must be stark mad.* "Forward," he ordered. He left the shelter of the de-stroyed tank and began to crawl up the slope. The ridgeline sparkled with fire. Andrey felt a ricocheting hit on his armor. The heat of it burned his arm.

Oh, Kat, he thought. *Was it like this for you?* Worse, he was sure. The bastards burned an arm and leg off. But she survived. She completed her mission and survived. Kat was like that. Even now she must be on the verandah at Ullah's Vista, watch-ing the rose-colored sun set into the Gulf of Aralsk. He felt an overwhelming sense of loss and sadness, knowing that he would never see his beloved sister or his home again.

The Nimmies on the ridge had the range now and the fire from their armored vehicles was unceasing. Andrey could not actually hear the detonation of the shells as they struck the black ground nearby, but he could feel the deep concussions through his armor. The explosions were white tinged with blue and superheated. The bastards had spent the last Interval as they had every Interval before it—creating ever more hellish weapons with which to attack the faithful—

The faithful. Now why had he thought of the Sharia that way just now? It was a conventional wisdom among Andrey's and Kat's fashionable friends that the War of the Twin Planets was about anything but religion. Even Peter Mornay, the holy Frenchman, new Metropolitan and friend of Andrey's youth, who was the example always held up to the Volkov siblings, would have said the war was really a *philosophical difference* between Sharia Christians and Sunni Muslims. One did not fight holy wars about philosophical differences, did one? Surely that sort of jihad was something the *Nostromo* colonists had left behind, light-years behind and long, long ago.

Yet I thought of us, the soldiers of Nineveh, as the faithful, Andrey thought. *How very odd. Even a bit frightening. Does some deep sense warn me that this close to death it is best not to take chances with the Universal?*

It might be, thought Andrey, *that his father, the twentieth Gospodin of Ullah's Vista, and the old Metropolitan Galen Mornay, had been right, after all, when they declared that those born Sharia Christians always die in the faith.*

Well, no matter now. The certainty was that Operation Skybolt was finished.

Oh, Kat, ask the God of our Fathers to let me die well.

Andrey raised his laze and fired at the armor on the ridge. He was gratified by the sight of a soundless explosion, fragments flying high into the black sky before spinning back in a long, low-gravity fall. Then the crawlers opened up again and the trooper on Andrey's right vanished into a ball of fragments and flame. Watching, Andrey savagely suppressed an urge to vomit into his suit.

There was one more thing left to do. *Potemkin* must be warned not to return for the attack force. She could be overwhelmed, captured or destroyed. The loss of a spaceship would be a terrible blow to the armed forces of Nineveh.

Andrey changed frequencies and tongued his microphone.

"Potemkin this is Skybolt. Do you hear me?"

There was no immediate reply. He had no idea how far to sunward the assault ship had moved to await the results of the battle.

"Potemkin, the attack has failed. There are only three of us left. Do you read me, Potemkin?"

The Nimmies on the ridge read the message well enough. They burst into another storm of laser and missile fire.

Andrey tried to dig into the rocky soil. He put his head down and waited for five minutes before transmitting again.

"We are finished, Potemkin. Do not come back for us. Do not come back for Skybolt, I say."

On the ridge crawlers separated and started down the hill to flank Andrey's position. *Textbook tactics,* he thought. Perhaps the Nimmies are really no better at this than we are. We shall see. He raised his laze and fired at the crawler on his right. The coherent light reddened the steel of the crawler's flank but did not penetrate it.

It is over now, Andrey thought. *Over.* He raised his eyes skyward, toward the stars dimmed by the dust and debris of the Rings.

What he saw made the breath catch in his throat. The image lasted for only a moment but as it moved across the sky it was blue shifted, then dopplering to red.

The Nimmies saw it, too. They stopped firing. They stopped advancing on his position.

It was a golden apparition. A thing shaped like a diamantine moth or butterfly, though with far too many wings, and all of them gleaming, golden mirrors.

It was impossible to guess how large it might be. There was nothing against which to scale it. But from wingtip to wingtip it stretched half across the meager sky of the black planetesimal over which he and the Nimmies were contesting.

Of one thing he was certain. It was an artifact. An artifact of such stunning, heart-rending beauty that his breath caught in his throat. Vast golden wings on a long and slender body and the whole glistening with threadlike lines of light that haloed the light of the Ross sun.

It appeared and vanished in a heartbeat, traveling at a rate of speed that seemed magical. Behind, it left a wake of sparkling light that lasted only for a moment and then dissolved into darkness.

A Goldenwing, thought Andrey, *a ship of myth.* No, that was not right. Goldenwings were real enough. It was a Goldenwing that brought Andrey's people to Nineveh, another that brought the Nimmies to the Accursed Twin. He wondered, as no modern man normally would, if the beautiful craft had come to take him and his fellow Sharia Christians to Paradise.

Traveling still at what was probably only a tiny percentage of the speed of light, the Goldenwing crossed the sky and was gone.

Faced with an event of near-supernatural dimensions, Andrey Volkov was not the fashionable atheist he had pretended to be at Saint Petersburg University. Invoking the ancient Sharia Christian formula, Andrey thought: *God of my Fathers. God the Merciful. I thank you for the gift of life. And if I must now die, I thank you for showing me such a wonder before I cross the river into the Dark Land.* . . .

The Nimmie crawlers began to advance down the ridge, and Andrey Volkov, regretfully, but with Russian submission, prepared to die.

3

A DAUGHTER OF THE FIRST ALIYAH

The coat of arms carved into the slates above the fireplace in the upper hall of Ullah's Vista bore the heraldic cross and crescent denoting the family's status as Sharia Christians, and the ancient sailing ship marking them as First Landers on Nineveh. The twenty thousand hectares of choice South Ararat wheat land surrounding the old stone house bore witness to the family status. Ullah's Vista was a First Aliyah grant, belonging to the Volkov descendants in perpetuity. There was no better in all Ararat, North or South.

Ekaterina Alexandrovna Volkova sat on the wide verandah, a nullgrav walker by her side. Silent in her old-fashioned wheelchair was Irena Yurievna, the old Volkova. The Volkov dowager had not spoken or walked since the death of the Gospodin, Alexander.

Kat, the present Volkova and Gospodina of Ullah's Vista, made a constant effort to involve her mother in family affairs and decisions. It was not an easy task. And when Kat, herself, a *malenki polkovnik*—"small colonel"—of the Ararat Territorial Guards, had been severely wounded by a Nimmie laze bolt, the society of South Ararat expected the old Volkova to release a tenuous hold on life.

She did nothing of the sort. When Kat returned to Ullah's Vista to recuperate, her mother remained as she had been since her husband's death, silent and wheelchair-bound. But her eyes glistened with attention and interest in all that took place at Ullah's Vista. She showed no sign of dying quietly as Nine-vite war widows were prone to do.

Recuperating from her war wounds, Ekaterina assumed the duties of Volkova and Gospodina. She established a routine suited to her mother's silence and immobility and her own painful rehabilitation.

With the present Recurrence now three years old and no end in sight, Ullah's Vista, like all the estates of South Ararat, was understaffed and showing the effects of heavy taxation and conscription. At this moment, Andrey Alexandrovich, the son of the household, was on active duty in the Rings with his company of Ararat Territorials. Fields lay fallow for lack of people to work them, and the raising of blood horses (the most ancient occupation for the holders of South Ararat) was in abeyance. Sperm and ovum of the most prized steppe blood-lines lay cryogenically stored in the underhouses and the ani-mals themselves roamed their pastures, aging and segregated to prevent unsupervised breeding. The horsemen of South Ara-rat dreamed of a return to their beloved avocations, the breed-ing and training of fine horses and the growing and harvesting of wheat. This would come, of course, only "when the Recur-rence ends." But since the shortest Recurrence of the War of the Twin Planets had heretofore lasted thirty planetary years, the aristocracy of South Ararat were not sanguine about any return soon to normal life.

With Ekaterina and Irena on the verandah stood young Peter Mornay, the recently elevated Metropolitan of Nostromo-grad. Mornay, regarded by most Ninevites as far too young for such a post, held the appointment by virtue of his filial rela-tionship to Boris Petrovich Mornay, until six months ago the Metropolitan of Nostromograd, and his descent from Galen Mornay, the chaplain of the First Aliyah.

Mornays and their ecclesiastical superiors, the Bokharas, had guided the Sharia Christian Mosque of Nineveh from the day the Goldenwing *Nostromo* broke lunar orbit for the Ross Twins with seventy-five thousand colonists in its cold sleep combs.

Peter Mornay, as he would be the first to admit, was not the churchman his legendary ancestor or his revered father had been. But he was an earnest and intense young man eager to do his duty to Nineveh.

He had grown up in South Ararat as a cadet in the Volkov household with Andrey Volkov and Ekaterina Volkova his close companions. He had returned to Ullah's Vista with a mission. But he had not yet nerved himself to speak of it to Kat, whom he had loved since childhood.

Some forty kilometers to the southwest, on the coast of the Gulf of Aralsk, lay the town of wooden Nostromograd.

Nostromograd had religious significance on Nineveh far beyond its size and commercial importance. It had been built at the place where Goldenwing *Nostromo*'s shuttles deposited the First Aliyah seven hundred Earth standard years before.

The golden mosque domes of the town (called "wooden" because even the streets were paved with the hard woods of the Ural Mountains) were visible from the ridge above Ullah's Vista. It was a town of mosques, one hundred and eleven of them, a mosque for every shade of the Sharia Christian faith that the colonists had brought to Nineveh. It was, in fact, the religious capital of South Ararat, and its Metropolitan was always premier cleric of the planetary Sharia Christian community of Ararat, second in rank only to the Metropolitan of Saint Petersburg, the capital city, on the northeast coast of the continent.

Small compared to Earth's continents, Ararat was the only habitable land on Nineveh. The Blasted Continent, an immense wilderness spanning a full third of Nineveh's south polar hemisphere, had risen from the deep ocean a mere three million years ago. It was a continent of volcanic rock and sand, snow and ice—fogbound for nine months of the Ninevite year—a useless, bitter wasteland.

The people of Nineveh speculated from time to time on the feasibility of developing the Blasted Continent, but the place was so inhospitable that the project never passed the talking stage.

At one point in the Twin Planets' history, there had been

a movement among liberal members of the First Aliyah to give the Blasted Continent outright to the colonists of the Second Aliyah. But the Recurrences discouraged any serious consideration of that plan. And by now, with the fifteenth Recurrence under way, no one on Nineveh was willing even to consider sharing a world with their unwelcome cousins of the second migration from Earth. The recent establishment of a Collective as their form of government on Nimrud was particularly distasteful to the Ninevites.

Kat Volkova regarded the nullgrav walker beside her with dislike. This enormously expensive device, meant to ease the difficulty of getting about on a regenerating leg, had been issued to her by special command of the Board of Military Ephors. It was intended to show her how highly she was regarded as a military commander. The South Ararat Territorials were the best troops the government of Nineveh could field, and the units commanded by members of the local boyarhood were the elite of the Territorials.

The wounding had been a terrible experience, taxing Kat's endurance to the limit. She had survived only because her battle armor did some portion of the job it was intended to do. Her executive officer, a dour outlander from Petersburg named Leonid Sergeivich Zaitsev, had done the rest with a pneumatic tourniquet. Zaitsev had been given temporary command of her battalion after she was invalided home, but he had died in the next engagement, the last before the unit was withdrawn from the Rings and rotated back to Nineveh for rest and rehabilitation.

Ekaterina had been told that the new leg, cloned from her own cells in the military Organ Bank, would soon be indistinguishable from the shapely limb she lost to the sharpshooting Nimmie laze gunner in the Rings. The cloned arm, from the same source, would reach maturity, the medics said glibly, in less time.

But at the moment, Ekaterina's right leg was shorter than her left by six centimeters and her right arm was a grotesque and undersized appendage. Both were the sexless limbs of a preadolescent. Kat found her treatment repellent. The immature limbs revolted her.

She was by training and inclination a *boyar,* a country noblewoman quite at home with assisting mares to foal and performing veterinary medicine on farm animals. But she was subconsciously offended by the idea of human limb regeneration as a medical technique of war. *Why was it,* she wondered, *that technology of all sorts flourished at the same time the population of the Twin Planets was dedicated to arson, mayhem and murder?* For some people, religion was able to supply answers. But not for Kat. She wondered if Peter understood this.

The late afternoon sun hung low in the southwest. Ross was an M6 star, ruddy and slightly cooler than the sun of Earth. Like most colonists, from Alpha Centauri to Epsilon Eridani, the inhabitants of Nineveh compared all things astronomical and geographical to Earth and the Sol system.

By this time Kat and her fellow Ninevites were totally acclimated and conditioned to life on the Blessed Twin. But they still made comparisons with a world their ancestors abandoned almost a millennium ago, a world they had never seen and would never see.

Here the seasons were longer and more severe than those of Earth. The air was thinner and less rich in oxygen, and the gravity was slightly less than the gravity of Earth, the mountains higher. Still, there was great beauty here. To the north, the Urals rose in snow-capped grandeur to the peak of Mount Ararat, at 9,750 meters. Sunsets, in the late fall of the year, were glorious in South Ararat. The pelagic airflow over the Planetary Ocean raised towering pillars of cumulus and cumulonimbus clouds that soared into the stratosphere on the rising thermals of Ararat's coastal plateau. When the setting red sun lighted these sky palisades, the effect was stunning.

It was said in Petersburg that what the Nimmies coveted on Nineveh was the Blessed Twin's glorious autumnal evening displays. Returning home after a long absence, Kat could almost believe it.

A south wind, carrying a hint of the winter to come from

the frozen antarctic continent, made wavelike patterns in the grassy plain below the ridge on which Ullah's Vista had been built. *In other times,* Kat thought, *instead of the grasses one would see square kilometers of wheat.* Wheat so fine that even the Nimmies would come to buy and carry the rich grain away to that other reddish body shining through the fading daylight: Nimrud. The Accursed Twin.

Ross 248 Beta was locked in an unbreakable astronomical embrace with its slightly larger and vastly more favored twin, Nineveh. Throughout the 370-day year, the Ross Twins maintained a mean astronomical distance from one another of 1,200,000 kilometers.

Nineveh was an oceanic planet, but Nimrud was a bleak ball of rock and dust. Millennia ago shallow, muddy seas had covered the surface of the planet. But some cosmic event, perhaps the planet's capture by Nineveh, or a severe Ring encounter, had drastically altered the climate. The seas were consumed by geological fracturing and tectonic collisions, sucked into the ground or blown off as superheated steam into space. Now liquid water was to be found on the Accursed Twin only at a depth of twenty kilometers or in the thin coating of ice to be found at the poles.

Life on Nimrud was not the life led on Nineveh. But it was there that Goldenwing *Resolution* deposited the forty thousand refugees of the Second Aliyah. *Resolution* died in fulfilling her contract, as did her eight syndics.

Peter Mornay was talking overmuch, Kat thought. She wondered whether it was the sight of her child's arm peeping out of the folds of her *boyar*'s robe or the presence of Irena Yurievna, who followed the conversation between her daughter and the young cleric with the attention of a small, silent bird of prey.

If either were true, Kat thought, *it would be a disappointment.* Peter had been away from South Ararat for several years, engaged in his ecclesiastical studies and assignments. But he had always been a welcome guest at Ullah's Vista, his cadet home. And he had never been shy about seeking the affection with which he had always been regarded by the Volkovs.

———

Arriving at Ullah's Vista, he had tried not to be shocked by the extent of Ekaterina's wounding. After seeing her, he questioned the wisdom of the errand with which he had been entrusted by Third Ephor Yuri Vukasin. It might well be true that Kat would be ready for a second tour of duty within the time specified by the medics at Odessa. Mornay did not challenge that. The new regenerative techniques were marvels of medical wizardry. But how willing to fight again would Kat be?

He looked covertly at the old Volkova, Irena. Her opinion of Vukasin had been set years ago by the Gospodin. Vukasin was shrewd, perhaps even intelligent. But he was a jumped-up *kulak*'s son. A parvenu and careerist. It was depressing to realize that his title of Third Ephor put him within reach of being Head of State. How would Kat take a direct order from him? *God befriend us,* he thought. If not for the Recurrence we wouldn't be faced with making such decisions. Why must Recurrences go on and on?

"Is it growing too chilly for you, ladies?" he asked.

Irena stared, a small erect figure in black widow's weeds.

Kat shook her head. "I like the cold, Peter. Have you forgotten?"

"Of course not." *I have forgotten nothing about you, Ekaterina,* he thought. *Nothing. Not your tall grace, your blond hair, your wide and generous mouth, your skin like pale satin. Not the way you laugh, nor the way you danced the Harvest Festival Eve away in the hall of this house with every young cavalier in South Ararat asking for a smile from you. Was it only six years ago? It seemed so much longer.*

"Do I depress you, Peter?" Kat asked. "The medics at Odessa claim I will be whole soon again."

"Nothing about you could ever depress me, Ekaterina," he said with feeling.

Kat regarded the new Metropolitan thoughtfully. Peter was a sweet man, rather handsome with his height, his sandy hair and beard, his pale blue Circassian eyes. Eyes much like Kat's own. But his melancholy face bore silent witness to the inner storms and doubts that had troubled his brooding Russian mind since childhood. Kat was well acquainted with the

Mornay *angst*. Peter and the Volkov siblings had been insepa-
rable before this last Recurrence.

Angst was not a Volkov trait. The Volkovs were of Georgian stock, a family devoted to straight talk and action. What
the Gospodin Alexander used to call "shouting names and
kicking ass."

She could see the thin red crescent of Nimrud, low on the
southwestern horizon at this latitude, dominating, as it always
did, the rose-colored sky of Nineveh. Each fifty-two-day month
Nimrud changed from a scimitar to an angry, bloody disk and
back again low on the horizon. As it had for all the years of her
life, Nimrud transited the sun a dozen times each month, cast-
ing a night shadow across the face of its more favored Twin,
raising the great tides of the Planetary Ocean.

The Accursed Twin rules our lives, Kat thought with bitterness. A million kilometers distant and as different from Nineveh as hell from heaven. She signed herself with the cross and
crescent, wondering whether she was indulging in what she
and Andrey called "Mornay gloom." It had to be the low
spirits that accompanied a long convalescence.

She suppressed a sigh and tried to concentrate on Peter's
account of his elevation as a Metropolitan of the Sharia Christian Mosque of Nostromograd, which he described in great—
near to tedious—detail. It was past time she commented on it,
lest Peter's feelings be injured.

"Prince of the Mosque. So grand a title, Peter Borisovich,"
she said formally, using his Christian name and patronymic.

The elevation had taken place in Nostromograd while she
was offworld. Andrey had seen it and had written to her about
it before leaving, himself, for the Rings: *"A grand sight, Sister.
A parade of long-bearded ecclesiastics winding through the streets of
wooden Nostromograd, laden with relics and ikons of the saints. And
our Peter, tall as a morning shadow, accepting his crown from the
hand of Grand Metropolitan Massoud Bokhara and his rod of office
from First Ephor Oleg Sergeivich Gordiev—our beloved, and somewhat senile, Head of State. Mother would have loved the singing."*

She glanced at the old Volkova. She was erect as a soldier
in her wheelchair. Her eyes bright and searching.

———

Irena Yurievna had raised and loved Peter Mornay as one of her own. But he now represented the state, which had taken her Gospodin from her. She refused to acknowledge Peter's presence. Her bright eyes seemed focused beyond him. It made him unhappy and uneasy.

The Gospodin of Ullah's Vista had been adamantly against the war, but when the Recurrence came (as Recurrences inevitably did) he was among the first to enlist for a cause in which he did not believe. For a bitter moment Kat wondered if *Polkovnik* Alexander had a grave somewhere on the Accursed Twin. Her father had not died, as most soldiers of Nineveh did, in the Rings, fighting for worthless planetesimals, but on bleak Nimrud, in an early, suicidal attack on the enemy's home planet.

The First Aliyah had been a quest for religious freedom. Seventy thousand Circassian and Georgian Russians, all devout Sharia Christians, abandoned Earth in the fifth year of the Fundamentalist Jihad and embarked on the Goldenwing *Nostromo* for the ten-light-year cold sleep voyage to the Ross Twins.

On arrival at Alpha, pleased with what they saw, and before they had explored either the Blasted Continent or Beta, the colonists dispatched word to Earth by radio for a Second Aliyah to embark.

The message took ten and a third standard years to reach its destination, and that time, added to the ten it had already taken the *Nostromo* to reach Alpha, was enough to have radically altered the situation on the home planet.

The *Nostromo* colonists had renounced Earth in a grand ceremonial quest. The colonists who embarked for the Ross system in Goldenwing *Resolution* were a very different sort of people, shaped by very different conditions.

Resolution had departed a world raped and left for dead by fanatics. The soldiers of the Prophet were spent with killing. The exhausted Jihad began a global retreat. Europe and Africa lay in ruins as the tattered remnants of the Muslim armies straggled back across the continent toward the Zagros Mountains whence the Jihad had come four generations before.

The colonists who boarded Goldenwing *Resolution* were ethnic Russians, but Russians co-opted by the Jihad. They were a polyglot assemblage of the driven and the desperate, collaborators abandoned by their fundamentalist Muslim masters fleeing the retribution of the Jihad's victims. Not at all what the members of the First Aliyah had in mind when they called for more colonists from "home."

The people of the Second Aliyah were neither farmers nor people of the soil. They were mechanics and technicians, folk of the urban ghettoes and refugee camps.

Given the nature of the *Resolution* colonists, their assimilation on Nineveh would have been difficult under the best of circumstances. But they were not destined to find the best circumstances. In fact, they never reached Nineveh, never reached the green continent of Ararat, which by now supported a population of a million wheat farmers and horse breeders. What the people of the Second Aliyah lacked in the social skills and graces they lacked also in luck.

The Ross 248 system's peculiar astronomy made it a solar system of asteroids and planetesimals. Plus the Twins. These two terrequivalent worlds orbited their central point in a ring swept clean of astronomical detritus in earlier epochs by the Twins themselves. By sheerest coincidence, Beta had done most of the sweeping. It had taken a fearsome battering in the process. It was now a world without oceans, without growing things, with only the most rudimentary indigenous life, a world of harsh landscapes, steep mineral-rich mountains and craters, thin atmosphere and violent climate.

Sunward from the Twins lay a half dozen belts of small bodies, planetesimals and asteroids too small even to be mined efficiently. Outward from the Twins lay the true Rings, asteroids and larger planetesimals rich in metals and elements extending out to the edges of the Oort Cloud, three light-days from Ross 248.

From time to time—astronomers on Nineveh had not yet

determined exactly at what irregular intervals—the Twin Planets encountered an edge of the outer Ring nearest them. When this happened, both Nineveh and Nimrud underwent a severe pelting from space in the form of meteor showers and falls of bodies massive enough to crater the ground and cause great damage. Within sight of Ullah's Vista lay the grassed-over and weather-softened contours of two such craters caused by strikes during the last Ring encounter a planetary century ago. Interplanetary spacecraft had often been lost during these events, and a deep planetary encounter with a Ring was a terrifying and dangerous event.

It was the bad fortune of the Second Aliyah to arrive at the Twins system at the height of a severe brush with a Ring. Goldenwing *Resolution* blundered into an unexpected field of debris and, unable to maneuver, was wrecked. The syndics, to a man and woman, died in the encounter. But the colonists, still in cold sleep, were launched into space in *Resolution*'s shuttles and sleds. A true, last act of heroism by the Wired Starmen who sailed *Resolution*.

When the sleds and shuttles made planetfall on automatic guidance, the cold sleepers were awakened by the mechanisms aboard the landing craft.

They were horrified by what they saw. They had expected to see pelagic Nineveh. They did not. The Second Aliyah had made planetfall on bitter Nimrud.

And there the people of the Second Aliyah established the same sort of refugee camps whence they had come, and later a series of experimental, repressive governments. Year after year, decade after decade, as the camps became bleak towns and then ugly cities, there was talk on Nineveh of allowing the *Resolution* colonists to complete their voyage and settle on some of the unoccupied land of Ararat. And failing that, on the Blasted Continent.

But even that bleak mercy was never granted. The Ninevites, who had long ago established science stations on Nimrud and knew the place well, now contended that Nimrud suited the character of the late arrivals. They answered petitions for resettlement with rebuffs. The message was clear.

"Remain on Nimrud amid your factories and communes. It is the world you built and it suits you."

By the time the colony on Nimrud was twenty local years old, the movement known as Gammah—"Justice" in the polyglot language of the "new" arrivals, was gaining adherents. It soon became common practice for the population of Nimrud to gather in late afternoons of Tenth Day to look up and chant curses at the large, ever-present globe of Alpha in their reddish sky. The Tenth Day Rage (an adaptation of the days of Sharia self-flagellation) swiftly became a tradition on Nimrud.

On the twenty-fifth anniversary of the wreck of the *Resolution,* the War of the Twin Planets began with an annihilating attack by Gammah terrorists on the Ninevite science stations on Nimrud. And save for the periods of exhaustion and the intervals of rebuilding and rearming, Recurrences of the war continued to the present time.

Until young Mornay departed for the Sharia Christian Seminary at Frunze in the far north of Ararat, Ullah's Vista had been his home: To Peter, the most wonderful place in all Nineveh. The Volkov family treated him with kindness, generosity, and respect for his ancient name. The Gospodin Alexander had toyed with the idea Ekaterina would one day marry Peter, who was destined for the Mosque. Daughters of the Volkov House often married churchmen. "Such matches smooth over the sin of our skepticism," the Gospodin liked to say.

Kat, though her feeling for Peter was no more than friendly affection, would have gone through with her father's plan. It was in the Volkov tradition to do as the Gospodin bade. But then came the Recurrence, and soon thereafter, the Gospodin's death in battle.

Ekaterina returned to her chair and sat down. Ninevites were acutely conscious of physical beauty—or the lack of it. Her Volkov vanity suffered each time she limped or stumbled. Peter was on the verge of making some soothing—and possibly offensive—remark. She forestalled it.

She said, "I've heard nothing recently from Andrey. His

unit is somewhere in the Fifth Ring. Have you had a letter?''

"Nothing," Mornay said. "But you know how he is about writing." He again glanced covertly at old Irena. The Volkova was staring at him as though reading his soul.

Irena Yurievna was a Danilov. The Danilov women were said to have the second sight. Did she know what message he carried for Ekaterina? Absurd, of course, or was it?

Mornay remained guiltily silent. In order to send troops to Ross 248's most distant rings of planetesimals it had been necessary to alter the molecular structure of men and women facing the voyage so that they could withstand weeks of constant three-g acceleration. That this treatment also shortened life expectancy from one hundred to fewer than seventy Ninevite years was not general knowledge. The Ephors had never permitted release of the information.

But Ekaterina knew. *Kat knew many things,* Peter Mornay thought; *she always had. From the place where we could find sea darts among the rocks at the Aralsk shore to the rules the Ephors passed in the secret rooms of the Kremlin in Petersburg, Kat knew.* How did she feel knowing that both she and her brother had laid years of their lives on the consuming altar of the War of the Twin Planets?

To live in the company of patriots, Mornay thought, *was difficult.*

"Can you speak about the war, Kat?" he asked.

"If I must."

"Are we any closer at all to an ending?"

The cool blue eyes probed. "You would know better than I, Peter. You speak to the Ephors, I don't."

"Ah, Kat, I am an ignorant man," Peter said in a rush of characteristic self-derision and melancholy.

"The Mosque doesn't choose ignorant men to be its Metropolitans. Or stupid ones either," Kat said. "Don't pretend that it does." She sounded tired and sharp. *Pain makes anger,* Mornay thought. He rubbed his palms against the spun wool robe of Earth Sky Blue that denoted his Metropolitan's rank. Long ago, the Greek Orthodox clerics who were the first revolutionary Sharia Christians wore robes embroidered with gold, silver and gems. That practice was stopped when the converts began applying the Islamic Sharia to their basic Christian concepts. In the black years that gave birth to the new faith, the imams and bishops hid from the spiritual leaders of the Jihad among the faithful. Thousands of Sharia Christians were slaughtered both by Muslims, who thought their adoption of Mohammed into the pantheon of saints was sacrilegious, and by Christians, who chose to believe that the followers of the new religion were demons of Mahound the Corrupter. Without the exodus and the Goldenwing *Nostromo,* the Sharia Christian faith would have perished on the home planet.

Kat was saying, ''The army is sound. There is not a soldier who would not die to protect Nineveh.'' She managed a rueful smile. ''That is the good news. The bad is that so many may have to. The Nimmies learn quickly and too well.'' She ran a long-fingered hand across her high forehead. Her eyes turned again toward the southern horizon. Out there, on the thin, sharp end of the continent of Ararat, lay the military district of Odessa. It was from the spaceport there that all probes, missiles, manned spacecraft and satellites, as well as the dozens of civilian flights to the hundreds of mining enterprises in the Rings, were launched.

The activity level at Odessa was very high these days. The army was lifting dozens of payloads into space. Even as she watched, a thin rocket trail climbed vertically into the dusty rose sky. Presently it turned eastward to utilize the rotational speed of Nineveh to help boost its payload into orbit.

Peter Mornay, who had never been offworld, looked at her searching expression and his heart seemed to turn over. *Have you left me behind, Kat?*

The satellite launch rocket's condensation trail was tattered by the onshore wind from the Planetary Ocean.

''Peter,'' she said, ''the war is in good hands. We are winning.''

''But the casualties. I must comfort the families of the killed and missing in action. I do my best. But there are so many, Kat. The dead and the maimed.''

''Like me, Peter?''

Mornay buried his face in his hands. Kat had seen him do that when a prized pony fell and had to be destroyed. For an instant she was angry at his lack of steel.

Peter stood and walked to the balustrade to hide his expression. Kat was immediately consumed with remorse for her bad temper. Peter had never been a soldier, had never heard the crack of bullets on a helmet or the horrid bubbling of lasers burning though the soft parts of your space armor. He had never been in space. He didn't comprehend the vital need to know, with absolute certainty, that one fought on the winning side.

Even, she thought, *if it was not so.*

Particularly if it was not so.

Kat stood again, steadied herself on the walker, and made her way to the balustrade next to Peter. The view was unobstructed under a sky turbulent with clouds stained bloody by the red light of Ross 248. A partial eclipse was beginning. The Accursed Twin was slowly taking a sliver of light from the setting sun. Like most colonists, wherever they found themselves, the inhabitants of Nineveh thought of their star as "the sun." They were still children of Earth.

"Look, Peter," she said. "This is our world. *Our world.*"

"Perhaps we could share," he muttered.

"Perhaps we could. But that does not alter the fact that this"—she struck the stone balustrade with her hand—"and that land out there. The sea beyond. The sky. All of it—is ours. That is our only truth. Would you have us let it all go? We did that once, on Earth. We won't again."

Mornay sighed and looked south. "It is truly Ullah's view," he said. Despite his Slavic face, the Metropolitan's features were said to have a Gallic cast to them. When they were children, Andrey and Ekaterina used to tease Peter about it, recounting the well-known (to most Ninevites) tale of Jean-Pierre de Mornay, a French officer captured at Borodino in 1812 by Kutusov's Hussars. De Mornay had remained in Russia, married, had become totally slavicized.

To this distant day any descendant of cavalryman Jean-

Pierre de Mornay, who became more Russian than a Tsar, was apt to be called "the Frenchman."

We have long memories, Ekaterina Volkova thought. *It is our burden.*

Peter's ancestor, old Galen Mornay, had been the Sharia Christian chaplain of the voyage of colonization. And it had been he, many years ago, who had climbed to the crest of this very hill with the *boyar* Yevgeny Andreyevich Volkov to inspect his friend's new grant of land. "From here," he was reputed to have told the about-to-become Gospodin, "Ullah can have his world in view." And Yevgeny Volkov named his house and estate Ullah's Vista. And many years later, when the Metropolitan Galen Mornay was near death, Volkov had caused a dozen hectares of hillside land to be deeded to the Sharia Christian Church, and on that land built the jewelbox Mornay Mosque, whose golden onion domes now gleamed in the late evening sun a half dozen kilometers from Ullah's Vista at a place where the road to Nostromograd crossed the Dnieper River.

Far to the southwest, in the direction of the Gulf of Aralsk, the ruddy sword blade of Nimrud seemed to rest with its point on the horizon. "Like a weapon planted on our land," Kat said with feeling. "Wherever we go, Nimrud looms over us like an evil spirit."

"No evil spirit ever can touch you, Ekaterina," Peter said in his most passionately ecclesiastical voice. Women and love confused the religious mind. They had taught him that at the seminary and he believed it. He understood why it was that in the early days on Earth clerics of the Sharia Christian sect were required to be *eunoukhos.* That had never been the case on Nineveh. Here even clerics were expected to contribute to the colonial gene pool.

He was no nearer to broaching the reason for his visit to Ullah's Vista. It was a matter so equivocal that he feared Kat's reaction. That was the trouble with the warrior caste. People born to military service tended to accrete the most archaic notions of tradition and honor.

The Third Ephor Yuri Vukasin, newly appointed to head

the Council of Strategy, was a man not much older than himself or Kat. The self-seeking son of a self-seeking family. (Was it his imagination? Or did it seem that the government of Nineveh was falling more and more into the hands of untried men of questionable character?) Vukasin's great-great-grandfather had been a peasant when he was awakened from coldsleep on Landing Day.

Still, it did no good to play the aristocrat with Kat. She had bloodlines better than most on Nineveh, but she never used her patrician heritage to influence the assignments she was given by the Council of Strategy.

Did she know that the Nimrudites had detected a Goldenwing approaching the Twin Planets? Almost certainly not. The scientists of Nineveh were better at biology and husbandry than at astronomy. Fortunately, less than honorable men like Vukasin had seen to it that the enemy chain of command was well penetrated by spies.

The Secret Intelligence Corps had produced the news of a Goldenwing's approach. But it was the Mosque, the Keepers of Records, who had been able to determine what cargo the Goldenwing was bringing down from the stars.

The devices the Goldenwing carried were from Barnard's, and the people of Barnard's made farm implements, but they also made weapons.

Whether that was enough to justify the Third Ephor's plan remained to be seen. The decision would have to be Kat's. Alexander Volkov had raised his daughter with a strict set of *independent* values.

As a religious man, Mornay had his own code of ethics. But the very idea of refusing a direct order from an Ephor chilled his blood. He regarded Kat's straight back as she stood looking out over the land her forebears had claimed on Landing Day and husbanded ever since. Surely Kat would do what she knew, what *he* knew, was right for Nineveh. Hadn't she as much as said so only moments ago?

There was one other consideration. Ephor Vukasin's order could be carried out only by an officer of the Territorial Guard able to campaign and fight in the space environment. On Nineveh now there simply was no one more capable than Kat to do what was required. She was not yet fit. But would that matter to the Ephors? To Mornay's knowledge, no such action had ever been fought. The very idea made sweat drip down his ribs.

To attack a Goldenwing was surely an act of almost unthinkable heresy.

Kat steadied herself on the walker. "Peter," she said, "what do I do if I reject these limbs? I am a soldier of Nineveh. What sort of soldier can a cripple be?"

For the first time Peter Mornay gave some thought to how Kat must be feeling. The pain in her eyes touched his heart.

"The medical staff at Odessa tell me that you are mending as expected. Recovery from serious wounds is not a simple matter," Mornay said.

Kat smiled bleakly. "You are an optimist, Peter. It must be the Frenchman in you."

"You *are* mending, Kat. You *will* be whole again."

"Is that the word of Ullah, Metropolitan? If it is, it's very gratifying. But Ullah should get on with it."

"Don't blaspheme, Kat. Remember who you are."

"I'm not likely to forget it," Ekaterina said, leaning against the balustrade. She studied Mornay's long face curiously. "Now tell me why you've come all the way from Nostromograd in mid-Gagarin just to see me."

Mornay was surprised at the directness of the question. The month of Gagarin was heavy with religious observances and agricultural rituals brought to Nineveh from Earth. The mosques were filled for the rites of spring common to most agrarian colonies. Even in wartime the Ninevites were very observant people.

"There is something I must say to you, Kat," Mornay said.

Ekaterina smiled thinly. "Official, ecclesiastical, or personal?"

"Official."

"Ah." Kat made her way back to her chair and released the nullgrav walker. The device bounced in the way nullgrav devices did, and anchored itself to Kat's chair.

―――

Irena turned her chair so that she could face her daughter and Mornay.

Peter hesitated.

"If it concerns me, the Volkova can hear it," Kat said.

"Very well. Last Eight Day I had a private meeting with Yuri Vukasin."

"I am filled with delight at your good fortune," Kat said drily.

"I know what the Gospodin, your father, thought of Vukasin," Peter said. "My own father did not rate him highly, either."

Kat's eyes took on a combative glitter. The Volkovs had never gotten on well with the Ephors. Alexander Volkov had tried to have several Ephors impeached. But his insurrection had stopped short of actual rebellion and he became a victim of the war he had sought to stop.

Yuri Vukasin, however, was very much alive and the senior member of the Council of Strategy, which meant that he was, in effect, military commander of Planet Nineveh's home forces. A military dictator without a shred of military experience or judgment, he nevertheless had to be listened to.

"I have been instructed to offer you a special command," Peter Mornay said.

Kat's eyes narrowed. "What sort of *'special command,'* Peter?"

Peter Mornay looked back into the main house. "Where are the servants?"

Kat said irritably. "Those the Ephors have left us are doing the work that needs doing."

Mornay moved closer to Ekaterina's chair and lowered his voice. "There is a Goldenwing coming, Kat."

It took Ekaterina a moment to assimilate what had been said. *A Goldenwing.* Instantly, her mind was filled with the image she had learned at her amah's knee, in her tutor's classroom. It was a vision of a giant golden butterfly, a creature of space shaped like the delicate creatures the colonists had brought with them from Earth, the black-and-gold Monarchs that flew in fluttering waves on the spring winds across the continent of Ararat. *Like* the Monarchs, but vastly different. The pictures in the old books showed *Nostromo* in orbit around Nineveh, an immense golden presence against the velvet black of space. Wings twenty kilometers long, a segmented monofilament body even longer. Skylar sails mirroring in gold the images of Nineveh, of Ross 248, even of angry Nimrud. To any child born on Nineveh, *Goldenwing* was a magic word. A creature of deep space so huge, yet so delicate, that the vision suggested poetry and music and far-seeking adventure.

In all the years the colonies had been established on the Twin Planets, no Goldenwings but *Nostromo* and *Resolution* had ever made planetfall in the Ross 248 system. And *Resolution* had paid for her planetfall with her life and the life of her syndicate. To this day, Kat realized, there were still drifting in the First Outer Ring bits and tatters of the ship that had brought the Second Aliyah from Earth.

"How do you know this, Peter?" she asked.

"A survey station on Nimrud has made contact with the Wired Ones aboard."

That jolted her. She was not accustomed to learning anything after it was first known to the people of the Second Aliyah. "Is it true? Not Nimmie propaganda?"

"No, Kat. There is a Goldenwing coming. To Nimrud."

He let himself fall silent, letting the import of what he was saying impress itself on Ekaterina.

"Ullah be merciful!" Kat made the sign of the cross and crescent on her breast. She was almost overwhelmed by the urge to demand the reason a Goldenwing should choose to call at Nimrud rather than Nineveh. It meant that the Goldenwing must have a cargo for Nimrud—and none for Nineveh. The implications were staggering to a soldier at war.

Kat's expression suddenly hardened. "You said Vukasin is offering me 'a command.' What sort of command, Peter?"

"A spaceborne force," the Metropolitan said.

"To do what?"

Mornay inhaled deeply and took the plunge. "To take the Goldenwing, Kat. To capture the starship and bring it here to Nineveh."

"My God," Kat whispered, and again made the sign of cross and crescent.

In the southern sky, the partial eclipse was ending, the Accursed Twin passing from the face of the sun. But the sky did not brighten. Instead, it seemed to Kat, the evening grew darker and the wind turned cold.

Peter Mornay said urgently, "The need is desperate, Kat. Gammah's pro-Nimmie killers are everywhere in Petersburg and in the mountains. They are trying to stop our shuttles from reaching the Rings, and we can't do without them. If our metal ore imports drop below a dozen flights a day we can't sustain the battle. We must do something. We have no choice."

Suddenly, unexpectedly, Irena Volkova's voice broke the silence. *"To attack a Goldenwing is to bring the wrath of God upon the people,"* she said. *"No excuse can justify the sacrilege."*

Then she turned her chair and wheeled it into the darkening shadows of the great house.

4

A CRY FROM THE DARK

Duncan Kr lay on the air of the inner skydeck—the large deck that had been designated (by ship-designers who were unclear on the concept) as a social center and observation lounge. No colonist had ever seen a skydeck, nor had one participated in any of the social doings the designers imagined as taking place during a voyage measured in parsecs.

The original charterers of *Gloria Coelis* would have been unlikely space-revelers in any case. They had been Christocatholics, most of them monks and nuns, fleeing the Jihad in its first terrible years. Between Planet Earth and their destination, Planet Aldrin, they had lain in cold-sleep deep within the Goldenwing's vast holds. No sodalities had ever met under *Glory's* transparent carapace. No colonial revelries had ever taken place there.

But the syndics who sailed *Glory,* generation after generation, delighted in the beauties visible from the deck where Duncan now floated, weightless, in the glinting, shifting, coruscating reflections of light from the nearby M6 star, from the tumbling objects buried within the Rings, and from the more distant stars seen through the glow of plasmas racing along the monofilament stays, shrouds, halyards and braces of the rig.

To the skydeck, it seemed to Duncan, *Glory* showed herself in all her finery, with a vanity that was almost human. His ship might be a machine, but Duncan Kr had long since ceased to think of *Glory* that way.

Duncan was born on Thalassa, a seaworld of gray rock and rainfall, a planet of the Wolf System, nine light-years from Earth. Though the planet bore a Greek name, its people were Scots, descended from the people of the Hebrides of Earth.

As a boy of twelve standard years, Duncan was given to the aging Starmen of the *Gloria Coelis* by the matriarch of the marriage group which nurtured him.

He grew to manhood on *Glory* and had been her Master and Commander for ten uptime years. He was tall, slender, with cobalt blue eyes and a commanding presence. A dour man, touched with melancholy.

He had reason.

Duncan allows himself to drift higher, closer to the thin transparency that divides him from deep space. Like the gray-green fabric of the ship, the transparency is only microns thick. *Gloria Coelis* is as fragile as a bird and swift as a beam of starlight.

A powerful empathic Talent, even un-Wired he senses the emotional sendings of those aboard his ship. He senses the pleasure of Anya Amaya, the Sailing Master from Centauri—at this moment engaged in sexual play with Damon Ng, the young Rigger from Nixon. Syndics are promiscuous, or nearly so. Duncan is not comfortable with that view of Broni Ehrengraf or Buele. He imagines that in time his rather prudish attitude will change. When Broni is older. When Buele is wiser.

Duncan can also sense the sendings of the ship's family of cats. Mira, who was born on *Glory* four shiptime years ago, is the last descendant of an Earthborn cat. She was taken from cold-sleep by Dietr Krieg, *Glory*'s Neurocybersurgeon, and given an experimental interface with *Glory*. Now Mira and the first litter of her artificially begot kittens have all been surgically "enhanced" by Dietr—fitted with radio-drogues linking them with the ship's computer. The results of this biological-cybernetic meddling delight the Neurocybersurgeon. He suspects he has done something significant. At this moment Mira and one of her kittens are outside in the plenum near the valve

opening onto the skydeck. The queen is seeking Duncan. To
Dietr Kreig's annoyance, the cat prefers the company of Duncan Kr to any of the other humans aboard the ship. Dietr has
sensed that Mira thinks of Duncan as *the dominant tom,* which,
Dietr reasons, is not far from the truth. Cats, downworld or in
space, have a well-developed sense of hierarchy.

Dietr is inordinately pleased with what he has accomplished with the cats. But he does not realize just *how* enhanced
his procedure and *Glory*'s computer have made them. Dietr
Krieg is a skillful surgeon, but not an imaginative man.

Duncan Kr has come to the skydeck to be alone, to indulge his
melancholy. Since breaking orbit at Voerster he has been silently grieving for the woman left behind there—Broni Ehrengraf Voerster's mother. On Voerster, nearly thirty years have
passed. The object of his romantic memory is gone beyond
recall.

Other Starmen have known this peculiar grief. Other Starmen have overcome it, as will Duncan. But it is hard.

Buele, who was regarded as retarded on Voerster, has been
following the kittens through the huge and empty holds. He
has been trying to use his own enhancement to communicate
with them. So far he has not succeeded in doing anything but
annoying Mira, who knows what he is trying to do and, catlike, simply does not care.

She announces herself from the outer valve to the skydeck
and her kitten repeats her trill. Duncan senses her near presence. Mira has a well-developed sense of propriety. She calls
before entering a private space. *Perhaps,* Duncan thinks, *she
imagines that humans are as sensitive as cats, and as easily startled.
She does us more honor than we deserve,* he tells himself.

He says aloud. "Come to me, Mira."

The cat is so at home in null gravity that she seems to
materialize at his shoulders. She clings there, somehow managing not to break the skin with her claws. She peers intently
into his face. Blue and golden eyes lock. The animal's projected personality is very strong.

Duncan carries Mira closer to the overhead transparency.

———

"Other worlds, Mira." He looks at the twin stars of Nimrud and Nineveh. He thinks of high clouds, of land beneath one's feet. *"Do you ever grow curious, Mira? Do you ever have the urge to prowl under an open sky? I do. I did it on Voerster. For a time."* His words are subvocalized in the near-silent way of empaths.

Mira replies with a jealous growl, as though she recalls Eliana.

"So you do remember her," Duncan says.

As swiftly as she appeared, Mira vanishes.

"It's my fate to be abandoned," Duncan says aloud with a twisted smile.

He is very near the transparent carapace. The scene beyond it is wondrous, even to a Starman. Close to, the masts and stays and braces look as though they have been spun of fine silver. St. Elmo's fire races, glittering, along these narrow paths, jumps to the yards and sail edges, like the etching of a fine golden pen.

Duncan remembers Black Clavius, the beached Starman who stayed on Voerster to interpret Eliana to the kaffirs. Clavius was a man at home with Scripture. The Book of Revelation had always been one of his favorites: *"And I saw a new heaven and a new earth: for the first heaven and the first earth were passed away. . . ."* Clavius was a tragedy and a marvel, Duncan thought. After ten long downtime years on the bitter beach among the kaffirs of Voerster, the old Starman still had the courage to reject what he longed for to stay on that benighted planet in Eliana's service. *Even loving her,* Duncan thought, *could I have done the same?*

I did not.

With an irritable, practiced motion, he sets himself to flying away from the light and down toward a drogue console on the fabric deck far below. He reaches it and connects to *Glory.* The computer informs him that it is time for him to return to the bridge and take over the watch.

Ten hours later Duncan was still on the bridge. At a distance of 352,000,000 kilometers from Ross 248, *Glory* was now moving at only a tiny fraction of her extrasystem velocity of approach. With Anya Amaya conning the ship and Broni in her pod, both women hard-wired to the computer, *Glory* followed a conical formation of six sleds and thirty shuttles moving like a shield through the debris at the edge of what the *Sailing Directions* called the Fifth Ring.

Duncan was not in his pod. Instead he floated at the main control console, connected to the ship by the thick cable of a drogue.

The bridge crew was receiving a series of micro-pulse transmissions from the auxiliaries' probes. Empathic reactions to the transmission governed the manner in which they trimmed *Glory*'s million square meters of skylar sails. Anya Amaya and Broni were teamed with the Master and Commander in what had proved to be the ship's best close maneuvering crew.

Glory's steep angle of approach to the Ross 248 system was recommended in the *Sailing Directions* as the least hazardous passage of the Ring through which it was necessary to move in order to reach the Twins at this time of the Rossian year. The *Sailing Directions* was once an actual book carried by seafaring captains describing in anecdotal terms the approaches to thousands of ports on the shores of the oceans of Earth. Aboard a Goldenwing, it was now a vast subdirectory of computer files, but in content and intent it had changed little. The information contained in the files was gathered from radio beacons and broadcasts, from reports and logs, and even from tales and rumors. All was compiled and evaluated by the mainframe's fuzzy logic algorithms so that when queried, the *Sailing Directions* responded by offering the spacefarer a consensus on the hazards and conditions to be expected along his course.

At best, this sort of sailing was meticulous and exacting work requiring the skills of a team of dedicated empaths. It was an art rather than a science. It sometimes produced flights of absolute fantasy synthesized from the minds of man and machine. At other times, the product was faulty and capable of producing moments of sheer terror—as when twenty hours ago a soccerball-sized rock, with a relative velocity of ten percent of the speed of light, struck the starboard mizzen skys'l, exploding the almost indestructible golden hectare of skylar into kilometers-long tatters capable of fouling the rig. *Glory* had staggered with the impact—the rig was still vibrating in harmony with the echoes of the strike.

Damon Ng, the Rigger, despite his acrophobia, or perhaps because of it, had gone EVA, and with a team of thirty monkeys had tamed the slashing and banging shreds of the huge skys'l. The loss of a sail was barely tolerable aboard a Goldenwing, and the need to salvage what remained of it was absolute. One could buy a small planet in some of the Outer Systems for the price of a single golden skys'l. *Glory* still tamed the tachyon coriolis winds with the same suit of sails she had worn outbound from Earth in 2199. Skylar was made now at only one place in Near Space, Planet Gold, second from the sun 61 Cygni C, parsecs from any port of call on *Glory*'s route for the next decade.

The destroyed sail was secured and coaxed aboard and into one of the unused holds which Damon had designated a sail loft. Perhaps it might be saved. But the important thing to Duncan was that Damon had conquered his fear of *outside* well enough to perform the task required of him.

The monkeys had had to be retrieved from the Monkey House, where they had been recharging and avoiding the effects of the gravity well into which *Glory* was moving deeper and still deeper. They had performed erratically but Damon had handled them well. They were now, once again, in the Monkey House.

On the bridge deck, in the semicircle of bridge-pods or simply hard-Wired and floating free, the syndics were merged into a multiple personality, each part of which consisted largely of *Glory,* herself. They saw with a collective mental eye, planned with a collective mind, and consulted with the ship's computer, in effect, with *Glory,* herself.

To the electronic mind of the ship, it seemed her bridge crew swam in space before her, like dolphins guiding an Earthly leviathan, cautiously leading her through the cubic kilometers of rubble.

Though none of the syndics left the bridge, the essence of

what and who they were was outside, guiding *Glory* through the perils of the Ring.

Duncan floated with one leg hooked over a railing. He was as naked as his female syndics and though the bridge deck was colder than the living spaces, he glistened with sweat. He worked exposed to the computer's interpretation of the space environment, feeling the sting of tachyons, the heat of the photons radiating from the Ross star, the unpleasant irritations of the space debris of the Ring's edge. He stared sightlessly at the console before him. His eyes were directed outward from the lead shuttle, alert for another hurtling piece of rock or cloud of dust.

In these circumstances, it was on Duncan that the heaviest work devolved. He checked the inputs sent to the computer by Anya and Broni. He was aware of the steady breathing of Buele, sleeping in his quarters, exhausted by a four-hour watch, and of Damon's restless sleep, troubled by half-dreams of falling into space.

Duncan was ready at any time to intercept, countermand or restate any sailing commands sent by the women.

The ship was his. On his command judgment his vessel and all aboard her lived or died. Of all her syndics through the years, Duncan Kr was closest to *Glory*.

Mira appeared out of a transit tube. She inspected the dark bridge, lighted by the amber glow of the digital repeaters. The cat could sense the tension of the Wired Ones in the pods. For a moment it concerned her. Then, catlike, she lost interest in a situation that did not require her intervention. She gathered herself and slowly leaped the ten meters between the tube opening and Duncan. She alighted easily and grasped the velcro strips put on the console for her convenience. Again she swept the bridge with a slitted-pupils look. Through her drogue she was aware that her kittens were safe. Some were sleeping in a hold two kilometers from the bridge. Others were in the nest of the foolish tom—Mira's designator for the boy, Buele. She refused even to try to measure things as the large ones did, but she knew to within a heartbeat how long it would take her to fly through the ship to her kits if there should be a need.

———

She clawed at the latch of Duncan's pod. The hatch opened and she slipped inside easily and stood weightless on the glyceroid gel. The pod was redolent of the dominant tom's odor. She arched her back. Circled three times and lay down.

Duncan had reacted to her presence on the bridge with a human greeting. *"Welcome, small Mira."* The cats seldom paid the slightest attention to the names the Starmen gave them. They were totally indifferent to human ways of identifying individuals. Dietr Krieg, ever probing Mira and her litter, had concluded that because their natural senses were so acute they had no need for identifiers in the human sense.

"How scientific, Dietr," Duncan had chided. "You mean that they easily recognize one another or us at a distance."

"A distance I suspect would stagger us if we dared quantify it," Dietr replied. Then, shrugging, "Of course they don't put a value on such things as 'distance.' If they want something and can reach it, they seize it. They are capable of marvellously fine judgments of the relationship between physical objects. But if 'it' is out of reach, it becomes an abstraction, and they lose interest."

Through the open hatch of the pod, Mira regarded Duncan with intent, unblinking eyes. That she thought of him as the dominant tom aboard *Glory* chagrined Dietr. "I made her and her brood what they are," the Neurocybersurgeon often said. "Why isn't the little beast grateful to me?"

Duncan thought that Buele's rejoinder was most apt. "It was God made them, Brother Dietr. You only meddled."

The remark was prototypically Buele, who, on Voerster, had been thought an idiot savant, a kind of human computer in the service of Broni's uncle, the Astronomer Select of Voerster. Now his computational skills challenged *Glory*'s own. And he was young as a Starman. He had a lifetime to grow. He was still, however, odd in his interpersonal relationships.

Near the computer, the cats' wire-thin antenna-drogues were vibrantly effective. It had become Duncan's habit often to conn the ship with Mira or one of the other cats in the pod with him.

Their feline senses helped extend Duncan's awareness far out into the stellar deeps englobing the ship. Possibly even into other spaces, other dimensions. Who could tell? None of the other syndics would venture a guess. It made the Starmen uneasy. There *were* things out there. Things that were there when time began.

Were they living things? *One had to define the term "living,"* Duncan thought. Not an easy task. But for Mira and her brood there was no question. The cats cared nothing for explanations and definitions. Were the things Mira sensed even really out there in the extragalactic dark? Duncan thought so. But the distances involved were so vast that a man would need to live a hundred thousand or a million shiptime years to cross them.

Out of reach? Well, perhaps, if Einstein was right.

But what if one day—always assuming one was free to cut up time in such arbitrary ways—mankind discovered that there were life-forms orders of magnitude larger, wiser, longer-lived, more swift, more savage, than man could ever be? Life-forms who simply ignored the limitations Einstein had codified for his fellow human creatures? What then?

Glory's cats, who declined to conceptualize any distance they could not cover in a single pounce, reacted to the emotional traces of the distant ones like hunting predators: with lowered silhouettes, standing fur, and angry clicks and growls.

But at the moment there was no intent to challenge in Mira. In swift images, she was thinking of her newest litter, some of whom had taken up independent residence in the vastness of Cargo Hold 3100. She was not concerned. The dark, empty spaces within *the-great-queen-who-is-not-alive* were all parts of Mira's world, the only world she had ever known, and a world as familiar as the scent of the dominant tom. Inside *Glory* all were safe. It was a safety Mira would fight to defend.

She could sense Buele. The foolish tom had just awakened and was at this moment trying to teach the four kittens with him how to use the food replicator. Mira saw the slack-jawed boy simply as a part of her environment, one with *Glory's* silent passageways and unused holds. He had not always been a part of Mira's world. He had appeared at the same time as the young queen with the strange sounds in her body.

Mingled with these shifting images was Mira's awareness of Duncan. At this moment, it was colored by a ferocious sexuality. Mira was coming into estrus again.

Broni, stirring in the next pod, felt the cat's awareness in her loins. The girl knew almost nothing of sex. She had spent her adolescence as a virginal symbol of Voertrekker virtue, too cloistered and too ill even to dream of sexual adventures. But becoming a syndic aboard the *Gloria Coelis* had liberated her. Life was challenge now, and excitement, and new sensation. For the first time in her short life, Broni Ehrengraf was a free human being.

Duncan was aware of Broni's alert interest in sexual matters. The girl was maturing swiftly. On Voerster a normal woman's life would have been impossible for her. Aboard *Glory* all that had changed.

Like her mother before her, Broni Ehrengraf Voerster had fallen in love with Duncan.

For Duncan the problem had a painful dimension. Not a day went by that he did not see Broni and remember Eliana, lost in the dilated time of *Glory*'s wake.

"Duncan." Anya Amaya was calling him back to duty, to attention. It was dangerous to allow alertness to flag inside a gravity well. More so when the well was filled with ship-killing debris.

The Sailing Master had sent a single probe ahead of the others toward the planetesimal Duncan could sense at thirty thousand kilometers off the bow. *"There's life there, Duncan,"* Anya Amaya said.

That was not unexpected. The people of the Twin Planets had been mining the Rings for generations. So said the radio transmissions. *Glory*'s Hold 1000 contained equipment intended to make the task easier for them.

"Broni," Duncan ordered, *"use two sleds and sweep from twenty starboard to twenty port. Look for a spacecraft in sensor range."*

In a star system where a long war was being fought, Duncan thought, *a strange ship should not surprise another in space.* He issued voice commands to Buele and Dietr Krieg.

"Surgeon and Supernumerary to the bridge. We need you here."

"Straight away, Duncan." Krieg's reply came also by voice, over the intraship communications net. Buele replied with a powerful empathic blast almost unmodulated by *Glory's* mainframe.

Over the internal com-net, acid-tongued Dietr said, "Buele's talent is inversely proportional to his good looks."

"Duncan, there is a ship moving sunward." The message came through the drogue from Anya Amaya. Her rich feminine personality underlay every mental image she put through the computer. *"I see an ion trail. The ship is powered and it is accelerating. I am not certain, but I think it's a warship."*

Duncan: *"Any sign that they are aware of us?"*

"None." The Sailing Master's guesses in such matters were always excellent. Anya Amaya was a shrewd judge of human intentions.

"Duncan?" Broni was joining the circle.

Duncan responded.

"There is something much closer. I think it is a call for help."

"How many people, Broni?"

"I'm sorry, Duncan. I can't tell." Both Duncan and Amaya could feel the girl's chagrin. She wanted to be perfect.

"I sense great distress. There has been a battle. There are three still alive, Duncan." Anya Amaya's empathic communications were precise, articulated with the Sailing Master's usual clarity. *"Listen."*

At Amaya's command, the computer amplified the transmission. It was very faint. *Perhaps,* Duncan thought, *from a suit radio. "What language is that?"*

"It is a dialect of Russian." Amaya said.

"Glory. Translate."

The transmission faded and hissed in the electronically confused environment of the Rings.

Then a man's voice: *"Potemkin, can you hear me? This is Skybolt. Potemkin, answer."*

"I think he is calling the warship that is moving sunward," Amaya said.

No reply. Hissing and the strange ragged beat of the stellar emissions from Ross 248. Then the voice again: *"It is an ambush, Potemkin. Don't return. Potemkin, do not return—"*

Damon Ng had awakened and come unbidden to the bridge. Duncan said, "Damon, Wire up and take over the helm."

"Aye, Captain." Damon Ng opened his pod, unshipped a drogue, and Wired himself into the computer.

"Broni. Look for debris," Duncan sent. *"Move a sled ten degrees starboard. It seems clearer there."*

"Aye, Duncan."

Damon stripped and settled into the gel, joining with Anya to manage the ship.

Duncan allowed his attention to shift back to the transmissions. The person transmitting continued to call the *Potemkin*.

It took him several microseconds to find and identify the exact origins. A planetesimal body a half light-minute from *Glory*, bearing 343 degrees. As the probes drew nearer, the sendings clarified.

Duncan shuddered. A battle was being fought on harsh, black soil under an airless sky. The Preacher on Thalassa used to speak familiarly of hell. To Reverend MacDow'l, hell had no heat. There was only black cold there. That was the image *Glory* presented to Duncan. There were a hundred recently dead men on a tiny planetoid. Three persons remained alive there.

"Potemkin, this is Skybolt. Do you hear me? Potemkin—"

"Glory," Duncan said. *"Shut that off!"*

Duncan did some swift, rough calculations. It was impossible to bleed off sufficient delta-V to bring *Glory* within sled or shuttle range of the planetesimal and the voice. At the speed Glory was making, it would take days to turn her around.

Duncan said, *"There is nothing to be done. Our speed is too high. Our ship is too cumbersome."*

He addressed Broni with deliberate calm, grimly aware that death was out there in the cold and dark.

"What should I do, Duncan?" He felt Broni's enormous desire to please.

He let his Talent take over, reassuring and comforting a new syndic. Her sending was calmer now, controlled. Duncan watched and waited as she slipped into a triad with Anya and Damon. *Glory* responded smoothly to the skill of her new combination of handlers.

I am sorry, Duncan said silently to the Russian-speaker in the dark. *The Laws of Motion doom you. We cannot help.*

"We could clear the Ring completely by changing course a further ten degrees right, Duncan," Amaya said. *'Then we might—"*

"Hold course."

"Aye, Master and Commander."

It was bitter to turn away from a cry for help. At such times as these, the informality among Starmen vanished and was replaced by the archaic language of the sea. The language of authority. It indicated that the Master now took responsibility for the events to come.

Like a living thing *Glory* responded to the combined forces of the tachyon wind from the galactic center and the photons streaming in a flow shaped by the magnetic mantle of Ross 248. *Glory's* mains, mizzens and courses were still set, but her skys'ls and jibs had been backed so that they turned concave surfaces to the reddish light of the star she was approaching. The resulting interplay of light gave the ship the look of a jeweler's artifact made of rose diamonds and beads of amber. Each time a flurry of microdust struck the tachyon-charged sails there were showers of silvery sparks so that the entire sailplan, all ten thousand hectares of it, came to electric life.

"I am here, Brother Captain." The boy Buele had drifted into the bridge without being noticed. He was already settled into a pod and Wired. The connection of his drogue gave him complete knowledge of what had transpired in the bridge since his last joining with *Glory.*

"Buele, is there a way we can fetch this planetesimal? I need to see if we can use a sled to go down there for a few minutes."

"There are people there, Brother Captain?"

"Yes."

But Duncan knew it was hopeless.

Long years ago, when the great clippers sailed the oceans of Earth, a sailor lost overboard was lost forever. The ships simply could not slow, stop, circle, change course. Wind and sea and the vessel's own vast inertia made it impossible to pluck a lost life from the sea.

Buele said, *"I am sorry, Brother Captain. There is no course we can sail to do what you want."*

Duncan closed his eyes momentarily. He already knew what the boy was telling him. But he'd had to ask.

Death came in many guises, he thought. For the survivors on the planetesimal it would come in battle or it would come in the dark, airless cold.

But it *would* come. That was what it meant to be at war.

Deeply preoccupied, Duncan disconnected his drogue, brushed by Dietr Krieg, who was just arriving, and moved down the dark plenum into the interior spaces of the ship.

5

A CELEBRATION IN NOSTROMOGRAD

For a hundred planetary years after First Lander's Day it was said the streets of Nostromograd were paved with gold. In actual fact, then, and for the succeeding four centuries, the streets of the town were paved with wood from the forests of the Ural Mountains. Colonial nostalgia, yearning for the cities and towns of old Russia, produced the name "wooden Nostromograd," by which the town was fondly known.

Built on the site of Goldenwing *Nostromo*'s landing, Nostromograd lay on the Dnieper River in the place where the mountain cataracts ended and the broad, deep and navigable reaches of the river began. The Dnieper was the largest river on the island-continent of Ararat, and from its source in the Ural Glacier under the peak of Mount Ararat, it tumbled to the steppe in the far south. From this point southwest to Nostromo Sound, the Dnieper carried the natural resources of Nineveh to the sea: magnesium, copper and iron ore, rare minerals and timber. Ararat's northernmost province of Siberia at seventy-four degrees north latitude, a land of taiga and marshlands, could be reached in winter only by iceboat. In summer the road from Petersburg was usually passable. Northern Sound, on the Siberian coast, and the Sea of Okhotsk, directly to the southeast, were icebound in all seasons save high summer. Four hundred kilometers from the coast of Okhotsk, on a granite plateau of lakes and forests, the colonists had built the governing city of Nineveh, a town of stone buildings and cobbled streets. Nostalgically, they named it Saint Petersburg.

South of Petersburg rose the first ranges of the continent-girdling Ural Mountains, densely timbered with trees indistinguishable from earthly conifers, but hermaphroditic and hard wooded. Only one settlement had ever been permanently established in the heart of the Urals. This was the town of Perm, in the shadow of Mount Ararat's 9,750-meter peak. There had been built the monorail terminal of the line from the north, and the northernmost post of the logging road to the steppe in the south.

From forty-five degrees north latitude to the southern tip of the continent at Cape Odessa, the land was austere. Winters were still severe at this latitude, but the climate of the Odessa District, where Nineveh had concentrated its military and space complex, was almost benign. In a star system with a warmer sun it would have been tropical.

Odessa lay between South Odessa Bay and the Sea of Aralsk, a body of water indistinguishable from the vast reaches of the Planetary Ocean to which it was contiguous.

North of Odessa, on the western coast of the narrow continent, lay Nostromograd, the southern reaches of the Dnieper River, and the Volkov estate, Ullah's Vista, in the southern foothills of the Ural Mountains.

Except for the ice-bound antarctic deserts of the Blasted Continent, and a few small islands, Ararat was the only land on Nineveh. It lay like a long island in the northern hemisphere of the planet, a land of ancient mountaintops and plateaus risen from the primordial ocean aeons before the eotemporal astronomical catastrophe that had produced the Blasted Continent.

The climate and geography of Ararat suited the ethnic Russians who had settled the planet. The climate was cold, with pronounced seasons. The sea was well populated with edible and useful fishes, and best of all, the southern steppe, covering a third of the continent, lent itself well to the growing of wheat and the raising of horses. These were the chosen occupations of the farmer-descendants of the colonists who stepped from the shuttles of Goldenwing *Nostromo* as the First Aliyah on Lander's Day.

———

*

Nostromograd, like most Ninevite towns and villages, was essentially rustic—a sprawling community of low-rise buildings and chalet-like houses with brightly painted wood facades and onion-domed cupolas. The town was unique on Nineveh as the only Ninevite settlement that had a city wall. The wall had been built when the human grip on Planet Nineveh was still uncertain, and it was not known that there were no inimical life-forms anywhere on the planet. But within seventy years of the Landing, the colonial leaders had determined that Nineveh was friendly to human beings, and no more walled towns need be built. Wooden Nostromograd remained unique.

The leaders, already called Ephors, concluded that it was now safe to dispatch a call to Earth for the fulfillment of a cherished dream—the summoning of a Second Aliyah.

The decision was made by political leaders anxious to enlarge the colony. The religious leaders of the Christian Sharia, those who had suffered most at the hands of the Jihad, remained suspicious. More cautious than the politicians, they counselled delay. The Blasted Continent, they said, where it was planned new arrivals would be located, seemed a poor reward for ten years in cold-sleep. They cautioned that a Second Aliyah, given the antarctic lands, fog-shrouded and inaccessible half the year, would not be grateful. But eventually the academics and politicians and liberals prevailed and the summons was sent back to Earth at lightspeed.

The arrival of the new colonists at the Twin Planets, twenty Ninevite years after the summons, was a disaster. *Resolution* never actually reached Nineveh, and by the time the new colonists recovered from the trauma of their shipwreck on the Accursed Twin, the welcome they had been led to expect was no more.

Nineveh's politics had changed. Meetings between the religious patriots of the First Aliyah and the collaborators of the Second went badly. Nineveh immediately limited immigration from Nimrud, even to the Blasted Continent in the far south.

———

The *casus belli* of cyclic war was established. It became the most important fact of life on the Twin Planets.

In times of trouble, it was to Nostromograd, true home of the Sharia Christian faith, that the Ninevite colonists looked for guidance. Technically, the premier mosque on the planet was located amid all the other government buildings in Saint Petersburg. But the people had never accepted that, nor had the hierarchy of the Sharia Christian faith attempted to enforce the primacy of Saint Petersburg.

Wooden Nostromograd was the city most loved and most reminiscent of ancient Earth. It was a beautiful town, filled with tall trees, onion-domed mosques, and surrounded by the *dachas* of the landed gentry of the south and of the high priests and imams of the Sharia, who performed many of their religious duties not in Petersburg but in Nostromograd.

Across the Urals that girdled Ararat and far to the north lay the government city of Saint Peter. There the Duma met—when it met, which was not often. All government offices were there, as were both the traditional University of Nineveh and the newer and more aggressive Polytechnic Institute.

On Nostromograd's Volkovskiy Prospekt, one found the Mosque of Nineveh, home of the Imamate and its present Hierarch, Grand Metropolitan Massoud Bokhara (an old man of legendary rigidity in matters relating to the Sharia). Hard by Nostromo Square stood the Seminary of the Sharia, the school that trained Nineveh's clerics, and next to the seminary stood the Mosque of the Landing, religious domain of Peter Mornay, the Metropolitan of Nostromograd.

It was to Nostromograd a politician would apply if he were seeking approval from the people of a particular course of action.

It was to Saint Petersburg a landowner went if he was seeking approval of a project or exemption from military service for his farmers. To discuss all that concerned the authority of the Ephors, one traveled from the south to Perm by road and then by monorail to Saint Petersburg. There was no civilian travel by air on Planet Nineveh. Most particularly since the start of the most recent Recurrence.

Before the arrival of the Second Aliyah, Nineveh's Great Russian settlers had found a talent for entrepreneurship. The periodic Recurrences had placed a great burden on Planet Nineveh's resources. They had also brought to a halt any enlightenment of the social hierarchy of the planet. A new generation of Ninevite *apparatchiks* who might once have been scientists, artists or business leaders, had devolved into a ruling class devoted entirely to the conduct of the war and to the protection of political perquisites. The generation to whom fell the current Recurrence of the War of the Twin Planets was a true *nomenklatura* that any mid-Twentieth-Century Soviet Russian citizen would have recognized, appreciated, and longed to join.

In the steppe of South Ararat, Saint Petersburg and the planetary government were regarded as bloodsucking burdens on the population. Some embittered southerners said (rashly, because it had become illegal to ''scorn'' members of the government) that the bureaucrats of Petersburg were the best friends that the ''worker ants'' of the Accursed Twin had had in almost a dozen Recurrences.

This was a harsh judgment, but it was accurate. This Recurrence was being more viciously fought than the previous ones; and the government of Nineveh (having defamed, mistreated and aroused the men and women of the Second Aliyah to war) had now become convinced that a just and equitable peace would be possible only after the latecomers to the Twins were forced into unconditional surrender.

Five hundred years before, this notion might have had some hope of success. It had none now, but the politicians of Saint Petersburg were convinced that if only some formula could be found, peace might be at hand.

It was not.

Peace had, in fact, never been so distant. What was approaching was an unheard of defeat for the soldiers of Nineveh and a possible occupation of their homeland.

*

Yuri Efrimovich Vukasin's greatest asset was an instinct for public relations. Long before other members of the *nomenklatura* had begun to think that they might be sitting on a volcano of political discontent, Vukasin had commenced mending his private fences.

That the war was going badly, only a fool could fail to recognize. Yet the Board of Ephors, the very governmental organ tasked to make the military decisions, was staffed by complacent, foolish, and self-satisfied men.

Vukasin, a solidly built man of forty Ninevite years, wore his antique Great Russian–style uniform uncomfortably. He was by training and inclination an academic. He disliked soldiering, even the little of it he was expected to do as Third Ephor, the senior officer of the Ninevite armed forces. Vukasin had never fired a laze, never marched a kilometer. He had never left the surface of Nineveh, and he had no desire ever to do so.

With his round, soft-featured face and deceptively gentle brown eyes, he was extremely popular with the wives and mothers of the Ninevite soldiers serving offworld. To them he addressed his assurances that he was doing his best to bring the Recurrence to an end and return their sons and daughters to peaceful living. He attended memorials with them, wept with them, and prayed in the country mosques with them.

Yuri Efrimovich Vukasin was a politician of a shrewdness not seen on Nineveh since the leaders of the First Aliyah. He had first been elected to his local Duma as a representative of the Polytechnic Institute of Saint Petersburg while he was still an Associate Academician. But instead of serving a term or two in the legislature, as most ambitious academicians were satisfied to do, he decided that he had found a home in "public service." He was a natural political careerist.

Within three years he was on the staff of the Board of Ephors as a technological adviser. Within four he had announced his candidacy for the first available vacancy on the Board. And the following year, two years before the incident that brought on the current Recurrence, he was elected Third

Ephor of Nineveh, in effect the commander of the military of Planet Nineveh.

At the time the forces consisted of a ceremonial guard Regiment of Infantry stationed in Saint Petersburg. Now they contained two-thirds of the able-bodied young men and women of Nineveh.

Yuri Vukasin was a calculating, perceptive and utterly ruthless man. He had no intention of following the trails blazed by generations of educators and scientists on Nineveh. He knew himself to be an indifferent researcher and an impatient teacher. He had no intention of ever returning to the academic life. He much preferred being the senior political commander of an armed force now grown to a million men and women. He intended to end the Recurrences and then to offer himself to the people of Nineveh as the political leader they sorely needed—had needed since the shuttles of Golden-wing *Nostromo* deposited them on the steppe of South Ararat.

The war fever that swiftly engulfed the planet promised rich rewards. Yuri Vukasin launched himself immediately on a feverish schedule of patriotic appearances, war-related fund-raisings, and political volunteerism. All things that previous Third Ephors had never done, it being beneath their soldierly dignity.

A natural lover of detail, Vukasin made himself a student of Russian military history and of the lives of successful wartime politicians dating back to Peter the Great. His new devotion to war was in sharp contrast to the attitudes of his fellow Ephors, who had seemed surprised and quite taken aback by the sudden onslaught of the present Recurrence.

What his fellow Ephors had never understood and refused still to understand was that the Nimmies loathed and despised the people of the Blessed Twin and that they intended, this time, to end the War of the Twin Planets with a genocidal cleansing of the descendants of the First Aliyah.

That, Yuri Vukasin did not intend to permit. But he also intended that his people of Nineveh should reward him for delivering them.

———

Chief Ephor for Life would be a suitable reward, Yuri Vukasin thought. One that he intended to have.

For the first time in many years, the gentry and the Sharia were not avid supporters of the war with the Accursed Twin. A policy split between Duma and Sharia appeared, and in that narrow crack, Yuri Efrimovich Vukasin found space to plant his ambition.

True to the Russian traditions that guided the First Aliyah on Nineveh, victories—when they occurred—were announced from the Kremlin wall in Petersburg by the firing of an antique cannon and the reading of a proclamation by the Marshal at Arms of the Duma. These events were at first met with jubilant demonstrations in the streets of Petersburg, but as time went on and the casualty lists grew longer, the people of the capital became less and less willing to turn out and dance on the cobblestones to thank the members of the Duma for blundering once again into war.

There was a First Ephor on Nineveh. There had always been one, ever since Lander's Day, when Piotr Ilyich Gordiev, the head of the Colonial Central Committee, was revived from cold-sleep to sign off the transport manifests and release the *Nostromo* syndicate. From that time onward, a Gordiev was effectively the Head of State of the Ninevite colony.

The present Head of State, by now little more than the Speaker of the Duma, Oleg Sergeivich Gordiev, was a direct descendant of the original Gordiev. But beyond that he was a man with little to recommend him. At the moment of the current Recurrence's exploding, Gordiev had been searched for and finally found in his fourth mistress's *dacha* on the eastern coast of Ararat.

In a fury of disengagement, Oleg Sergeivich had signed over most of his seldom-exercised political powers to the Board of Ephors. They in turn appointed Yuri Vukasin temporary governor of Ararat, effectively putting populated Nineveh under martial law.

On that day Yuri Vukasin had, without asking the consent

of the Board of Ephors, announced his appointment with antique cannon volleys from the Kremlin wall.

That event was the first "victory" to be announced on Nineveh from the Kremlin wall with a cannon. Now, almost a full year later, Yuri Vukasin had traveled across the waist of the continent of Ararat to transfer the business of celebrating victory to the shrine of the Ninevites—wooden, traditional, holy Nostromograd.

Ephor Vukasin, a man with a considerable talent for measuring the public pulse, had sensed early that the people of Nineveh were not willing to make the war effort that would be required to blunt the military skills of the inhabitants of the Accursed Twin. The victories announced in Petersburg had been small ones. In some cases they had actually been defeats. It did not trouble Vukasin's conscience that he and the other Ephors were misrepresenting the course of the Recurrence. There had been, after all, many Recurrences before, and not all of them could have been victories, he reasoned. But the Kremlin still stood, no enemy spacecraft had appeared in the skies over Ararat—or even over the Blasted Continent. It followed, then, that since Nineveh had never been defeated, she never would *be* defeated. His studies had taught him that Russians were, and had always been, masters of the passive defense. On Earth, at the start of the Nineteenth Century, the Tsar's general, Kutusov, had, at enormous cost, bled the French Grand Army to death on the wintry steppes of the ancient Motherland. Others such as Voroshilov, Timoshenko, and above all Stalin, had done the same to the armies of Hitler's Third Reich. Russians were always willing to make great sacrifices.

What remained, then, Vukasin believed, was to reap the enormous benefits to be won by such stoic sacrifices. For this, the skills of a politician were far more useful than the skills of a soldier.

In private consultation with Alexis Menshikov, the Minister of Intelligence, he devised a plan that would be completed when the office of Head of State was reformed into a seat of real power, and when it was occupied by the one man in the government of Nineveh who understood the true uses of power—himself.

A peripheral, but important, project was the removal of the victory celebrations from Petersburg to Nostromograd. Menshikov, an astute judge of his fellow Ninevites, believed that the men and women of Nineveh were still Russian enough, and emotional enough, to respond to military festivals of the sort that once lighted the skies over Old Moscow with pyrotechnics. "We are all children at heart, Yuri Efrimovich," Menshikov said. "Show and pageantry lighten our hearts and feed our fighting spirit. We love to display our confidence in our power as soldiers. Even if we feel none."

"How cynical you are, Alexis," Vukasin replied. "And how right."

Accordingly, Vukasin and Menshikov had persuaded the Board of Ephors to develop a duplicate military display for each victory at Saint Petersburg and at Nostromograd. To that purpose, the Artillery Complex at the new Kronstadt Armory on the Gulf of Aralsk had been commissioned to produce seven hundred cannon in the style of the field artillery of the Great Patriotic War. These guns, together with more than two hundred thousand blank charges and five thousand light rockets, had been shipped to Nostromograd over the course of the last three months. Now, at the end of the month of Gagarin, a time fraught with subtle significances for the agriculturally oriented Ninevites, the first of the Great Celebrations of Victory at Holy Nostromograd was about to begin.

Therefore it seemed natural that the Ephor Yuri Vukasin and his shadow, Alexis Menshikov, should have come from Saint Petersburg to preside over the military ceremony, which (not by accident) coincided almost exactly with the eight hundredth anniversary of the founding of Nostromograd.

The sharp wind blowing off Nostromo Sound snapped the flags banked around the three-hectare wooden expanse of Nostromo Square. At the northern edge of the square stood the Mosque of Nineveh, a Sharia church of dark, polished timbers with brightly painted walls and gilded domes glistening in the cold, early spring midday. The Orthodox Cross and Crescent sharing the tallest staff on the highest belltower were both fashioned of solid gold: a half a metric ton of the metal, gleaming in the cold, ruddy sunshine.

Facing the Mosque, on the southern perimeter of Nostromo Square, a long colonnade fashioned of native timbers carved with images of terrestrial vines, formed the facade of the Town Hall, the site of such territorial and civic discussions and decisions as were allowed to the municipal government of Holy Nostromograd.

The boundaries right and left of the Square were lined with shops and civic buildings: the Municipal Library, the Territorial Administration Building, the Territorial Theater and the Central Ararat Territorial Armory. By the most conservative count, ten thousand men and women milled about Nostromo Square, inspecting the ranks of ceremonial cannon aligned wheel to wheel in four ranks across the Square. Each gun was attended by a crew of six Territorial Guard Artillerymen, all resplendent in dress uniforms of dark blue, scarlet and gray. As the noon hour approached, mosques among the *dachas* on the outskirts of the city prepared to toll their bells. One errant bellman misstruck his giant bronze, and the sound was carried on the wind across the roofs of the city, down the timber streets and finally across the crowded Square paved with polished wooden blocks.

The detachment of police standing to parade rest in front of the Mosque of Nineveh came to attention uncertainly, expecting the clerics within to begin pouring from the Mosque and into the street, as they had been informed the great ones might at the first sound of the Ephor Vukasin's approaching sikorsky was heard.

There was no exodus from the Mosque, though a number of junior clergymen did appear with poled portraits of the Lord Jesus and the Lord Ahuramazda, both of whom would be saluted during the military ceremony. A third portrait, discreetly smaller, of the Third Ephor Vukasin, was also being prepared for the procession.

Coached by excellent crowd inciters, a large group of people in the Square began to sing patriotic songs.

> *The winds of freedom blow*
> *Over the land given our Fathers*
> *By Ullah, to hold for Eternity.*
>
> *Ullah is great, His Sharia is*
> *A sword in our hand*
> *And our forebears' ghosts are*
> *In the ranks beside us. . . .*

There were other verses, dozens of them. The folk of Nostromograd, many already roaring drunk on the native vodka,
had formed a human serpentine and danced about the wooden
Square, singing and drinking. It was a scene the ancestors of
the Ninevites would have recognized and instantly joined.

The men in the passenger cabin of the sikorsky—the Ninevite
name for a helicopter—had been discussing a man called
Krasny.

"I worry about Gammah, Your Honor," Alexis Menshikov said smoothly. Menshikov, a youngish man already
balding and putting on weight, looked harmless in his police
uniform of dark blue blouse and colonel's silver shoulder-
boards. He made it a point to wear exactly what the street
constables wore, displaying only a modest number of the medals Ninevites so dearly loved to display. But the fact was that
Menshikov was one of the most important men on Nineveh,
and his organizing genius was likely to make him even more
so.

The years Vukasin had spent in acquiring the credentials
of a Ninevite academician, Menshikov had spent organizing
political cadres within the police force. The Recurrence—and
Vukasin's sponsorship—had increased his power.

The people of Nineveh were uneasy with their inability to
put down the (as they saw it) repeated aggressions of the Gammah and the troops of the Accursed Twin. Frightened people

tended to empower policemen. In addition to his skills and opportunism, Alexis Menshikov had chosen to ally himself closely with Yuri Vukasin, the most dynamic politician in Ararat.

"I worry about Gammah, be assured of that, Alexis." Vukasin shifted his weight on the upholstered bench of the jet sikorsky the Ephors had allotted him. He grimaced at Menshikov's statement of the obvious. Everyone worried about Gammah. But he understood with great clarity that a political leader could not display a fear. The people of the First Aliyah had an almost fanatical devotion to valor.

"I have told the Gammah messenger in Petersburg that I am a man of peace and willing to risk a great deal for a truly *productive* meeting in Nostromograd," he said. "But I have no intention of risking an accusation of treason, Alexis. These meetings could become an assassination try. That is why you are here."

"You do me honor, Ephor," Menshikov said.

"Spare me the obsequiousness. I would be a foolish man not to know that if the Gammah meeting goes badly, I may find myself dead. Or accused."

"By whom, Ephor?"

"By you, of course, Alexis Sergeivich." Vukasin regarded his companion with a rictus grin. It was an expression that transformed Vukasin's pleasant, almost foolish face into a steel mask.

"Never," Menshikov said.

"The Chinese of Old Earth had a saying: 'Say *never* only when the time is *now.*'"

Menshikov remained silent, his gaze fixed on the mountain landscape below. Nostromograd lay on the horizon, and beyond lay the silvery expanse of Nostromo Sound, a part of the Planetary Ocean. The sikorsky was minutes away from touchdown in Nostromo Square.

"Fortunate for me, Your Honor, that I am not Chinese," Menshikov said. He felt cold and rigid. It was the way fear affected him. Oddly, he relished the feeling. One did not truly value life unless it was at risk.

Vukasin favored him with a softening of the death's-head grin. "You are a realist, Alexis."

"I hope I am, Yuri Efrimovich," Menshikov said. "But there's no dreamer in me. Note that I am here, with you, and not with the old dodderer."

The reference was to Oleg Gordiev, the weakest Head of State in half a thousand years.

"A suggestion, though, Ephor?"

"About Gammah?"

"Yes, Your Honor. Why don't we restrict offworld traffic? If they cannot move to and from the Accursed Twin, the bombings will stop."

"You disappoint me, Alexis," Vukasin said. "It is not so simple as putting a cork in a bottle. Fifty shuttles or more leave Nineveh for the Rings every day. As many or more return. We cannot survive without their cargoes. A secret flight for Gammah can leave from the highlands or the steppe or even from the Odessa spaceport at any time. We haven't the force to police every one. I know it, and Gammah knows it. So should you."

The light over the communicator snapped on. Menshikov touched the switch. The pilot's face appeared on a small screen. "We are beginning to descend, Polkovnik Menshikov." Menshikov was a strict believer in subordinates' use of military titles. Perhaps among a more warlike people the formality might not be needed, but the centuries in the Ross System and the repeated attacks by the Second Aliyah had not made Ninevites more respectful of rank. Quite the contrary. The people of the north of Ararat were rebellious and disrespectful by custom. Only the aristocrats of the southern grasslands remembered ancient Great Russian military traditions.

"Very well, Leytenant," Menshikov said.

"Circle Nostromo Square once before landing," Vukasin ordered.

"Yes, Your Honor."

Vukasin spoke to Menshikov calmly. "Krasny will be well supported in Nostromograd. I want you to see to it that his entire gang of thugs and arsonists are identified and kept under surveillance. Prudence, Alexis. Prudence.''

"Rely on me, Your Honor."

"Oh, I do, Alexis. I do."

6

A DIPLOMATIC DISCUSSION

The man known as Krasny had come down the river from the wilderness above the Dnieper cataracts in four days of sleepless travel. He was accustomed to hardships, but the journey down the river between fields of growing wheat had wearied and angered him more than it should have. *It was rage that sapped his energy,* he thought. Rage at the ordered, peaceful landscape through which he had traveled since leaving the mountains. But mingled with his rage was fatigue. Years of fighting a guerrilla war—of losing comrades, a wife—had taken its toll. Krasny was near to the breaking point, though he refused utterly to believe it.

This was his first major operation since becoming Krasny, his first major operation in South Ararat since the Nimmie security forces ambushed and killed Jamallah and her cadre. *Krasny* was the old Russian word for "red"—the color of explosives bursting, the color of blood. *A fitting choice,* Krasny thought, studying the wooden square from his tiny window in the flank of the belltower of Old Nostromo Mosque.

The center of the Square had been most laboriously mined by a team of totally dedicated agents who were now, almost without exception, totally dead. But the bombs now in place were very much alive.

Thanks to Allah the Compassionate, Krasny thought, *for the medical skills used to ensure that the heart would fibrillate to the point of death before one could be forced to betray the Movement.* Nevertheless this Recurrence, as successful as it seemed, was taking a fearful toll of Gammah fighters. There were times when Krasny wondered about the price the Second Aliyah was paying for what was rightfully theirs.

It was stuffy in the tiny belltower room, which smelled of old wood, dust and dead insects. Krasny, a slope-shouldered muscular man with sallow skin, a full head of pale hair and a beard, wore the clericals of an acolyte of the Sharia Mosque, shabby and worn as one would expect of a would-be religious. The examinations the Sharia heretics had devised for the clergy were so complex and deviously written that there were literally dozens of perennially disappointed acolytes of Krasny's age and older. These disappointed ones tended to remain in and around the mosques of Nineveh, performing menial tasks and studying in garrets and cellars for the glorious day on which they would once again be subjected to trial by the Mosque examiners.

In many ways, Krasny thought, *the failed acolyte was the perfect persona for him to assume.* Other Second Aliyans of his generation were in the field, out in the Rings, with genuine military commands. But the Ayatollahs on Nimrud had chosen to keep Krasny underground, bombing lev-trains and murdering politicians. "It is what you do best," he was told. "On Nineveh you will be Krasny." It had become a title rather than a *nom de guerre.*

A disciplined freedom fighter did not complain of his assignments, and Krasny was a very disciplined man. He was descended, like all his co-Second Aliyans, from the Russian stock brought to the Ross System by the lost *Resolution.* On the homeworld, where he wore a kaffiyeh and robe, his woman, Jamallah, once said that he resembled the old pictures of Saladin, the legendary Sultan who defeated the Christian warrior-king Richard.

Jamallah was only a memory now. She had joined him in the ranks of Gammah, and she had given her life to the struggle. Occasionally, when he was most bitter and lonely, he wondered what "the struggle" was accomplishing. He had no answer. Jamallah had died at the end of a rope in Odessa Military Prison. She was taken in a roundup of Gammah assassins after the murder of an Ephor.

She had lured the pompous butcher to bed and one of her men had cut the man's throat. *The struggle,* Krasny thought. *The endless struggle.*

He let the shutter fall back into place across the tiny window. From below came the sounds of music. Drums, pipes, brass instruments. Schoolchildren were singing.

That morning there had been a partial eclipse. At this season of the year each eclipse blotted out more and more of the sun until, in deepest winter, the sky grew dark enough to see stars as Nimrud transited the ruddy disk of Ross 248.

Eclipses seemed more benign on this fat world, Krasny thought. Nimrud experienced the same number of eclipses as Nineveh, but there the darkening of the sun seemed filled with danger and celestial malice.

The malignity was imagination and years-long resentment at work, but nevertheless all Second Aliyans felt it. In the course of each long month there were a dozen or more eclipses on both worlds, but the explanation was astronomy, not politics or witchcraft. The Twin Planets orbited an epicenter which in turn orbited in the plane of Ross 248's ecliptic. Had not the match been less than perfect, there would have been two total eclipses every eighteen days, the period of planetary revolution around the epicenter. As it was, only a dozen of the eclipses out of the yearly one hundred and four were total, these coming at midsummer and midwinter on both worlds.

Krasny scowled, remembering how the children of Nostromograd had greeted the darkening of the sun with songs and dances. That was not the way of things on Nimrud. There the ritual was one of prayers for revenge against Nineveh for stealing even the light of the sun.

At the far end of the room, near the trap in the floor through which ran the wires connecting the bronze bells above with the Sacristy below, Simon Egonov, a Gammah convert and Ninevite traitor for a dozen years, squatted listening to a hand-held telecommunicator. Simon had been a communications specialist in the Ural mines before he had deserted his Gospodin, a labor broker of Perm in the central Ural Mountains. He had performed his terrorist apprenticeship there in Perm, under the loom of Mount Ararat. It had mostly consisted of setting up radio-bombs to bring down monorail pylons in the northern mountains and placing booby traps to kill road crews working on the road from Perm to the south. He had had some transient experience as a field communicator in the wheatlands of the steppe, but his true talent was technical murder.

Krasny had tested Simon severely before accepting him into the cadre that might find it necessary to blow the center of Nostromograd, along with a third of the town's celebrating men, women and children, into bloody splinters and tatters.

How dare the bastards celebrate? What cause did they have to rejoice? Krasny wondered grimly. The Recurrence was almost three years old and the soldiers of the First Aliyah had yet to win a battle. All they could manage in the Rings was survival. Even that would not be permitted for much longer.

Simon Egonov said, "Comrade Krasny, the Ephor's sikorsky is circling the town."

Simon was a man of much *orgotish*. This was a Nimrudite word meaning a mingling of bravery, slyness and sulking pride. Such a man was valuable. In battle he was more willing to die than the ordinary man. In secret work he would break the poison tooth long before reaching the point of betrayal under torture. The Ayatollahs preached that to die in the company of such a man was to start well on the journey to Paradise. *Perhaps,* Krasny thought. But though he valued Simon Egonov for his coldness, his ruthlessness and his conviction that he was, now and forever, *right* in his view of the universe, he did not fancy him as a companion on the voyage to Eden. Even if the trip was a short one.

But I might have become such a man, Krasny thought, *had I not known Jamallah.*

The bells in the Mosque of Nineveh in Volkovskiy Prospekt began to ring. The bells overhead in the tower took up the pealing. Krasny grimaced against the clangor. Other bells began to ring throughout the town. Krasny could also hear clearly the whacking noise of the official sikorsky passing low overhead.

"Not so low, stupid son of a bitch," he muttered. "I need Vukasin alive."

Egonov fiddled with his black box and the sound of the bells grew muffled as he set up a small stasis field around the belltower room.

"Thanks be to Ullah for small favors," Krasny murmured.

"Ali and Hammad have their men all in place," Egonov said listening to his handset. "What now?"

"We let the bastard land and make his speech. Then we'll make ourselves known and see."

"Will you be going down to the Square, Comrade?"

Krasny showed yellow teeth in a smile. "I wouldn't miss it for the world. Has Hammad tested his link with the public address system?"

"He can override the Ephor whenever he chooses," Egonov said.

"Let's go then." Krasny straightened with an effort. He had been crouched at the shutter since dawn and his legs were stiff. His stomach ached. He had had nothing to eat since last night's Spartan meal in the Sacristy—bread and beer stolen from the Mosque's refectory.

He stepped through the narrow door to the steel steps that spiraled down the interior of the belltower.

The smell of candlewax and incense assailed his nostrils. Old memories flooded back. The mosques on Nimrud smelled the same way, and though there were no idols or images in the mosques, the stink of holiness was the same. Krasny, an orphan raised by desert workers on the Accursed Twin, had spent many years in surroundings like these.

He held his dusty blue robes tightly around him as he made his way down the tower. Above him, Simon followed. For a moment Krasny succumbed to apprehension. If Simon were a betrayer as well as a death commando, he could deliberately fall from the ladder and carry Krasny to his death on the flagstones below. He chided himself for doubting Egonov's *orgotish*. That was the kind of error in judgment and a lapse of faith one expected from a Ninevite, not from a commando of the Gammah.

At the ground level, Krasny paused to adjust his acolyte's robe. He could hear the rumbling of the crowd just outside the Mosque. *Perfect,* he thought. When the bombs were exploded the panic following the carnage would be enormous. He shivered slightly, remembering his last engagement. A high-explosive package under the tractor of the Petersburg-Siberia mag-lev. The grasslands had been awash in fire and blood. A thousand people had perished. Perhaps more, despite what the Ephors published about a failed terrorist action. The mines under the wooden pavements of Nostromo Square would kill at least as many, perhaps more.

Crossing the Sacristy with Simon, Krasny felt a touch on his shoulder.

"Your blessing, pilgrim." The speaker was a young soldier in the uniform of a South Ararat Cossack Regiment.

Krasny, veiled by his blue kaffiyeh, lowered his eyes and made the sign of cross and crescent. "Ullah be with you, warrior."

"A word, holy one?"

Krasny was impatient to make his way out of the Mosque and mingle with the throng in the Square. But he said, "How may I serve you, my son?" He kept his eyes properly averted. Acolytes of the Sharia Christian persuasion were expected to practice extreme modesty.

"Confess me, holy one."

Krasny raised his eyes at the slightly ironic tone. The soldier's eyes were pale, hard. *Security Force,* Krasny thought. The young man's grip tightened on Krasny's wrist.

All's lost, Krasny thought.

The breath exploded from the soldier's pallid lips in a human body's primeval protest of a death blow.

Simon, dusty cloak spread to hide his movements, twisted and withdrew the stiletto from between the security man's ribs. He caught him as his knees went loose, and carefully lowered him to a seated position against one of the pillars supporting the Moorish groins of the Mosque's star-gilded ceiling.

Krasny looked about swiftly. There was no one inside the Mosque but himself and Simon. Early morning worshipers had left before sunrise in order to see the Victory Guns being ceremonially rolled into position at dawn.

With Simon at his side and his heart pounding, Krasny slipped through the metal-studded Mosque doors, out into the Square, to lose himself and his companion among the celebrating citizens of Nostromograd.

The large sikorsky settled onto the wooden pavement before the Nostromo Mosque with a beating of rotors and a sigh of hydraulics. The flying machines kept by the government in Petersburg tended to be old and overused. Yuri Vukasin was relieved as his transport settled on the wooden pavement of Nostromo Square.

A delegation from the Mosque had gathered a respectful distance from the sikorsky, and they stood there sheeplike, their robes flapping in the wind raised by the spooling rotors. Behind the clerics and all around the sikorsky was a solid sea of the people's faces. Vukasin studied them speculatively. He had learned always to look at the populace that way. Most of the inhabitants of Nostromograd were reasonably well disposed, one could see that on their faces. They expected to be cajoled by an important man. The folk of Nostromograd, after all, had a finely developed sense of their importance. They paid their taxes and gave their sons and daughters to the Recurrence without complaint. A man in Vukasin's position owed them his serious attention. One never knew when or how their support might become vital to a politician's survival.

Yet there was an element of unrest in the Square. Vukasin could sense it. The people of Nostromograd wished to be patriotic, but above all else they wished to be reassured that the war was going well, and that it would soon be over.

"What is it, Your Honor?" Menshikov asked. "Is something troubling you?" Menshikov was tense. Knowing that

Krasny and his thugs were in the town, and that Vukasin had agreed secretly to a meeting was disturbing. An attempt on the life of an Ephor could mean disaster for the men charged with the Ephor's protection. He spoke into his hand-held communicator, urging his agents to a higher state of alertness.

"Smile and wave, Menshikov," Vukasin said irritably. "It is expected."

"Yes, Your Honor." Menshikov did as he was told, feeling the fool as he waved to the mob beyond the sikorsky's windows.

The pilot let himself down the outside ladder and stooped to extend the steps leading from the passenger door down to the pavement.

The door was opened and Vukasin stepped out, hearing the cheers. *A modest demonstration,* he thought. *But good enough for now, considering that the* boyars, *gospodin and clergy were the real powers in this old town.*

From the Mosque came a procession of Sharia Imams, led by young Peter Mornay, the Metropolitan of Nostromograd. Flanked by attendants swinging censers, he extended his hand so that Vukasin and Menshikov might kiss his ring.

Vukasin lifted the hand, rather than lowering his mouth to it, and performed the obeisance perfunctorily.

"If you will follow me, Your Honor," Mornay said, and turned to lead the way to a dais that had been raised in front of the Mosque.

He gives himself airs, does young Mornay, Vukasin thought. *But he follows orders. The virtue excuses the fault.* He watched dourly as Menshikov carefully inspected the entire length and breadth of the dais. It was an insult to the people of Nostromograd and they might very well react badly to it. But with the crowd stiff with agents of the Gammah, caution became a matter of life and death.

Gammah on Nineveh was largely composed of planetary natives. That made it a bitter pill to swallow. In earlier Recurrences there had been nothing like it. The thought of First Aliyans turning traitors against their homeworld sickened

Vukasin. It was his destiny, he secretly believed, to stop this endless cycle of attack and killing from the Accursed Twin. To this end he was willing to take risks.

Metropolitan Mornay raised his hands in blessing to the crowd in the Square. The people responded with a humming mantra of devotion. It was strangely stirring. Vukasin's researches into the history of the Sharia Christians had informed him that in the early days of the faith, when church and mosque were feeding upon one another, there had been heavy infusions of Far Eastern cult doctrine into the Liturgy.

There were many contradictions. At one time cross and crescent were contending symbols. Bitter wars had been fought on Earth. The antagonism between Sharia Christian and Sunni Muslim had an ancient and confused provenance.

The Metropolitan of All Nineveh, Massoud Bokhara, had stepped to the edge of the dais. Bokhara was, himself, a contradiction, a worldly cleric. Not only was he worldly, his ancestry was closer to Krasny's than to any First Aliyan. Yet a First Aliyan was what he was, descended from the first and most aristocratic imam who had, in the mists of early times, abandoned the faith of the Prophet Mohammed to take up the cross and crescent. The history books of Nineveh mentioned the Bokhara family as exemplars of the *genuine* true faith of the Prophet Mohammed, the holy man who bestowed upon Ullah the cognomens Merciful and Compassionate.

Bokhara, now in his sixties, was a robust warrior of a man, dark eyed, swarthy, heavily bearded. He was the present heir of a family who had never claimed Russian descent, a line without Circassian eyes or pale skin, a clan, in fact, descended from desert Arabs of Earth.

Krasny hated Massoud Bokhara for his betrayal of his bloodline. It did not matter to the Nimrudite that the betrayal, if betrayal it was, had happened centuries ago.

Krasny watched the clerics from his place in the shoulder-to-shoulder crowd. Men like Bokhara could have demanded justice for the colonists of the Second Aliyah. As holy men they should have done so. But they did not. That was unforgivable.

After the blessing, Peter Mornay reclaimed the speaker's position and launched into his introduction of the Third Ephor. Krasny studied him carefully, eyes bright between veil and kaffiyeh. Had the young cleric seen him yet? Did he remember that they had met in Petersburg University a few short years ago when Krasny was a Gammah organizer there?

Krasny had enjoyed his stay at Petersburg University. The Recurrence had not yet begun. The teachers were friendly to poor students from the Accursed Twin. It was academic pressure that had caused the establishment of the many scholarships available in those days. And much of Krasny's knowledge of history was acquired at Petersburg.

One of the most activist professors, Eduard Orgonev by name, had lectured glowingly about a Russian government that once had flourished on the home planet. A marvellously conceived state devised to take "from each according to his ability and to provide to the many according to their need." But the ancestors of the Mornays and the Volkovs and the Bokharas had destroyed it, smashed it into a jumble of quarreling fragments. When the Jihad drove them from Earth, they brought their sin with them: the sin of pride, of intolerance, of bloody-minded bigotry.

Orgonev had died in a student riot in Petersburg a half dozen years ago. But Krasny remembered him as a great man.

Vukasin stepped forward and began to speak.

You have much to pay for, you arrogant bastards, Krasny thought.

On the dais Vukasin was well into his exhortation. *The man was a spellbinder,* Krasny thought, *you had to give him that.* The crowd had begun the festival in the Square uneasily, ready to question. It had been warned of hellfire and damnation by the clerics, and now here was the Ephor, pretending to be a soldier and telling the people of Nostromograd that they were the chosen of Ullah, a folk for whom Jesu the Christ had died on the Cross while the Crescent moon wept in the sky over Lost Jerusalem. It was a fantastic performance. If only the man had been born with the courage to do more than strut in his Military

Ephor's uniform, the son of a bitch would have been worthy of the Gammah.

Vukasin, limned against the ruddy light of the Ross sun, slipped easily into the bad medicine he had come to Nostromograd to dispense. He had started listing victories, naming places in the Rings that no longer existed, having been wiped out by the technologically superior military machines from Nimrud.

Krasny, a trained observer, noted with interest the gray-faced despair with which Mornay seemed to face the mention of the Territorial Guard from the southern province where the Volkov family ruled.

What had he heard? He tried to recall it accurately. Something about a small formation of First Aliyans destroyed on what Nimrudites called Planetesimal Aleph-1008. A unit commanded by one of the young gospodins of the district, Andrey Volkov.

"The battle was fierce, but our troops fought like tigers and the planetesimal remains under the Cross and Crescent of Nineveh—our seven hundredth victory of this bitter war!"

It was incredible, Krasny thought, feeling the sweaty swaying presence of people close by. *The idiots were cheering themselves hoarse, yet the man was without* orgotish. *Every word out of his mouth was a lie.*

The cannoneers were preparing to begin their victory salvoes. Vukasin spoke on. Krasny's mind was filled with the certainty that Nineveh was a world of liars. Nineveh had never been closer to losing the War of the Twin Planets.

Krasny began to push his way through the crowd to the less populated side street leading to the stone park where he had agreed to meet with the Ephor.

Vukasin was like a piece of meat ready for broiling. But he needed a bit of tenderizing. He thumbed the device in his kaffiyeh, sending the code for option number two. The response was almost instantaneous.

"Attention! Attention people of Nostromograd!"

The message was coming from the same public address

speaker that had, a moment ago, been resonating to Vukasin's false hosannahs. *That should shake some of the hubris out of the bastard,* Krasny thought.

The unexpected interruption of the Ephor's speech shattered the emotional unity in Nostromo Square. The people milled about in confusion.

"People of Nineveh! This is the Voice of Gammah! You are being lied to. You are told that there have been victories. This is untrue. There have been only defeats. Many thousands of your young men and women will not be returning to this fair world you keep for your own. Ullah's wrath is upon you!"

For lack of any better instructions, security forces were converging on the dais. Badly shaken, they didn't know where to search for the source of that strident voice haranguing them in the harsh accents of the Second Aliyah. *Simon's friends had done well,* Krasny thought. Each moment the mystery remained unsolved and the people on the dais showed their confusion was a victory for Gammah.

"Now hear me, People of Nostromograd! Nostromo Square has been mined with explosive charges. If it suits the purpose of Gammah to blow up the charges thousands of you will die!"

The crowd began to mill about in earnest. There was the beginning of a rush for the streets leading from the Square.

Not enough, Krasny thought savagely. *Not nearly enough.* He pressed the call for option three.

"So that you will know that Gammah can reach you wherever and whenever—" The public address system went silent. The security people had found the power source. But the threat hung in the air like poisoned gas.

There was a flat boom, without echo, muffled by the press of bodies it destroyed. At the far end of the Square a single satchel charge had been exploded by remote control. The explosion crushed, lifted, dismembered and scattered. There was a collective scream from the people in Nostromo Square.

That was one, Krasny thought savagely. *There are forty more.*

But they would not be needed. Yet. The throng between the Mosque of Nineveh and the smaller Mosque of the Nostromo, where Krasny had been hiding, turned into a panicked, surging river of humanity boiling out of the Square seeking the safety of the side streets.

Krasny looked across the rabble at the dais. Of course all the notables had vanished. But Vukasin would be at the meeting place. Krasny had made a study of the man, and he was confident that the explosion in the Square was just the correct amount of coercive force to apply to the Ephor.

Now, Krasny thought, *we are ready for a civilized discussion.*

The woman who opened the door to Krasny had the look of a security service agent. *Or a jailer,* Krasny thought. There was something millennial about these Russian descendants. The Cheka, the OGPU, the KGB were ever the role models for them. Was it the result of a conscious effort to remember their bloody past? Or was it simply in the blood?

Two more security agents appeared out of the shadows and made as though to search Krasny and Simon. The Nimrudite decided to put an end to this exercise in dominance before it even began.

"Don't let priestly robes deceive you Ninny pigs," he said. "Keep your hands in sight or the rest of Nostromo Square goes up in splinters."

The male agents looked stupid enough to test his threat. Which was real enough. Gammah trained its people never to bluff. He was struck by an errant, uncalled-for thought. *Is there a Paradise?* Krasny—and he was sure others as well—had their doubts about this. But as a pillar of Gammah discipline, the Muslim belief in Paradise was vital.

The woman agent snapped. "Pass them through to the Ephor. Get on with it."

Laze pistols drawn, the men escorted Krasny and Simon down a stale dark hallway into a low-ceilinged room with splintery wooden walls. They gave a brusque order to wait and left the room.

Simon Egonov, with a fanatic's patience, leaned against the wall, hands in his cuffs, finger on the switch that would alert the Nimrudites still hidden in the square.

"Are they listening, gospodin?" he asked.

"Of course," Krasny said. "Let them. And never call me gospodin. It's a White term." This was immediately understood by the First Aliyan Gammah. Once, very long ago and very far away, Whites had fought Reds across the steppes of the Russian homeland.

"Perhaps they should understand that my communicator has a dead man's trigger," Simon said.

Krasny nodded. "They do."

Minutes crawled by. The heavy air in the room smelled of stale cooking. Krasny forced himself to think of the cold, hard deserts of Nimrud. *We have fought so long and hated so hard that we tend to forget that Nimrud's austerity has a kind of beauty these Ninnies would never understand.*

There was a sound behind the door. It opened with a crash and a squad of five uniformed security troops tumbled into the room, laze weapons ready. They took up stations around the room.

Krasny found himself hoping desperately that the enemy had, indeed, been listening to Simon Egonov's statement about the dead man's trigger. In the Gammah manner, the commo device was doubly protected. First the message to the hidden bombers would be sent, then the device itself would detonate, killing anyone within a dozen meters of it. "Steady, Simon," Krasny whispered.

Simon seemed to require no encouragement. His pale blue eyes were fixed on the security troops with an expression of undying hatred. *No one can hate authority quite the way a Russian can,* Krasny thought.

The door opened again and Yuri Vukasin, looking somewhat dusty and disheveled, marched into the room followed by Alexis Menshikov, his Chief of Security. Krasny had never before met Menshikov face-to-face. The man seemed unremarkable, but Krasny knew better than to judge a policeman by his appearance. Some of the most vicious killers of history masqueraded behind accountants' faces.

Vukasin, red-faced, began without preamble. "There was

no need to explode one of your filthy bombs,'' he said in a voice shaking with anger.

''I don't agree with you,'' Krasny said. ''You had to be shown.''

''Murdering bastard! You killed a dozen innocent people.''

''There are no innocent Ninevites,'' Krasny said. The statement was steeped in loathing.

Vukasin forced himself to draw a calming breath. ''We agreed this meeting was to discuss a possible peace. Was that just a another Nimmie lie?''

''I am here,'' Krasny said coldly. ''Talk.''

''I should have you killed now,'' the Ephor said.

''You won't. So don't make threats. You want to make an offer? Do it now.''

''What does Gammah want?''

''Don't be stupid. You know what Gammah wants. We have wanted it since *Resolution* marooned us on Nimrud.''

''You want land.''

Krasny's thin lips curled with scorn. ''Not just any land. Not a hundred thousand hectares or a million on the Blasted Continent. We want our just share of Ararat.''

Simon Egonov shifted his weight and the security troopers edged forward. They were stopped by a gesture from Menshikov.

''Tempting,'' Krasny said thinly. ''But not possible, policeman. Not if you value your precious Nostromograd.''

Vukasin said, ''Let's stop this, Krasny. Let's stop it now. I can't just give you what you want, but I can give you a chance to ask for it.''

''Ask? When we are ready to take?'' The Second Aliyan's scorn was palpable. Menshikov glared.

''Yes, ask,'' Vukasin said. ''The government of Nineveh is run by reasonable men. Wars should not be measured in centuries. It is too much.''

''Go on.'' Krasny's voice was uninflected, under tight control.

''Can you speak for Nimrud?''

''Say what you propose.''

———

"Or even Gammah?"

"I am a soldier, not a politician."

That brought a narrow smile to Yuri Vukasin's thin lips. "Oh, I think you *are* a politician, Krasny. Your people have made a racial career of the politics of victimization. Your status as a bereaved lover might win you something from the Board of Ephors, but I doubt it. You will have to have concrete proposals to make. But no matter for now. I suggest a meeting between a member of your Communal Council and our Minister of Foreign Affairs in some neutral location. Can we at least agree on that?"

Krasny's eyes blazed with hatred. This pig of a man and his like killed Jamallah. Now he was boasting of it. *That will cost you more bodies in the Square, Vukasin,* Krasny thought. The whip hand. Never lose the whip hand. Not even to rage. "To what end?" he said. "More talk. During the last Recurrence there were Peace Talks that lasted six years and accomplished nothing."

"This time it could be different."

"Why should we talk? We are winning the war."

"You cannot win the war. You can only lose it. Again."

Krasny stared at his opponent. It would be so simple to kill the man. A thrown knife. A laze fired from beneath his acolyte's robe. But what purpose in that? The man was anxious to make an agreement. That much Krasny could risk. There is always time for killing, he told himself.

"I offer you a meeting with Gordiev and Massoud Bokhara," Vukasin said.

"An old man and a heretic."

"Sergei Gordiev is Head of State. Massoud is no heretic, but the Sharia Christian Grand Metropolitan of every Mosque in Ararat."

Krasny stood silently, listening to the murmurings that came through the thin walls from the people still milling about in the streets, shocked and confused by the explosion set by Gammah. Krasny looked from Vukasin to the tight-lipped Menshikov and to the armed security police standing against the doors.

———

"It might be considered," he said slowly.

"That's a start," Vukasin said.

"Where could such a meeting take place?"

Vukasin's eyes remained steady and unblinking. "On the Goldenwing that is coming."

Krasny stared at the Ninevite. So they knew. Well, why not? There was no way to keep an astronomical fact hidden.

And how much more did the Ninevites know? Were they aware that Nimrud and not Nineveh was the intended port of call for the Goldenwing? "Well?" Vukasin seemed impatient now, anxious for Krasny to make a commitment. Would his word be enough to give me safe passage out of here now? Krasny wondered.

"I will carry the message home," Krasny said.

"Then do it."

Krasny regarded Vukasin contemptuously. What was there about academics that always shone through the facade? Weak men with the hard-but-brittle crust of the politician.

Menshikov looked as though he were in pain. Obviously, he had come here hoping to kill or capture Krasny. *Another day, butcher,* Krasny thought.

Krasny signalled Simon to move toward the door. Menshikov signed for the security men to retreat.

"I will expect your acceptance within a tenday. Can you arrange that?" Vukasin said.

"Yes."

The Ninevites parted, allowing Krasny and Simon Egonov to reach the long hallway. Would there be a neck-shot so beloved of these damned Whites?

No, Vukasin was anxious to play this farce out to the end. *How much weaker than we realized their situation must be,* Krasny thought. As he moved toward the door into the street, his mind was racing. Where would the greatest advantage lie? Was it worthwhile trying to kill Vukasin and Menshikov now? He longed to make the attempt. Longed for it as he longed wearily for the key to Paradise where the Faithful claimed Jamallah would be waiting for him in a garden of milk and honey.

———

But a meeting with the old Gordiev and Massoud Bokhara on the Goldenwing. That could be vastly more rewarding.

They reached the street. People were still running to and from the Square. Krasny turned to look again at Vukasin. *Am I underestimating him?* he wondered. It didn't matter. The heat had to be turned up under him and all the Ninny aristos who kept the Second Aliyah from its proper destiny.

"When we reach the corner, Simon," he whispered, "go east and then signal the others to blow two more sections of the Square."

It would not do to let these bastards keep their balance. *Killing is what has brought us this far,* Krasny thought, as he strode along the narrow street. *Killing will carry us through to the end.*

At the edge of the Square the men separated. Krasny looked to see if Simon Egonov was being followed. It didn't matter. Simon, like himself, like Jamallah, like any soldier of Gammah, was expendable.

Krasny crossed the square and walked swiftly down the Street of Weavers toward the river, where another Gammah safehouse lay.

Presently he was satisfied to hear and feel the boom and then the thump of two more explosions.

Until we meet again, Vukasin, he thought. *On the Goldenwing.*

7

OVERBOARD

Duncan Kr, high in the port mizzen rig, anchored himself with careless skill to the mizzen tops'l spar and studied the planetary duo ahead through his gold visor's magnifying field. *Glory* was still two days from orbit around Beta but near enough to planetfall for both Twins to exhibit their radically different faces.

Glory was well clear of the cluttered space of the Ring, making it possible for Duncan to see Nimrud, *Glory*'s destination.

The planet had a Martian tint to it, a ruddiness made ruddier still by the rose-colored light of the M6 Ross sun. Duncan could see that Nimrud was a world without true mountains or bodies of open water. There were no rivers, although there were deep scars left on the land by floods that had taken place millions of years ago and were now eroded. Once, he thought, studying the sere planetary surface, a sudden rise in temperature had melted the deep permafrost, causing inundations on a planetary scale. *The chaos must have been devastating,* Duncan thought. Had there been life on Beta then? Probably not. Neither Nimrud nor Nineveh had ever produced much in the way of native life, so the *Star Guide* said. But, of course, the *Guide* was as vague as the *Sailing Directions*. What it contained came mostly from the same highly anecdotal sources. Nineveh (from this angle half-hidden by its red, angry twin), had a superficial resemblance to the images Duncan had seen of

Earth. But there were only two continents; one, spread across the antarctic, as barren as the surface of Nimrud, the other, with a kinder ecology, was a long and narrow mega-island shaped like the blade of a kaffir's *assegai*.

Why, Duncan wondered, *am I still thinking in such terms? Glory's* Voertrekker adventure was light-years behind her in distance, and decades past in Einsteinian dilated time.

Duncan regarded the planets ahead. Had the Ross system been colonized in a less politically correct era, the twin worlds would probably have been called Castor and Pollux. But on Earth, at the time of the discovery of the Ross planets, the academic fad of denigrating Western intellectual traditions was again in vogue, and the syndics of Goldenwing *Nostromo* had idiosyncratically indulged the conventional wisdom of the day by naming the Twins Nineveh and Nimrud—Near Eastern names that were, for the moment, more correct than those of the Greek twins.

Duncan shifted his mass on the light-alloy spar. *I am having a run of grim luck,* he thought. His disappointment at having been unable to rescue "Skybolt" was unduly profound. Voices came seldom out of the darkness of space; when they did a man should be able to respond. But celestial mechanics were merciless. It would have been impossible to shed enough velocity to make a stop, or even a slow-down in the vicinity of Skybolt's little planetesimal. Still, the memory of the lonely voice on the radio was haunting. What faction had Skybolt favored? For what set of images were he and his people perishing? Duncan had no idea. Perhaps that was the true nature of war. It was a strange happenstance that the syndics aboard *Glory,* who had sailed so near to so many conflicts, and who were, in fact, who and where they were because of the Great Jihad, had never actually seen war.

A thousand meters below him, through the intricate monofilament web of the starboard mizzen, he could see Broni and Buele inspecting the rig from aboard one of the small cargo sleds. Buele was instructing her on the management of the sled. He had been Wired before her, and so was senior. He was

———

skilled, too. Duncan noted with approval the ease with which he guided the sled through the maze of monofilament shrouds and stays.

The play of starlight through the spidery rig gave the impression that the two young syndics were trapped by the vast web, but only for a moment. The sled rolled inverted and angled away from the mizzen. Light reflected from the polished metal surfaces of the small machine. Attitude thrusters flickered and flared as Broni maneuvered the sled.

The girl wore a skinsuit of amber and gold, something designed for her by Amaya, who amused herself by turning out fantastic space costumes for *Glory*'s people. Duncan, himself, wore one of her creations, a surreal pattern of space black and silver points. "Night and stars for the captain," Amaya had said. Buele wore a skinsuit of flame red streaked with yellow. He glittered in the ruddy light of Ross 248.

Duncan watched the sled veer away in the direction of the portside foremast. Broni was showing considerable talent in piloting the sleds. Soon she would be ready to start flying the larger, more powerful shuttles used for landing cargo from orbit. The artificial heart Dietr had implanted in her was more than adequate for work in zero gravity. Whether she could be risked downworld was something about which Dietr still had his doubts.

The sled vanished behind the mizzen courses and swiftly reappeared inverted above the mizzen fores'l. Clearly, the adolescent girl was larking. Duncan tuned his com to the sled frequency. Immediately he could hear Broni's liquid laughter and the admonitions to take more care so near the masts coming from the Wired Anya Amaya, who was acting as remote safety pilot for Broni and Buele.

"Broni, be careful near the masts. Watch what you are doing. What is your relative heading?" Anya was having some difficulty overriding the bubbling good spirits of the two straddling the open sled.

"I am heading seventeen degrees right. I am well clear of the rig, Anya."

"We have plenty of clearance, Sister Anya." Buele habitually

backed Broni against any implied criticism. Duncan smiled at the idiot savant's use of the term "Sister." Osbertus, the old Astronomer Select, had once told Buele that men who wrote the Holy Books of Voerster taught that all men and women are brothers and sisters. From that moment on, Buele had addressed everyone, old or young, high or low, as Brother or Sister. It did not appear that he would ever desist. Dietr Krieg found the habit irritating, but it amused Duncan. Who could say that Buele, who could do orbital mechanics equations in his head, was wrong?

Laughing, Broni sent the sled into a steep spiraling climb, opening distance between herself and the mizzen foretops'l, a full thirty kilometers from *Glory*'s hull. It was the sort of exuberant play in which Duncan, himself, had engaged when he was new to space.

There was an abandon about the way the girl piloted the sled, forming the suggestion a knot of concern in Duncan's belly. If the sled should collide with the mast or spars it could be flung off into space at a speed and in a direction that it would be impossible to calculate in time for a retrieval. Or if the sled struck the monofilament rigging, the long, single molecules of the shrouds and stays could slice the sled and its riders into bloody rashers of mingled human flesh and steel and alloy fragments. Such accidents had taken place on other Goldenwings.

Duncan tongued his transmitter and called, *"Broni. Buele. Slow down and stay well clear of the rigging."*

Broni's reply was instantaneous. *"Duncan? Is that you? Where are you?"*

Duncan cast himself free of the spar and moved clear of the rigging before replying.

"I am in the port mizzen rig," he said. Then, speaking directly to Anya Amaya on the bridge, he called, *"Anya, is that sled equipped with a locator beacon?"*

"Of course, Duncan. I'm not careless, you know." Amaya sounded offended. Un-Wired, Duncan could not be certain of her feelings. He heard the voice of Dietr Krieg in his helmet.

———

"Gently, Master and Commander. Broni is tethered and in no danger."

Duncan spun angrily to look above him. There, wedged comfortably into a lubber hole, was the Neurocybersurgeon, Dietr Krieg. He was holding a medical telemetry scanner.

"She is perfectly safe, Duncan."

Suddenly irritated, Duncan snapped, *"What are you doing outside?"*

"The girl needs proper exercise and she needs to work on her piloting skills." Dietr raised the scanner. *"I want some readings on her pulmonary efficiency. Ergo—"* He shrugged the shoulders of his skinsuit. One that Anya had made with a white skeleton on a red suit. "The Masque of the Red Death," Dietr called it. It was like Dietr to have memorized chapters of Poe.

Duncan looked across the space between the port and starboard foremasts. Broni and Buele had taken the sled ahead of the ship, beyond the bowsprit, out of sight below the dolphin striker. Duncan suppressed his sudden apprehension. If the sled were to lose power and weigh out there beyond the tachyon field that protected *Glory* from the forces of inertia, both sled and riders could be suddenly rolled under by the vast swift mass of the ship.

"Broni," Duncan said, *"return to deck level straightaway."*

"Duncan! Come join us! Please. Duncan?"

Duncan reined in his sudden anger. Broni was only doing what every young syndic did, stretching her limits, surfeiting herself with the vistas of space and the complexity of the glorious craft in which she served. Duncan, himself, after so many years, still played similar games with *Glory*'s auxiliary craft. It was one of the things syndics did to find that joyous personal connection with their Goldenwing. A connection to be found only in space, where one could see the ship all around, feel her presence. It helped, too, to see the stars and feel the tachyons tingling on one's cheeks.

Duncan started down toward the hull. Hard on the starboard bow lay the disk of Ross 248. The rings of dust and debris that formed the major part of the star's companion system caused a heroic and shimmering rainbow of zodiacal light that made the star appear to have wings spreading to infinity. Ross 248's near stellar neighbors, Alpha Centauri, the Luytens, and Epsilon Ludi were bright, but ringed with the haze caused by the Rings which formed most of the system's mass.

Glory had moved inside the outer Ring and sailed now through a great interstice almost totally cleared of debris by the multi-millennial sweep of the Twins. In this open area the outer stars shone without haloes, burning with fierce intensity.

Far to starboard Duncan could make out the nebulosity of the Greater Sagittarian Cluster, an extragalactic system of stars packed so tightly together that they were believed to collide and explode into supernovas on a prodigal scale. The effect was one of unreal beauty, of churning motion frozen by time and distances so gargantuan the human senses could not truly perceive the scale. To short-lived Man, such events in space seemed motionless, eternal.

It was all there, Duncan thought. Everything for which he had left Thalassa and the Great Sea, everything for which he had given up the dour comfort of the group marriage that had borne and reared him in that bleak village called Chalkmere by the Thalassan Sea parsecs from where he was at this moment.

The demands of a Wired Starman's life had never seemed excessive, Duncan thought, until he had met and loved Broni's mother. Now that Eliana was irretrievably lost, was he having doubts? And was his uncertainty driving him to overprotect Broni? The girl had to be dealt with as an adult now. She was a syndic and a Starman, socketed and Wired. She was no longer Eliana Ehrengraf's daughter, but a member of *Glory's* crew. *Like any one of us,* he thought. He deliberately did not look again for the girl and the boy Buele on the sled. *She is not my daughter,* Duncan thought. *She is not my property. She is what the Earth poet Rilke called* niemandskind—*no one's child. No one's child but* Glory's.

As he fell in slow motion toward the great curve of *Glory's* hull, the proximity alarm in his suit pinged the note that indicated micrometeors nearby. The standard technique in such a case was to return to the mast and access one of the myriad hatches that opened into the sail storage compartments within the shaft. At this level above the deck the mizzen was four meters in diameter and made of titanium alloy 109 microns in thickness—ample protection from all but the swiftest micrometeoroid.

The inconvenience was that the alarm in the skinsuits was unsophisticated. It gave the wearer no information about the size of the approaching objects. Anything smaller than one thousandth of a gram in mass could be stopped by the material of the suit, anything larger than one hundredth of a gram could be seen and either avoided or destroyed by the multiple lasers scattered throughout the rig.

Duncan searched the area the alarm indicated as the source of the meteoroids and found nothing. Here in the rig, where a thousand reflected beams of light from the sails crossed and recrossed amid the shrouds and stays, even small objects could usually be detected by eye as they plunged though the maze of lightbeams.

He reached the mast and turned for a last look before opening the sail storage shelter. Far forward, he saw that Buele and Broni had done the correct thing, securing their sled to the foredeck and taking shelter at the bow. There was an instrument locker just aft of the cathead, but neither Buele nor Broni had as yet had reason to know this.

He called them on the com, but they had not activated their suit-coms after leaving the sled from which they had been drawing power.

"Dietr, do you hear me?" He called the physician, but Dietr had retreated into shelter the moment his own suit alarm warned him. It was a first principle. When a Starman received an alarm, he took shelter first, then looked to aid others. It was a procedure descended across millennia from the Age of the Clipper Ships. *"One hand for the sailor, one hand for the ship."*

The pinging stopped and he hesitated in the process of opening the storage hatch. Instead, he unshipped an unused halyard and fastened it to his harness, then he turned and began a powered descent toward the foredeck, still far below.

"Duncan, what the hell are you doing?" Anya Amaya's voice was in his ear, amplified by *Glory.*

"It's all right. I'm tethered."

"Like hell it's all right. We have a microswarm coming in from eleven o'clock. Get under cover!"

It was not too surprising. The swept wake of the Twin Planets was clear of debris only in comparison to the clutter of the Rings. Space, even space considered clear, was filled with the debris of aeons—the Dark Matter astronomers had been seeking ever since astrophysicists discovered that the parts of the Universe that were visible accounted for only a half of the assumed total mass of the cosmos. Dark Matter came in planetary masses and in nanomasses.

Duncan called to Buele and Broni again and received no reply. Duncan felt the g-force as he reached the end of the tether and began to swing through the bottom of an arc toward the foredeck.

As he reached the nadir of the arc he had achieved a substantial delta-V, but his swing was slow enough so that he could see Broni and Buele sheltering under the titanium housing of a halyard winch.

"Brother Duncan . . . !" Buele called.

"Stay under cover," Duncan commanded.

He swung through the bottom of the arc and out over *Glory*'s starboard quarter. It was at this moment that the swarm struck *Glory,* pelting the spread sails, parting a few shrouds and stays, and severing the halyard Duncan was using as a tether.

In a single spinning, tumbling pair of seconds, Duncan Kr was a hundred meters from the ship, trailing a whipping, angry monofilament line. In four seconds he was a kilometer from *Glory,* still spinning wildly, and the distance growing with shocking speed. By the time Duncan had stabilized himself and could see more than streaking starlight and the wildly gyrating disks of the Twins and their reddish sun, he was five kilometers from his ship and almost out of com range.

It took him another six seconds to free himself of the tangle of the parted halyard and orient himself in relation to

Glory. Then he realized, with sinking heart, that the lashing halyard had smashed his com port.

Glory had never looked more beautiful or inaccessible. She was like a silver-and-golden butterfly against the black of space, her golden wings spread to the light of the Ross sun. Even as he watched, he could see the distance between himself and *Glory* increasing as their vectors diverged.

Duncan felt a surge of panic. Starmen were known to have died this sort of lonely death, but he had not imagined it was going to be his fate. He forced himself to think calmly and without passion. *Everyone dies,* he told himself, *everyone who ever lived.* Why should it be different for Duncan Kr?

He set his life-support to human minimums and activated his locator. He had a fleeting memory of the times he and Mira had imagined they encountered those immensely distant ''Others'' in the interstellar reaches.

There was nothing like that in a gravity well so near a sun. *But,* he thought ruefully, *there will come a time—and soon, very soon—when I will yearn for the companionship of even imaginary things.*

He watched helplessly as *Glory*'s diamantine shape grew smaller. And smaller still.

8

THE SHIP'S CAT

The shrill note of the meteoroid alarm changed abruptly to a wail. Anya Amaya's drogue pulsed with an emergency message, as ancient as it was frightening: *Man overboard!*

Glory repeated the message three times in rapid succession. In the time it took her to do that, Duncan Kr had drifted a further five kilometers from the ship.

Anya reacted with convulsive alarm.

"*Dietr! Damon! Wire up!*" Then: "*Broni, Buele! Duncan's adrift. Did you see anything? Report!*" Even before she finished issuing orders, she began the maddeningly slow business of backing more sails, using the light pressure from Ross 248 to slow the ship. As she did so, her apprehension grew. She had herself once been struck from a spar and flung into space by a psychotic shipmate. She knew from personal experience the terror of seeing the gap between ship and drifter grow wider as difference in mass and delta-V translated into meters and then kilometers of separation.

Of the syndics still aboard, Anya Amaya was the senior deck officer. Without hesitation, she assumed command and began a dialogue with *Glory.*

"*Do you have him?*"

"*I am receiving Duncan's locator signal. But it is weak, probably damaged.*"

"*How far out is he now? Rate of separation?*"

"*Thirty-one kilometers. Separation increasing by nineteen meters per second.*"

"Initialize a sled. I'm taking it out."

Glory's logic was ruthless. *"Not recommended. By the time a sled launches Duncan will be out of range."*

Sometimes Glory *could be obtuse,* Anya thought exasperatedly. *"Then a shuttle. Initialize now!"*

Anya pulled the drogue from the socket in her skull and shouted into the com. "Damon, Dietr, get up here fast! Move, damn you!"

The physician and the Rigger appeared, breathless, from the main plenum. Amaya's orders were crisp and sure. "Wire in, Damon. Take the conn. Dietr, you're with me. Let's go!"

Mira and two of her offspring appeared on the bridge, eyes wide, backs arched, tails stiff and bristly as bottle brushes. Amaya extracted a remote drogue from a locker in the bulkhead. *"What does the cat know, Glory?"* she asked.

"She reads him, Sailing Master."

"Explain."

"An explanation is beyond my programming, Sailing Master. But she knows where he is and that he is in danger."

Dietr said, "It is possible, Anya. The beasts have capabilities I have only just begun to plumb."

Amaya caught up the cat and launched herself into the plenum toward the hold where the auxiliary vehicles were kept. Dietr Krieg followed.

Glory said, *"The Astroprogrammer and Supernumerary have left the deck."*

Anya Amaya's temper flared. *"Broni! Buele! Damn you to hell, follow orders! Get inboard!"*

There was no reply from the apprentice syndics. Mira growled and dug her claws into Amaya's wrist. Amaya had a blurry mental image of a large, shadowy cat, aggressively male, in a posture of aroused defense. *"Where is he, Mira? Can you find him?"*

Mira uttered a bloodcurdling shriek of rage and clung to Anya's skinsuit. The Sailing Master had a surging impression of possessive fury ablaze with fear.

At the lock into the hold used as a hangar deck, Amaya

spoke again to *Glory*. *"Pressurize and open the hold. Have you still got a lock on Duncan?"*

"Sixty-two kilometers and the signal is breaking up. There is debris between us. Initialization of the shuttle will take a further four minutes."

Amaya suppressed an urge to shout with anger and impatience. *"Have the apprentices come inboard?"* She knew the answer to that. She had been working closely with Broni Ehrengraf, who had a well-developed mind of her own.

"The apprentices are now ten kilometers out. Their separation rate is one hundred seven meters per second."

"Track them. That's a priority command."

"Aye, Sailing Master. The shuttle hold is pressurizing now."

Anya and Dietr Krieg waited in the plenum, watching the fabric bulkhead of the shuttle hold expanding as *Glory* pumped air into the normally empty cavern.

"Is your Wire working properly, Dietr?" Anya Amaya asked.

Dietr, who seldom used a remote drogue, replied through *Glory*'s mainframe, *"I believe so, Sailing Master."* He deliberately used the formal method of address. Even though he, and currently Damon, were sharing sex with Anya, in situations such as this easy familiarity would be in bad form. Despite his exalted position as Neurocybersurgeon aboard *Glory*, Dietr Krieg retained a Teutonic sense of discipline that made it possible for him to subordinate himself to Amaya in all matters pertaining to sailing and flight.

The hold bulkhead expanded to its limit as *Glory* pumped air into spaces normally left without.

In the first days of *Glory*, her holds had contained the cold-sleep combs of colonists, thousands of them, on her colonizing voyage to Aldrin. Later, most of the holds were stripped and converted into spaces for Goldenwing cargoes—machines and tools no longer suitable for high-tech societies, but adequate for less advanced colonies, terrestrial animal embryos, plants in biostasis. Goldenwings carried other things, as well, many of them on speculation. Books, musical instruments, works of painting and sculpture, bolts of exotic fabrics, films and tapes and holographs.

But no Goldenwing sailed with anything like a full load now. There were spaces inside *Glory* that had remained empty and unvisited since the days of the first Wired syndics. No starcraft powered by anything other than starlight or the ubiquitous tachyon trades could be used to carry on trade between the stars. To drive a reaction-engined ship to the speeds attained by *Glory* would have required nuclear fuel and reaction-mass ten thousand times the mass of the ship herself.

It was said that one day the ''children of the Goldenwings'' would return to Earth in faster-than-light ships powered by principles yet to be discovered on the colony worlds. Laymen and downworlders said that. Starmen knew better.

''Glory. Do you still have a lock on Duncan?''

''I do not, Sailing Master. There is too much debris for clear signals.''

Anya suppressed an urge to cry out in impatient rage. But no matter how distressed one might be, it did no good to shout at *Glory.*

The valve began to dilate and Anya, Mira clinging to the shoulder of her skinsuit, shot through. Dietr followed into the dark hold.

It was two kilometers from forward to aft bulkhead. The shuttles had been lined up facing the now-retracted launching ramp. There were thirty shuttles in *Glory*'s complement, ceramic-clad wedges twenty meters from stem to stern and powered by ion rocket motors ranged across the blunt stern. One shuttle stood open, ramp lowered, red interior alight. A rotating beacon sent spears of light searing through the cold darkness of the hold.

Anya arrowed without hesitation into the initialized shuttle, ordered Dietr into the flight engineer's station, and recycled the ramp. *''Now,* Glory. *Open the hold and give me the last bearing you had on Duncan.''*

''I can give you a bearing on the sled, Sailing Master.''

Anya wondered if she were being reprimanded for having

all but forgotten that Buele and Broni were out there, somewhere.

A band of starlight appeared as the hold's door started
down. The atmosphere in the hold fogged momentarily as
temperature and dew point touched, then whooshed from the
cavernous interior. Anya touched the ion control and shot
through the opening into space and away from *Glory*.

Dietr, who seldom went EVA, sucked in his breath at the
sight beyond the ceramic glass of the forward carapace. Beyond
the golden curves of the skylar sails could be seen a dusting of
diamantine stars, the brilliant young suns of the outer Orion
Arm.

A single ping appeared on his CRT. It expanded into the
symbol for an EV sled.

"Anya. Do you see it on your board?"

For reply, the Sailing Master sent: *"Broni! Have you a bearing on him?"*

The girl's reply was almost unreadable. It seemed that
every piece of debris between the rig and the orbit of the Twins
had a magnetic field, and that magnetic field was spoiling
communications.

Dietr heard Broni say only, *"We are on . . . bearing, I think
. . . Buele . . . says . . . seven, mark twenty . . . not sure . . .
following—"* The signal faded completely, but not before Anya
turned the shuttle and fed power to the maneuvering thrusters.
Dietr Krieg saw *Glory*'s golden shape receding, then it was lost
as the shuttle turned. The Neurocybersurgeon cautioned himself not to succumb to fear of the Outside. Many Starmen did
if their duties kept them perpetually inboard the Goldenwings.
He watched as Anya activated the proximity alarm and set it to
broadcast into space every thirty seconds.

"Are you going to rely on the apprentices' observations?"
Krieg asked.

"Have you anything better?" Anya asked sharply.

The physician remained silent.

*

"We are in danger, Sister Broni," Buele said earnestly. "The Brother Captain will be angry with me." He straddled the stem of the sled, feeling the pulsing of the reaction-motors against his short legs.

Broni made no reply. She was at work with the range detector attempting to pick up the sendings of the locator beacon in Duncan's helmet. She had been aboard *Glory* long enough to understand that Duncan was in mortal peril, a peril that grew with each passing second. But she steadfastly refused to consider the actual possibility that Duncan could not be retrieved. And even farther from her mind was the danger which Buele was so correctly announcing.

"Duncan will be angry with us both, Buele," she said. "But first we must find him."

"Of course, Sister Broni. Have no doubt."

Broni wondered what it was Buele meant by that cryptic statement. But many, even most, of Buele's pronouncements were as eliptical as that. One could only assume their meaning by measuring them against what one knew of the boy who uttered them. Of one thing Broni Ehrengraf was certain. Neither on Planet Voerster nor aboard *Glory* had she ever seen Buele afraid. She remembered his Spartan conduct aboard *Volkenreiter* on the home world. The Voertrekker-Praesident's dirigible had found itself in a mortal storm, surrounded by the crags of the Shieldwall, and Buele had helped the Luftkapitan-pilot to guide the vessel to a safe landing. If anyone was going to retrieve Duncan, it was likely to be Buele. *And me,* she amended the thought. She was pleased to realize that she felt no fear herself, despite the alarm she had heard in the Sailing Master's voice.

She ran through a swift check of the reaction-mass available. The sled was down to eight percent. That meant that if Duncan were as far as thirty kilometers from the ship, the sled could reach him—but not retrieve him. It would be stranded at least twenty kilometers from *Glory*.

But there was a ghost on the scope. It almost certainly had to be the mass of a shuttle, Anya's shuttle, closing in on them at five meters per second. Relative speed had to be kept low because the space around them was littered with dust and debris.

"Anya? Anya, can you read me?" Her com was cluttered with the clicking, hissing static characteristic of a debris field.

The reply from Anya Amaya was indecipherable. Radio reception had deteriorated badly in a short time. Anya would correct that if she could by boosting power. But the interference had a pattern. Broni flogged herself to remember her lessons with Duncan. The tone and volume of the radio trash meant that both shuttle and sled were transiting a cloud of micrometeoroids, size unknown, extent unknown. But the individual parts of the cloud had to be submicroscopic to produce the fine-grained static she was hearing.

She warned herself that such submicro swarms often contained a few "giant" particles, some as large as two micrograms or even larger.

She turned to look back at *Glory*. Their tracks were inevitably diverging. The ship already assumed a different aspect, and was probably as many as thirty kilometers from the sled. She sucked in her breath as the angle changed and *Glory* appeared as the central object in a sky-spanning zodiacal light, golden, accented by the glowing filaments of the rig and sailplan, and blazing with the golden reflections moving across the golden skylar sails.

"It is very beautiful, Sister Broni," Buele said. *The boy's empathic ability was remarkable,* Broni thought. He was like some of the cats aboard, with the ability to step inside one's personal space and share one's most secret emotions. *Such a Talent was valuable,* Broni thought with more maturity than her years suggested. Or dangerous. All Starmen were talented, all were empaths. But what else might Buele be?

Duncan would know. *Therefore,* the girl thought with controlled precision, *it was necessary to retrieve Duncan and return him to* Glory.

"I think I am getting a signal from Duncan, Sister Broni."

"Do you just think or is it so? Concentrate, Buele."

"The reception is very bad," Buele said, as though deflecting criticism. That was not like him. He was changing, gradually

changing. Was it simply because he was maturing, or was the change deeper?

"I hear him, Sister. In my head."

"Does he know?"

"I don't think so, Sister Broni."

"Follow him, Buele. Never mind our fuel state. Anya is coming behind us in a shuttle."

Again the girl calculated the separation between the sled and *Glory*. The Goldenwing was diminished in size so that it resembled a jeweled and gold butterfly against the black of space. *How beautiful she is,* Broni thought, *and how frightening to see her so far away.*

A loud transmission from Anya reached Broni's com. *"You must be on the right course, Broni. Mira is going crazy."*

The cheet, Broni thought. No, that was not right. Mira and her litter were not Voersterian cheets, no matter how much they resembled the familiar animal she knew. Mira was an Earth beast, a cat, ancient in the homeworld's history and legend. A critter believed to possess magical powers. That part of the cat's legend had not adhered to the Voersterian look-alike.

"How is your fuel, Broni?"

"We have enough to last eighteen minutes more," Broni said.

"We are right behind you." Even the hissing of the cluttered sky did not disguise Anya Amaya's concern. *How wonderful that was,* Broni thought. On Voerster, her mother, the Ehren-graf, had loved and guarded her. But to her father, the Voertrekker, Broni Ehrengraf Voerster had been a political token, a piece to be moved on a chessboard. Here, in deepest space, she had the love and support of every syndic aboard the Goldenwing. It was a remarkable and sustaining fact of existence.

The girl thought about Duncan Kr, by whose strength and authority she had become a Goldenwing syndic despite her infirmities. *I love you, Duncan,* she thought.

"What did you say, Sister Broni?"

Was Buele an example of the New Man the geneticists of Voerster had always contended would one day arise from the people of Voerster? Unlikely. The Voersterian medics envisioned something much grander.

"Don't lose him, Buele."

"Never, Sister Broni," the boy said. *"Never."*

9

KAT

Ekaterina Volkova regarded her companion with a mixture of suspicion and reluctant admiration. Tempering her customary tendency to make harsh judgments was the secret gratitude she felt for his part in returning her to active duty.

Her original response to the message Peter Mornay had brought to Ullah's Vista on the second tenday of Gagarin had been shocked disbelief. In that it had not been very different from the reaction of her mother, Irena, who still refused to leave her quarters and would accept visits only from the local imams of the district. She had even closed herself off from Peter Mornay, by right and rank her confessor, because he had been the source of the sacrilege.

And now, of course, with the ponderous, ironclad logic of the older generation, Irena was convinced that Andrey's death in the Rings was Ullah's punishment for the Volkov's part in the Ephors' scheme to attack the approaching Goldenwing.

Yet Kat, who disliked Yuri Vukasin for many reasons— some sensible and others not—found herself grateful for an opportunity to avenge her brother's fate. She knew intellectually that revenge was a poor motive for anything, but emotionally she yearned for action.

The day had been spent on the Odessa paradeground, performing the military rituals that went with the assumption of command of the Tenth Battalion, Territorial Guard.

The people of Nineveh, though they thought of themselves as only part-time soldiers, were, in fact, professionals. The endless cycle of Recurrences made each generation of Ninevites soldiers in turn, and each Recurrence required of them a higher level of military professionalism.

The fact that both Kat and Andrey had selected the service in which they intended to fulfill their military obligation at the age of thirteen was a measure of how pervasive in Ninevite life the martial ethic had become. It also accounted for the dubious regard in which Ekaterina Volkova held the person of Third Ephor Yuri Vukasin. Try as she might she could not rid herself of the conviction that Vukasin was a parvenu and a man unqualified for the military post he held. Until the bombings by Gammah at Nostromograd she had thought him a physical coward, but no longer. The lowborn academic-turned-politician-turned-soldier could no longer be dismissed simply as a jumped-up opportunist.

Kat and Vukasin sat at table in a private dining room of the Officer's Club of Odessa—a room Kat had not even been aware existed in the old-fashioned castle on a hill overlooking the causeway to the islands of Odessa Spaceport and the Sea of Aralsk. *Rank, quite obviously, had privileges,* Kat thought.

The dinner had been quite lavish, considering the restrictions and blue laws made active by the Recurrence. Kat could feel the slight tension in the muscles of her face that a stasis field always caused. There were only two reasons a ranking officer would order a privacy field surrounding a dinner for two, and one of them was, to Kat, unthinkable. The other was a powerful need for military secrecy.

But Vukasin seemed in no hurry to do more than exchange civilities with the new full colonel of the Tenth Battalion. His round, almost clownish, face seemed out of place on a man wearing the uniform of Nineveh's highest military officer. It reminded Kat of one of the animals brought as frozen embryos to Nineveh along with the First Landers. It had been a food animal called a pig, a stump-nosed, foolish-looking beast that for some reason had not done well on Nineveh.

But there was nothing foolish about the intense scrutiny of Vukasin's small, bright eyes. He projected a shrewdness and alertness that was rare in South Ararat.

"Ephor Gordiev and the others were impressed with how smoothly you assumed command of your new unit, Polkovnik Ekaterina," Vukasin said. "There are very few women colonels in the Territorial Guard, as I am sure you know."

"I do know, Your Honor," Kat said. "Though I have never understood it."

"I belong to a new class of the *nomenklatura*, Polkovnik Volkova. We are trying to change things," Vukasin said.

"Has recruiting become so difficult?" Ekaterina asked wryly. She felt she needed to get through Vukasin's contrived social armor. Did the academic life teach him to be so self-protective?

He lifted a wineglass and regarded its golden color. "A white Pinot," he said. "From the eastern highlands." His small eyes lifted to lock with Kat's. "Our lands are varied, Ekaterina Alexandrovna," he said. "But they are *ours*." He lifted the glass and drained it. "Now, let us speak of more pressing matters. Are you well? How near to grown is the arm?"

Kat extended her arm, flexed her still childish hand. "Strong enough to hold a weapon," she said.

"And the leg?"

Ekaterina bridled at the intimacy. She hated discussing her injuries with outsiders. "Complete," she said shortly.

"I will take your word for that. But the regrowth medics must clear you. That is understood?"

"I haven't come this far to spend another six months recuperating," Kat said firmly.

"How much did young Mornay tell you?"

"Very little."

Vukasin said flatly, "I understand that the Gospodina Volkova has taken to her rooms because of what was said."

"My mother is an old-fashioned woman," Kat said. "She may have taken to her quarters because of what she heard the

Metropolitan say. But she stays there because my brother was lost in the Rings.''

Vukasin's eyes became steely. ''I have held off stationing a garrison at Ullah's Vista because the Volkov reputation earns you that courtesy. But if it becomes necessary I will isolate Ullah's Vista from the rest of Nineveh. The Goldenwing operation is most secret.''

''Security troops are not required to keep my mother discreet, Ephor,'' Kat said coldly.

Vukasin inclined his head. ''I will accept that.'' He poured more wine. Kat left her glass untouched. ''There is something you must know before we proceed further,'' Vukasin said. He paused for what seemed a long while. ''Your brother Andrey is alive, Ekaterina Alexandrovna. He and two other survivors of Operation Skybolt were captured by a scout crew from Nimrud.''

Kat felt a great burst of joy and hope. ''You know this for a fact, Ephor?''

''I do.''

Kat sketched the sign of cross and crescent. *Thanks be to Ullah the Merciful,* she thought. ''How do you come by such information?''

''Krasny,'' Vukasin said.

''*Krasny?*'' Every Ninevite knew that name, and hated and feared it.

''I met with him in Nostromo,'' Vukasin said. ''The day his Gammah assassins exploded three bombs.'' He regarded Kat steadily. ''And we have communicated since. Perhaps I should be less forthcoming, but you have a right to it all.'' He paused and then said carefully. ''You belong to a class of society with a great many archaic notions, Gospodina. Are you willing to sacrifice a few of them for the cause of victory?''

It seemed to Kat that his porcine face was no longer softly contoured. It seemed carved from granite. An amazing transformation. It was, she realized, a moment of decision. For her. Vukasin's decision had been made long ago. That was obvious.

"Yes," she said.

"The Goldenwing will arrive in orbit around the Accursed Twin in four tendays. I have been bargaining—haggling, if that suits your opinion of me better—with Krasny. I have convinced him that I—we—are ready to open negotiations with the Accursed—and with Gammah as well—but mainly with their ruling collective—"

"About what can you negotiate?"

"Land."

"The Blasted Continent? That's been tried—"

Vukasin shook his head. "Land on Ararat."

If Kat had been told that Ararat would be swallowed by the Planetary Ocean, she could not have been more dismayed. *Ullah the Compassionate,* she thought, *in what treachery have I allowed myself to become involved?*

Vukasin raised a warning hand. "I have no intention of ever giving land to the Nimmies. I lied to Krasny. I intend to do worse. I am not asking you to betray our country. But I am asking you to betray your honor."

Ekaterina stared at Vukasin. There had once been a French general on Earth, a cavalry leader, whose single dictum in war was: *"L'audace, l'audace! Tojours l'audace!"* Was Vukasin such a man?

"Very well," she said. "You intend to meet aboard the Goldenwing. And you intend to use my battalion to take the starship. What else should I know?"

Vukasin nodded slowly. "That I have never been under fire, Gospodina."

Ekaterina said, "If my brother is alive, he must be at the Black Desert prison on Nimrud. I would join your plan much more readily if I knew that he was out of that hellhole and aboard the Goldenwing. Am I making myself understood, Your Honor?"

"And am I being threatened, Gospodina?" The Black Desert prison was the Nimrudite death camp. It was seldom mentioned, and never escaped from. Ekaterina Volkova was making her price perfectly clear. It was the act of a harlot, he thought with lower class prudery. But the price was payable. In fact, Kat's gambit appealed to the charlatan in him.

"Service for value, Ephor," she said. "It is the way we live on the steppe."

"I was about to ask Ullah to give me *orgotish*," Vukasin said, using the Nimrudite word deliberately. "But He has already given you enough for both of us. Can you train your force in three tendays?"

"What will the opposition be?" Kat asked.

"From the Goldenwing syndics, no opposition. They sail with very few in their crews. Six, perhaps. No more than seven. They carry no real armament. It is not their tradition to go armed."

"Are you so certain of this?"

"Unless Goldenwings have changed since the wreck of *Resolution*," Vukasin said. "Change is not likely. It is in the nature of their calling that they remain as unchanging as can be. Intelligence guesses that they need stability to keep their mental balance. The Einsteinian equations force them to live as time travelers."

Like all colonial descendants, Kat understood the fact of the Einsteinian equations and what near-lightspeed travel did to relative time. She did not accept the popular fantasy that Goldenwing sailors were time travelers or immortals. But it depended on one's perspective. To a planet-bound colonial, it did appear that Wired Starmen were a different breed of folk. One could only guess what they might do in any given situation.

Kat asked: "How many Nimmies will escort the Accursed Twin's negotiators?"

"As few as I can arrange. Absolutely no more than twenty nor fewer than ten. I will insist on an equal number of our Territorials. I expect you to prepare a force of at least five times stronger."

Kat regarded the Ephor with increasing interest. Soft on the outside and steel on the inside. Did the Board of Ephors and the Council of Strategy realize what they had in their midst?

"Will you meet my condition?" Ekaterina asked.

———

Quick anger appeared in the Ephor's eyes. "*Condition* is a harsh word."

"Request, then, Ephor."

Vukasin remained silent.

Kat took a deep breath and said, "A prisoner exchange to show goodwill. Aboard the Goldenwing."

"We have no Nimmie prisoners to exchange, Polkovnik Gospodina Volkova. You know that as well as I do," Vukasin said.

"You and I know it, Yuri Efrimovich, but do the Nimmies?"

Vukasin's eyes grew speculative. "I've underestimated your gift for treachery, Ekaterina Alexandrovna."

The Ephor stood and walked to a nearby window. The night had cleared and the nearby stars glittered in the wind. The thin scimitar of Nimrud had appeared once again, emerging from the shadow of Nineveh.

Vukasin stood for a moment looking at the vast sky over the dark Sea of Aralsk, and at the bright stars of Nineveh's sky: Almach, Mirach, Alpheratz, Deneb. Kat moved to Vukasin's side, standing taller than he. She wondered if her height made him uncomfortable, as it did most men of her acquaintance.

He said, "It might be arranged."

"It must be arranged, Ephor."

"I did not expect so much steel in an aristocrat, Gospodina."

"Then find it instructive, Ephor," she said coldly. "I want the survivors of his detachment as well."

He looked for a long while at the blade of light formed by the Accursed Twin in its new phase. "The astronomy of our system is beautiful, don't you think?"

"It is all I know, Ephor."

He turned on Kat with the face of an executioner. This was a White matter. Gammah and the Nimmies spoke of things Red and things White. When dealing with aristocrats, certain Ninevites did the same. A consideration of *class* crossed all lines. "No, Gospodina, you know a great deal more than that. Don't take advantage of it with me again. Not ever."

10

THE DOMINANT TOM

G *lory* now resembled a moth frozen in black amber, a tiny brilliance against a vast starshot dark. Duncan's spinning motion had slowed almost to a stop. Despite the fact that he was moving through space at nearly the same speed as *Glory,* he seemed motionless in an enormous bowl of black night.

Due to the angle at which he was traveling, the twin disks of Nineveh and Nimrud lay forty degrees off his apparent course. Nimrud reddish and angry, Nineveh a cool, pelagic blue.

If this is prelude to dying, Duncan thought, *I cannot fault the Almighty's taste.* Trite phrases—"gems on black velvet," *Glory* "a jeweler's masterpiece"—arose in his mind to describe a scene of vast, unreal beauty.

"Dunc— can you— If you can— please . . . reply—" The broken transmission came from a shuttle, from Amaya, Duncan thought. That was bad news. It was unlikely that the radio gear aboard one of *Glory's* shuttles was faulty. By simple elimination, that meant that his own suit's receiving com unit had been damaged by the lashing halyard that had smashed his transmitter.

He tongued the com system and said, "I am receiving you badly, Anya."

The words died inside his helmet. Death inched closer.

I wish I were a religious man, Duncan thought. *My family group tried to make me devout on Thalassa.* "There always comes a time when one must rely on the power of prayer, Duncan.

Prayer and faith." His mother, clan leader Glendora Kr, said that. How long ago? To a Starman, did that question make sense?

He closed his eyes and imagined that he stood on a high cliff overlooking the Planetary Ocean of Thalassa. Gray sea, gray land, gray sky overburdened with the mighty shape of the moon, Bothwell. Cold struck into him, into the very marrow of his bones. *Was that the proximity of death?* he wondered. His suit's life-support was still functioning, but the cold was *deep*.

A phrase Black Clavius had been fond of using on Voerster formed in Duncan's mind. *"Innocent of the ways of the world."* It was so archaic, so Middle Centuries Earth Victorian, that he was forced to smile. But in simple truth, Duncan knew almost nothing of what the black Starman had called "the ways of the world." Any world. He had been born on a nearly empty continent by a frigid, empty sea. When the Starmen came on Search he had become a ship's boy aboard a Goldenwing. Then through the years he had sailed *Glory* among the Near Stars, from Barnard's to Sirius to Epsilon Indi and back across the known sky to Tau Ceti and Struve 2398 and Alpha Centauri. But little of that time was ever actually spent downworld, among the colonists and their ways.

Only on Voerster had he learned anything of "the world." There he had loved Eliana. There he had lost her, as he had known he must. He opened his eyes and looked around him. Distance steadily diminished the image of *Glory*.

He managed a sketch of a smile. "This is the way, then. I die ignorant of the ways of the world," he said aloud. "A virtually virtuous virgin."

"What is that you said, Brother Captain?"

Buele's transmission was strong, nearby. Hope surged. *"Buele, can you hear me?"* Duncan asked.

"Not very well, Brother Captain. Your transmission is breaking up again."

"Can you receive my locator beacon?"

"No, Brother Captain. Have you a flare?"

One, Duncan thought. *Just one*. He had failed to replenish the suit's supply before going EVA. Carelessness, the killer of Starmen. *Or do I have a death wish? Have I lived too many years?* How Amaya would bridle at that dour Thalassian notion.

"I'll save it for last, Buele," Duncan said. *"Are all your sled lights on?"*

"Yes, Brother. Can't you see us?"

Duncan used his attitude jets to rotate slowly in three dimensions. There. Almost lost in the glare of the Twins. Three small points of light. Red, green and amber.

"I see you, Buele. Rotate your sled right. Slowly."

The lights rotated, angles between them changed. The amber dorsal light vanished. The sled was head on to Duncan now. *"Hold now and ease forward. One meter per second."*

Buele complied. But *Glory* had diminished even more. Her shape was losing definition, the reflected starlight from her fluttering, backing sails made the image twinkle, as though she were shining in air.

"Broni. Can you read me?"

"I hear you, Duncan. Your transmission is very poor."

"How much reaction-mass have you remaining?"

"One hundred ten grams."

Duncan tasted bitterness. Far too little to get them back to *Glory. So I have killed them, too,* he thought. *I should have known they would come after me no matter that they were ordered to remain on the Goldenwing's deck.*

"Can you see us now? I'm so glad we've found you, Duncan."

The young ones, Duncan thought, listening to the sound of her voice saying: *I am new and immortal.*

The sled's light grew brighter. They would reach him at almost the same moment the last of their reaction-mass was expended. Then they, and he, would drift for eternity in Ross 248 space.

"Broni. This is Anya. Are you talking to Duncan?"

Duncan rotated himself, searching for the shuttle from which the last transmission came. He could not locate it, but the strength of the transmission overwhelmed the faults in his com system.

"We have found him, Sailing Master." Broni. Being the cool Starman. He was lost in space and we have found him. A triumph for the children.

An image formed in his mind. An image not of his creation. It was a projection, powerful and terrifying.

He saw himself crouching in a dark place. He was large and powerful, armed with teeth and claws and a surging, raging mixture of fear and anger. He twisted his helmeted head to look behind him. His movements seemed incredibly stiff and restricted, not strong and fluid as he knew they should be. He could see the dusty light of the Rings, now millions of kilometers away. But between the Rings and himself was a shade, a vast, twisting darkness that was blacker than black. Some instinct told him it was an opening and that something was flowing through it hungrily—

"What's happening to me?" The cry was torn from him. He could feel his claws flexing, his black lips drawn back to bare saber-shaped canines.

The images collapsed, leaving him gasping and trembling with unused adrenaline.

Aboard the shuttle, Anya was defending herself against the attacks of a terrified and infuriated cat.

Dietr shouted, "Look at the power of that transmission from *Glory*! That was a ten terawatt surge!"

"Dietr! For God's sake, hold Mira!"

The cat was like a bundle of barbed wire. Her pupils were dilated, her fur extended, her ears flat against her skull. She was screaming with rage and fear. Her mental images, powered by the burst from *Glory,* were reaching out to the dominant tom, the protector of the pride, the mate of the-great-queen-who-was-not-alive.

The thing pouring through the dimensional warp presented itself to Mira as something wolfish, vast in size, armed with overpowering malevolence. Mira clung to the velcro bulkheads and shrieked for Duncan. All *Glory*'s syndics, aboard and adrift, heard her and understood the core of her cry with a primal instinct.

"Good God, she's calling him!" Dietr gasped.

Amaya, half recovered from the shock of Mira's attack, thumbed the com switch on the controller.

"*Broni. Buele. Can you hear me?*"

Broni sounded out of breath. "*Yes, Anya. What happened?*"

"*You felt it?*"

"*Oh, yes. What was it?*"

Amaya chose not to guess. "*Is Duncan in sight yet?*"

Buele spoke up. "*I see him, Sister Anya.*"

"*Are you out of reaction-mass?*"

"*Almost, Sister Anya.*"

"*Use what you have to reach the Captain. Then boost your locator beacon.*"

"*Yes. Sister Anya.*"

Anya looked from Mira, still clinging defensively to the bulkhead, to Dietr. "She did that, Dietr."

"She. And ten terawatts from *Glory*. My God, Amaya! What a breakthrough."

"But what *was* it?"

"What could it have been? An image in a cat's brain. A primal feline fear—"

"You don't believe that for a minute."

"I don't want to believe it, Anya. I don't want to share space with whatever she sensed. I don't want it to be real." He reached out with uncharacteristic gentleness and brought Mira against his chest. "It's all right. *Hab' Mut, Katze.* You have found him for us." *And perhaps much more,* he thought.

11

WHO GOES THERE?

At 950,000 kilometers the Twins loomed, seemingly just beyond the rig. Sunlight danced through the web of monofilament stays and braces, sending arrows of reflected illumination through the curving transparency of the carapace to pattern the fabric skydeck. The double planet system filled a third of the sky: two great orbs—one the color of sand and dust, the other the brilliant blue and white of clouds and sea.

The syndics were gathered in the carapace deck in extraordinary session.

Duncan had specified that this meeting be delayed for at least thirty-six hours following his return to the ship aboard Amaya's landing shuttle. He wanted calm judgments and considered speculations about what had happened to him and to Amaya, Krieg, Buele and Broni, in space.

Damon, who had stayed aboard *Glory* with the conn while Duncan was adrift, had felt the effect, but less strongly than had the others. The tremendous surge of computer power *Glory* had projected at her spaceborne syndics had been tightly beamed. Even Duncan, who knew *Glory* best, marvelled at the Goldenwing's unsuspected ability to absorb a mental imprint and hurl it into space like a giant spear.

Until this moment no one on the skydeck had said aloud what was most disturbing. *Glory*'s computer had accepted the angry image from the brain of a *cat,* and had, for a moment, made Mira's small, intense mind capable of transmitting a clear—and terrifying—picture.

At Duncan's explicit order, Mira had been brought to the carapace deck. She sat like a statue of Bast in the center of the circle the syndics had formed to begin their meeting.

They floated in the chill air. Shadows of the rig made intricate patterns on the fabric deck. The silence grew palpable. Mira sprang from the circle to Duncan's shoulder, from which vantage point she regarded the circle of Starmen with feline inscrutability.

Duncan said, "First, from Dietr. Tell us exactly what you believe Mira's capabilities are."

The Neurocybersurgeon said, "She's a *cat*, Duncan. What else can I say?" For one so driven to experiment, Dietr Krieg became strangely restless and uncomfortable when confronted with the true implications of his work.

"Well, then, let's see what we know," Duncan said. "Mira's drogue. What is the range?"

Dietr said, "I always assumed that the range was limited. Not more than a thousand meters, if that."

"Did you ever conduct tests?" Anya asked. She had donned a skinsuit for the meeting. Duncan had ordered no distractions.

"Of course, Anya," the Cybersurgeon said in a defensive tone. "It was only a surgical exercise, *lieber Gott*. Why would anyone need to do engineering tests? I never intended that Mira nor any of the other cats would leave the ship. It just didn't occur to me to test the range of their implants."

"Why did you operate on the cats?" Broni asked.

"I told you, child. It was an experiment. An exercise."

"Are they more clever now than before you made the implant?" she asked. "Or is it only that they can communicate with *Glory*?"

"Of course they are cleverer, Sister Broni," Buele interjected. "We are all enhanced by *Glory*."

Damon said, "Goldenwings' computers are all self-repairing, self-aware. They always have been."

"The computers are *machines*," Dietr Krieg said sourly. The experimental whimsy of which he had been ironically proud had opened a gate that frightened him—frightened them all.

"So are we all machines," Duncan said. He looked at the circle of faces surrounding him. "Now I ask you all this question. Does the phrase 'great-queen-who-is-not-alive' mean anything to any of you?"

The syndics looked baffled. Mira stared into the dark shadows of the large compartment.

"All right. Dietr," Duncan said, "rank us according to our latest empathic readings."

"That is bad policy, Duncan," the Cybersurgeon said.

"To hell with policy, Dietr," Duncan said shortly. "Just do it."

"Very well, Captain. First, you. Next in order, Broni, Buele, Anya, Damon and me."

Anya shot a quick, momentarily resentful look at Broni Ehrengraf Voerster. Dietr shrugged as if to say, *He insisted.*

"What about Mira?" Duncan asked.

"Duncan, that's a meaningless question. One cannot rate an animal on a human scale."

"Why not? We are all animals, too, Dietr. You must have made empathic measurements. It would be unlike you not to. I ask you again. What about Mira?"

"This is very unscientific," Dietr complained.

"Damn it, Dietr. You were in the shuttle. You felt the blast *Glory* emitted. The leading edge of that carried Mira's perceptions. And we've spoken about that many times. Now tell me what your tests of Mira and her brood showed."

"I can't be held to this, Duncan. The scales don't match in any way that makes sense. Apples and oranges. Man and beast."

"Don't be so damned species proud, Doctor," Duncan said. "Not out here. What did your tests tell you?"

"The cats are highly empathic. Say *extremely*."

"Tell us something we don't already know," Amaya said.

"Maybe more than merely empathic." Dietr made an uncharacteristically vague gesture. "How can anyone be certain?"

Duncan said, "No one is asking for certainty, Dietr." He lifted Mira from his shoulder and held her, looking into her golden eyes. Was she receiving input from *Glory* at this moment? There was no way to interrupt the flow of information between *Glory*'s mainframe and the cat's brain. Dietr had not equipped the radio-drogue with a shutoff switch. Mira and those of her brood that Dietr had enhanced would remain in contact with *Glory* until one or all of them moved out of range or died.

"What did you see out there, little queen?" he said aloud. Was it, he wondered, one of those entities she sometimes "saw" lurking out beyond the galaxy's edge? And were those images of a real thing? Or were they shadows out of the depths of a beast's mind? Then again, was Mira vulnerable to a mass delusion brought on by the stress of mortal danger? *We are both Terrestrials,* Duncan thought, *does Gaea whisper to us both when we are at risk?*

But the images, he thought. *Vast, blurred, distant, and so incredibly malevolent. Have we finally made that first contact that has stirred the imagination of Earth's creatures for so long? Only to discover a malevolence beyond our imagining?*

Damon said, "I was not Wired when the power surge left the ship, Duncan. But I felt an overspill from *Glory*. I don't know how else to describe it. I was afraid to connect until all of you were back aboard. I heard some of what you said on the shuttle voice com link. Did I do wrong?"

Duncan shook his head. "The ship comes first, Damon. Always."

Buele twisted in midair next to Broni. "But what was it we—saw—felt?"

"You tell me, Buele," Duncan said. "Describe what you saw."

"Something black. It blotted out the stars. It came out of a rift, a tear, something far away and nearby."

"Make sense, boy," Dietr Krieg said testily.

"No, he's right about the distance. It was and was not in any *place*. It could have been upon us or it could have been at the galaxy's edge. The terms have no meaning," Duncan said.

"It would be like trying to localize a dream—a nightmare. No place or time. Just *there*."

"I saw *you*, Duncan," Broni said.

"Of course you would," Anya Amaya murmured.

"You were a shadow, but it was you, Duncan," Broni said firmly. "You were—" She stumbled. Stopped.

"What?" Duncan demanded.

"You were a cheet. Huge. But that's what I saw. You were protecting us."

"Yes," Buele said. "It was like that. A shadow, something dark. Claws. Teeth. And there was something else. Something *looking* at us. It wanted us dead, Brother Captain."

"Perhaps, Buele. We don't know that."

"I know it, Duncan," Amaya said. "Whatever it was, we are less than nothing to it."

Mira continued to stare disinterestedly at the syndics.

The Neurocybersurgeon regarded her from his superior height. "Attention span almost nil. We are boring the little monster."

"Yes, I think we are," Duncan said. "All right. Everyone Wired now. Buele, get the drogues."

The boy dropped to the deck and opened a section of the bulkhead. The heavy drogue cables snaked out. The syndics gathered, each collected a drogue, Wired themselves to *Glory*.

But there was nothing. Mira settled into Duncan's lap, curled herself like a nautilus shell, closed her eyes.

Duncan probed back along the track *Glory* had traveled. He could feel the gentle sting of tachyons, sense the spaceborn detritus of the Ring's edge a million and a half kilometers astern. Probing ahead Duncan felt the heat of Ross 248, and the sunlight reflecting from the glittering blue sea covering most of Nineveh. A sandstorm was moving across the ruddy face of Nimrud. In space between the Twin Planets Duncan could feel the presence of a small spacecraft, a transport little larger than a shuttle.

"Anything, anyone?" he asked.

"Nothing, Brother Captain."

———

"Nothing, Duncan." Amaya, trying hard to be more empathic than Broni.

Broni: "It is gone, Duncan. But it was there."

Duncan probed space back to the co-ordinates of the cube of space in which he had earlier lost himself. There was nothing. No, wait. Not nothing. An empty echo, a tang, a taste of something *different* that had been there. How long ago? Time was meaningless.

"Mira," Duncan said. "Wake up. Help me."

For an instant, all in the carapace deck felt the visceral response from the cat. Each felt a stirring of her sexuality. She was near to estrus. Her hormones were preparing her for another mating. She had no interest in tangs, and former presences. *It* had gone, had retreated back into the time and dimension that spawned it.

She swiftly lost interest in what was not there, what was not threatening her or her brood or "the-great-queen-who-was-not-alive."

Mira burrowed more deeply into Duncan's lap and closed her eyes. She wanted to sleep and there was no dissuading her.

Duncan removed his drogue. Simply by being a cat, Mira discouraged any intimate probings. *Later, little queen,* Duncan thought. To the syndics he said, "This meeting is over. Disconnect and make *Glory* ready for approach to Beta."

—————

12

AT BLACK DESERT

The Black Desert Prison Camp lay in the center of what the Nimrudites, with perverse pride, called "the worst place in the world." It took its name from the black basaltic rock that ran in a major geologic upthrust from latitude 10 degrees north to the equator and from 122 degrees east to 139 degrees east longitude.

There had been a time, two hundred years earlier, when the Black Desert had been thought to contain diamond deposits. In the ten years Nimmie geologists had suffered this delusion, five thousand civil prisoners had died in the camp. The myth was that they had expired from "environmental deprivation." A few had succumbed to the rigors of equatorial Nimrud, but most had been either worked to death or killed trying to escape.

There were few escape attempts from the Black Desert Camp these days. Since the last Recurrence, camp wisdom—handed down from prison generation to prison generation—had reached a fine degree of development. Known to the inmates simply as "Understanding Hell," it had effectively curtailed attempts to escape.

As the camp staffers asked with such satisfaction: *"Escape to where?"* The Black Desert Camp lay 2,000 roadless kilometers from the nearest town. The nearest *city* lay 1,900,000 kilometers away on the world of Nimrud's enemies.

Each day, from dawn to midafternoon, the hot coriolis wind blew over the Black Desert and the ruddy light of Ross

248 burned down on the works. Despite this, the seventy thousand prisoners (most of them Nimmie misfits) labored in the open pits to extract the only wealth the Black Desert contained, copper ore with small deposits of vanadium and platinum.

The operation was far from economically sound. It cost the Commonwealth of Nimrud three times what it brought in. But the Black Desert's reputation cowed even the most determined of Nimmie would-be miscreants and lawbreakers, and during a Recurrence it served as an absolutely secure prison camp for captured Ninevites, whom the Nimmies regarded with pathological suspicion and class hatred.

Andrey Volkov strained to lift his share of the one-hundred-twenty-kilogram slab of basalt that he and his work-gang had been laboring most of the suffocating day to release from the substrate of black schist. He was normally a slender man of ordinary strength and power, but two months of confinement in the Black Desert had reduced him to skeletal proportions and a mass of cuts and bruises—some inflicted by the camp guards, others by the Nimmie criminals with whom he and the survivors of his company had been confined.

Since reaching this hellish place Andrey had made it his duty to share the worst tasks and the greatest deprivations with the Territorials who had survived Operation Skybolt. Maida Ulanova, the peasant girl from north of Nostromograd, who he had been certain would die from her wounds, had surprised him with her determined recovery. Since arriving at Black Desert she had been repeatedly raped by Nimmie prisoners until Andrey had thrown discretion to the coriolis wind and killed her most recent assailant with a jagged fragment of schist. He had been horrified by his own action—the act of a criminal, he thought—but one apparently well within the code of conduct for Black Desert prisoners.

Two other survivors of Skybolt had made it to Black Desert. Piotr Komorovskiy, who had lived in Odessa, and Timon Timoshenko, who had once worked as a horse-breaker for Andrey's father, the Gospodin.

Andrey had retaken command of "his" people and

formed them into a work-gang for mutual protection and against the day when they might make an attempt to escape. This last dream was a source of much nasty merriment among the Nimmie prisoners who learned of it. There were no walls or fences at Black Desert—only around the execution yard. Prisoners had vanished from the camp many times. None had ever reached any other place. Their bones petrified in sand drifts around the camp. At first Andrey had feared that the guards might take special precautions to thwart a prisoner who dreamed of escaping. He soon discovered that no special action was *ever* taken against would-be fugitives. "It is simply another form of suicide," the Watch Captain told him after a routine beating. "Why should we care?"

By now Andrey realized that there would never be a time to escape from Black Desert. Only peace and a wholesale repatriation would ever get the remnant of his destroyed company back to the Blessed Twin. But that needed peace, and when, or if, that might be, no one could say. The last Recurrence had lasted for fourteen planetary years. In the repatriation that followed, no Ninevites had returned from Black Desert.

The crew had worked since before dawn to free the huge rock from the schist. No one could imagine why the guards wanted it moved. None of the work performed at Black Desert was ever useful. Its purpose was to keep the prisoners occupied, and eventually to kill them. The people of the Second Aliyah were not great believers in rehabilitation. Given their history, it was not surprising. Somehow, over the years, the *Resolution* people had come to the conclusions that the Ninevites had been responsible for the Ring Encounter that stranded them on the Accursed Twin. Survival had demanded of them total submission to a repressive, highly collectivized, society that did not welcome back ex-transgressors. For the few war prisoners who survived long enough to reach Black Desert there was even less sympathy.

A normally ruddy sun glowed an angry red through the dustclouds raised by the coriolis wind. Andrey and his people huddled in the poor shelter of the boulder that had occupied their morning, taking advantage of the quarter hour they were allotted for eating their midday meal.

This consisted of a thin gruel made of chaff from the poor grains the Nimrudites had managed to grow in the temperate regions of Ross Beta. With the gruel was served a small cup of dusty water and a liter of liquor squeezed from the thick leaves of an aloe-like plant brought from Earth on *Resolution* and saved in the catastrophe of Lander's Day. The aloe-squeeze had some slightly psychedelic effects that the camp administration thought helped keep the inmates in a biddable condition.

Andrey had insisted that his people mix the squeeze with water, stretching the water-ration and diluting the effects of the aloe liquor. The Nimrudite inmates of the camp block found this precaution a source of nasty amusement. Timon Timoshenko had received a knife cut across the ribs when he resented the comments of the Nimmies.

Maida Ulanova, who now considered herself the gospodin's woman, huddled as near to Andrey as she could manage and still remain sheltered from the wind by the rock they had been wedging and cursing for the ten hours since dawn.

"Why are they doing this, Your Honor?" Piotr Komorovskiy asked plaintively. "Why don't they just kill us and have done with it?"

Andrey sighed at the note of quintessentially Russian mournfulness in Komorovskiy's voice. There was little hope of escape from this hell, but it did the group great disservice to carry on as though one were totally without hope.

It was true there was no escape. It was also true that a repatriation was, at best, a distant, outside chance. It was also true that given the conditions and the food in the camp, it was not likely that any of the Ninevites at Black Desert would greet the New Year. But there was still one's responsibility to the group. Surrender by an individual only made the group weaker.

"Killing us, Piotr, would only give them momentary pleasure," Andrey said. "And perhaps they are curious to see how big a rock soldiers of Nineveh can move from this place to that.

Eat your slop and drink your horsepiss. This afternoon something wonderful may happen, who knows?"

Timoshenko, a slope-shouldered horseman originally
from a village in the Urals, showed his broken teeth in a smile.
"You tell him, Your Honor. Why, this life is nothing compared
to life in the Ural horse camps in summer. There we had to fish
and hunt and screw and ride all the day long. Nothing at all like
the fine pastimes the fucking Nimmies give us here."

Andrey grinned gratefully at the horse-breaker. Timon
had once had a fine set of white teeth. The Nimmies had
broken them, even before disembarking from the warship that
had brought them back to the Accursed Twin.

Hate, Andrey thought. *Hate is good. It can keep you alive
when all else surrenders.*

He was thinking about hate and the Nimmies when he heard
the sikorskys overhead. He raised his eyes to try to see beyond
the stinging dustclouds. There were two sikorskys, one a big
transport, the second a gunship.

Fixed-wing aviation had never really succeeded on either
of the Ross Twins. On Nineveh the continent was too small and
the ocean too great to make fixed-wing flying useful. Ararat,
though technically a continent, was really no more than a
medium-sized island. The Blasted Continent was larger, but
remained uninhabited. Everything else on Nineveh was covered with water, making ocean flights into flights to nowhere.
Vertical takeoff and landing machines had served the colonists
well ever since Lander's Day. And what was true on Nineveh
was also true on Nimrud, though for different reasons.

On the Accursed Twin flying of any sort was extremely
dangerous, the weather made it so. And though the reasoning
was perverse, the inhabitants of Nimrud had adopted the aero-
nautical habits of their rivals. Sikorskys—known on Old Earth
as helicopters—were the chosen method of transport on Nimrud, because their ability to land anywhere, and at once, made
them attractive transports.

Transports to where? Andrey wondered, watching the two
machines losing height to land on the rim of the pit.

———

"What's happening, Your Honor?" Maida asked.

"Visitors, I would guess," Andrey said. "I doubt it has anything to do with us."

But he was wrong. Less than a quarter hour after having seen the sikorskys descend, one of the Nimmies' ugly armored cars appeared on the rim next to the sikorskys. It squatted like a turtle at the edge of the slope.

A squad of five Nimmies, dressed in nullgrav battle armor, flew down the slope and over the work-gangs in the pit. Their reaction-engines stirred clouds of black dust and flying bits of rock. When they reached the area where the Ninevites were working, they landed and signalled to the armored vehicle. The cannon mounted in a turret atop the flat carapace swivelled to point at Andrey and his work-gang.

"What the hell," Timoshenko said darkly, "are the bastards up to?"

"Are they going to murder us, Your Honor?" Komorovskiy asked plaintively.

"Of course not," Andrey said. "Don't let them see you are afraid."

The Nimmie troopers standing like statues looked as formidable as had the ones Andrey and his people had faced during Skybolt. Andrey Volkov moved to take the psychological advantage away from his jailors. He stood, raised a grimy bandanna to cover his nose and mouth, and advanced to face the squad. They were soldiers, not jailors, Andrey noticed. The armored face-plates made them resemble machines.

"Volkov?" The filters made the voice sound artificial.

"Yes."

"Yes, *sir*."

"You care about that? All right. I am Volkov. Sir."

"Come with us."

Andrey looked back at his troopers. They seemed stricken. The generations of colonial life had not made the Ninevites independent. Nineveh was a society rigidly organized along class lines, and the Ninevites relied on it.

Andrey sucked in a gritty breath and said, "Not without my people."

"You bloody fool," the armored jailor said. "I could blow you away where you stand."

No, you could not, Andrey thought. *They don't send sikorskys and troops for expendable prisoners.* "Do it then," he said. "My people stay with me or put your money where your mouth is."

Andrey's survivors had gathered around him. He felt vastly pleased and proud of them, even lugubrious Piotr Komorovskiy.

The armored car on the ridge emitted a shrill, impatient whistle.

"Allah damn all Ninnies. All right, form a line and let's go." The iron face stared sightlessly at the prisoners. "You wouldn't be so anxious if you knew who you were going to see."

"But you are just dying to tell us, aren't you?" Andrey said.

"Try Krasny. Of Gammah."

Suddenly Andrey Volkov's defiance seemed less than he had intended it to be. But he had no real choice in any case. The squad rose into the air, weapons unlimbered, and the tattered Ninevite Territorials began the long climb up the steep talus to the rim. The armored Nimmies hovered over them, weapons ready.

13

CAMP RESOLUTION

Camp Resolution lay at 70 degrees south latitude and 89 degrees east longitude. Here the coriolis wind was a near-constant ingredient of the weather, as were the fogs and ice storms that swept up from the south at the time of the winter solstice. These storms would begin within the month. They were never late and seldom early, but they were always severe.

All the towns and cities of Nimrud carried the designation "Camp." It was the disfranchised Russian way of remembering the history of the Second Aliyah. A "Red" thing. On Ross 248 Beta there were two compelling preoccupations: remembrance of past grievances, and a dedication to redress and revenge. On Nimrud, *revanchism* was a way of life. The brilliant blue planet that dominated the skies of Nimrud, eclipsing the sun hundreds of times a year, was a constant reminder of the people's victimhood.

Camp Resolution sheltered nearly a million inhabitants, and it was located at the very place on the planet's surface where the shuttles of the wrecked *Resolution* had deposited the First Landers of the Second Aliyah.

It was a city, but it would not have been recognized as such by anyone other than a native. To visitors from Earth, or even Nineveh, the place would qualify as a suburb of hell. The Nimmies took pride in the unpleasantness of their world.

The mean temperature in winter was − 34 degrees Celsius and in summer it might rise to 40 degrees. For 300 days of the

386-day year sandstorms blew off the equatorial desert at 60 to 150 kilometers per hour. In the short seasonal intervals of good weather, electrical storms and a threatening aurora australis turned the night sky into an arena of demented, terrifying beauty.

The celestial displays, which had been, due to the Ring event that destroyed Goldenwing *Resolution,* even more spectacular in the year of the First Landing, had driven the colonists underground. It had been the first conclusion of the shocked remnants of the Second Aliyah's Muslim contingent that Nimrud was their punishment for having been collaborators of the Jihad, and for having fled Earth instead of remaining to accept a swift trip to Paradise at the hands of the raging, liberated, ruined populations left behind and alive by the retreating remnants of the Holy Warriors' armies.

After landing, the matter was considered most carefully and strictly by the imams and Ayatollahs. It wouldn't do, they concluded, for the common people to be exposed to the new planet's furious weather and celestial pyrotechnics. Study of the K'uran and other sacred books would be required before the will of heaven could be known. In the interval, the Second Aliyans would build a settlement below ground, and there they would live.

There they still lived, centuries after Lander's Day.

Hardship had reduced the power of religion over the people of Nimrud. Some even came to take joy in the security of an underground existence. The populace had come to the conclusion that there was no other practical way to cope with their diabolic planet.

The government of Nimrud had taken many forms, none of them democratic. Fifty years ago there had been a revolution. Since then the government had been known as "the Collective." It consisted of an Outer Committee (of ninety members), an Inner (of ten), and a Revolutionary Council of four members. Clinging to the political habits learned as adherents of the Jihad on Earth, the Nimrudite elite ruled by the dictum that political power is best restricted to a few members of a single class. Their history had made the people of the Second Aliyah suspicious, secretive, hostile and extremely efficient under difficult conditions.

Political and military decisions were discussed by the rank and file in Camp Meetings. Discussion produced consensus, and consensus invariably passed the decision-making authority on up the social pyramid until it reached the top.

The Revolutionary Council was anonymous to all but members of the Inner Committee, decisions of the Council were absolute. Rule by the Revolutionary Council was strict, silent and severe.

This suited most Second Aliyans. For those whom it did not suit there was Black Desert or a lazebolt in the back of the neck. Political opposition on Nimrud was so rare as to be practically unknown.

During a Recurrence, the Collective made it a practice to rotate its venues among the towns of Nimrud: Camp Dzerzhinsky, Camp Black September, Camp Stalin-Bekaa, and the capital, Camp Resolution. The reason given was safety from possible attacks from space, but the truth was that the Inner Committee's suspicion of its own citizens demanded that meetings of the Revolutionary Council be secret.

Camp Resolution was a fully industrialized city built on four levels. Its construction had taken a hundred years and thirty thousand lives. The Russian-descended people of Nimrud were not, by inclination, heavy laborers. But like all colonists, they acquiesced to the pressures of colonial life and did what needed to be done.

On this date in the month of Ramallah, the Council sat in session within one of the seven domes that protruded from the buried city, and through which its business with the upper world of Nimrud was conducted.

Hussein Ballator, the Designated Speaker of the Revolutionary Council, had just completed a reading of the operational orders to be given to the spaceborne military units that would be called upon to guard the meeting the Krasny, the leader of Gammah, had arranged with the Ninnie traitor Vukasin. One point of discussion among the four councilors was the effect the presence of Wired Starmen might have on the proceedings.

Ballator was a veteran of both the current and the most previous Recurrence, an elder of enormous personal courage and fierce dedication to Nimrudite rights. But his courage faltered when he used the phrase "Wired Starmen." Neither he nor his peers knew what they might expect from the syndics of the Goldenwing that could now be seen in Nimrud's orbiting telescopes.

In another time, he knew, he would have greeted the coming of the *Gloria Coelis* as a visitation from Paradise. But the truth was that Hussein Ballator no longer believed in gods, even the Allah of the Holy K'uran. Such things were for the masses.

Yet the idea of actually coming face-to-face with Wired Starmen was daunting. All his life he had heard of the starfaring sailors. Information reached Nimrud in radio whispers from the worlds of the great diaspora.

Had such fabled beings really come across the light-years to deliver to Nimrud a shipment of nuclear-powered mining machines? Or was there some other, darker reason? The Nimrudite Head of State who had placed the order for the machines was two hundred years dead and gone. With his mind Ballator understood the oddities of Einsteinian time dilation, but emotionally he shied away from it as unnatural. *Mortal men ought not live forever,* he thought. And though he knew that viewed from their point of view, Goldenwing syndics lived no longer than other men—to downworlders such as himself and the other men in the hive-shaped chamber, the Starmen were near immortals.

No Nimrudite had seen a Starman since Lander's Day. They knew of them only from the histories and from the faint radio signals that reached the Ross 248 system from other "nearby" stars. The men and women of Nimrud had trained themselves to be at home with advanced technologies, but with their Muslim hearts they knew and feared crimes against nature. People who lived according to a different (and more favored) time scale were aliens, changed over time into something other than human beings.

Envy burned in Ballator's Nimrudite soul. His was a tradition that had turned Earth's Holy Land into a desert by destroying not only his enemies but their families, their livestock, their vines, their gardens and their forests.

Ballator said, "The Krasny assures me that the syndics will regard us—if not as friends, then certainly as persons to be dealt with honorably. In any case, the plan provides for a squadron of attack craft to join the starship in orbit. If there is treachery from the Ninevites or from the people of the starship, the delegation will be protected."

"Or dead," murmured Bandar Abbas, the most junior of the Committeemen.

"I do not intend to risk the members of this Council. I will attend the meeting as sole representative of the Council of Four. So be at ease, Bandar Abbas," Ballator said in annoyance.

The younger man exchanged glances with the remaining two members of the Council.

Mohammad Ali Raschad, who had lost an eye in battle with the Ninnies, had a familiar expression of suspicion on his scarred face. A man of enormous *orgotish*, Raschad commanded the police apparatus on Nimrud. It made him nearly invulnerable, and Ballator disliked having colleagues he could not discipline.

Abou Jamil, who had been trained as an ayatollah and used his bigotry with the skill of a laser-swordsman, remained silent and uncommitted.

It was like this every time the Council met, Ballator thought. Not an immediate clash and battle for dominance, but such a contest was never far beneath the surface of what passed among Nimrudites for civility.

He indicated to the roboclerk of the meeting that it should stop recording. To his peers, he added: "Those of you who are carrying secret recorders, be good enough to disable them now." His glance was almost metallic as he waited. Presently, he said, "It ill becomes you, Abbas, to have suggested that the meeting the Krasny has arranged is a trap into which I intended leading the Council."

The challenged councilor said stiffly, "If I am mistaken, I apologize."

Abbas protested, "Is it wise even to risk yourself?"

Ballator's manner was cold. "It is necessary." His dark eyes glittered malevolently. "And if any of you believe that I am in some sort of collusive combine with the outworld syndics, you had better be prepared to prove it to the Committee of Ten."

Abou Jamil, the almost-ayatollah, said in his sibilant, chilling voice. "Our Brother Ballator is in command for this trimester. We will support him in the name of the Compassionate, as the Holy K'uran commands."

Ballator regarded Jamil contemptuously. He had the face of a prophet, long, bearded and gaunt to the point of emaciation. He cultivated the ascetic look. While other men studied the scientific works brought from Earth, Jamil drew his arguments from the holy books of the Jihad. The man was an anachronism who would have been better suited to life on Earth in the Seventh Century.

How ironic it was, Ballator thought, *that we are the Second Aliyah of a mass movement set in motion by the very Jihad that dominates our intellectual life. But we have come far—in thought and distance. The sorry history of human beings on the home planet was no longer of interest in the Ross system. Here there was one struggle, a battle for survival and domination. Here only the fittest would survive. And we are the fittest,* Ballator thought. *We are the inheritors of the Twin Planets.*

The Speaker touched a com button in the stone table. A door opened and a human attendant, one of the few cleared to serve so near the Council of Four, appeared in the opening to the stone hive.

"Bring in the charts," Ballator ordered. Then to his peers he added, "Before this meeting progresses farther, let us be unanimous in what we will and will not accept from the Ninnies."

Jamil said, "I want to discuss the question of religious

observations. We cannot live side by side with the Sharia Christian heresy."

"Jamil, we cannot eat the feast before we have set the table," Ballator said, quoting an old Nimmie proverb.

The one-eyed Raschad grunted agreement. He turned to Ballator and said, "Not spoken like a peacemaker, Speaker."

"Peace is an objective, not an imminent reality," Ballator said.

"If what you intend is obtaining a foothold, then I am with you. But the forces will need to know what comes after." The old warrior's single eye glittered like a bit of black steel.

Bandar Abbas, a mass psychologist by training, was an expert in the art of determining what degree of effort and sacrifice could be extracted, and by what mix of persuasion and force, from the population of Nimrud. "To maintain an effective expeditionary force on Nineveh will require extreme sacrifices and effort from our people," he said. "They must be shown that there will be rewards."

The attendant who had been sent for the charts of Nineveh appeared with a large folio.

"Leave it," Ballator said.

The attendant put the folio on the stone table and withdrew.

"Look at this chart, if you please," Ballator said. He stood and extracted a large-scale chart of Nineveh's eastern hemisphere and the island-continent of Ararat from the folio.

On Nimrud, the military cadre from which each Recurrence's officer corps was reconstituted was a product of the one hundred military families. Nimrud was never fully demobilized. The military families were periodically searched for special skills and special aptitudes and the qualified then trained to commando standards. Gammah's guerrillas and terrorists came from this source.

Ballator had spent days on a military protocol that would serve as the guideline for a swift invasion (in the guise of a survey of territories on Nineveh for which the Nimrudite negotiators might be willing to cede without a fight). Once established on the continent of Ararat, Ballator was sure, a strong and well-trained military force of Nimrudites would be impossible to dislodge.

"According to plan, the Krasny's meetings with Vukasin have held out the strong possibility of peace," he said, his knuckles resting on the continent of Ararat. "The astonishing thing is that no one of our previous leaders ever discovered that the Ninnies would entertain the idea of negotiations." He looked one after another at his peers. "We are not in a striking position yet, but I believe that we shall soon be. The Golden-wing *Gloria Coelis* will assume orbit around Nimrud in days. We have a picket craft in low orbit scanning for a visual sighting. We have also exchanged messages with the offworlders." He essayed a thin smile. "They are fulfilling a contract made two hundred years ago by our predecessors with the syndics of a different Goldenwing entirely. Remarkable." He paused for a thoughtful moment. "I must caution you all not to confuse ethical behavior with weakness. What their warfighting skills may be, I do not know. But they are star-travelers and their technology is in many regards superior to our own and cannot be disregarded. For that reason we will put the warship *Khomeini* in orbit near them, and we will go aboard their ship with a large force of assault troops. We have explained to the Ninnies that this is customary among us, and they have made no objection."

"We pulled a Ninnie officer and two troopers out of Black Desert on your orders, Ballator," Raschad said. "Explain."

"Vukasin asked for their release as a gesture of goodwill. I saw no reason not to comply."

"A bad precedent," Jamil said, scowling.

Ballator ignored the man and returned to the chart on the table. He placed a covetous hand over the green-tinted steppes of southern Ararat.

"It seems a small price to pay, Holy Man," he said. "Very small, indeed. For a reward such as this."

Bandar Abbas, who was shrewd and opportunistic beyond his years, asked, "Who, exactly is this precious Ninnie Vukasin wants returned?"

"His name is Andrey Volkov," Ballator said. "A steppe aristo with, one supposes, influential friends in Petersburg."

"It makes no difference," Jamil declared. "We must not establish the precedent of returning soldiers of the exploiters."

Ballator suppressed an urge to shout at the ayatollah. He did not take exception to the man's bigotry for moral reasons. He objected to it because it was invariably an obstacle to Ballator's ambitions for Nimrud. "No precedent is being established, Jamil. The Krasny made that clear," Ballator said. "And before you ask me, I admit that the present Krasny is without experience in space. But consider—" He extended a thumb in the Nimrudite way of counting. "One. The Krasny has lived among the Ninnies for thirteen years. He knows them better than any man on Nimrud. Two—" He extended the index finger. "He is at the end of his usefulness as a Gammah guerrilla leader. The Ninnies killed his wife in a guerrilla action. He lives for vengeance. But the Collective is powered by ideology, not emotion. Three—" Another finger extended. "He has dealt skillfully with the Ephor Vukasin. Vukasin is an academic by training. A low-born one at that. Our psychological profile on him suggests that he may have a secret sympathy for us. Tenured academicians are often moved by guilt to support the dispossessed. And four—the Krasny's name is legendary among our soldiers at this moment. They have enormous faith in Gammah and the people who have been fighting on Nineveh. It is unlikely that the Krasny will ever see his Gammah guerrillas again. But having him martyred would not necessarily be a bad thing." He looked around at his peers. "Does anyone require more?"

Jamil frowned. The others shook their heads.

Bandar Abbas asked, "If they discover what we intend, will the Starmen support us?"

"They will not oppose us," Ballator said. "They never take sides."

"Never?"

"Never. Over time the Wired Ones have developed an ethic, a way of dealing with colonial societies. In its most basic form it enjoins them from unduly influencing the societies they encounter in Near Space.''

''Do they honor their ethic?'' Bandar Abbas asked.

Raschad scowled at the younger man. ''Always.''

Abbas reacted to the tone by staring at the old warrior's scarred face for a silent moment. Raschad stared back.

The youngest Councilman secretly thought the old fighter past his prime and a liability to the Collective. The man was a veritable mine of sentimental, stupid judgments, all heavily influenced by his old warrior's *orgotish,* which in Abbas's secret opinion was a combination of the most cumbersome and out-of-date Muslim and Russian traits.

Ballator had returned to the map of Ararat. He regarded the green and brown elevations on the chart with a covetous intensity. *The island-continent resembled an elongated protozoan,* Abbas thought. Brown lines of elevation showed the rising ground of the Urals with their crowning peak of Mount Ararat. Wasn't there some ancient Earth legend about Mount Ararat? Didn't the drunken prophet Noah fetch up on that mountain after the Flood?

In the north, the Ninnie protozoan seemed to be extending pseudopods to the northeast, to the north and to the northwest, as though beckoning to the Northern Ice half an empty water world away. In the south, archipelagos extended feelers toward the far closer Southern Ice, while encompassing the near enclosure of Odessa Bay, the Sea of Aralsk, and Nostromo Sound.

Little wonder Ballator became greedy when he regarded the charted land on Nineveh. Compared to the deserts that generated the storm now battering the domes of Resolution, Nineveh was a veritable Paradise. A far more attainable Paradise that the one described in the holy book of Islam.

Drawn by his own cupidity, Bandar Abbas joined the others around the table to help plan the division of the spoils to which he, no less than any Nimrudite dispossessed of his due by the accursed inhabitants of the *other* Twin, was entitled.

BOOK TWO

14

APPROACH

Bleeding off excess delta-V, *Glory* passed over Twin Alpha at 660,000 kilometers. From this distance the Planetary Ocean was a beautiful pattern of ever-changing swirls in shades of blue from cobalt to turquoise. White clouds outlined a vast weather system sweeping northeastward out of the fastness of the southern ocean toward the narrow island-continent of Ararat.

Duncan, with the conn, lay in his pod, Wired to the ship. Beside him slept Mira, her paws and legs twitching in some dream-chase through green jungles she had never seen. Since Duncan's adventure overboard, the cat had not moved far from his side. She guarded him the way a senior lioness might watch the pride's lead male.

At this moment *Glory* was presenting Duncan with a magnificent view—experience, really—of the planet below. It seemed to Duncan that he flew, naked to the wind and sun, many thousands of meters above the alien sea. Directly below him, he could make out a sandy bottom dotted with forests of waving, thick-fronded kelp. Brilliant blue-green flowers attached millions of schooling creatures like tiny fish in silver armor.

The Starman wondered if any of the colonists inhabiting Nineveh had ever actually seen what he was seeing now. It was possible that they had not. Ararat lay on the distant horizon— five thousand kilometers away. With an ocean so vast and unbroken, there was little incentive for much oceanic exploration by the colonists. In time, there would be, of course. The Ninevites had the means: boats and helicopters. But for the incessant warfare between the Twins, the sea of Nineveh might have been colonized by now.

There was nothing to prevent it, Duncan thought, *and it was a thing that badly needed doing. But to judge from the broadcast fragments from both Alpha and Beta, the war—the "Recurrence"—took precedence. Always and forever,* thought Duncan bitterly. What would the quarrelsome colonists think when he told them of the Others, those beings without time, without distance, shape or mass, but nevertheless *there,* waiting. Or waiting no longer? Perhaps they had wearied of waiting while man explored a space they considered theirs.

I am a Starman, Duncan thought. *Not a diplomat. Not a soldier. More the point, not a god. I can only tell them what I believe is out there.*

In dreams Mira tracked his thought and snarled softly. *You know, little queen,* Duncan thought. *You know but you cannot tell me. We lack the words in common. Why have we waited so long to learn the languages of the creatures with whom we shared the Earth?* Duncan wondered. *Have we waited too long?*

"Be patient, Duncan. We are slow learners."

Anya Amaya's thought, tinged with the essence of *Glory,* came clearly through the drogue. Duncan smiled. His image of her bypassed his eyes, which stared sightlessly at the bridge overhead. His point of view shifted from the set of imaging cameras in the rig to the one in the chartroom, where the Sailing Master was physically inspecting a replica of an old chart from the computer's bubble storage, a chart made by the surveying Goldenwing *Eratosthenes* fifty years before *Nostromo* left lunar orbit with the First Aliyah.

From a high angle in the overhead the camera watched Anya Amaya bent over the table. Her drogue cable, anchored in her black hair, hung in air between the table and the chartroom socket.

Anya was half nude, as was her preference. Her hips and legs were sheathed in dark green skinsuit tights. Her back was slender and muscular, *café-au-lait* skin occasionally suggesting the fine bone structure over which it was stretched. From time to time, as she straightened to consider the chart from a distance, her full breasts quivered.

A half dozen ship's days ago Duncan had resumed his casual and needful affair with Amaya. His return to the easy promiscuity of life aboard a Goldenwing had lessened his melancholy somewhat.

Anya, with *Glory's* help, kenned his thought and looked up at the camera eye to say aloud, "I am glad of that, Duncan."

Duncan made no response. None was required. He had no doubt that it had been his experience adrift that had jarred him from his self-imposed isolation.

It was an undoubted fact that Broni's mother, the Voertrekker lady Eliana Ehrengraf, now lay forever beyond Duncan's reach. Someone once said, "The laws of God and man are harsh." To which a Goldenwing sailor had replied, "But the laws of Einstein are harsher still." Eliana Ehrengraf was a memory, lost to the hard demands of time dilation. And a man must live on, Duncan knew. Wired Starmen did not willingly surrender life, no matter how bleak it seemed.

"Link to an outside camera, Anya," he ordered. *"Let's compare that chart with what we see."*

In the chartroom, the Sailing Master made the required reconfiguration. Now she saw Nineveh as Duncan did, from a vantage point in space. Point by point they examined the reality and compared it with the ancient *Eratosthenes* chart.

"Nothing has changed in over a thousand years."

A thousand years is an eye-blink, Duncan thought. *A moment, no more. The Universe does not live by our racing time-scale.*

"That is what makes it so grand," Anya thought. Her image was filled with star-flung majesty. Duncan remembered Black Clavius, who, aching to return to space, had remained, duty bound, on Voerster. *"The heavens declare the glory of God; and the firmament sheweth his handywork."* How often Clavius quoted those words, Duncan thought.

"An old friend remembered," Anya said aloud.

Mira stretched and opened her eyes. *What does she see when Glory commands her senses?* Duncan wondered. *And shouldn't we rethink our definition of ''life''?* Several times he had caught the strong impression from Mira that *Glory* was, to Mira's kind, an *entity.*

The paradox of a commanding, nurturing entity who was the-great-queen-who-was-not-alive plucked at Duncan's human reason. *What a limited species we are,* he thought. *So broad in intellect, so narrow in— What? Vision? Imagination?* Mira knew, and could not, or would not, say.

He returned to his scrutiny of the continent below, now vanishing swiftly astern as *Glory* swung, influenced by the planet's gravity, into line with the course needed to establish a low orbit around Beta. The second twin filled a third of *Glory's* sky while Nineveh, herself, still occupied more than half during this low pass.

What Amaya said was quite literally true. The island continent of Ararat, noted only as ''Land Mass One'' on the survey chart, had not changed an iota in a millennium. This was the land the two Aliyahs were disputing. According to the broadcasts detected over time from Nineveh, there had been fifteen Recurrences fought over a share of that small island continent. Duncan watched Ararat disappear over the rim of the Planetary Ocean.

''Duncan,'' Amaya said. *''We were scanned by radar as we made our fly-by.''*

''I expected that,'' Duncan said. But it was disturbing.

The Sailing Master said, *''Are you so certain we should not establish contact with the people on Alpha?''*

''Not before we discharge our cargo on Nimrud,'' Duncan said. *''We are bound by the terms of the original contract.''*

''Won't that make us seem to be taking sides?''

''It may. We will have to repair that impression before we leave Nimrud.''

''If we can.'' Duncan caught the nuances of her sending. Doubt. Concern. A subtext of anger. As a native of New Earth, a planet of Proxima Centauri, Anya was a hair-trigger feminist. One ignored her soldier's perceptions at one's risk.

She said, *''There are at least fifty satellites in low orbit around*

Nineveh. Some are weatherbirds, but a great deal of the other hard-ware is military. And several larger bodies. Shuttles, I think.''

"Brother Captain. Sister Anya.'' The two older syndics felt the "join" of the youngest aboard, Buele, as he socketed him-self and pushed innocently into the rapport between Duncan and the Sailing Master.

"May I see the chart, Sister Anya?''

"Study these. They are charts of where we are going.'' Amaya substituted a chart of Nimrud. She was tolerant of the new syndics, but she was irritated by Buele's lack of tact. New Earthers tended to be prickly about manners. She savored her moments alone with Duncan Kr.

Buele, in his quarters, repositioned the chartroom camera. *"Show me, Sister.''*

Amaya reshuffled the chart images and produced one that was all shades and swirls of red, orange and black. The plane-tary map of Nimrud, the Accursed Twin.

"The white dots are towns. They call them cities. They are mostly underground,'' she said.

"The one in the left center is a prison,'' Buele said.

"How did you know that?'' Amaya demanded aloud.

"I don't know, Sister Anya. But it is a prison. I can feel it. It is like the Friendly Isles on Voerster. But much worse.''

Wild Talent, Duncan thought. *And this is what the Voertrek-kers had called a retarded child.*

"Give Buele a full briefing,'' Duncan said. *"I am breaking contact now. Damon is here to take the watch.''*

Damon appeared in the valve from the plenum. Duncan opened his pod and sat erect. He disengaged the drogue from his skull-socket. Immediately he felt the familiar diminish-ment of his perceptions. It was a sensation akin to grief, this loss of contact with *Glory* and the living vastness through which she sailed.

Mira stood, stretched, and regarded him reproachfully. The cat never completely lost touch with *Glory.* Dietr Krieg was anxious to change the syndics' cyberneural connections to the system he had used to enhance the cats. *It had a certain appeal,*

Duncan thought. No drogue cables. No switching in and out of rapport with the ship. But his native caution urged him to go slowly. Mira and her brood were basically changed from what they once were. They were still cats, to be sure, but they were permanently combined with *Glory*'s computer in ways the humans aboard were still far from understanding. Dietr had *committed* the cats. The men and women aboard would have to choose for themselves whether they wished to alter their humanity so radically. *In time,* Duncan thought, *perhaps.*

Damon prepared his own pod and said formally, "I relieve you, Master and Commander."

"Carry on as before," Duncan said. "Course is set. Speed is set. Courses are furled. We sail under jibs and t'gallants."

"Good night, Captain." Damon Ng settled into the pod and closed the hatch after himself. There he would stay until Anya came to relieve him in four hours.

Duncan swung himself in the nullgravity and slipped through the valve into the plenum. Mira followed. Man and animal swam easily and familiarly down the long fabric entrail. Presently they reached the section containing Broni's personal compartment. At the valve, Duncan stopped and touched the annunciator pad in the bulkhead. "It's Duncan," he said.

"Come in." The valve dilated.

Broni hung in the air before the Astroprogrammer's personal console in the fabric wall. She wore a skinsuit and her blond hair, weightless, haloed her head. She had been Wired; now she disconnected and turned to greet Duncan. Sometimes she so resembled her mother that Duncan's heart ached.

"I've been studying, Duncan," she said. "Our Russian language program is adequate but only just."

"*Glory* will learn from the colonists," Duncan said.

Broni made a face. "I was never good at languages. At home we spoke only Afrikaans and Bantu. Kaffir, that is."

"There's no negotiating to be done. Only a delivery."

"Will I be in the landing party, Duncan?" she asked.

"You know better than that, child," Duncan said.

Broni touched her chest almost angrily. "The heart. Can't

Dietr make another with more volume, or whatever it is it needs?''

She was not so unsatisfied when she came aboard, Duncan thought. *But then, neither was I.* Eliana had still not made the choice to return to her people.

"Dietr will do what he can when he can, child,'' Duncan said.

"I am not a child, Duncan. I'm eighteen standard now. Wired and a full syndic.''

"Point taken, Astroprogrammer,'' Duncan said quietly. "Now, have you done the history survey I ordered?''

Broni allowed the drogue to retract into the bulkhead. "Yes. It's far from comprehensive, because I compiled it entirely from radio broadcasts dating back almost to their Landers' Day. But it should be useful. Maybe it can help us deal with these strange people.''

"Strange, Broni?'' It was not a word Wired Starmen customarily used. It was, in the language of the directive-writers, too *judgmental.* It was the opinion of the people who wrote the rules for starship sailors that nothing should ever be thought truly "strange.'' But Broni was still a Voertrekker.

"What sort of people could have spent the last few centuries fighting the same war over and over again?'' the girl asked.

"That's not quite accurate, Broni,'' Duncan said. "Each Recurrence has been slightly different. Different causes, different tactics, different weapons.''

"Still the same war,'' Broni said positively. "Colonists shouldn't fight one another. They have no *right—*''

Duncan regarded the girl ironically. "Have you forgotten the history of the Voertrekkers and the Great Kaffir Rebellion?''

Broni frowned.

"Well?''

"I seem to have done. I'm sorry, Duncan.''

Mira arrived and floated to Broni's shoulder. The girl caressed the cat's small head.

"I should know better,'' Broni said.

"You have a right to wonder what sort of people spend centuries at one another's throats out here.''

———

"My people fought a terrible war. But they *did* end it," Broni said.

"We humans are a strange species," Duncan said. "I used to think we were the cruelest predator in the Universe. That was a terrible conceit. Now I fear there is something far worse out there."

He noted immediately the way Broni seemed to flinch from his statement. Dietr, after a long session with his psychoanalytical programs, would classify her reaction as denial.

"Duncan, we were so afraid," Broni said. "We thought we might have lost you. Isn't it possible that it could have been imagination or—"

This must stop, Duncan thought. *Now. At once.* Glory's *syndics could not be allowed to deny what* Glory *and Mira had shown them.*

"We don't know *all* that it could have been, Broni. But it is real and it is out there. We approach it and it loathes us for it."

Broni stared hard at Mira, who returned her gaze inscrutably.

"She is only a cheet, Duncan," Broni whispered. "What *Glory* showed us might have been some feral image in her mind."

Duncan shook his head. "That won't do, Broni. Mira is a cat, not a cheet. She is a much more highly developed animal. Together with *Glory,* she is something formidable. All the cats may be. It depends on what Mira teaches them. But whatever and wherever *It* is, it is real and we must eventually face it—or retreat back to Earth and simply wait."

He had not meant to be so frank, but it was as well. Broni's generation of syndics might be burdened with a totally different, and horrifying, sort of war for human survival. He would have to speak with the others, as well. Until this conversation with the Voertrekker girl, he had not allowed himself to notice that talking about *It* was difficult. *We have all been slipping into denial.* He felt Mira's steady, solemn look. It was like a touch. No denial there. The tiny predator's willingness to challenge prey kept her steadfast.

"She knows, doesn't she?" Broni said softly.

———

"I think she does. Maybe *knows* is not the right word. *Feels,* perhaps." Duncan smiled mirthlessly. "It may be we are the only beings in the Universe with a *need* to know. Others may operate on a purely emotional level. But however we meet our challenges, we do meet them. We must. There is no other way for us."

"What are you going to tell the system people?"

"The truth. That they must stop fighting one another," Duncan said.

"Will they listen? We can't compel them, can we?"

"No. We cannot."

A light flashed on the computer console.

"*Glory* wants attention," Duncan said.

Broni reconnected to the ship. Duncan extruded a second drogue and did the same.

"*The surface of Beta is sending a message to the Commander.*"

"*Pass it through.*"

The voice from Beta spoke the expected derivative "Near-abroad" Russian post-Soviet dialect.

"*I am Hussein Ballator, Speaker of the Committee of Four of the Collective of Nimrud. I wish to speak with the Master and Commander of the Goldenwing approaching Nimrud. In the name of Allah the Compassionate. Can you hear and understand me?*"

"*I am Duncan Kr, captain of the* Gloria Coelis. *I hear and understand you. How can I serve, Speaker?*"

"*As you know, Amir, we are at war by the will of Allah.*"

"*I was not aware it was by the will of Allah,*" Duncan sent. Broni listened intently.

"*The persons of the First Aliyah ran from the word of Allah many hundreds of years ago. But I am not calling you about history, Amir.*"

"*I am listening, Speaker.*"

"*You will assume orbit around Nimrud in thirty hours?*"

"*Nearer twenty. But yes. In slightly less than one planetary day.*"

"*I ask a favor, Amir.*"

"*I listen, Speaker.*"

"*We are opening delicate negotiations with our adversaries on*

Nineveh. We need a truly neutral site for these discussions to take place safely. There is much animosity and suspicion, Amir. We ask that our first meetings take place aboard your magical ship.''

Duncan glanced at Broni, wondering if she caught the odd turn of phrase and understood it. Technologically, the Twin Planets were far advanced over the Voertrekker girl's rural homeworld. Yet it would never have occurred to any inhabitant of Voerster to call the *Glory* "magical." Broni smiled and shrugged her shoulders.

"How many of you, Speaker?" Duncan asked.

"Twenty from each side, Amir. Perhaps some few more.''

Duncan paused thoughtfully. Space was no problem. There were hectares of unused hull-space aboard *Glory*. But Starmen often bridled at the idea of downworlders in the vast spaces of their ships. Syndics were human, after all. They resented "short-timers" on their ground. *"On their turf,''* Old Earthers used to say. A corps d'elite's reluctance to be truly open with lesser mortals? *We are going to have to change that,* Duncan thought. *The coming conflict would demand more unity than men and women had ever managed to attain in all their history. Not exactly a comforting idea,* Duncan thought.

"How maneuverable are your short-range spacecraft?" he asked.

"Quite maneuverable, Amir. May we bring them aboard as well?''

To Broni, Duncan sent: *"Interesting that he has already assumed we will allow them aboard.''*

Broni's return: *"Will we?''*

"Yes,'' Duncan said.

To Ballator he sent: *"You will be welcome aboard, Speaker. Do you want your cargo landed first?''*

"In the interests of peace,'' Ballator said, *"I think the meeting should take precedence, Amir.''*

"Yes,'' Duncan said. *"Very well, then. We will notify you of our orbital parameters.''*

"That will not be necessary, Amir. We will know them. I bid you good-bye for now in the name of the Prophet and Allah the Merciful.''

Glory reported: *"Transmission completed, Duncan.''*

Indeed, Duncan thought. A simple, straighforward request. Or was it? There was a quality to the transmissions from Hussein Ballator that set Duncan's nerves on edge.

The First Arrivers in the Ross 248 system wanted more colonists like themselves. And the Second Arrivers thought they had been promised a piece of Paradise. Both had been disappointed. Not a happy beginning.

"He makes me uncomfortable," Broni said. The Voertrekker girl was an empathic genius and should be listened to. But how could a Goldenwing syndic ethically refuse a request like Ballator's?

"I am inclined to be cautious, Broni," Duncan said aloud. Except—" He paused, grimly thoughtful. "Except that we've had an epiphany. One we must share. One that might just end their war."

15

A MATTER OF *ORGOTISH*

The man known as Krasny wore space armor uncomfortably. It was restrictive, cumbersome and physically distressing. Moreover Krasny was discovering, to his dismay, that he was a borderline claustrophobic, and being confined in battle gear plucked at the sinews of his self-control and courage.

Krasny had spent much of his adult life on Nineveh as an officer of the Nimmie cadre of saboteurs and terrorists the armed forces of Nimrud maintained on the Arrogant Twin. At the age of forty he had lost track of how many of the enemy he had killed or directly caused to be killed. He had destroyed mag-lev trains in the high Urals, sikorskys at the various air bases of the slothful and careless enemy. He had lost track of how many bombs he had exploded in civilian crowds. He had fought the kind of war his sort of man had relished for a thousand years, from Earth to Nineveh.

Why, then, he wondered, did a mere phobia of being confined in armor suddenly make him sick to his stomach, cause him to think of the mountain of corpses for which he was responsible, and bring to life all the unquiet dead who waited for him to arrive among them in hell? He hunched, drenched in sweat, lungs empty and gasping, eyes filled with the horrible emptiness of the void that surrounded him, ready to break into his shell and suck the breath from his lungs and the blood from his veins. How had he not known it would be like this?

I gave Ballator what he wanted, Krasny thought shakily. *I reeled in Vukasin like a fisherman a mountain gar. Why am I here in space? What more is required of me?*

This was not like blowing up trestles in the Urals or planting explosives in peaceful towns. But surely the psychologists who had tested him over and over again must have known that he was phobic. The Ninevites were naive when it came to fighting a real war, but the Nimrudite medics had to have known that in this environment terror would make him impotent.

He stood unsteadily in his armor, anchored to the deck of the attack shuttle with his magnetic crampons. He could not force himself to do more than glance out of the open ramp of the shuttle. The starfields, so bright and disorienting, could have been within touch or at the edge of the galaxy. It required a controlled mental state to make such judgments, and his mental state was far from controlled. He could feel moisture leaking down his leg. The lights of his wrist console betrayed him, announcing his fear to anyone with the skill to read them.

The shuttle was rotating slowly, causing the stars to move from top to bottom of the lowered ramp. The sight made Krasny's gorge rise. A second warning light on his wrist console winked on. It warned of incipient nausea, which could result in vomiting and a choking death inside battle armor.

Krasny felt the crash of an armored fist on his helmet. The attack-master, a sergeant-colonel of the unit belonging to the shuttle, loomed in the glinting darkness.

"Use your puke-stop, man!"

Krasny had been briefed on using the features of the battle armor. There had been something said about an auto-injection of some anti-nausea agent.

He had missed most of the information in his growing anxiety. He had known from the beginning that he would become part of the cadre assigned to escort the Speaker aboard the Goldenwing.

"Third left on the tongue console, asshole!"

The sergeant's voice on the com was really angry. Clearly he was one of the Nimrudite regulars who did not consider Gammah a legitimate fighting force. This same sergeant-colonel had called Gammah "baby killers" only last night before lift-off from Camp Resolution.

With bile rising into his throat Krasny thrust his tongue into the third pressure socket in his tongue console. Immediately he felt the blow of an airgun shooting drugs into his arm. The effect was miraculous. His breathing steadied, his salivating stopped. He felt still afraid, but almost human. The respite allowed him to organize his thoughts.

What he had not realized was that because the starship was so different—so ancient—it would be necessary for any visitors to make the transfer from battle-shuttles to Goldenwing in the extravehicular mode. But Hussein Ballator had known it well enough.

The big sergeant touched his face-plate to Krasny's so that he could communicate without using the com system. "This is only an exercise, Gammah. To help you and the troops get it right. I don't want the Speaker embarrassed. Have you got that?"

Krasny nodded.

"Answer me aloud, you fucking ground-pounder. I can't hear you bobbing around inside that suit. I said, 'Have you got that?' "

Stiff with anger, Krasny looked through the two face-plates. "I have got it, Sergeant," he said. *You bloody bastard,* he thought. He could hear nothing as the big soldier moved away, but he could see his triumphant smile and read his lips. It was a choice and scornful obscenity the soldier used.

In the opening to the rear of the shuttle's troop compartment, the red disk of Nimrud appeared, descended like a executioner's blade toward the deckline.

Krasny looked at the others in the open bay. Thirty troopers and a half dozen Gammah fighters. He had imagined, when arranging the meeting with Ephor Vukasin, that Gammah would be in charge of the operation. He did not for one moment believe that the troops were aboard this shuttle to protect Hussein Ballator. The operation called for more than that. He was accustomed to operating with sketchy information. The nature of a guerrilla organization made that a fact of war. But there was something more happening here, and Krasny was not reassured. He had an intuition that suggested he had been chosen for inclusion in this mission *because* of his secret weakness, not despite it.

They had even taken Simon Egonov from him. He had assumed that the Ninevite would make the journey to the starship with his Krasny. He had assumed too much. He was alone among strangers.

"Now hear me, all of you." The sergeant-colonel stood at the head of the bay, a vast titanium robot of a man, armored arms akimbo. *"This is the way this exercise will be carried out."*

He had turned on his facial illumination so that the troops could see his expression. The effect was unreal, a thick, cruel face, red and bearded, suspended so as to appear that it was looking though a hole in the dark space of the open bay.

"You Gammah pay particular attention. I know your experience of real fighting is limited—" The sergeant-colonel's dark eyes burned into the Krasny. *"This is a drill. A simple landing drill. We will shortly overtake a barge—a large one. It has been fitted out with what the boffins think a Goldenwing's rig looks like. It is waiting for us in synchronous orbit just beyond that horizon."*

Krasny saw with a lurch of his tortured stomach that the shuttle had stopped turning and now flew stern first, ramp gaping like a mouth. The horizon of which the sergeant-colonel was speaking made a convex line across the upper half of the opening. Krasny realized that not only was the shuttle traveling stern first, but relative to Nimrud, it was inverted. The medication the suit had administered lost some of its efficacy.

"The shuttle will make a single low pass over the barge. This unit will move out the ramp and into near-freefall. The impact when you hit the barge deck should not be more than your armor can handle." The lighted face within the helmet gave the assembled men a horrible grin. *"If your suit fails, we'll give you another. All right? Questions? Good—"* Without waiting, Krasny noted. *"For you from Gammah. Your suit was hand-picked by regulars. Jump when I tell you, land like I showed you in the simulators."* Again that ghastly grin. *"Just think of it as a walk through a garden on Nineveh, right? Eleven minutes to drop time."*

The sergeant-colonel stationed himself by Krasny. He touched helmets. "Any questions?"

"Yes," Krasny said. "Why am I here?"

"Because the Speaker wants you here. Any other questions?"

"You have special orders about me."

"I said 'questions,' not 'statements.'"

Krasny stared at the big soldier with genuine hatred. "You have orders to shop me to the Ninnies," he said. "I'm a goodwill gift to the enemy."

The sergeant-colonel's large face regarded Krasny though the two face-plates. "A man could be condemned for talk like that, hero. Just do as you are told and you might even come out of all this alive. You are not important enough to shop." He moved away, mingling with the troops, checking equipment.

"Three minutes." The word from the flightdeck came in harsh Nimrudite tones. Why was it, Krasny asked himself, that I never noticed how unpleasantly some words of Nimrudite sounded?

"Two minutes. Have ORGOTISH, *comrades."*

The Krasny thought, *I am a Nimrudite, like the officer on the flightdeck, like the sergeant-colonel. Yet he has great* orgotish *and I have none. I did not know until now. I thought I had* orgotish. *When I killed, I revelled in it. When I issued orders, I had pride, arrogance, a commanding presence, a sense of obligation.*

Yet all that is gone and I am left with nothing but a terrifying leap into space, he thought. He closed his eyes and uttered the most sincere prayer he had spoken since childhood. *Allah the Merciful, Allah the Compassionate, protect me in my hour of need.* But the prayer was false, unreal. *We are not true Muslims,* the Krasny thought. *We pretend to be, but we are heterodox. We are collectivists and have been since our time on Earth. We use whatever words are at hand, but Allah is the state and the Prophet is whoever speaks for the Collective.* It was a bitter self-discovery, one that left no semblance of warmth or comfort.

"One minute. Target in sight."

In spite of himself, Krasny raised his eyes to look. A gray construct of dull metal floated in view.

———

"Thirty seconds."

"Stand to the ramp!" The sergeant-colonel's order roared in Krasny's com phones. He forced himself to move toward the open ramp. The barge looked like a slippery sheet of scrap metal against the stars. The bright, cruel, distant stars.

"Execute!"

Krasny watched two troopers, spreadeagled against the stars, drop from the shuttle. Suddenly the void was at his feet. From the right of the open ramp the disk of Nimrud began to appear. The limb. The half disk. The terminator. Bright orange-red and the blackness of night, the dark atmosphere streaked with the familiar snaking bolts of lightning.

The sergeant-colonel took an armored step in Krasny's direction. *He is going to push me into space,* Krasny thought. No man of *orgotish* could permit such a thing.

He stepped into the darkness and fell.

———

16

THE DOWAGER VOLKOVA

The Metropolitan of Nostromograd, Peter Mornay, left his ground-car at the bottom of the hill and climbed the broad stairs to the verandah of Ullah's Vista. The dappled winter sunlight made the day bright, but gave scant warmth. Mornay felt the bite of the frigid air even through the quilted garments he wore.

For a careless moment he wondered how many centuries his people had been making such garments. The practice began among the Mongols on the Russian steppe long before there *were* Russians. *What a basically conservative people we are,* he thought. *Despite our grandiose claims to scientific preeminence we still wear the clothes our forebears wore when they were subjects of the Great Khan.*

He paused for a moment to catch his breath and look up toward the sprawling house on the ridge above him. His careless moment faded. Without Kat in residence the place seemed still and lifeless. From the big, empty house, the dowager Gospodina Irena Volkova ran the estate. She would have preferred to retire from the world. She had made that very clear. First she had taken refuge in what the folk of Nineveh called ''Widow's Silence.'' Women of the aristocracy often stopped speaking when their husbands died. It was an act hallowed in the Sharia.

Then, when Peter had brought the Ephor Vukasin's offer of a space command to Ekaterina, the dowager had broken her silence to voice her outrage. In the process, she had divorced herself from her fosterling, Peter Mornay.

Mornay's repeated pleas for an audience had been shunned until now—a mere three days before Kat and her troops were to embark at Odessa Spaceport.

When the dowager's summons finally arrived, Peter had been attending to his clerical duties in Nostromograd, but he had dropped them immediately to rush to his foster-mother's side. He barely allowed himself to hope that the dowager Gospodina of Ullah's Vista had forgiven him. Forgiveness was always in short supply among the colonists of Nineveh.

Perhaps, he thought, *it was about the official view that Andrey Volkov and some of his soldiers were going to be returned aboard the* Gloria Coelis *by the Nimmies as a gesture of goodwill.* He hoped that story was not what the Gospodina wanted to interrogate him about.

Mornay did not believe in Nimmie goodwill. Among the inhabitants of the quarreling Twins, there was no such thing. There had never been. But the prospect of liberation for her brother must have had a great deal to do with Kat Volkova's willingness to fall in with the Ephor Yuri Vukasin's plan.

But if this whole affair ever ended before an ecclesiastical court, the results could be devastating. A Goldenwing was a Holy Object. It was written in the Sharia. It had been many years since Sharia Inquisitors had held court, but an act of piracy against a Goldenwing might just bring out the musty red robes and death-caps.

Mornay reached the top of the long staircase and stood on the wide verandah. He had spent his cadet years in this house at the top of the long stone staircase. He had played here as a child with the Volkov children. He had fallen in love with Kat here, under the stern eye of the Volkov matriarch. Stern, yes, he remembered. But she had given him more love than he had ever had from his distant father's third wife.

Peter Mornay was filled with a sense of fate. A sense, truth be told, of his own mortality. He had an almost superstitious need of the Gospodina Irena Volkova's approval. Perhaps, he thought, it was because Andrey and Kat had treated him with such open affection that he thought their blood was blessed.

What foolish nonsense, he thought. *We fought and squabbled the way any children anywhere did.* But now, at this moment, both Kat and Andrey were fading from his life. Without them he would become, in time, a desiccated, bookish religious, his life at an end before his thirtieth year.

On the way from Nostromograd, Mornay had stopped to pray at the golden dome of the Mornay Mosque. Not, truth to tell, he thought, because he was such a pure and religious man, but because it made him feel closer to the Volkovs.

The sexton had been overwhelmed at the appearance of the Metropolitan of Nostromograd, whose family name was carved into the grillwork above the altar beneath the Golden Dome. Since the Recurrence, services at the Mornay Mosque had been restricted to once a week, when the circuit-riding imam stopped to read the Sharia to the local inhabitants. He had asked Peter to preach a sermon, but Peter had pleaded a lack of time and hurried on his way to Ullah's Vista, leaving a disappointed sexton who wished that young Mornay (who was one of the locals, after all) had more spirit.

Peter stood on the verandah looking at the familiar southern vista. The hills, the grasslands, rolling plains, and finally in the winter distance the Planetary Ocean, gray in this light under a ceiling of swiftly moving clouds.

"Welcome to Ullah's Vista, Your Honor."

At his elbow stood Oleg Lavinovich, a lame overseer brought from a veteran's hospital in Perm. Lavinovich was a small, wire-sinewed man of fifty years who had learned his task of overseer on one of the Mosque estates under the supervision of the Grand Metropolitan of Nineveh, Massoud Bokhara. The same Bokhara who was at this moment preparing to join the delegation assembled and led by the Ephor Vukasin.

Peter Mornay distrusted the Grand Metropolitan Massoud's devotion to religion. He suspected the old man of having dreams of the glory of ancient times, when the Mosque Militant dominated Ararat. During his seminary training, it had been Massoud Bokhara who had insisted that Peter serve a tour of duty as a military chaplain in the Rings, a duty Peter had despised.

"Welcome to Ullah's Vista, Your Honor," Lavinovich said again, with a correct tug at his sparse hairline. "The Volkova has asked me to greet you and see to your comfort." He hesitated, shrugged and said bluntly: "Until yesterday I was under orders to turn you away from the estate. But the Volkova appears to have changed her mind about seeing you. I am most pleased, Your Honor. Follow me."

The overseer led the way into the cavernous old house. It seemed darker than it had been when Peter had last visited. *But of course,* Mornay thought, *that was because Kat was not here.* To Peter Mornay, the presence of Ekaterina Volkova was like sunlight. Not much sunlight today, Mornay thought as he followed Lavinovich up a long, curving staircase toward the family rooms. The illumination in the house shifted and darkened as banks of clouds moved low overhead, driven by the seawind off Nostromo Sound.

"Is the Volkova well?" he asked Lavinovich.

"Reasonably so, Your Honor. She is most distressed at the thought of Polkovnik Ekaterina returning to active duty so soon, of course."

"Of course," Peter Mornay said humbly.

They had reached one of the upstairs parlors. In a house as large as Ullah's Vista there were customarily three or four such rooms of diminishing size. The dimensions of the room to which a guest was conducted were a measure of how intimately he was regarded by the family. Close friends and relatives were entertained in small, warm rooms. Others were greeted in larger, colder surroundings.

It was a measure of how badly out of favor Peter Mornay was with the dowager Gospodina that he had been ushered into the largest of the three upstairs parlors, filled with unpleasant memories from his cadet days. Here, the Volkovs dealt with politicians and other riffraff, as the old Gospodin used to say.

Taska Marenko, a personal female retainer of the Volkova's who had come to Ullah's Vista as a part of Irena Volkova's bridal party forty-six years before, appeared carrying a samovar and crystal glasses in silver chalices.

Peter Mornay's spirits sank. His foster-mother was choosing to receive him as though he were Metropolitan of Nostromograd, and nothing more. His beloved surrogate mother, the woman who had, in effect, raised him, was dealing with him as a *personage* (of whom she now disapproved) rather than as the surrogate son he had been in this house for most of his juvenile years.

Taska placed the samovar on an ancient mahogany table—a relic of Earth—and regarded Peter with cool formality. "The Volkova will be with you presently, Your Honor. May I pour you tea?"

This, Mornay thought, from a retainer who had bandaged his scraped knees and brought him snacks sent by Kat when he was being confined in his rooms for some infraction of cadet discipline. The Gospodina Irena must be very angry, indeed.

"Yes, Taska. Thank you. I should like some hot tea. I have had a cold journey."

The old woman poured the steaming tea without the slightest show of interest in whether his journey had been hot or cold. It was a custom that high-ranking visitors were always greeted with courtesy by the servants at Ullah's Vista. But courtesy, too, could be either cold or hot on Nineveh.

Lavinovich bowed. "If you will excuse me, Your Honor. I have duties to perform."

Taska presented Mornay with his silver-mounted tea glass and placed a decanter of iced vodka on the table next to the samovar.

"With your permission, Your Honor." She bowed and prepared to leave the parlor.

"Stay, Taska. Tell me of your family. Is Yevgeny well?" It had been her husband, Yevgeny, who had been entrusted with the serious task of teaching Andrey and Peter to carve the great goose-like birds that were eaten on holidays in the steppeland estates.

"Yevgeny has been made a field overseer, Your Honor. It was his choice when the Recurrence began."

I should have known that, Mornay thought. *I should have remembered from the last time I was here.*

"Taska," he said. "There is no need to be so formal. You know me too well for that."

"You are Metropolitan," she said.

"I am also almost a foster-child of yours," he said with a slightly forced smile. "Is that nothing?"

"Of course not, Your Honor. But the Volkova thinks—"

"Please, Taska. I have a feeling I shall shortly know exactly what the Volkova thinks." He looked about him at the uninviting, elegant room. "I did not expect this," he said. That was untrue, of course. Actually he had feared worse.

Taska stood silent, with folded hands. It was foolish to look for a warm welcome from Taska or from any of the Ullah's Vista people so long as the Volkova was displeased with him.

He made the sign of cross and crescent and extended his ring for Taska. She kissed it with relief, curtseyed and left the room. *This visit is going to be even harder than I imagined,* Peter thought. *May Ullah damn and blast you, Yuri Vukasin.*

Peter walked to a tall, narrow window facing the mountains to the northeast. Wind chuckled under the broad eaves and rattled the locked-back storm shutters. The sky over the mountains was turning into a solid bank of silver streaked with black. The green of the Urals' southern slopes was dark green-gray, the color of the native conifer-like trees that forested the immense terraces of rising ground. The ranges rose in a steady procession, that dark green-gray patterned with white-gray shields of granite. In the far distance Peter could make out the metallic glint of the river Dnieper as it fell from the high reaches, flowed across the granite terraces, fell again in shimmering silver falls to the Plain of Perm, a land of lakes and streams where the Dnieper flowed in broad, looping meanders toward the steppe.

On an exceptionally clear day one could stand at Ullah's Vista and see the vast conical mountain that rose to a height of 9,750 meters and the peak of Mount Ararat. Ararat had never been climbed. The last thousand meters of the peak was a cone with sides near to vertical and the last five hundred quite literally pierced the sky, extending beyond the tropopause and into the stratosphere of Nineveh. Scientific and signalling devices had been placed on the summit of Mount Ararat, but by machines dropped from space, never by climbers. Ninnies were proud of their colossal mountain.

"Good day to you, Metropolitan."

Peter Mornay turned to face the Volkova of Ullah's Vista. Though she was a small woman, no more than 152 centimeters tall, she stood like a spearman, erect and austere in black cloth.

"*Matyachka*," Peter Mornay said. Alone with the Volkova, he fell easily into the habit of referring to her by the local corruption of the Old Russian "Little Mother." It had always been his habit as a child to address her so when they were private. "I thank you for seeing me."

The aged blue eyes held no hint of affection. "Offer me your ring, Imam," she said.

He did so and she took his hand in hers. Her skin felt delicate and papery to the touch. She touched her lips formally to the Metropolitan's ring on his forefinger.

"Bless me, Imam," she said.

"Always, *Matyachka*," Mornay said, and signed the cross and crescent.

"Did you have a pleasant journey from Nostromograd, Imam?" Irena Volkova asked.

Does she care at all whether or not I did? Peter wondered.

The Volkova lowered herself stiffly into a straight chair. Her Circassian-blue eyes remained fixed on Mornay.

"I am very pleased that you sent for me, *Matyachka*," Peter said. "But I wonder why."

"You wonder? This is your home."

The Volkova was not an ingenuous woman. Nor was she given to making simple statements.

"I am grateful you feel that way, *Matyachka*. But I am still perplexed," Mornay said.

"You may properly wonder why I entertain an associate of

Yuri Vukasin," she said. "*That* may be a source of your perplexity."

"So it might be," Peter said warily. He should know better than to press the dowager Gospodina for explanations. Even her husband had never been able to succeed at that game.

"When did you become a partisan of the Ephor, Peter?"

"You misjudge me. I am not his partisan," Mornay said.

"I am pleased to hear that. Yuri Vukasin is a parvenu," the Volkova said. Her posture seemed to grow even more erect as she spoke of Vukasin. "He was a schoolmaster. Did you know that? I even hear that he was rather a good schoolmaster."

"He is Third Ephor, *Matyachka*," Peter said.

"And that makes him master of the world?"

"Of course not, Gospodina," Mornay said, beginning to sweat.

"*Dowager* Gospodina, Peter. The true Gospodina of Ullah's Vista is Kat."

"Of course, *Matyachka*."

"I am concerned." The Circassian-blue eyes were like glacier-ice. "Her recovery from her wounds is far from complete."

"*Matyachka*," Mornay protested, "Ekaterina is the best judge of that, surely."

The finely limned eyebrows arched. "I spoke to the medical staff at Odessa. Regrown limbs take a full year before they are strong enough for active service. You were a chaplain. I would have expected you to know that."

"Forgive me, dowager Gospodina, but we both know that I was a very bad chaplain."

The eyes seemed to brighten. "I have never asked you this, though I have wondered, Peter. Are you a coward?"

The question, so bluntly put, shocked him. "I do not believe so, *Matyachka*."

"I expected you to say that, Peter. And you always do what is expected of you."

"That is so," Mornay said gloomily.

The dowager Gospodina stood and walked to a small

table. She took a key from her bosom and unlocked a drawer. When she turned to face Mornay, she held a lazegun in her small fist.

The Metropolitan stared at her.

Irena Volkova returned to her chair and seated herself.

She fixed Mornay with the look of a delicate bird of prey. The lazegun she leveled at his chest.

Peter's mouth felt dry.

"We share many similar ideals, Imam," the dowager said. "That is true?"

"Yes, *Matyachka.*" The breath seemed to congeal in his chest. A bolt from a lazegun would burn though flesh and bone like a white-hot spike. Smoke would curl upward to the exposed rafters and in an instant the charcoaled edges of the wound would burst into flame. Blue at first, then yellow, and finally the fire would gutter out leaving a charred hole as big as a fist through a man.

"Do you know what the penalty for heresy and blasphemy is, Peter? Let me tell you. It is death by laser fire."

"*Matyachka—*" Peter sat very still.

"The defilement of a Goldenwing is blasphemy, Imam. But you know that, of course."

"I do, *Matyachka,* but no such charges have ever been brought against—"

"Anyone?"

"There is no record of any such punishment."

"We are speaking here of Andrey and Ekaterina. The last of the Volkovs."

"Yes, *Matyachka,* I do understand—"

"Do you, Peter." Watching the dowager Gospodina was like watching a cold fuse burn down. Peter could not take his eyes from her.

"I want you to understand, Peter Mornay," she said. "It is not for lack of love for you I do this."

She raised the lazegun until it was level with his eyes.

Ullah protect me, Mornay thought, *she is really going to kill me.*

———

"This is what my other children, the future of the Volk-ovs, are facing."

Peter watched in fixed fascination as the delicate fingers squeezed the stock of the lazegun. He saw the muzzle glow and then release a beam of coherent light, red as a ruby, red as blood.

He did not move.

The beam burned the air a centimeter from his temple and struck the stone wall behind him, loosing a shower of sparks.

Irena Volkova put the lazegun in her lap and folded her hands primly. "Now, Peter," she said, "let us talk of important things." She refilled his vodka glass with vodka and tea from the samovar and did the same for herself.

She lifted her glass. "To life," she said.

"To life," Peter Mornay whispered, and drank down his spiked hot tea. It was as though he had died and the stuff of life was being poured back into his empty body.

"To life, *Matyachka*," he said again, "To life."

17

LIFT-OFF

A t the head of her troops, Ekaterina Volkova crossed the gangway onto the deck of the hovercraft which lay, floats awash, in the surging surf at the pierhead.

It was customary for Ninevite Territorials embarking for a lift-off into combat to be dispatched with all the military pomp and color the base at Odessa could contrive. Honor guards, regimental colors massed, a band playing. That was the Ninevite style. *A small enough inducement,* Kat thought, *for embarkations into a war in which the troops often took forty percent or higher casualties.*

The Great Russians who gave the Ninevites their military traditions were a breed with a finely developed taste for martial show and glitter. Kat had begun to wonder if the Ninevite taste for such things had not cost the colony too dearly in blood and treasure, and her doubts did not make the bleakness of this secret embarkation any more palatable.

The shores of the embarkation area were barren, black rock washed by a gray sea. On the Launch Island One to the south their battle-shuttle stood in its gantry illuminated by banks of floodlights. At this distance could be seen only the bluish-white glare. It did little to dispossess the gray winter dark.

Kat wondered if the political delegation were already aboard the shuttle. Ephor Vukasin's list of participants was a short one. Few of the personages Kat expected had been included. Except for the Grand Metropolitan Bokhara, it was a company of strangers waiting for the troops to arrive and be stowed in the troop compartment of the ugly, stump-winged shuttle.

Some few of Kat's commandos had donned their medals for the departure—she had not had the heart to discourage them. But it made a pitiful show, a few bits of ribbon and metal on the black, thermal jumpsuits made to be worn under battle armor. Not what soldiers of Nineveh fancied. Not at all.

At the head of the gangway, Vasili Gorchenko, the captain of the hovercraft, returned her clenched-fist salute and made room for her on the narrow platform where the officer of the deck normally took station.

Gorchenko was an overage leytenant with a failed mustache. He frowned at the sky, measuring the chances of a sudden squall—of which there were many in these southern latitudes at this time of year—troubling his noisy, ungainly craft. Gorchenko disliked irregularities. He had, with difficulty, managed to seduce a middle-aged petty officer in the Supply Depot. It was his custom to visit her each eightday at midmorning. But it looked as though this day he might be forced to change his plans. This made him testy.

It also made him incautious. "They aren't giving you much of a send-off," he said. "Did you cross your legs to someone important?"

Ekaterina Volkova was not amused. Even after four hundred years of service in the armed forces of Nineveh, women still heard such remarks. Usually from noncombatants like this ferryboat driver.

Kat touched the golden wheat sheaves on her collar points. "Do you see these, Leytenant?" she asked coldly. "Do you know what they mean?"

"Yes, of course." When his reply was greeted with an icy and aristocratic contempt, he blurted, "No offense, Colonel."

"Offense taken, Leytenant. Now get my people on board and under cover and forget the social commentary." There were rumors about secret Nimmie surveillance satellites in orbit around Nineveh. If they were true, a body of troops moving purposefully in the open could betray Vukasin's entire operation.

"Sah, Polkovnik!" Gorchenko shouted. It was the traditional reply of a junior who had just put his foot in his mouth and felt the flash of a flamethrower aimed at his military ass. He swiftly descended to the deck to stand under the shrouded air-screws from where he bawled orders at his six-man crew.

Kat lost interest in him. She flexed her still-aching arm. The regrowth process was nearly complete. Her leg, too, had healed well, though from time to time it throbbed a warning.

Her executive officer, Yevgeny Orgoniev, reported to her with a salute. Her battalion saluted often. With reason. Kat had decided when training began that a mission so fraught with potential disaster had to be run under strict discipline. Her troops had taken to calling her "Sweet Colonel Ironass." She rather fancied that. It was just disrespectful enough to indicate good morale and readiness.

She wondered if Yuri Vukasin, who had appeared frequently at Odessa while the battalion trained to watch her preparations, understood any of this sort of thing. She doubted it. Like most politicians, he did not make the connection between the mission and the men and women who had to complete it.

The battalion filed aboard, laden with weaponry, single file on the gangway above the ten-meter tide. In an hour this floating pier would be aground. Tides on Nineveh were savage.

The troops looked at her, some fearfully, some with a childish faith that she was invulnerable and would make them so as well. Occasionally one of the young men or women caught her eye and smiled. Some questioned silently. She did this herself. *Is what we do right? Is it possible to do it at all? What will the butcher's bill come to?*

Yuri Vukasin had caused the engineering troops to build a mockup of a Goldenwing on the plain north of the Odessa Weapons Range. Nimmie spy satellites were routinely shot down by Nineveh's armed shuttles, but Kat wondered whether or not the purpose of the Potemkin villages on the northern plain had gone undetected. Secure or not, Kat and her commandos had trained on the mockup, but not only was security questionable, no one really knew if the mockup bore any true resemblance to the real thing they would be assaulting. There were drawings of the *Nostromo* in the museum at Nostromograd, but the curator was of the opinion that the renderings were made long after the ship had departed from the Ross system. There were some photographs taken from unloading shuttles and sleds in low orbit, but the images were indistinct and without *scale*. The starship could have been twenty meters long or twenty thousand. At the time of the landing the colonists and syndics had had other things to consume their time.

It *was* known that Goldenwing *Nostromo* had been described as a small vessel. The engineers had used what information they had and Kat's people had made do with what was available. She soon realized that taking a starship, large or small, with a small unit would be very difficult if anyone opposed it. But simply adding bodies to her force would not answer. What she had needed was intelligence. And of that she had almost none.

She watched the grenadiers file aboard laden with their Hellfires. She had seriously questioned the wisdom of using Hellfires aboard a Goldenwing. The grenades were small enough to appear nearly harmless, but the explosive was so violent that a single grenade could eviscerate a shuttle or a main battle tank. Goldenwings were made of monofilament fabrics and titanium frames and spars. A single Hellfire might destroy the Goldenwing. Kat had no way of knowing. Yet *threat* was everything. *Guerrilla terrorist tactics,* Kat thought. *Has it come to this? What if we are forced to use our weapons? What then? Dare we really wreck a Goldenwing?*

After the grenadiers came the rocketmen, a section of gunners and their recoilless light artillery. Such troops had been successful against Nimmie armor in several Ring engagements. But again, Kat was unsure whether they were going to carry out a coup or fight a declared and angry war against the Wired Ones.

———

That possibility was a daunting one. As far as Kat knew, no colonist had ever raised a weapon against a Goldenwing. And who knew what weapons the mysterious "syndics" had acquired in their timeless wanderings among the Near Stars?

The heart of the force, the light infantry, marched onto the steel deck. The gangway was hauled aboard and the idling air-screws advanced. The hovercraft moved away from the dock and into the chop of Odessa Bay. The lifting fans began to whine, inflating the high-pressure area under the skirts. The craft lifted onto its air cushion and began to move more swiftly. Gorchenko had retreated onto the flying bridge with his helm and throttlemen.

Kat felt the relative wind increase as the hovercraft picked up speed for the forty-kilometer journey to Launch Island One. She moved to the bow and stood behind the low spray shield. The cold spume stung her cheeks. She stripped off her red beret and let the wind blow her hair.

The low clouds were tinged with red. Unseen above them, the Accursed Twin was entering the shadow of Nineveh, as it did a dozen times each month. Kat closed her eyes and tried to imagine how the phenomenon was being experienced on Nimrud, where the eclipse would be an annular eclipse of the sun.

So many experiences in common, she thought, *and we spend our lives trying to murder one another.* She recalled a verse from the Sharia Book of Revelation often quoted by the dowager Volkova: *"There was war in heaven; Michael and his angels fought against the dragon: And prevailed not."*

Why did I remember that now? she wondered. Was it as Andrey used to say: "Years pass and we watch ourselves turning into our parents." He always said it with a grin. But somehow Kat did not feel like smiling. With a heavy heart she left the windy foredeck for the breathless compartment she shared with her troops.

On Launch Island One, the ferry's destination, the ground crews moved about the pad, men and women dwarfed by the massive fins and tail surfaces of the battle-shuttle in the gantry.

Liquid oxygen overflows made plumes of white in the gray

morning. The stink of hydrocarbon fuel persisted around the spacecraft despite the wind. Compartments on wheeled carriers awaited their turn to connect to the crane-lifts and be stowed aboard the shuttle.

The embarkation was running behind schedule and Ephor Yuri Vukasin was hard put to maintain his patience. The members of the peace delegation were aboard; their luxurious compartment component had been one of the first put aboard the battle-shuttle.

Vukasin was displeased and disappointed at the skepticism with which his talk of a peace meeting had been received by the *nomenklatura* in Petersburg. He had hoped to have both old Oleg Gordiev, the Head of State, and Massoud Bokhara, the Grand Metropolitan, as members of the delegation. Having both aboard would have been almost irrefutable proof of good intentions. The Nimmies would have been forced to accept such a gesture.

But Gordiev had temporized and then backed away at the last moment. Yuri Vukasin suspected that the old man's private intelligence network had discovered the full scope of Vukasin's plan.

Gordiev might be thought senile by members of the Board of Strategy, but he proved far too wise in the ways of Ninevite politics to allow himself to be embroiled in so equivocal an enterprise. He had declined the honor of heading the delegation to the Goldenwing.

Well, thought Vukasin, *so be it.* If the enterprise succeeded and at long last the Recurrences came to an end, Yuri Vukasin would not need to share the credit with Gordiev. The Ephor would stand alone at the apex of Nineveh's political pyramid. *Let Gordiev deal with that when the hour came,* Vukasin thought.

So it was that, aside from Massoud Bokhara, the persons of the delegation were nonentities, second rankers dragooned by Yuri Vukasin. But did it matter? Neither the Nimmies nor the Starmen were likely to guess that Vukasin's "peace" delegation lacked political muscle. What the Nimrudites thought would not matter.

They would be surprised by Ekaterina Volkova and her

Territorials, and that was what was important at this moment. Vukasin gained stature by the fact that he would use real force to bring the Goldenwing to Nineveh.

The *Gloria Coelis* herself, and the military and political rogues of the Nimmie Collective who would accompany the Krasny to the Goldenwing, would be a haul of enormous importance. The hostage people alone might be enough to bring an end—on favorable terms—to the current Recurrence.

Young Andrey and his few surviving Territorials were only a lever he, Yuri Vukasin, might need to use to control Kat Volkova—who was not, it seemed to Vukasin, as committed as one might wish to the enterprise.

The thought of the younger Volkova was curiously engaging. Vukasin stood on the periphery of the launch pad regarding the bay. He had been careful on his way up the academic and political ladder. His family bloodlines were insufficiently aristocratic for him to be granted the license bestowed on the better born. He had avoided marriage because the quality of woman he could command was not the sort that would advance his career. But when success opened the field of really eligible Ninevite females to him, that would be another matter.

He considered Kat. Perhaps still too well born to lie within his purview now. *But what a political partner she would make,* he thought.

She did not love him. That would be too much to ask. He knew himself to be less than heroic in appearance. That was a pity. Ninevites loved heroes who looked like heroes. But an Ephor who outwitted the Second Aliyans and brought peace to the Twin Planets might look rather more heroic than other, more handsome men who had accomplished less.

One of his aides ran across the concrete ramp with a message from Launch Island Control. "Sah. The Harbormaster reports the hovercraft is on the way. Estimated time of arrival is thirty minutes. Is there a reply?"

"I'll come," Vukasin said. It would do no harm to greet Kat on the dock. It was the sort of gesture Ninevites approved. It might even impress her.

*

The battalion filed aboard the crane-mounted loading compartment in the shadow of the shuttle's massive tailfin. The pie-shaped component was blind save for three heavy glass ports around the curving outer bulkhead. Like every part of the battle-shuttle it appeared heavy—too heavy for a spacecraft—and invulnerable. Heavy it was, Kat knew, but far from invulnerable. A number of Ninevite shuttles had recently been lost. The battle-shuttle on the pad at Launch Island One was the best and newest spacecraft the techs of Nineveh had contrived. But the Nimrudites, less numerous than their enemies, were clearly better at creating the weapons of war. There had been suspicions of this before, in earlier Recurrences, but Kat feared there was now proof in the number of Ninevite spacecraft missing.

Her soldiers route-stepped up the loading ramp and into the compartment under the leadership of Lieutenant Orgoniev. She turned to Vukasin, who stood by her clad, inappropriately, she thought, in the dress uniform of a Ninevite general.

"The Controller will lower an elevator for us," he said. "The others are already aboard. Level One."

"I'm sorry, Ephor. What did you say?"

"I said the Controller will lower an elevator, Volkova."

"I won't be riding with the political party, Ephor."

"Surely you don't intend to ride in the troop compartment?"

"Yes, of course. They are my soldiers."

Vukasin seemed shocked that a daughter of the steppe aristocracy would choose to ride in a troop compartment where men and women were stowed aboard like so many fish in a tin.

"The Metropolitan Massoud Bokhara expects to see you," Vukasin said.

"Please offer my regrets to the Metropolitan and tell him that I look forward to seeing him on the Goldenwing."

The last of the battalion had vanished into the compartment and the lights on the top of the crane were flashing amber, indicating that the segment was ready to be lifted aboard. Kat saluted the Ephor and climbed the ramp to the open valve in the compartment's curving flank. She vanished into the pie-tin and the valve slammed shut. The crane began immediately to lift the section up the two hundred meters to the forward fuselage of the massive war-shuttle. Vukasin stared after her with mixed anger and admiration.

He used his com to call the Controller. "Well, send the elevator down and be damned quick about it." Shouting at an inferior always made Vukasin feel better.

Inside the troop compartment, the men and women of the battalion swayed as the compartment was lifted.

"Everyone on a G-bed!" Lieutenant Orgoniev shouted. "Tie down!"

Ekaterina moved to the G-bed on the periphery where her gear had been stowed for her by her orderlies. It was a place nearest one of the windows. The armor glass was smeared and dirty, but through it she could see the girders of the gantry passing by as the section rose toward its place in the spacecraft's hull.

She lowered herself onto the bed and used the tie-downs. She was suddenly thirsty for a glass of the cold fruit juice the field kitchens had prepared for her before the march to the hovercraft. No such luxuries here. She had nothing but water in her canteen. She controlled her thirst and waited. The canteen would have to last for fifty-two hours, the flight-time to orbit around Nimrud.

The troop section reached its assigned place and plungers from the gantry seized the docking latches and began to slide the unit into place like a piece of a giant child's puzzle. The titanium hull banged and creaked. Loading troops was not a gentle operation.

The troops had a number of colorful things to say about the launch and loading crew.

"All right, let's settle down." The gravelly voice of Yelena Markova, the battalion sergeant-colonel. "Babushka-to-us-all," the troops called her.

Kat both heard and felt the locking bolts slam shut as the pie-tin became part of the shuttle. There was a hatch between the apex of the pie-slice and the central plenum of the war-shuttle. From there any life-supported section of the spacecraft could be accessed. Kat wondered wryly if the Ephor Vukasin was so taken that he would appear here in the troop compartment. The "Tiger-cage," the troops called it.

Soldiers had special names for everything and every place. It made war-fighting—if not familiar—at least bearable.

A breath of cold, fuel-smelling air struck Kat's face. The section was on ship's life-support now, everyone breathing internal air. Soon the oxygen content of the air would be increased. A higher oxygen level meant that the internal atmosphere could be kept at a lower pressure—a safety measure. All the troops had undergone the long-duration, high-G voyage treatments and could breathe low-pressure air without discomfort.

Like my still-undersized limbs, Kat thought, *a gift from our devoted medics. A gift paid for with years taken from our lives. How strange,* Kat thought, *that the Mosque countenanced that. What did Ullah the Compassionate think about such contempt for life?*

"Ten minutes to lift-off." The voice of the bridge-crew. Kat tied herself down more securely. These big battle-shuttles lifted brutally, hard and fast.

"Give me your attention, Territorials," Kat said into her com. Her words emerged from each trooper's command radio. "We are flying to meet a Goldenwing. Don't be awed. When the time comes, we will take possession of it in the name of Ullah and Nineveh."

Kat was pleased and surprised to receive a murmur of approval.

"We have the force to do it," she said. "There are only a half dozen syndics aboard and they are not warriors. We do not know the number of soldiers the Nimmies will bring aboard, but we are a match for any Nimmies." She felt no compunction saying that because she believed it fiercely. "Now settle down for lift-off, and huzzah for the Nostromograd Territorials!"

The troops cheered her.

The gantry turned, positioning for lift-off. An errant shaft of sunlight, leaking feebly through a tiny break in the heavy overcast, sent a beam of light across the compartment.

Against the far bulkhead of the compartment, Lieutenant

Orgoniev was helping a tall, black-clad trooper with a chaplain's cross and crescent on his breast stow his equipment.

Recognition shocked Ekaterina. It was Peter Mornay who met her eyes guiltily.

The Metropolitan of Nostromograd was the last man on Nineveh she had expected to see here and now. Combat in space was simply not Peter Mornay's proper environment. What had brought him here?

She spoke into her com unit. "Metropolitan Mornay, I will speak with you when we are under way."

The first rumbling of the booster rockets made the heavy, ungainly war-shuttle tremble as the final tie-down alarm came from the ship's intercom.

The spacecraft rose from Launch Island One on a narrow cone of flame and smoke. To those few on the ground who had seen the ancient history tapes, the launch was reminiscent of similar spacecraft launches on Earth, in the dawn of spaceflight.

At an altitude of fifty-five kilometers the shuttle was inverted and still thundering skyward. At ninety kilometers the booster rockets reached burn-out and separated from the shuttle and its fuel tank. They tumbled, smoking and spinning, toward the now-solid undercast, broke through the cloud deck and vanished to plunge into the sea.

Kat felt the booster's main engines shut down. At three hundred ten kilometers or thereabout, they would be used again for the transplanetary injection into a long elliptical orbit that would carry the warship eventually into orbit around Nimrud.

The first sensations of weightlessness struck her and she controlled the familiar liquid bitterness in her throat that was her own personal warning of space-sickness.

"Hear this, troopers," she said into her com unit. "Anyone who feels ill, use a Beta patch."

It was really not necessary to mother such experienced troops, but it was her duty to see to their well-being. Besides, it took her mind off her own unsettled stomach and postponed the moment she would have to move across the compartment and talk to Peter.

What could he had been thinking about? she wondered. It was the prerogative of any Mosque cleric to attach himself to any outbound unit he chose. This was a Sharia tradition that dated back to the days of the Jihad on Earth. But he had taken Kat so unaware that it had never occurred to her personally to check all the supernumeraries attached to her battalion. What most surprised Ekaterina Volkova, who had always held the beloved Peter in a tiny bit of contempt, was that he would do such an apparently quixotic thing.

Kat tried to assign a political reason to it; she could not. Peter was not a man active in politics. No, his presence here was almost certainly personal.

But because she and Peter had known one another almost as brother and sister since they were children, she did not come up with the true one.

18

PLANETFALL AT NIMRUD

Duncan Kr lay on the air of the bridge watching Anya and Broni put the final touches to the sailplan configuration that was keeping *Glory* in low orbit around the red planet below. With him was Dietr, present, as he often was, to watch the interplay between *Glory* and her sail handlers. Sailing was an art that forever escaped the physician, and that made it fascinating to him.

In the holograph *Glory* was projecting in the center air of the bridge-deck the image of Nimrud boiled with duststorms. Surface features were obscured. Duncan considered the image thoughtfully. Under the best of circumstances it would be difficult to examine the Beta Twin carefully. The weather of the planet was abominable, with nearly continuous storms and electrical displays, boiling red clouds and one-hundred-kilometer-per-hour winds. *Was it always like this?* Duncan wondered.

He had noted that even the areas of the planet below that were not hidden by the filthy climate were impossible to scan with any accuracy. Some sort of shield against electronic probing? Given what *Glory*'s database provided in the way of intelligence, a shielding device would be very much in character for the Nimrudites.

There were a plethora of objects in orbit around Nimrud. Most were obviously military satellites. Capabilities unknown. Other, larger objects appeared to be scientific orbital stations or lain-to spacecraft.

"Look at those, Dietr." Duncan spoke quietly in the humming, living dimness of *Glory*'s bridge-deck. "How would you date them?"

"Early Twenty-first Century Earth," Dietr said. "But they look somehow more capable."

"I agree," Duncan said. He drew a drogue from a bulkhead enclosure and Wired himself. "*Glory*. What can you tell me about the shuttle in grid 133429?"

Glory, when she spoke to Duncan, spoke Anglic tinged with a Scots burr in the voice of a young woman of Thalassa, Duncan's homeworld. The *Gloria Coelis* was one of the last Goldenwings to be built in lunar orbit. Her technology encompassed many such niceties. They were assumed to make the Wired Ones feel less isolated as they moved from star to star and from year to year.

At the time *Glory* was constructed, the Jihad was weakening itself by internal, intersect conflicts. But the religious torture and persecution of European and North American Christians continued unabated. It was said by the colonists who abandoned Earth that "the Twentieth Century endured for two thousand years." Since even the histories were burned by the rampaging Ayatollahs, the aphorism could be literally true.

Glory zoomed in on the holographic image of one of the winged shuttles. She was locked, mind to mind with Duncan. But for Dietr Krieg's un-Wired benefit, she spoke aloud through the com system. "The shuttle is larger than similar craft on Earth. Sixty thousand metric tons. Much of the mass appears to be titanium armor. The craft was built for war."

Glory's voice seemed laden with disapproval. *Was that possible?* Duncan wondered. *Could the-great-queen-who-was-not-alive have such feelings and express them?* Duncan knew he would have to be a far more intuitive cybernetician than he was to even guess intelligently at the answer. Generations of syndics had never really measured or understood the ancient ship's total abilities. When constructs with self-enhancing and enlarging computers such as *Glory*'s "lived" for centuries they became something quite beyond human *kent*. Duncan, reverting to his Scots roots, felt the old Gaelic word was the right one to use.

Anya Amaya and Broni stirred sightlessly in their pods. Outside, in the ruddy light of the Ross sun and the even redder light reflected from the world below, *Glory*'s square kilometers of skylar sails completed the automatic "fisting" into the tightly furled configuration required to house the golden foil within the spars. Only the foremast jibs and mizzen skysails remained spread to balance the light pressure of Ross 248 against the ever-present coriolis wind of tachyons that flowed out of the galactic center and dominated the nearly empty sky.

The tachyons now impacting on the ship had begun their journey eighteen billion years before in the dark maelstrom of the star-devouring black hole at the center of the Milky Way Galaxy.

It gave one perspective on the nature of time, Duncan thought, and filled one with wonder at the wisdom of the ancient geneticist Haldane's insight about the Universe: *"My suspicion is that the universe is not only queerer than we suppose, but queerer than we* can *suppose. . . ."*

"Captain?" Damon's voice came from the speakers mounted in the fabric walls.

"What is it, Damon?"

The Rigger was in Hold 9002 loading the cargo consigned to Nimrud into a trio of landers. The shipment for the Beta Twin consisted of a number of atomic generators designed to be used in deep mining operations. The machines were unsophisticated, even by the standards of the Aldrin colony that produced them six shiptime years before. But the radio calls from Nimrud had been persistent and demanding ever since the Nimrudites became aware that *Glory* had penetrated the Oort Cloud of the Ross system. They seemed to feel that the appearance of a Goldenwing at just this time was more than fortuitous. Duncan was beginning to suspect that the primitive fusion generators had little to do with the eagerness of the Nimrudites to greet *Glory*.

With Damon in the near to empty cavern of Hold 9002 was Buele, who had been put to work as cargo assistant. Buele took delight in moving heavy machines about in free-fall.

Damon said, "Do we have landing coordinates for the freight, Captain?"

"Not yet," Duncan said. Damon was anxious to command the shuttle-train that would leave *Glory* with the mining gear and power generators. Duncan suspected he was getting ship-bound. He had not been downworld for three ship years and he needed a break in routine. Unfortunately, Nimrud was an unattractive place for shore-leave.

Duncan said, "I am going to make radio contact as soon as Camp Resolution comes over the horizon, Damon. I will let you know as soon as I know myself." He suspected that using *Glory* as a venue for a peace conference was going to be both troublesome and tedious. *There was nothing in the Twin Planets to attract the restless sailor,* he thought. But that was the way of it. Pleasant shore-leaves were uncommon for Starmen. He spoke to Dietr. "I suspect we are being tracked and watched by one or all of those shuttles, but since there has been nothing from them on the radio, I shall assume that the people here prefer that I make contact with representatives of the downworld government first." He steadied himself on the edge of the pod holding Broni. "I sense that these folk are suspicious almost to the point of paranoia." He caught the Cybersurgeon's covert smile and said, "All right. That may just be Physician Kr's diagnosis. But the observation stands until further notice."

"As it should, Duncan. I have been monitoring our exchanges with the downworld government. Their attitudes make one shudder."

"Even you, wise one?"

"Even I, Master and Commander. When you deal with them watch your six o'clock—as they used to say in the army of the European Reich." It was a matter of both pride and sardonic amusement to the physician that he had once, a very long time ago, served in the medical service of a European army that had existed for a brief time during the last years of the Jihad. It gave Dietr a whisper of military credentials. Which was a whisper more than anyone else aboard Goldenwing *Glory* might claim. In fact, it fascinated and excited Dietr Krieg that *Glory*'s port of call was in a society that had been, to all intents and purposes, at war for a thousand years.

Duncan said, "I want you to make certain we are swept clean with antibiotics and whatever else is needed. I don't want any Nimrudite coming down with even so much as a cold he caught from us. They are capable of thinking it a weapon." He essayed a thin smile. "They have elected us the site of a peace conference, and I want to make damned sure it stays peaceful."

"I will have us polished, Duncan," the physician agreed. "But what about them? We can stand a few exotic bugs, but Broni can't."

"Quarantine her," Duncan said.

Dietr Krieg said, "Thank you, Master and Commander. But that is an assignment better suited to you than to me."

Duncan essayed a wry smile. "It may take the best efforts of the two of us," he said. He studied the hologram thoughtfully. "Has it occurred to you that perhaps we may need just exactly the skills that make these Twin Planet colonists so unpleasant?"

"Mira's monsters?" Dietr said.

"They are real, Dietr."

The Cybersurgeon visibly suppressed a shudder. "Maybe. I don't feel sure enough of my facts to dispute them with you."

"She sensed something out there. I did, too," Duncan said. "It terrified me."

Dietr shrugged. "You are the most empathic of us all. Except, perhaps, the Voertrekker boy. If you say there is something out there, I am willing to accept it. What does that get us? How far "out there"? Do they exist in our space? Are they sentient beings? *Lieber Gott,* Duncan. How big are they? As big as a breadbox? Or big as a star? You see where we begin to run into problems?"

"I have no answers," Duncan said. "No descriptions. No definitions. No time-scale. But one day, Dietr, we are going to meet. When that happens everyone will be needed."

"I devoutly hope, Duncan," Dietr said, "to be dead and floating in space by then."

In the gel of her pod, Broni stirred. Her synthesized voice came through *Glory*'s com system. *"Our orbit is stable, Duncan; we can send the parameters to the Nimrudites,"* she said.

"I concur," said Anya's voice.

"A single watch-keeper will do for the next four hours. You have the duty, Broni." Duncan disconnected from the computer and allowed the drogue to retract into the bulkhead.

"The downworlders are very anxious, Duncan. They are hailing us," Broni said aloud.

"It appears our hosts can't wait for you to make contact with Camp Resolution," Dietr Krieg said.

The images in the hologram changed as the transmissions were received. The hails were coming from a large, brutish-looking shuttle closely escorted by another.

"Aboard the Goldenwing, do you hear us?"

"We are receiving you," Duncan said.

"This is the captain of the war-shuttle *Astraris*. I have a high-level delegation aboard. How shall we approach you?"

"I will open a hold so that you can bring your vessel aboard. Have you that capability?"

The voice seemed to bridle at being asked the question. "We have that capability, *Gloria Coelis,* and a good many others. What are your instructions?"

Off the air, Duncan said quietly. "Bring them inboard to Hold 3100, Anya. Without offending their sensibilities, if possible."

"Aye, Master and Commander." The Sailing Master fell easily into shipboard formality.

"And we, Dietr," Duncan said. "We had better purify ourselves and put on some clothes to receive our guests."

19

GOLDENWING!

The compartments aboard the Ninevite war-shuttle designed for the comfort of very important persons were far from luxurious. Space aboard such craft was strictly rationed, and not always along lines the Ephor Vukasin thought proper.

But despite the discomforts, Massoud Bokhara, the person aboard most likely to be saluted as a personage, was enjoying his venture into space with a schoolboyish enthusiasm Yuri Vukasin thought unseemly in a septuagenarian clergyman.

The fact was that though the Bokhara clan had provided the Mosques of Nineveh with clerics for eleven generations, those Bokharas who had escaped the duty of imamhood had lived lives of high adventure as explorers and warriors. Massoud, himself, had been a second choice for the clerical path. An elder brother destined to be Metropolitan of All Nineveh had died by assassination before Massoud could escape into the military service.

As a student and monk and later as an imam, Massoud had done his best to live his clerical life as his blood dictated. He had been one of the first chaplains actually to go into space on war missions with Nineveh's soldiers. In the last Recurrence he had demanded—and almost received—command of a military force to fight in the Rings. His ideal imam had been the ancient Earth Templar Jacques de Molay, who had fought in the Holy Land only to be savagely betrayed by the French King Philip and Pope Clement, and who had died calling for his tormentors to meet him before the throne of God to answer for their crimes against the Holy Sharia.

But Nineveh had no place for crusading warrior priests and Massoud Bokhara had been denied his command of soldiers and sequestered for many years in the Mosque of Saint Petersburg until he was liberated by his election as Grand Metropolitan of all Nineveh.

Now, for the first time in many years, Massoud Bokhara was in space. Brought there, it was true, by the political maneuvering of Yuri Vukasin, but still in space and about to take part in a grand adventure. The old man's ebullience rasped the Ephor's stretched nerves.

Ekaterina Volkova, summoned from the troop compartment to occupy the churchman by the tense and edgy Vukasin, half smiled as she watched the old would-be warrior peering excitedly from the shuttle's thick port seeking a first glimpse of the mystic vessel they were about to encounter.

She was well aware of the Bokhara's dreams of military glory and she pitied him for his ignorance of the true nature of war. But she had known him all of her life and felt a deep affection for him.

She had shed her armor—a thing field troops never did in space. But this was not an ordinary mission. She had still refused to don her military finery as the Ephor had done. Life aboard a war-shuttle was uncomfortable enough without the dinging and jingling of medals and badges in zero gravity.

"I tried to get Peter Mornay up here, Father Massoud," she said. "He refused to budge from the troop compartment."

The imam turned to look at her impatiently, as though he was in no mood to hear about the foolishness of the Metropolitan of Nostromograd. "If he had come I would have had to reprimand him, Gospodina. Whatever else Peter might be, he is not unintelligent. What will you do with him if there is fighting?"

I might ask what should I do with you, *Father Massoud, if there is fighting,* she thought. But familiarity did not permit impertinence. Besides, she was well aware that the Grand Metropolitan was aboard because Yuri Vukasin's scheme needed high-level approval. Or complicity?

"I shall try to keep him out of harm's way," she said. "I appreciate his feeling of being honor-bound, but he has done me no favor by attaching himself to my battalion."

The imam braced himself against the transparent port so that he was limned against the ruddy glow of the planet below. "I appreciate that our people have a long tradition of allowing their women into battle, but I must say it distresses me when the women in question are so handsome as you, Ekaterina."

Dear old man, she thought, *compliments don't help lessen the load on my back.* She was only too well aware that she was the only person aboard in a position of authority who had any experience of fighting in space. The training sessions she and her troopers had undergone again and again on the plain at Odessa had left her unsatisfied and apprehensive. How was it possible to train for a mission against an objective no soldier of Nineveh had seen for a millennium, give or take a dozen decades?

The Metropolitan's bright blue eyes under a thatch of white hair were far more youthful than they should have been, Kat thought. The Bokhara was in his seventies. By Earth standards (and colonists never failed to compare what they had or what they were with what they had once been), Massoud Bokhara would be counted an old man. The Russians who colonized the Ross system were not so prejudiced against age. They valued it and honored the old with positions of command.

Perhaps it was a kind of innocence that kept Bokhara so fresh, Ekaterina thought. The old man reminded her of her brother Andrey—whom she might soon see, if the Ephor Vukasin could be trusted. Even that made her uneasy. Was the ancient enemy suddenly become honorable?

Massoud Bokhara said, "How can I help you, my daughter?"

"Peter went to visit my mother, the dowager Volkova, before he reported to Odessa," she said.

"Do you find that odd?" Bokhara asked. "After all, he was

a cadet in your house, Ekaterina. She is his mother in all but blood.''

"That is as may be, Imam. But Peter is here now, on board this shuttle.'' Kat held herself in place against an inertial shift. The shuttle was beginning a roll maneuver. "Mother was there when Peter first mentioned this mission to me at Ullah's Vista,'' she said. "Peter being here is the Volkova's doing.''

"Knowing your mother, I am not surprised. You should not be either, my daughter.''

She yearned to know how much of Vukasin's plan the Grand Metropolitan knew and had actually approved. The Metropolitan of All Nineveh was an honorable and chivalrous man. Had he signed onto an act of war against a Goldenwing? Normally, to pry into the old man's secret knowledge or ignorance would be unthinkable. But this was not a normal situation. She nerved herself to speak.

Outside the port the disk of Nimrud had disappeared as the stars wheeled. A flash of red sunlight from some incredible span of gold sent spears of living light into the compartment.

Across the chamber she heard Vukasin suck in his breath and utter a cry of surprise and awe. The Grand Metropolitan had turned to stare out the port as the flashing, shifting spears of light played across his face.

"God's mercy,'' the Metropolitan whispered. "That I should be allowed such a sight!''

In low orbit around Nimrud, *Glory*'s furled hectares of skylar were largely hidden within her yards. But those few sails left spread to steady her in her flight across the sky were more than enough to present her to the new arrivals in a blazing splendor of reflected sun and starlight.

And her size! Kat stared breathless. The pitiful mockup on which she and her soldiers had trained was like a toy, overwhelmed by the reality.

As the war-shuttle drew near her, *Glory* filled the sky with her overwhelming presence. Her spars seemed to reach to the stars, her rigging made a haze of gleaming, shifting silver as the angles between Goldenwing and shuttle changed.

There was no scale, nothing against which to measure her.

She was vast, and she seemed to grow even more as the Ninevite spacecraft approached. Her hull was like a sculpted planetoid, long sheer lines and graceful curves.

"She is the most beautiful thing I have ever seen," the
Metropolitan whispered. "She is touched with Ullah's own
glory."

Kat had an uncertain urge to laugh aloud as she remembered that the shuttle's crew had rather loftily asked the hidden
syndics whether or not they could take aboard the war-shuttle.
The Goldenwing could take aboard a hundred such craft, perhaps a thousand. She glanced over at Yuri Vukasin. He was
pale with shock.

As the shuttle reduced the distance, the Goldenwing
loomed, dimming the stars. Kat drew a cold breath. But a ship
that size was what was needed, wasn't it, to carry enough
humanity to populate a world?

And it was empty. Or as near as made no difference. And
crewed by seven human beings. Kat steadied herself. Seven
very special human beings.

She heard the voice of one of them speaking to the shuttle
pilots. The Ninevites had piped the exchange through the shuttle's communications system.

*"We are opening a hold for you, shuttlecraft. The valve is open-
ing abaft the starboard mainmast. Do not let your final approach
delta-V exceed two meters per second."*

Strange mixture of the language of space and ancient salt
seas. The Starmen used an antique Russian dialect.

Kat moved to the port for a better view. The darkness of an
opening in the long hull finally gave her a sense of scale. It
looked like a black coin.

Ullah protect us, she thought, *we are still a dozen kilometers
from her.*

Vukasin and members of his staff drifted across the compartment and stood with the Grand Metropolitan at the port.
Moments ago they had been engaged in spirited conversation;
now they were awed and silent.

"Have you any ideas, Yuri?" the Metropolitan asked, not

taking his eyes from the fantastic craft glittering in the light of sun and planet.

Vukasin, a man seldom at a loss for words, shook his head.

Ekaterina said, "I'd better get back to my people. They won't know what to make of this. We gave them no warning."

"We made available what information we had," Vukasin said defensively.

"It was not very good information, Ephor," Kat said. "I would need a division to take that ship. It's bigger than most of the planetesimals we fight over."

"There are only seven syndics, Gospodina," Vukasin said.

"And enough starship to hide Nostromograd and Petersburg, too," Kat said. "I must return to my troops."

As she dropped through the central plenum of the shuttle and moved through the valves into the troop compartment, she sensed how correct she had been concerning the state of her troops. The battalion was gathered around the three small viewports in the outer bulkhead. There was fearful talk and some pushing and crowding. The sergeants and Lieutenant Orgoniev were doing their best to maintain order, but the very scope and span of the Goldenwing in orbit was eroding discipline.

"Attention Territorials! Hear this!"

Her sudden appearance stifled the incipient panic.

"All right," Kat said. "It's big. Very big. Does that frighten you?"

The troops muttered and clung to one another in the zero gravity. *Like children frightened by a fairytale,* Kat thought. Only the overpowering construct out there was no fairytale. What must she be like with all her sails set, reaching for lightspeed across the void of deep space? Her name was *Gloria Coelis,* and that was what she was. The glory of heaven. Ullah's gift and savior of the adventurous ones who had spread from Earth to the Near Stars. What an irony that cognomen was. Near Stars, indeed. The farthest star reached by the Goldenwings was Epsilon Indi. Light leaving E. Indi would not be seen on Earth for eleven years. Man moved about those stars contained in a tiny box of space in a universe billions of parsecs wide. He called what that box contained the *"Near"* Stars. What arrogance. What humility. *Ullah forgive us,* Kat thought.

"Yes, troopers," she said. "So the Goldenwing is large." She glared at her troops. "What does the size matter? She is a spacecraft sailed by seven ordinary human beings."

"Ordinary, Polkovnik?" One of the older women in the unit was not afraid to speak. *We Ninevites are an outspoken people,* Kat thought. Our blessing. Our curse.

"Bukova, isn't it? Yelena?"

"Yes, Polkovnik."

"Ordinary, Bukova," Kat said. "Men and women. Not angels or devils."

"Men and women fly that?"

"That and others like it. It is how we came to live under the Ross sun. Goldenwings exist to serve us."

Was that even remotely true? Kat wondered. If it was not, who could even imagine what she and her people faced?

"Look, we are going in there!" Someone was pointing at the opening in the gigantic hull. The war-shuttle closed the starship at a slow deliberate pace.

Let our pilots be good, Ekaterina Volkova prayed. *Let them not embarrass us.*

With steadily decreasing delta-V, the shuttle approached the open hold. The opening that had so resembled a dark coin before now loomed like an open mouth. Within the Goldenwing's hull there was a soft radiance.

"Bring your shuttle inside and reduce power to zero."

That odd, archaic dialect of Russian. *Did they speak to each colonial race in its mother tongue?* Kat wondered.

The labia of the open valve were broader than she had imagined. The opening in the Goldenwing's hull must be close to a kilometer broad and half a kilometer wide. *What sort of ships had once delivered their cold-sleeping cargoes into this radiant darkness?* Kat wondered. *What sort of men and women flew them? Had they remained at home on Earth to die in the Jihad?* To a Ross colonial, a member of the First Aliyah, all that was ancient history. But to the syndic commanding this enormous star sailer? They were not like other men, no matter what she had told her troops. They were *Starmen. The Wired Ones.* Mysterious. Aliens, yet made of our blood, our life, our history—

The shuttle passed the threshold of the cavernous hold and hovered above a softly pulsating deck. Deeper, deeper into the half-light. Then a stillness of the attitude jets. No more flickering reflections of lights from the semi-golden surrounding.

"Polkovnik! The door is closing!"

The sky with its scattering of stars slowly vanished as the valve closed.

There was a soft, susurrating silence.

The Ninevites were in the belly of the beast.

BOOK THREE

20

ABOARD THE *KHOMEINI*

Hussein Ballator sat belted to a padded chair gimballed above the bridge-deck of the warship *Khomeini*. It was a position of nominal tactical command, but the Nimrudite realized that at the moment the Goldenwing rose above the warship's horizon, his command, political though it was, was passing from his hands to those of Mohammad Ali Raschad, the old warrior imam.

The original scheme had been for the Nimrudite force to be carried to the starship by an ordinary shuttle. But radar images of the Goldenwing had so alarmed the Committee of Four that changes were made in the plan. Instead of a single commando company, the fighting contingent was increased by a factor of five. Heavier weapons were requisitioned. And the entire expedition was loaded and launched aboard the warship *Khomeini,* the most powerful spacecraft in the Nimrudite arsenal of ships.

The commandos now numbered two hundred. They were crowded into the warship's spaces wherever they could be accommodated. The prisoners of war had very nearly been left behind at Raschad's insistence, but Ballator, who regarded them and the Krasny as vital to the operation, refused to leave them behind on Nimrud.

Sitting high above the bridge crew in his command chair, Ballator replayed in his mind all of the decisions and deceptions of the last few weeks.

When the Four met over the map of Ararat in Camp Resolution it had been obvious to those present that the plan to call a peace conference aboard the starship was little more than a fig-leaf for a military seizure of the great vessel and a swift application of the power that gave Nimrud. But for the Krasny and the rank and file of the Collective it had been convenient to maintain the fiction that no real inconvenience to the starship or her crew of Wired syndics was contemplated.

The radar images had changed all that. The Goldenwing incited not only superstitious reverence among the colonists of Nimrud, but naked fear. For days Ballator had struggled to save the essence of his plan. In the end he had had to agree to a substantial enlargement of the strike force, and to the appointment of an experienced soldier as tactical commander. Mohammad Ali Raschad had been the only choice.

Now, situated above the bridge-deck in a circle of viewing screens that gave Ballator access to the troop compartments of the *Khomeini,* the Speaker should have been able to exercise the direct command he had envisioned when the plot was begun. He could not. The warship was crowded with men and materiel, all jammed aboard in a nervous, fearful rush. He had not been able to locate the Krasny, whose position it was to strengthen the troops with the experience gained in so many years among the enemy people. "You will convince our force that the Ninnies are farmers, peasants without military skills or organization," Ballator had told the Krasny. Though now that the Speaker recalled the interview he was uncertain that the Krasny's enthusiasm for his part in the venture was all that it should be. And the time had grown too short for withdrawing the Krasny. To do so would damage morale among the troops.

A student of war of Old Earth had once written that "no plan survives a meeting with the enemy." The people of the ancient homeworld had many faults, but undue optimism was not one of them.

Ballator was also troubled by the treatment the military people aboard had given the Krasny. The man was the only person available who had any firsthand knowledge of the Ninevites, yet he had been badgered and hazed by the troops and treated with contempt by Mohammad Raschad. The old warrior's *orgotish* seemed to surge whenever he was confronted by anyone who fought, as the Krasny had done, for many years in the shadows. The one-eyed warrior regarded the Krasny as a contemptible man, one who fought by stealth and treachery. This was an attitude Ballator found absurd. It simply confirmed his belief that Raschad and those of his generation were ignorant of the people's history. How did the old fighter imagine the ancestors had survived in a land possessed by their enemies and surrounded by oppressors?

At the moment, Raschad was inspecting the troop bays, presumably to make certain that the sight of the ancient starship did not frighten the assault force. *It was a frightening enough spectacle,* Ballator thought. If he had been vouchsafed a glimpse of the *Gloria Coelis* before being shuttled up to the *Khomeini* it was just possible he would have scrubbed this whole operation. He had no doubt that among the followers of the Christian Sharia the effect of the starship's enormity would be taken as a measure of the accomplishments of Old Earth's Western Christians. On a descendant of the rejected adherents of the ancient Jihad the effect was very different. The very size of the Goldenwing stirred a deep, ancestral resentment. The fear that lay just beneath the surface made the resentment greater and more bitter.

At a distance of ninety kilometers, the Goldenwing spread across half the sky. Sunlight and the reflected ruddy glow of Nimrud's day side made the vast vessel seem a living, changing thing. What wonders did that great ship contain? What technologies could be taken from it to increase the power of the sons of Nimrud and the Prophets?

An airlock opened below and Mohammad Ali Raschad floated in, looking for all the world like some modern-day reincarnation of Great Saladin in his battle armor. The man's authority seemed hugely enhanced by his surroundings. Ballator's lips made a thin line as he recalled still again that it was he who had supplied Old One Eye with a stage for action. On Nimrud the old were not so honored as on the Favored Twin.

On Nineveh, Ballator thought, *Raschad might well be far more than he was on his homeworld.* A fact which gave Speaker Ballator pleasure.

He realized he should not so personalize the situation. The purpose of this entire operation was to snatch for Nimrud a power and prestige that would forevermore make Recurrences things of the past. The struggle for life on Nimrud was so difficult that Nimrudites made their decisions on the basis of political equations. What was good for Nimrud and bad for the despised inhabitants of the Twin was a balance a Nimrudite politician understood, a thing that needed doing. At whatever cost.

Raschad looked up at the Speaker in his gimballed chair. Without preamble, he launched himself upward to brake against the chair's setting circles.

His visor was open, and his single eye was baleful.

"Have you had a good look at what you propose we seize?" he asked.

"Of course I have," Ballator said.

"Look at it, Speaker. *Look* at the accursed thing again. We are still a hundred kilometers from it and it covers a third of the sky." Raschad's eye blazed angrily. "You should have known. It was your duty to know."

Ballator swung his chair so that he could confront Raschad directly. This was an engagement he had hoped to avoid. Without Raschad's convinced approval, an attack on the Goldenwing became a matter of enormous risk. The stories told of the size of Wired crews were, after all, just that—stories that could as easily be false as true. And even if there were, in fact, only seven syndics aboard that sky-spanning monster, who could guess at what technology they commanded? It was Ballator's experience that technological advance sprang from the compost heap that was war. Were the syndics aboard the *Gloria Coelis* warriors as well as starfaring sailors? He glared furiously at Raschad, hating him for undermining his trembling self-confidence.

"I know my duty, Imam," Ballator said. "But it is up to you to tell me whether that ship is protected by Allah or only by men. Or doesn't your knowledge of the Holy K'uran extend so far?"

To attack Mohammad Ali Raschad on the basis of his religious learning was to enrage the old warrior. He often said that had it not been for the military needs of his world, he would have found a lifetime of joy roaming the deserts of Nimrud as a teacher of the scriptures. In Raschad's mind Ballator was too young, too ambitious, and too irreverent to be a trustworthy leader.

"It is written: *'To whomsoever Allah assigns no light, no light has he.'* You are a man without light, Ballator," Mohammad Raschad said.

"I fight better in the dark, old man," Ballator said thinly. "How are the troops?"

"Concerned. It is a perilous thing to break a truce aboard a Goldenwing. It has never been done."

"It has never been done here, under the Ross sun. That is all you can, in conscience, say. There is a vast universe out there to which we have been denied access." This was a subject near and dear to Ballator's heart, though he had not thought of himself as a potential "liberator" until the astronomers informed him that a Goldenwing was approaching the Twin Planets.

"What are you thinking, Speaker?" Raschad asked suspiciously. "This adventure has grown very grand suddenly. From a straightforward meeting to discuss peace with the Ninnie Ephor and his people to something else. *What* else?"

"The thing that most annoys me about would-be imams and ayatollahs is the way you confuse ingenuousness with holiness," Ballator said. "You come here trying to frighten me with nervous words about the size of that ship. I do not frighten so easily. Tell me the truth. Has it never occurred to you what Nimrud could accomplish with that vessel? Think of it if you dare. *We* could learn to sail a Goldenwing. *We* could travel to the Near Stars."

Raschad looked shocked. "In the early days," he said, "if a man spoke blasphemy and heresy, his tongue was split and he was staked out to die in the desert."

"Old man," Ballator said, "you may have noticed. These are not the early days."

Raschad turned from the Speaker to look at the television screen in the pilot's console. A full crew manned the warship's controls: first, second and third pilots, navigator, first and second engineer, and four political observers. The image on the screen stretched from frame to frame. The radio detection and ranging equipment counted steadily down. Eighty-five kilometers, eighty, seventy-five . . .

What weapons does she carry? Raschad wondered. The *Khomeini* was the most powerful spacecraft ever built on Nimrud, a vessel designed to carry troops to the Rings. But it was without artillery. Nimrudite weapons engineers had devised an entire new class of infantry lazeguns, but they required long charging in the light of Ross 248. A satisfactory way of mounting these new weapons on a spaceship had not yet been developed. All such weapons were still being mounted on tracked armor for use on asteroids and planetesimals. *Khomeini*'s main weapons were the lazeguns of the men aboard her.

"Speaker!" The officer at the communications console shouted to get Ballator's attention. "The Starmen are hailing us."

"Ask what they want."

"They want to know whether or not we will enter a cargo bay."

The Speaker and Raschad had watched the opening and closing of a valve aboard the *Gloria Coelis* when the Ninevite shuttle was taken aboard. Nimrud's defense satellite network had been shunting images to the *Khomeini* for hours.

Raschad made a swift and negative signal. "Tell them we prefer not to take our ship aboard."

"*Why?*" Ballator whispered, as though he feared being heard aboard the Goldenwing, now a mere thirty kilometers away.

"I want our men deployed where they can command the largest area of the ship."

"Two hundred men, a vessel twenty kilometers from bow to stern?"

"The bridge-deck is amidships. See? Where that crystal dome lies flush with the deck."

Ballator subsided. Mohammed Ali Raschad's lifelong specialty was not war on shipboard, but infantry war on bodies smaller, for the most part, than the monster starship they were approaching.

Ballator spoke into his com link. "Tell the Goldenwing we cannot maneuver closely enough to go inboard. Ask on which deck we can dock without damaging their vessel."

The message was conveyed. The reply was a long silence. The *Khomeini* slowly overtook the orbiting starship. The masts and spars of the thing appeared to reach to the end of the sky. With its golden sails still set on the fore and aft masts, the Goldenwing reflected a scintillating light. The reflective surfaces appeared to magnify the light of the Ross sun.

Presently the communicator came to life again. "You may dock your craft between the mainmast and the mizzen. We will light a landing area for you."

Immediately a circle of flashing lights appeared on the humpbacked deck. It seemed absurdly small for a ship as large as the *Khomeini*, but as the distance between the space vessels diminished, the Goldenwing—and the landing circle— appeared to grow in size.

Ballator's mouth felt dry. "I will want the hostages and a small guard to move with me into their ship. The Krasny, too. He will have to deal with Vukasin. The rest of the force must stay armored and ready to leave the ship when I signal."

"Yes, Speaker." Raschad stared evenly at his superior. "It seems, then, that you have abandoned any idea of talking peace."

"Was there ever a doubt, Imam?"

Without further words, Mohammad Ali Raschad released

his hold on Ballator's gimballed chair and dropped into the central plenum of the *Khomeini*.

In the troop compartment and under heavy guard, the survivors of Andrey Volkov's battle in the Rings and the prison camp at Black Desert watched what little they could see through the crowd at the narrow viewport in the shuttle's flank.

They had caught only a glimpse of the Goldenwing they were approaching, but that glimpse had been enough to fill them with awe. Maida Ulanova, the peasant girl from the Nostromo steppe, had fallen into a reverential silence. Periodically she made the sign of the cross and crescent on her breast. Like most of her Ninevite compatriots, she had heard all of her life about the wondrous golden starship that had brought her people across the depths to settle under the Ross sun. Though Ninevite history remained intact, even after a dozen or more Recurrences, the passage of each year, decade and century embellished the reputation of the great ship that had saved the people from both the Jihad and the cold of deep space. This was a sacred sister of that vessel.

Maida Ulanova derived some satisfaction, if not much comfort, from the restless fearfulness of the Nimmie soldiers in the compartment. She understood that to the inhabitants of the Accursed Twin religion was a matter of devil and demon worship (she was unaware that her attitude reflected attitudes prevalent during religious wars on Earth from earliest times). If the Nimrudites believed they had conjured the Goldenwing out of emptiness to now fill their skies with light, she understood how they might be misled into believing that the starship belonged in their hagiography rather than in that of the true believers of the Sharia. Her feeling of superiority went far to lessen the panic, wonder-driven, that clawed at her hard-earned self-control. The Goldenwing was the largest and very nearly the brightest object she had ever seen, downworld or in space. It was also the most beautiful. She thought it looked like a golden creature emerging from a chrysalis of light.

Andrey Volkov, behind her, spoke to Piotr Komarovsky in

a whisper. "They have done it, then. They have enlisted Wired Starmen in their cause." For the first time since leaving Black Desert, Andrey's spirits were plummeting. His knowledge of the Goldenwings was more nearly complete than Maida Ulanova's, or for that matter, that of any of his surviving soldiers. But like all colonial knowledge of the sailing starships, it was based on ancient history, religious parables, and the imagination of teaching imams.

Komorovskiy, a city man from Petersburg, murmured back, "Because we are approaching it does not necessarily mean the personages aboard the Goldenwing are serving the Nimmies. And we are out of Black Desert, Your Honor. Anything is better than Black Desert." He moved closer to Andrey. The Ninevites were the only people in the compartment not armored against space, a fact that the practical Komorovskiy noted with some concern. "Did you know, Your Honor, that the Krasny is aboard this war-shuttle? In this very compartment, in fact. They have the murdering bastard masquerading as a soldier."

Andrey glanced around the compartment. He could not recognize any of the armored Nimmies as the infamous terrorist leader who regularly harassed Nineveh. But then, he had never actually seen the man, who was reputed to be a renegade Ninevite as well as a bomber and criminal.

The rumors had been circulating like lice among the Nimmie troopers since lift-off. By now it was common gossip that the members of the Nimrudite *nomenklatura* had lost their minds and were about to attempt to hijack a Goldenwing under the guise of a peace mission. The purpose of the captive Ninevite troopers was insurance against the resistance of whatever Ninevite forces might be landed on the Goldenwing in response to the Nimrudite *coup-de-main*. What remained for the prisoners to do was limited, but Andrey intended something, anything, to disrupt the Nimmie plan.

The Ninevites had been allowed to mingle freely with the troopers. They were unarmed and unarmored and could do no harm whatever to the heavily weaponed Nimrudites.

Andrey presented himself to the Nimmie sergeant-colonel. "It appears as though we are going to rendezvous with the starship," he said.

The sergeant-colonel, like all Nimrudites, hated officers of whatever sort. He had a particular loathing for enemy officers. "That's not your affair, Ninnie," he said. "Get back with your kind."

"What happens to us?" Andrey demanded. "You're armored, are you going EVA?"

"I said get back with your own people."

Andrey, weakened as he was by his incarceration at Black Desert, could still play the martinet. He came to the role naturally, by birth and training. "I asked you a question, Sergeant-Colonel. Unless you are too ignorant to know the answer, or too stupid and untrained to know how to deal with an officer, be good enough to answer me. What happens to us?"

The sergeant-colonel glowered and said thickly, "You will be notified." He shoved his way through the soldiers still gathered at the port and stationed himself before the thick glass panel. "All right, you men. Step away from this viewport and inventory your weapons. You hear me?" he shouted when his troops did not respond immediately. "Then, *do it!*"

The area cleared as troopers moved reluctantly away from the fantastic image beyond the window.

Andrey was aware of an armored figure beside him.

"Don't let the sergeant clod distress you. He does not know as much as you do."

The speaker was a man in battle armor, his helmet racked between his shoulder-blades. Andrey regarded him suspiciously. It was not a Nimrudite practice to fraternize with Ninnies.

Andrey regarded the stranger cautiously. Gray hair, gray skin. Gray eyes. *A monochrome man,* Andrey thought. The sort of man who could vanish in a sparse crowd. The thought struck him full-blown. *This* was Krasny. The old enemy of every Ninevite. The arsonist and incendiary and murderer.

"Are you going to attack the starship?" Andrey demanded.

"That is nothing to you."

———

"If this ship takes a laze hit and my people have no armor, we're dead."

"You will get space armor when you need it."

"That's Nimmie bullshit," Andrey said. "We need it now."

The gray eyes looked past the Ninevites and fixed on the sergeant-colonel with a rage of spine-cracking intensity. *What could have occasioned such hatred?* Andrey wondered.

"When you can serve a purpose. Not before." The eyes refocused on Andrey. It was as though an android lived behind those eyes. An android with a full spleen of loathing for the sergeant-colonel? Perhaps.

Then the eyes moved to Andrey's face in a disciplined scan. Andrey felt a chill work its way down his back. The armored Nimrudite put a metal-clad hand on Andrey's bare arm. With servo-assist working the armored gloves, Krasny could crush the Ninevite's arm to bloody jelly. The touch was bruising, but not flesh-and-bone destroying.

"You will have your chance, Ninnie," the Krasny said. "And I will have mine." The low, guttural voice was like the growl of an animal.

21

BOARDED

---

*I*n the fabric plenum between the outer deck and the hold containing the Ninevite shuttle, Mira snarled and cuffed angrily at her offspring. Mira identified the young cats by sight and sounds and smell, a method that was absolutely accurate over a spectrum of impressions that would have required terrabytes of memory to store in a computer. Mira and her offspring formed what would have been a pride ten thousand years ago on the Serengeti Plain. All had been enhanced by the experimenting Dietr Krieg, and in even more subtle ways by the overpowering presence of the computer-mind of Glory.

In the cat's dealings with the humans aboard, however, names were sometimes necessary. Mira was irritated by the cumbersome need, but human limitations made it necessary to think of Krieg as he-who-cuts, of Anya and Broni as the old and young queens (who oddly were always in heat and signalling the human toms with gestures, tones and pheromones).

Duncan, of course, was the dominant tom, Damon the fearful one. Buele had no cat-name. His mind was so similar to Mira's that no name was necessary. She almost thought of him as a subordinate member of her pride.

At the moment Mira felt the near presence of other, strange humans. Their sensory signatures came through the fabric walls of the hold that contained them. They were frightened and angry and unpredictable. Their proximity and the emotional spillage agitated every member of Mira's pride. This translated into a great deal of snarling and growling, which annoyed the already distressed matriarch.

The humans behind the fabric bulkhead were all primed with

---

fight-or-flee hormones. Mira understood humans' ability to inflict damage on other creatures. He-who-cuts had tried not to hurt the cats when he handled them and did things to their heads. But he had no way of knowing that there is pain animals can feel that humans, far from their arboreal antecedents, cannot. Their oversized brains had cost them much that was useful out where the Others stalked and hunted life.

Still more humans were coming. They were dangerous to the-great-queen-who-was-not-alive and a threat to Mira's pride.

The cat raised her eyes to the overhead and growled in her throat. The humans came like predators making the final rush. Many. Her feline mind made swift, angry judgments.

The few men and women who lived inside the great queen were acceptable, part of the paraphernalia of home. But the strangers in the hold raised the human presence to Mira's level of tolerance and the approach of more from outside exceeded it.

Others were listening, watching, scenting the soft black empty wind. Human emotions spilled into the darkness were like the smell of blood in the night to Them.

Mira opened her mouth, baring white, needle-sharp teeth. She uttered a furious screeching challenge.

There was no reply from the Others.

She arched her back, raised her hackles and howled with such rage that her offspring were frightened and scattered up and down the plenum, scrambling through the air like bats in the nullgravity. Mira started for the bridge-deck in long flying leaps. She needed to be very close to the-great-queen-who-is-not-alive.

Floating in free-fall on the observation deck, Broni and Buele watched, fascinated, through the transparency as the large spacecraft from the planet below approached *Glory*.

"How ugly it is," Broni said. "Even uglier than the one that came inboard."

Buele squirmed uncomfortably. The approach of the colonial spacecraft, both of them, troubled him. When the first vessel had disappeared under *Glory*'s tumble-home, his stomach had heaved and ached as though from motion sickness. It was not motion sickness. It was anger laced with fear, though

Buele scarcely recognized it. Much of his young life had been spent at the observatory of Sternhoem, on Planet Voerster. Alone with old Osbertus Kloster on the only mountain in the *Grassersee,* he had often wondered about the nature of life and the emotions he felt. He was no nearer a solution now than he had been then, but one kind of knowledge had come to him on this voyage. He had sensed a great evil somewhere Out There— and he hated and feared it. Even without form, it loomed and threatened him. All the syndics felt it, but Buele felt it most acutely. Buele and the ship's cats.

Somewhere nearby, Mira and her kittens were reacting to the same stimuli and Buele could *feel* their distress, which was as strong as his own.

He looked at Broni. She had been terrified during the retrieval of Duncan. But she was not so gifted as Buele. Mercifully, her fear retreated into the shadows of her mind. At this moment she felt only interest and excitement.

She floated slightly above Buele, her hair spreading like a fine net of spun gold about her head. A net that glowed with the sunlight reflected from *Glory's* skylar sails.

Buele looked closely at the spacecraft closing with *Glory*. He could see the tiny spurts of reaction-mass being expelled from maneuvering jets. The ship turned and Buele could make out the script painted on the flank.

Broni asked, "Can you read that, Buele? What does it say?"

Buele, whose talent encompassed all of symbology from mathematics to languages, said, "It's Old Earth Arabic. It says *Khomeini.* I don't know what that means, do you?"

"Perhaps it is a place name. Or a fancy." Broni remembered fondly the dirigible used by her family for transport on her homeworld of Planet Voerster. The airship had been called *Volkenreiter,* "Cloud Rider." A fancy of her mother's.

"It is a warship," he said.

"Oh, Buele. How do you know that?" the girl asked chidingly.

"I don't know *how* I know it, Broni. But I do. It's a ship made for fighting," Buele said.

"Perhaps it is," the girl said. "They do seem to spend a great deal of their time fighting. Or so *Glory* says." Broni and Buele had taken, as syndics will, to personifying *Glory*. "Where are Duncan and the others?"

"I saw them going down to meet the ship," Buele said.

"I think they should wait to greet the colonials until both sides are on board," Broni said firmly, secure in the knowledge of protocol her training as a Voertrekker-Praesident's daughter on Voerster had given her. "One must be evenhanded." She turned, startled. "What was *that*?"

"Mira and the other cats," Buele said. "They are very upset. It's because of *them*."

"The colonials?"

"Partially. And something else."

"What, Buele? I wish you wouldn't be so cryptic."

"You remember what we all felt when Duncan went overboard and got lost?"

"Oh," Broni said. "I wouldn't let Duncan hear you saying that. Goldenwing captains do not get lost."

"You don't want to talk about it, do you? No one really does. But you remember. We all do. There is something terrible out there. Mira knows what it is."

"But she can't tell us," Broni said tightly.

"She 'sees' it, senses it, something she can do, something all the cats can do that we can't. Not very well."

Broni shivered in her skinsuit.

"So Mira sees beasts," she said. "What do you see?"

"Ghosts," Buele said. "The sort of spirits kaffirs raised at home on Voerster."

"There's no such thing as ghosts," Broni said positively. "I am surprised at you, Buele. Uncle Osbertus taught you not to believe old kaffir tales."

"Maybe not ordinary ghosts, Sister Broni. But things that live like ghosts. Distance doesn't exist for them. Neither does time. The cats know. We had a glimpse."

Broni felt a chill move down her spine. Buele was right. They had all felt the approach of things unimaginable, things who lived in a different space and time. Who fed on fear? Was that what had drawn them?

We should never have come out this far, Broni thought. The thought was unformed, instinctive, but it stimulated her powerfully. She both heard and felt the soft, swift hissing of her artificial heart. *It is metal and plastic,* she thought. *It cannot fear.* But the part that is Broni Ehrengraf Voerster can. Oh, yes . . .

"Glory," Duncan said aloud.

"Yes, Captain?"

"Can you extend a plenum out to that ship when it steadies down on deck?"

Uncharacteristically, *Glory* hesitated. Her program's contact with Duncan was firm but shallow. It would remain so until he settled a drogue into the socket in his skull.

Duncan and Dietr Krieg moved down the fabric entrail leading to Hold 3100, where the shuttle from Nineveh now rested.

"I am activating all the top-hamper cameras and probes, Duncan," Glory said.

The two men were dressed in skinsuits with breathing helmets closed up for safety. Neither man had been in this part of the ship for years.

Duncan said, *"Glory'*s gone on alert. Did you feel it?"

"I'm not the empath you are. But common sense tells me that you have put us at a disadvantage, Master and Commander."

Duncan stared at the Cybersurgeon through two thicknesses of transparent plastic. "Would you like to tell me what other choice I had?"

"No, Duncan, I would not. And better you than me."

"They are landing now. I will extend a dock and plenum," Glory's computer said.

Duncan said, "You are treating the ship inside and the one landing as though they are a danger. Explain."

"There are more people aboard the ship from Nimrud than their manifest states."

Duncan opened a panel and extracted a drogue. When he

had Wired himself into the system he could see though the imaging cameras in the rig that the vessel from the planet below was substantially larger than he had judged it to be.

"How many more?" he asked.

"I cannot say with certainty. But near to two hundred," Glory said.

"Lieber Gott," Dietr gasped. "They asked to bring twenty."

Glory reported: *"They have landed on deck. They are not waiting for a plenum, Duncan. They are debarking."*

Duncan snapped out an order. *"Syndics! Wire up and stand by!"* He extracted another drogue from the bulkhead and gestured for Dietr Krieg to take it.

"What is it? What's wrong?" the Cybersurgeon demanded.

But Duncan was no longer psychically present in the passageway. He had released his hold on the bulkhead, and his body floated free and hung in the softly blowing air, tethered to *Glory* by the drogue in his skull. His perceptions were outside, in the rig, looking down at the armored figures spilling from the vessel below. An alarm rolled through the twenty-kilometer length of the ship.

Glory announced, *"The Nimrudites are exiting their spacecraft. They are armed with energy weapons, and they have breached the hull into the observation deck. Warning. Broni and Buele are on that deck and the internal air pressure is dropping."*

22

ATTACK!

The first touch of a cutting laser to *Glory*'s hull breached the integrity of the observation deck and set off a series of clangorous alarms throughout the ship—alarms long forgotten by *Glory*'s mainframe and included in the software to alert ten thousand ghosts in the empty cold-sleep holds.

In moments like these the Goldenwings remembered that they were machines, built and programmed around the sanctity of human life. The cut from above instantly melted the skylar fabric. The moment the first hot light penetrated the observation deck, the air in the compartment began to rush into space. Focused by the narrow opening, the explosive pressure blew the laser-minicannon and its crew from the deck and sent both armored Nimrudite soldiers and their weapon pinwheeling into space.

This set off a flurry of confused orders among the Nimrudites. At Speaker Ballator's command the valve in the side of the *Khomeini* was swiftly cycled closed, splitting the debarking force. Those outside grew alarmed and retreated from the incision in the deck to form a defensive perimeter around their vessel.

For several minutes there was more confusion as Mohammad Ali Raschad struggled to reform his force. This was not the way he had envisioned the start of the Nimrudite coup.

Meanwhile, within the *Khomeini*, Speaker Hussein Ballator watched angrily through a port of armored glass. Ballator had donned space-armor, but he had no intention of stepping

---

out of the *Khomeini* until the Goldenwing was secured. This, as he saw it, was not a matter of cowardice, but a simple requirement of common sense. Of the Council of Four, only old Imam Raschad relished actual combat.

Ballator spoke into his com set, calling to Raschad in what he hoped was an authoritative voice. "What's the matter? Why have you withdrawn?"

"I have not withdrawn, Speaker." The reply was tense and testy. *Clearly the situation was taking a toll on the superstitious old warrior,* Ballator thought.

Raschad ordered a squad to unload a small sled and attempt to retrieve both the laser cannon and the three-man crew who serviced it. There was little chance of success and he knew it. The weapon and its crew were already out of sight. The force of the air escaping through the damaged deck was shockingly powerful. *How big was the compartment into which they were attempting to break?* the old warrior wondered. *How many cubic meters of air were spilling into space?*

The first move in this fight, Imam Raschad thought, had been a wrong one. The result of hasty planning. He needed to proceed more slowly. This was no battle on a grain of sand in the Rings.

"Sections one and two," Raschad ordered. "Approach the breach and use hand weapons to enlarge it. But tether yourselves to each other and to some of this equipment on deck."

He wondered for what purpose all the machines in sight on deck were used. They looked like winches and power modules. He looked up at the mainmast and was almost overcome with vertigo. The spar was so tall it appeared to curve toward and over him, vanishing in a mad perspective that could indicate a height of a hundred meters or a thousand. Limned against the ruddy mass of Nimrud, it was impossible to judge distances or dimensions.

Raschad had a feeling he had never had before in battle. It was as though something or some*one* were watching him, judging him. *War fever,* he thought. Nimrudites often succumbed to angry suspicion when faced with danger or the unknown. The people of the Second Aliyah were an angry,

emotional folk. It was a characteristic the old warrior sometimes thought devil inspired. In other days, Mohammad Ali
Raschad had used these berserker traits of his people as weapons in battle.

He hoped he would not have to do it again. Reaching deep
into the dark pit of human hatreds for power was a dangerous
business. If Allah were truly the Compassionate, surely He did
not approve of satanic methods.

Wired to the ship through the drogue in the plenum outside
Hold 3100, Duncan reacted violently to the break in *Glory*'s
hull-integrity. The slicing of the laser cannon used by the Nimrudites felt like a burning cut in his flesh. Dietr felt it, too,
gasping with pain and shock.

On the bridge, where Anya Amaya and Damon Ng had
only just connected to *Glory,* there was a flash of blue sparks as
Damon's violent reaction tore his drogue free of the computer
interface. Anya uttered a scream of agony and went into con-
vulsions. Elsewhere in the ship, the cats howled with pain and
fury, scrambling through the interior spaces in a futile attempt
to avoid the burning touch of the Nimrudites' weapon.

It had been many shiptime years since *Glory*'s syndics, any
of them, had been in mortal danger from outside, but *Glory*'s
military programs, buried under many layers of subdirectories,
began to load. A less ordinary way of describing the ship's
reaction to the assault would be to say that *Glory* grew angry.

Aboard the war-shuttle in Hold 3100, the activity on
Glory's weather deck overhead created an explosion of consternation. The Ninevite communications officer, monitoring—as
he habitually did in action—the radio exchanges between the
Nimrudite enemies, heard the electronic commands given by
Mohammad Ali Raschad upon the loss of his laser cannon and
its gunners. He immediately tripped an alarm that connected
him with the Ararat troopers in the compartment below and
with the Ephor Yuri Vukasin.

"The Nimmies have put an attack force aboard!" His outrage
was genuine, and effective with the troops.

In the troop compartment below, the battalion Kat had

spent so long in training was stunned by their loss of any tactical advantage, and by their suddenly menaced position inside the vast interior of the Goldenwing.

Ekaterina Volkova stood on a bunk and called her troops to attention. *"All right, listen up, troopers!* We aren't quite dead yet, so remember who you are and what we came here to do. A few Nimmies crawling about on the outside of this ship are not a conquering army!" She judged the disconcerted faces she saw around her and called for Peter Mornay.

Mornay, clumsy in his battle armor, shuffled forward. When he reached Kat, she gave the order for some of the regulars who had formed around her to lift him up beside her.

"Kat," Mornay whispered in confusion, "I'm not good at inspirational speeches."

"Inspirational speeches are your stock in trade, Peter," she said. "I want one now. The Volkova sent you for a reason."

"What shall I do, Kat?"

"Tell them Ullah is with us."

Mornay said, "The Volkova put a laze bolt past my ear, Kat. She was like a Fury." *And so are you,* he thought.

He looked at Kat standing in her armor and weapons. Was it possible that this war goddess was the girl he had grown up with on the grasslands of Ararat?

He turned to look out at the faces of the battalion gathered around its commander. It had leadership. What it needed now was faith. Perhaps this truly was what the dowager Gospodina had intended when she charged him to join Kat's battalion and play soldier?

Ekaterina put her lips close to his ear and whispered, *"God is with us! Tell them!"*

Was it as simple as that? Mornay wondered. How many generations of his family, followers and preachers of the Sharia, had done their most important work standing before an army of simple folk and telling them that Ullah blessed them, and guaranteed their victory?

"Soldiers of Nineveh!" he shouted. *"Ullah has blessed your arms!"*

A rustle of approval came from the troops. Some made the sign of the cross and crescent. *The same sign,* Peter thought, *that I wear on the breastplates of my armor.* ''We came here to this starship in good faith. We came to protect a holy Goldenwing. We came in the service of God and the Holy Sharia!''

He did not look at Kat. He knew what was expected of him now: a sense of righteousness. It was a thing men of religion had been supplying to warring humankind since the species worshiped stones and water.

''Our enemies have betrayed a truce. They are trying to seize this holy vessel—'' He felt a small surge of feeling in his chest. As he spoke it grew. It was like the rare times when his sermon in the Mosque caught at his spirit and lifted his heart. He had a momentary flash of arrogance as he thought of the Wired Starmen. Were they really so naive and helpless as it appeared they were? Was it really possible that Ullah intended that Nineveh should *own* a starship?

''It is written in the Holy Sharia that 'he who bears the shield of God cannot be overborne.' I say to you all, on the word of a Mornay, *that we bear the shield of Almighty Ullah!''*

Kat stepped forward and raised her arms for silence. *''Territorials—troopers of Ararat—we will now seek our enemy and destroy him! Form up for debarkation!''*

Yuri Vukasin, listening on the bridge-deck, signalled to the war-shuttle's crew. The sudden betrayal by the Nimmies was no less than he had been expecting. The Third Ephor had one great gift. He knew how to seize the moment. *''Soldiers of Nineveh! Debark the troops! And Ullah be with us!''*

Inside *Glory*'s observation deck Broni and Buele were being flung by escaping air-pressure against the overhead. Buele found himself pinned to the structural members supporting the deck above. His ears were popping painfully as the pressure in the compartment plummeted.

Broni clung to the suddenly open cover of a storage space containing a drogue. She seized the drogue and fixed it into the socket in her skull. Immediately she was assailed by the pain and confusion of her crewmates.

———

Damon and Anya lay unconscious in their pods on the bridge. Dietr floated stunned in the plenum leading to Hold 3100, Duncan beside him, blank-eyed with pain and struggling to stay in command of himself. *Glory* transmitted the information that there were intruders on deck and that many men and women were pouring out of the shuttlecraft in Hold 3100.

"Glory! *Open the valve to the observation deck,*" Broni commanded.

The valve cycled open and immediately became a wind-tunnel as air rushed in from the plenum to replace that which had been lost through the rift in the overhead.

Broni launched herself upward toward Buele. She reached him with a jarring collision.

"Hold on to me, Buele!" the girl commanded.

"I can't, Sister Broni. Call the others."

"They can't help us. Hold me around the waist, you foolish boy. *Just do it.*"

Buele wrapped his arms around Broni's waist. His lips were turning blue with anoxia. Broni's chest had begun to ache and she felt the panic reflex snatching at her throat.

No, damn it, no, she thought. *Don't act like a peasant kraal girl,* she thought. *I was a* Voertrekkersdatter.

She pulled the drogue free and used it to haul herself and Buele down to the storage compartment. From there she had to crawl through the open valve. When both of them were in the plenum she cycled the valve closed with the last of her consciousness and she and Buele floated senseless in the suddenly still air.

23

MANEUVER

The first strange sensation that struck Kat as she touched the deck of the Goldenwing was the organic way the deck gave even beneath her slight weight in the minimal gravity. It sent an odd, unpleasant thrill through her, as though she had become a small parasite on the body of some great animal.

The Wired Ones had not greeted them and, Kat guessed, they were unlikely to do so now that the Nimmies were debarking their own boarding force. She could not guess what weapons the syndics had at their disposal or how willing they were to use them on people who were, after all, descendants of the colonists Goldenwing sailors had once been dedicated to protect. *It was,* she told herself, *unlikely that the people of the Twin Planets could count on any such altruism.* Massoud Bokhara's favorite sermon, often delivered in the Great Mosque in Petersburg, could be summed up in one statement: Live by the sword, perish by the sword.

It was a wisdom as old as the colonies in the Ross system, and it seemed probable that it would be applicable to this peculiar situation. *Then why am I here?* Kat asked herself as she marshalled her soldiers near the shuttle. *Why have I come bearing a sword?* Her soldier's judgment caused her to add mentally that her sword—and the Nimmie commander's—was probably blunt and dull compared to the weapons of the people of this vast ship.

To Peter Mornay she said, "Stay by me." She felt a mixture of emotions looking at his incongruously armored figure. Concern, affection, exasperation.

She gathered her people about her and assigned tasks swiftly. The sergeant-colonel and a half-squad were sent to the dimly lighted right with instructions to search for an escape from this vast place.

Kat looked about her without the night-vision glasses fitted into her armor. Only moments ago this hold had been flooded with golden light. Now it was dark.

"You are to find us a lock, a portal, a doorway out of here and into the ship," she commanded. "It could take any form. Don't expect it to be familiar. These people have been in space for longer than we have lived in Ararat."

Leytenant Orgoniev was dispatched with a company to the left on the same mission. It was imperative that the Ninevites—all of them, even those still aboard the shuttle—evacuate this cul-de-sac into which they had been brought.

"Colonel!" The shuttle's communications officer's voice came through her earphones. The soldier's voice was pitched high with excitement. *"The Nimmies' force is at least a regiment. Maybe more. They have done some damage on deck. Com doesn't know how much. There is no response from the syndics."*

"Patch me into the Nimmie com-net," Kat ordered.

Her com set repeated the Nimmie messages the shuttle was picking up. The Nimrudites had tried to cut their way into the starship. Com did not know if they had been successful.

"The rest of you," Kat said to her troops, "follow me."

She struck out across the line of approach that had brought the shuttle to rest. She assumed this would be movement across the beam of the Goldenwing, and she was right. Three hundred meters from the shuttle a light gleamed on a heavy shape. Kat called for the battalion technician to accompany her and moved forward.

Distances were deceptive. How large was this cavern in which they found themselves? In the semidarkness and without either landmarks or scale, it was impossible to say. As Kat and her tech approached the light she realized that it was not on a bulkhead but on an enormous cylindrical shape that sprang from the fabric deck and vanished in the upper gloom.

"What is it, Gospodina?" the trooper asked in a hushed voice.

Kat stared. She had seen something like that before, but where? Then it came to her. Years ago, aboard a sailboat on Nostromo Sound. The *Viggen,* it was, and the pride of the merchant Rokossovsky family: an eight-meters-long sloop built a hundred years ago from plans brought to Ararat aboard the Goldenwing *Nostromo* in what amounted to the dawn of history for the colony on Nineveh.

Below deck on the *Viggen* there had been just such a shape. Far smaller, but its shape and placement between overhead and deck made clear its function. It was a small part of the belowdecks portion of a mast. In this case, a spar so huge that it towered a dozen kilometers and more above the weather deck of the *Gloria Coelis.*

"Leave it," Kat ordered, and continued across the soft deck for another two hundred meters of empty space.

Through her com set she could hear exchanges between the Nimrudites and their ship. *Ullah protect us,* she thought as she heard the name—*Khomeini. They have landed their newest and most powerful ship,* Kat thought. What weapons did it carry? There had never been a naval engagement in Ross space. The local technology would not support such an effort. Had that changed?

"Are you hearing all this, Peter?" she asked Mornay.

"Yes. What does it mean?"

"It means we must get out of this place to somewhere we can defend ourselves."

The company sergeant presented himself. "There is a high bulkhead just there, Polkovnik," he said, pointing off into the darkness. "And a control panel of some sort. I think there is a valve in the bulkhead."

"Let's see," Kat said.

She used her maneuvering jets to move swiftly. So swiftly that she collided with the bulkhead before she could react. The bulkhead gave softly and rebounded. She steadied herself and sank to the deck.

She spoke into the com set. "Yevgeny. Bring your company here. Sergeant, set a light for the others."

The sergeant ignited a flare and set it in a vanadium heat-resistant dish. The glare danced through the vast chamber. In the distance could be seen the Ninevite shuttle.

Kat spoke into her com. "Let me speak with Ephor Vukasin." To the tech at her side she said, "See what you can do with that control panel, but don't open the valve until I give the order."

"Sah!"

On a second channel she could still hear the exchanges between the Nimmie soldier and the ship on the deck. They had lost a weapon and some men and they were confused. She took no comfort from this. Nimmies grew particularly nasty when they were confused or frightened. Was there resistance from the syndics? It was impossible to tell from the angry, excited Nimmie communications.

The com-net came to life. *"Ephor Vukasin here, Polkovnik."*

Kat said, "We have found what appears to be a passage into the ship. I intend to open it."

Vukasin replied, "Is that wise? We have tried to speak with the syndics, but have not been successful."

Kat suppressed her irritation. How typical it was of a politician—most particularly one who intended treachery—to complain that the tables had been somehow surreptitiously—unfairly—turned. "They have us trapped here," she said shortly. "If they intended to harm us they would have done it before now." It seemed to her that if there were only seven syndics aboard their first concern would be the Nimmies racing about, unconfined, on their deck.

"Have you debarked the remainder of the battalion, Ephor?"

"They are forming now outside the shuttle."

"Where is the Grand Metropolitan?"

"With the troops. He insists."

"Leave a reinforced squad to guard the shuttle. Then you had better join the battalion and assemble here. I will leave a guide by the flare."

"What are you planning?"

"I am planning to improve our military situation, Ephor," Kat said in exasperation, and broke the connection.

Her tech was by her side. "The control panel is some sort of manual override, Polkovnik. I believe I can operate it. Orders?"

"Give me a chance to deploy some lazegun people and then open it. Make certain all in your team are fully armored."

"Sah!"

Peter Mornay moved closer to Kat and said softly, "Shouldn't you wait for Massoud Bokhara, Kat?"

"For what?" *All the well-oiled plans were going badly off-track,* Ekaterina thought, *as they were almost bound to do. We are honorable warriors and we do treacherous things badly. As usual the politicians had miscalculated and put soldiers at serious risk. And where were Andrey and his people? Were they truly aboard the Nimrudite ship clinging to the starship's deck like some sort of ugly limpet? Or had that been a Vukasin lie, too?*

"Third Company," she ordered. "Deploy around the valve, weapons out and ready."

Her troops reacted swiftly, grateful for familiar things to be done in this frightening and mysterious place. The lines formed, troopers supine and lazeguns charged.

"Open the valve," Kat said.

An aperture appeared. There was no light beyond. Kat moved to the threshold, her own weapon ready.

"Cast some light in here."

Several beams pierced the darkness of a passageway.

"Look!" Peter Mornay said through his armor mask. "There's something there."

Two men's bodies floated in free-fall.

They were tethered to a panel in the wall of the passageway by heavy, coiling cables socketed in their skulls.

The troops murmured with superstitious dread. Even Kat was shocked by the reality of the ancient myths. The beings floating in the passageway were Wired Ones, the Starmen the Sharia described in such loving, and frightening, detail.

"Are they dead?" Peter Mornay asked.

Kat ignored the question and called for a medic. She used the ancient dialect word for "nurse" which over the centuries of recurrent war had come to mean a military medic. *"Sidyelka! Over here!"*

The Territorial Battalion's medic was Oskar Goritsin, a tall and thin former wine grower with sad brown eyes and pale hair. He was from Perm, in the Ural Mountains.

Peter Mornay pressed forward. To the *sidyelka* he said, "Don't try to remove that thing in their heads. The Sharia forbids it."

Goritsin, face-plate open, looked at him with a twisted smile. "I don't believe it contains their souls, Imam. Only their link to this ship."

"Thank you for the lesson in theology, Oskar," Kat said. "Now tell me whether they are alive or dead."

If the Starmen were dead, Kat guessed that their fellows would blame her and her troopers and there would be retribution. Judgments were made just that simplistically in wartime. She had no wish to antagonize the star people more than was absolutely necessary to carry out her orders. If there was to be any hope of moving the Goldenwing into an orbit around Nineveh the enmity of the syndics must be kept to the lowest possible level.

Goritsin listened to the men's breathing through the stethoscope in his hand-armor. He tested their temperature, but could not guess if the thirty-six degrees Centigrade he found was normal for these human variants.

"What's the matter with them?" Kat asked.

"I think they are in shock, Your Honor. But they seem to be coming out of it with no help from me."

"Can you immobilize them?"

The medic frowned. "I would be reluctant to do that without knowing more about their physiology."

Kat looked down at the younger of the two men. He was tall, very sinewy, with a deeply lined face and long, dark hair.

His clothing consisted of a strange suit that fit him like a skin. He was, she noted, very masculine. Not at all the ascetic holy man the Sharia led one to expect to find aboard a Goldenwing.

His eyes opened. He seemed fully awake and mentally alert. As Kat watched, the muscles in his throat moved as he subvocalized some unimaginable message to some even more unimaginable destination.

Keeping her voice calm and steady, Kat asked, "Who are you?"

He spoke Russian with a stilted, learned accent. But it was intelligible. "Duncan Kr," he said. "I am captain of this ship."

Ekaterina Volkova spoke formally and with great, careful courtesy. "Then I regret to inform you, Captain Duncan Kr, that for the moment, you are my prisoner."

24

SYNDICS

Damon hovered over Anya Amaya's open pod on the bridge. His violent reaction to the touch of the laser cannon's beam on *Glory*'s deck had ripped the drogue he wore from the computer panel and saved him some of the agony that had convulsed the Sailing Master.

He toggled the audio com system and called urgently for Dietr Krieg and Duncan, but there was no immediate reply. He located a syringe of tranquilizer in the bridge medical emergency kit, filled it, and used the compressed air driver to inject the chemical directly into Anya's carotid artery. She uttered a moaning cry and began once again to tremble as she approached consciousness.

"Anya. Speak to me. Please, Anya." Damon's voice was dry and rasping. His head ached and he still felt the image of a burning cut on his back. Dietr had suggested to all the syndics long ago that serious damage to *Glory*'s structure while one was Wired might be translated into physical pain or even serious injury to the drogue wearers. "It is an interesting concept. One we should test and with which we should experiment," Dietr said. *How typical that was of the man,* Damon thought fearfully, removing Amaya's drogue with great care.

The Sailing Master's eyes opened, rolled back, focused with difficulty on Damon's face. "Oh, God—" Her lips trembled with latent shock before she could speak again. "Where is Duncan?" she whispered.

"I've called him," the Rigger said. "He doesn't answer."

He resisted the image forming in his mind, an image of Duncan and possibly Dietr and the two younger syndics all somehow obliterated by some untoward event or accident. For the first time since coming aboard years ago, he had a mental image of *Glory* as something fragile and vulnerable—a gossamer construct that barely held at bay the unimaginable risks and dangers of deep space.

With that thought came another—the memory of whatever it was *out there* that had so unnerved *Glory*'s people while they were searching for Duncan. He had a clear impression not that *It* was responsible for what had happened—that had been clearly the fault of the colonists who had landed on the deck—but that the thing or things *out there* were somehow drawn nearer to *Glory* by the fear and consternation he was feeling. It was unreal, impossible. By any science Damon—or any aboard—knew, there could be no sentience at the edge of space capable of "drawing near" to *Glory* in anything less than a million lifetimes. *Unless,* Damon thought, It *did not exist in the universe of laws and rules. Could* something move faster than light? Were there universes where the rules men knew did not apply?

"Damon. *Damon!*" Amaya had gripped the Rigger's arm and was pulling herself out of the gel in the pod. "Damon. Locate the others."

She reached for her drogue. Damon moved to stop her.

"No," she said. "*Glory* will have compensated for whatever it was."

Damon was about to protest but realized that if *Glory*'s "mind" was damaged, she could not be sailed. That would be a death sentence for her crew.

"Shall I Wire too?" he asked Anya.

"Yes. But watch me first."

She inserted the drogue in her socket and immediately assumed the semicomatose attitude of a Wired syndic. Damon watched apprehensively and after a moment extracted another drogue from the panel on the computer panel. He drew a deep breath and seated the drogue in his skull.

"*Duncan?*" Anya queried the captain.

"Yes, Anya. Are you all right?"

Damon picked up the sending. The breath eased from his tightened chest. Duncan was alive.

Duncan's images came through with preternatural clarity. He and Dietr were in the plenum outside Hold 3100. They were surrounded by armored figures with weapons. A woman was saying to the captain that he and Dietr were prisoners. The enormity and arrogance of that statement made Damon's pulse race.

Duncan subvocalized: *"Be calm, Damon. Be very calm. Where are Broni and Buele?"*

Amaya said: *"They were in the observation deck when the colonists on deck breached the hull there. It is airless now."*

Duncan: *"Glory. Locate Buele and Broni."*

When *Glory* did not immediately respond, the syndics on the bridge felt a flash of fear—an image of Broni and Buele spilled into space through the breach opened by the colonists on deck.

Duncan ordered, *"Glory. Search the plena around the ob-deck."*

Dimly heard voices, voices just below the level of the audible, came through Duncan's connecting drogue. A female voice speaking an archaic Russian dialect. *Colonists, damn them,* Damon thought. The woman was asking Duncan questions. Duncan was answering them calmly. *It did not matter,* Damon thought. *The female invader did not know what questions to ask.*

Duncan again to *Glory*: *"What is happening on deck?"*

"The intruders have discovered the Monkey House."

"That should cause some puzzlement." There was actually a hint of sardonic amusement in Duncan's sending. Damon wondered at the calmness, the silent grasp growing stronger. At weapons-point? Yes, that would be Duncan's way.

"I am getting an indication from Mira," Glory sent. *"She has found Buele."*

"Condition?"

"Shaken. But alive."

"Is he Wired?"

"No. His drogue is damaged."

"Tell Mira or one of the other cats to find Broni."

More voices.

"They want me to disconnect," Duncan sent.

Anya Amaya protested, *"Why?"*

"I think they imagine Dietr and I are hostages."

"Barbarians," Amaya said. *"How many of them are there, Duncan?"*

"I have seen twenty or thirty. There are more. The ship we took aboard is filled with troops, I think."

Damon could not contain himself. *"They moved their stupid little war onto our ship!"*

"It's stupid, but it's not a little war, Damon. I must disconnect. Stand by to get under way, Anya."

"Under way? To where?"

"Out there if we must."

"Oh, my God." Amaya's sending was sharp and painfully clear.

Damon succumbed to a pang of sheer angry malice. *"It serves them right. Let's see how powerful they are when* Glory *begins to leave this star system."*

The Krasny waited, fully armed and armored, for the signal to join the troops filing out of the *Khomeini* onto the exposed deck of the Goldenwing. He stood with an apparent composure he did not feel.

The bullying malice of the sergeant-colonel of the assault troops had not ceased. It had grown steadily worse. The Krasny's fear of empty spaces that had become obvious even before the practice assaults in training for this mission had grown into a full-blown phobia. Now the thought of moving down a ramp to the open deck of this gargantuan vessel was almost more than he could bear.

Through the port in the troop compartment the Krasny could see the horrifying spectacle of Nimrud hanging beyond the incredible spars like a scimitar spanning the whole of the black sky. Down was up and up down and nothing made any sense. He could scarcely take a step in the near-to-null gravity without losing his balance and having his throat swim with bile. It was all getting worse. There was no end in sight. He had been brought on this mission as a concession to the Ninevites—specifically to the Ephor Vukasin—and now the Krasny had begun to realize that he was being kept in reserve as a bargaining chip to be traded away if the need should arise. A Krasny, wanted for terrorism in nearly every town and village in Ararat, would be worth much to the Ninnies.

The Krasny had no qualms whatever about using the Ninevite soldiers aboard in exactly this way, but war and treachery were not games one played with any sense of turnabout decorum. Only Nimrudite politicians and Ninevite aristocrats conducted conflicts according to rules. The Ninevite aristos used the quaint rules of earthbound chivalry—a code of conduct centuries obsolete when the *Nostromo* left the solar system—and the Nimrudite politicians used the rules of the slums of Camp Resolution or the solitary cages of Black Desert. The former were fools for their naïveté, the latter for their bureaucratic addiction to rules and regulations.

The war the Krasny had spent fighting as an undercover agent in Ararat had been a blood sport. Until this moment he had not realized how shortsighted he had been. He had shown a Ninevite ingenuousness as he harassed all Ararat. He had imagined that made him a Nimrudite hero, to be given consideration and choices. Now he realized that a terrorist who bombed mosques and mountain monorails was unlikely ever to become anything more than an expendable assassin.

It was that, he now understood, that was the source of the sergeant-colonel's contempt and hatred. Regular soldiers everywhere and in every age loathed men who did not do their fighting according to a proper military book of rules and regulations.

He could see through the armored port that the soldiers who had been disembarked had fallen back against the *Khomeini* in a defensive posture. The laser cannon and its crew had vanished, somehow irretrievably blown off the Goldenwing's deck into space. The thought was enough to make the Krasny's sphincter go into spasm.

*

New orders were tumbling from the com speakers. The sergeant-colonel's subordinate corporals were shouting orders for the next batch of soldiers to make ready to leave the *Khomeini*. The Krasny's mouth felt sandy. He looked for the Ninevite hostages. He felt, somehow, that he was entitled to stay near them. They had been moved into the upper compartment with Hussein Ballator and the *Khomeini*'s operating crew.

The valuable people, the Krasny thought bitterly. If only he had known that day in Nostromograd when he spoke with the Ninevite Ephor how little he would be valued. A bit of forethought would have urged a sensible man to make special arrangements for survival. But, of course, he had no idea that he would be regarded as fair game by a brute of a soldier, a military bully who had hated him on sight.

The Krasny shuddered. The man had no face, no name. His eyes glared from a suit of armor's mask and his name was never used by any of the troops. This, he supposed bitterly, made the sergeant-colonel into the perfect soldier—the apotheosis of the soldier of Nimrud.

He was overwhelmed by an urge to leave the compartment and find safety. He abandoned his place near the rear bulkhead and climbed the narrow ladder to the hatch between decks. The barrier sensed his armored presence and queried the crew members on the upper level. The cycling indicator asked for an identity.

The Krasny punched in his title and military number. The indicator flashed red with the message ACCESS DENIED. He felt an armored claw on his shoulder. One of the corporals held him firmly. "Leaving us?" he asked.

"I need to see the Speaker." Anything, the Krasny thought, anything to put space between himself and the exterior hatch.

"The Speaker doesn't need to see you. Button up your armor. We are next out."

It came to the Krasny. A realization of the way the game was being played. It was the higher-up's *intention* that he should die in this action. On Nineveh there must already be another active Krasny, taking over all the activities of the Gammah terrorist movement on Ararat. He had thought of this before but abandoned the idea as too horrible. He could no longer do that. The fact was, *must be,* that *this* Krasny was no longer useful to the Collective, and rather than arrest and execution—which might need an explanation—death in battle had been chosen as a solution. Indulging the bullying cruelty of the sergeant-colonel was a dividend—a gift to a loyal soldier.

For this I spent my life blowing up trestles and tunnels and murdering civilians, the Krasny thought. *For this I lost Jamallah.*

On the far side of the compartment the cycling alarm of the exterior lock began to howl and flash amber.

"Face-plate!" the corporal snapped.

The Krasny closed up his armor and dogged the mask into place. Inside his virtual gloves his hands were slick with sweat. *Kill someone,* he thought. Even in extremis, the act of murder had always brought relief. Find an enemy and kill him.

On deck, forward of the mizzenmast, a trio of armored Nimrudite soldiers pushed their way into the Monkey House. They stopped abruptly, startled by the banked ranks of cybernetic organisms. Hundreds of brown chimps' eyes sheltering behind bubbles of clear plastic stared back at the intruders.

"What the hell is this?" a trooper asked.

The monkeys were quiescent, each drinking power from leads fed by a bank of solar cells high in the rig. But their eyes followed each movement made by the three troopers.

So near to Ross 248 the monkeys cybernetic balance was disturbed by the star's radiation, and they had been secluded in the Monkey House for recharging and protection.

But the threatening shape of the intruders frightened them and an unsteady ripple of fear ran through the ranks.

There were no instructions from the Starmen, and none from *Glory.* The monkeys grew more confused. They had no innate sense of time and they had been confined in the Monkey House since *Glory* entered the Ross system.

"Dwarfs," a trooper said. "Or worse. I've never seen anything so ugly." Native Nimrudites were virulently xenophobic.

A sending suddenly took shape from Damon Ng, the Rigger: *"Be still. Do nothing. DANGER."*

The sending was well-meant, but it was laden with emotional overtones and fear. The weakest of the monkeys, those who had not taken aboard their full ration of power and slipped into stand-by mode, reacted to Damon's alarm. They disconnected from the power-feed and extended limbs as though to begin a climb into the high spars.

"Allah protect us! Look out!" One of the troopers caught the movement and leveled his lazegun. His aura of sudden fright was detected instantly by the monkeys. They backed away from the intruders in a wave of cybernetic consternation.

The Nimrudite fired his laze. A beam of ruby-colored light decapitated a monkey. Blood globed into the airless space, brilliant as a giant ruby.

Glory reacted. Defenses not enabled for a thousand years loaded into memory. In milliseconds a grid in the deck of the Monkey House, built to control undisciplined and untrained cybernetic organisms when *Glory* was still in orbit around Earth's moon, went live with twenty thousand volts.

The three troopers' armor crackled with electric blue fire. Temperatures within the armor soared to a thousand degrees Centigrade. It boiled away the Nimmies' juices in a half dozen seconds.

In the bridge, Damon felt an urge to vomit. In the plenum outside Hold 3100 Duncan pulled his drogue loose and looked at Dietr. The Neurocybersurgeon looked ill. Both men had felt the hot touch of the troopers' death.

"Duncan—did the monkeys do that?" Dietr Krieg asked.

"It was *Glory.*"

The intruders surrounding them looked perplexed. From down the darkened plenum came a shrill cry of a cat.

"Lieber Gott."

Duncan looked at Dietr in the dim light of an intruder's torch. "That's why these systems were never used for war," he said.

The handsome woman in the bulky space armor was looking at Duncan closely. Did she understand what had happened? he wondered. Probably not.

But *Glory*, the-great-queen-who-was-not-alive, understood everything and she was alarmed. *Glory* began to mobilize her powers.

25

ASSAULT

Hussein Ballator, still braced in his gymballed chair above the control consoles of the *Khomeini,* heard the short, cut-off cries of the soldiers who had blundered into the Monkey House. There had been a momentary flash of information from one of the troopers' shoulder camera, but that image lasted less than a third of a minute before the voltage absorbed by the armor to which it was attached charred all electrical connections.

The Speaker shouted into his com: "What's happened there? Why is my picture gone?"

One of the engineering officers at the consoles below tried to re-establish the link and failed. He switched to Mohammad Raschad's personal channel and asked for a report for the Speaker.

Old Raschad's voice was ragged with frustration. Nothing was going as it should. His men were still in a defensive posture surrounding the *Khomeini.* The laser cannon and its crew were gone—by this time they had become three small satellites of Nimrud. The old warrior hated losing soldiers without recompense, and the laser cannon crew were now faced with a peculiarly nasty and lingering death. As to what had happened to the soldiers sent to investigate the deckhouse abaft the huge spar planted in the oddly flexible deck, he could not imagine. He had heard the startled exchanges and comments from the men and then the ominous silence. They were casualties, too. He was sure of it. And the worst of the situation

was that he still had no clear idea of what, or who, he was
fighting.

Had he made a serious mistake in lending his reputation
and his presence to Ballator's "peace" move? He had expected
fighting, but not so soon, and not against invisible enemies.

He tongued his com and spoke directly to Hussein Ballator
in the *Khomeini*. "I suspect we have lost five men and a piece
of ordnance, Speaker," he said. "I suggest we reembark the
troops and withdraw the *Khomeini* to station-keeping distance
until we can re-evaluate the situation."

The reply from the Speaker was swift and angry. "I expected better of you, Raschad. I ordered you to break into the
starship and locate the Ninnie delegation. Why are you suggesting retreat?"

Outside, under the loom of the planet overhead, Raschad
crouched with his men. He was stung by the tone the Speaker
took. What did the man expect? All his blather about peace
talks aside, what Ballator had intended from the beginning was
the seizure of a Goldenwing. It was the current equivalent of an
attempt by ancient pilgrims to seize Mecca and the Kaaba—the
shrine containing the black stone given by Gabriel to Abraham.
Success meant immortality and a place in Paradise; Failure
meant a blasphemer's eternity in hell.

"I am ordering the remainder of the troops out," the
Speaker said. "I want you to find a way into the Goldenwing.
The Ninevites are already inside. The Starmen invited them in,
but not us. That cannot be allowed to stand, Imam."

Ballator would *use a religious title in these circumstances,* Raschad thought. *Not that there was one religious bone in the man's
body. We are half religious zealots, half political fanatics. And the two
characteristics can blur and intermix.* In the underground passageways of Camp Resolution, Camp Black September, Camp
Bekaa—in all the deep warrens of Nimrud zealotry and fanati-
cism were always in conflict.

A call on the com-net originated in the perimeter guard
around the *Khomeini*'s cycling valve.

"They are coming out, Imam."

The *Khomeini* resumed disgorging armed men. Another

report came from far down the deck. "There is an open panel here, Imam."

The Speaker, listening, spoke from within the *Khomeini*: "Is there a valve? An airlock?"

The fellow was hungry to risk his men inside the alien starship, Raschad thought angrily.

"Yes, Speaker," the flank guard replied. "I can see into the first chamber of an airlock. A very large one." Then: "Everything is huge, Speaker."

"Raschad," the Speaker said, "we are being invited inside."

"That is an unjustified assumption, Speaker Ballator," the old warrior protested. "This is a time for extreme caution."

"I want at least a company inside this orbit," Ballator said. "I need to report to the Collective on the next transit of Camp Resolution."

"I do not agree, Speaker. It is too dangerous."

"Mohammad Raschad, have I made a mistake by giving you command of the assault force?"

Allah's compassionate curse on the man, Raschad thought. *May the Almighty protect soldiers from politicians.*

"Are you listening to me, Raschad?"

"I hear you, Speaker."

"Then obey my orders."

"Yes, Speaker."

Raschad gave the needed orders. It was obvious that the starship was largely automated. Handling a vessel of this gargantuan size would require thousands of men otherwise. Automation on such a scale required an impressive technology. Even if the technology was ancient, it was still a power to be respected. That was Ballator's main failing. He respected nothing.

Raschad stood and stared off down the enormous deck on which he, his men and his ship all stood. It was like a mountain plateau. A plateau with a half dozen monster trees springing from the woven soil. The red sunlight of Ross 248 gleamed through a woven myriad of monofilament lines and stays which helped to support the breathtakingly high masts and spars. *Perspective played tricks on the eyes and the mind,* Raschad thought. It was a scene of surpassing strangeness, but equally surpassing beauty. For some reason it brought to mind the Aliyan tales of Paradise—beauty, vastness, an emptiness filled with light.

He watched as the last of a company vanished into the opening in the deck. The place where the laser cannon had cut into the fabric of the ship was almost healed— *Why that particular metaphor?* he wondered. Because it was the most apt. So far, the Nimrudites had seen no living being aboard this titanic vessel. Yet somehow Raschad knew that human eyes watched his every move.

A flash of reflected sunlight glinted across his face from above. He raised his eyes to look up into the intricate web of stays and spars.

A golden hectare of brilliantly reflective skylar was extruding from within a spar. Others of even greater size were emerging from other, larger spars.

From the *Khomeini* came an immediate message: *"Raschad! Do you see?"*

"Yes, Speaker." The imam stared in wonder.

"What's happening?"

Raschad thought for a cold and terrifying moment of the interstellar deeps whence this ship had come. "May Allah have mercy on us. I believe they are getting under way, Speaker."

Ballator's voice turned shrill. *"Well, stop them, you old fool! Stop them!"*

Raschad ordered the troopers nearest him to laze the skylar emerging from the rollers inside the spars. A crisscross of ruby beams flashed from the deck up into the rig. A few stays and halyards parted, lashing with released tension. But as the shafts of coherent light struck the mirror surfaces of golden skylar, they were refocused and reflected into harmless fans and starbursts of bloody, golden light. The sails continued to deploy. Light pressure and tachyon energy began to alter *Glory*'s velocity.

Hussein Ballator screamed orders into the com-net. *"Ras-*

chad! Get your men inside and stop what the Starmen are doing! Kill them if you have to, but don't let them take this ship out of orbit!''

Mohammed Raschad, responding to a lifetime of warfighting, ordered the remainder of his command to abandon their useless lines about the *Khomeini* and follow and reinforce the company he had sent to face the enemy within the Goldenwing.

Broni regained a precarious consciousness floating in the dimly lit plenum outside a valve to the observation deck. The cable of a drogue had been dragged through the aperture and the valve had closed on it, the thick O-ring deforming to make a seal between plenum and compartment.

The girl had a confused memory of a fiery break in the overhead, through which she and Buele had been watching the Beta colonists and their ugly ship. The barbarians had actually cut through *Glory*'s hull fabric, damaging the ship's integrity and very nearly killing her and Buele.

She looked swiftly about her to locate the boy. For a moment she could not, and her anxiety flared. Broni, who had grown to young womanhood on Voerster with a heart so damaged that she ran a daily risk of death, was not easily frightened. But the thought that the savages from the red planet above might actually have killed Buele, her close companion since becoming a syndic, inflamed both her anxiety and her Boer intolerance.

Broni had lived as an aristocrat on a world where class and color mattered desperately. Buele was of Voertrekker stock as she was herself, though not nearly from so elevated a class. But Broni had learned to love the strange boy as the brother she never had, and the notion that some warring colonists might have caused his death outraged her.

She caught sight of Buele and her anger abated. He was not dead. He was, in fact, alive and clinging like a limpet to the fabric overhead of the half-deflated plenum connecting this section of *Glory*'s inner hull to the main passageways between the ob-decks and the bridge.

A watch panel on the bulkhead next to the closed valve

was flickering between amber and green. *Glory* had repaired the break in the hull and was replenishing the air in the observation deck.

"Buele," Broni called. "Are you all right?"

"I am well, Sister Broni," the boy responded. "Are you?"

"Yes. We must report to Duncan." Broni noticed that Buele had socketed a drogue from a wall panel in his skull. The boy—whom Dietr Krieg insisted on referring to as an "idiot savant," was different from the other Starmen. They all including even Duncan, seemed otherworldly when Wired. Broni was, herself. The enormous power of *Glory*'s computer widened mental parameters by so much that Wired Starmen existed more in virtual than in logical reality.

Broni found that an awkward way to think of the effect, but it suited her. *Glory* gave Broni's interface with the logical universe a dreamlike quality. But Buele reacted differently when Wired. He became more precise in his speech and as aware of his actual, as of his virtual, surroundings.

Mira and her pride reacted in much the same way, Broni thought. She looked up and down the empty plenum. Where were they? She remembered with a shiver the images the cats had projected while they searched for Duncan in space. Whatever those images represented, they were drawn toward the logical reality by fear. Human and animal fear. The virtual universe had been laced with hatred and terror. Everyone had felt it.

It frightened Broni to wonder if what she and quite probably the others aboard *Glory* were feeling now was once again attracting those virtual threats.

Buele drifted down to her, still Wired. "There are other people aboard *Glory*, Sister Broni. The folk Duncan and the others allowed to come aboard into Hold 3100. They have Duncan and Brother Dietr."

Broni had a fluttering, errant thought. For almost a year now, Buele had habitually referred to everyone with the honorific "Brother" or "Sister." Now he was modifying his form of address from time to time. Duncan was no longer "Brother Duncan," but "Captain" or simply "Duncan."

What social development was taking place inside Buele's macrocephalic brain? And why? Was the fear of beyond forcing him into new and strange ways of thinking? Buele was by far the most empathic of *Glory*'s syndics. Was he being molded by a reality none but he could encompass?

Duncan had suggested that those Others might exist in a different space and time. In a different *sort* of space and time with rules and limitations different from those of the familiar universe. The possibilities were—what? Terrifying? But thrilling as well, thought Broni. *To travel with the speed of thought rather than at the laggard speed of light— What sort of reality would that create?*

For an instant Broni hung in nullgrav space entranced by her Epiphany.

"Sister Broni. We are wanted on the bridge."

Broni was on her way, bounding through the long plenum with swift low-gravity leaps before she realized that Buele had communicated telepathically with her while she was un-Wired and after he had disconnected himself from the great-queen-who-is-not-alive.

So familiar did the figure of speech seem that Broni was unaware of its origin.

26

PREDATORS

Mira, clinging to the fabric bulkhead of the plenum between Hold 3100 and an unused observation deck under the foredeck, mewed to collect her pride, but not all of the males responded. She could feel their excitement. The-great-queen-who-was-not-alive was very powerful at this moment. It reinforced Mira's authority as leader of the ship's pride. But still the young toms were not responding to her calls.

Out there in the darkness the predators rushed to and fro in a kind of feral, demented dance across enormous distances too great for Mira to grasp, too great for the humans aboard to contemplate.

Mira had reacted with hostility to the invasion of the spaces of the great queen by human strangers. The invaders were similar to the beings with which she had spent her life, yet different. The thought images and auras they brought with them into Mira's territory were very different from those of the syndics. They were unfamiliar and uncomfortable to be around. Mira had fled from the newcomers as had all the members of her pride. But the young toms lacked her discernment. The invaders were only humans—distant relatives, Mira knew instinctively, of the creatures who normally raced about through the rig doing work no feline would ever consider doing. But the pride's toms tended to confuse them with the far more deadly predators who were being drawn out of the outside dark toward the-great-queen-who-was-not-alive. Damage to her and to the pride of the dominant tom was unacceptable. Mira would kill to defend her.

There was a stink of fear and anger in the air. It came from the strangers who had come inside. There were two prides of them, different but the same. Angry, distrustful, with all the killing instincts of humans very near the surface of their minds.

Mira called again. This time two of the young toms nearby replied. Mira released her grip on the plenum bulkhead and moved toward the sound of her adolescent offspring. One, a large gray tabby, appeared and presented himself. Mira cuffed him sharply across the muzzle and hissed a reprimand. The tabby's black companion approached her, belly to the deck, tail low, asking not to be cuffed. Her feline sense of the fitness of things did not allow her to excuse a breach of pride discipline. But the cuff she delivered was only a token. The black was not one of He-who-cuts' best experiments. He was brave but needed direction.

The hungry things outside were very near now. They leaped and whirled and raged. Their thoughts were beyond Mira's understanding, but in the way of her kind, the small queen dismissed complexities. The-great-queen-who-was-not-alive was more than Mira's world. The great queen led her own Great Pride which encompassed Mira and hers, the humans, the strange, empty half-beings who climbed and scuttled in the rig—all living things aboard the ship. The Great Pride must be defended at all costs.

The cat arched her back in alarm and let the hair along her spine and on her tail stand on end. The aura of the furious creatures outside penetrated the body of the great queen in infuriating waves. Far down the darkened plenum three of Mira's offspring reacted to the psychic pulse and screamed out fearful challenges.

Mira saw the predators as vast angry beasts that to humans— had humans her perceptions—would have appeared as smilodons out of Earth's violent prehistory. She rose onto her hind legs and bared teeth and claws. The young toms dropped to the deck in positions of submission.

Mira sent a message. In human language it would have said: I know you. You have been out in the dark night since time began. You live on emotions and psychic energies. Time and distance mean nothing to you. But speed and thoughtless rage mean nothing to me. Go! You are not welcome here.

Outside, streaming though the rig in great, near-to-invisible pulses, the Outsiders who had come vast distances probed at the ship, sucking at the life within.

———

27

SKIRMISHES

Buele said, "I am feeling something from Mira."

Without slowing her progress through the narrow plenum, Broni said, "That's impossible, Buele. You are not Wired."

"Nevertheless, Sister Broni, Mira is trying to tell me something."

Broni felt a flare of irritation. How could the boy play these foolish games at a time like this? "Buele, stop this foolishness. I know you are more Talented than the rest of us, but you cannot talk to the cheets. You simply cannot."

"Cats, Sister Broni. Not cheets."

Broni bridled when Buele corrected her. It was her history, her class, her heredity. Her intemperance shamed her. Duncan would not approve. "You cannot talk to the cats, Buele. You must not pretend that you can," she said.

"Sister Broni, let us stop at a com panel and Wire. You'll see."

Broni's lips tightened. *The thing was,* she thought, *that Buele might just be right.* He spent hours in the company of Mira and her brood. He talked to them, played with them, fondled them, fed them special tidbits from the food synthesizers. Was it possible? Did Dietr Krieg's enhancements of the cats mean they could learn human speech? With the help of *Glory's* computer, was it possible? The cats were *always* Wired. The Neurocybersurgeon had seen to that with his UHF radio links.

Broni came to a stop at a plenum junction. Actually, she

was confused as to the right way to go. *Glory*'s interior spaces were vast and immensely complicated.

"To the right and up, Sister Broni," Buele said.

"Yes, *I know*," Broni said fretfully.

"No, you were not sure," Buele said. "It doesn't matter. *Glory* wants us to lead the people from outside into Hold 3100."

Broni held his sleeve. "*Mira* told you that?"

"In a way, Sister Broni."

"Damn you, Buele. In *what* way?"

"I don't know, but it was Mira who told me."

"How?"

"A picture, I think. She put a picture in my mind." His face broke into a puzzled smile. "I didn't realize how strange everything looks from fifteen centimeters off the deck where the cats usually live."

"Never mind where the cats live. Mira told you what *Glory* wants?"

"Yes. Those things are outside, Sister Broni."

"The colonists from Nimrud?"

"Oh, no, Sister Broni. The bad things we remember from before."

"From before?"

"When we were looking for Duncan."

Something savage brushed across the girl's mind. It was like a spray of blood. Broni smelled death. She sucked in a terrified breath. Was that what Mira meant? All the syndics had experienced the cats' sensitivity to unknown forces.

The horrid touch seemed to have opened a door. Broni shuddered. "Come *on*. We must find Duncan."

Buele said, "Duncan can't help us, Sister Broni."

"Then Amaya—Damon—anyone—"

"You and me, Sister Broni," Buele said, and took the lead.

With increasing speed as they rose higher within the hull, Broni and Buele plunged through the plenum. The tube seemed to vibrate slightly as it did when newly spread sails first felt the kiss of tachyons. "Buele," Broni said, "I think we are getting under way."

"Yes. We are. I can feel it. So can Mira and the others. But the things outside won't fall behind."

"How do you know that?"

"I just do, Sister Broni. We can never leave them behind, Sister Broni," Buele said. "They are faster than tachyons."

"That is impossible," Broni protested.

"I know it is. But they are faster, nonetheless. They are creatures of a different night, not the one we know."

Broni felt fear, like a hand crushing her artificial heart. *Duncan once told me,* she thought, *that such things might be possible. That there might be speeds attainable that would make time dilation irrelevant.*

It was only a dream, Duncan said. A fantasy to carry home to Earth in some distant future time.

The bloody touch came again, fetid and redolent of death. *Not like this,* the girl thought. *God, not like this.*

Hussein Ballator watched with deep misgivings as the last squad of his troops disappeared through the open hatchway into the hull of the starship. None of this operation had developed in the way he had expected. It was an example of the warriors' cliché that "no plan survives combat."

That was well enough for military mechanics like old Mohammad Raschad, but it wouldn't do for a leader intent on ending a thousand-year-old war with a victory. Once again, as with much else in Nimrudite life, it was a matter of *orgotish*. A leader of society simply did not allow matters to run uncontrolled.

Still reclining in the safety of his gimballed chair above the *Khomeini*'s operational consoles, it occurred to him that he had completely lost track of the Krasny—whose value as a bargaining chip had diminished to nearly zero.

He activated the imaging cameras on the outside of the *Khomeini*, aiming them to study—with enormous misgivings—the steadily spreading skylar sails.

Ballator had spent all of his adult life as a politician. First as a commando cadet, then as a political cadre chosen in competition with the brightest and best of his generation, young people most adept at accommodating Marxism and Islam. All had been intended to place him where he was now, as Speaker of the Collective and leader of the Council of Four. He was now the nearest thing to an absolute leader the cutthroat competition at the top of the Nimrudite pyramid allowed.

And suddenly, he thought, *I am in the wrong place at the wrong time.* There was no question about it. The Goldenwing was acquiring speed and moving deliberately out of orbit around Nimrud.

Ballator, who in his most daring days had never been (or wished to be) a spaceman, considered the vastness beyond the Rings with a hollow fear in his belly. His undergarments were damp with sweat.

All the force that remained aboard the *Khomeini* were the half dozen men of the bridge-crew and a skeleton guard force still in position outside on the deck.

"Speaker," the First Pilot said, "you must decide. If we stay where we are we will soon acquire too much velocity for a return to Nimrud."

It was a decision Ballator was reluctant to make. The inflexibility of the laws of celestial mechanics offended his politician's soul. He tongued his armor's com and called the troop commander. *"Raschad, where are you now?"*

"We are in a passageway that appears to lead to the bridge, Speaker. We have encountered no Ninnies and no syndics."

"Have you any idea how long it might be before you establish control of the starship?"

"No, Speaker." The old man's voice was laden with sarcasm. *"But at any moment now."*

Ballator's lips thinned as his mouth compressed into a frown. He felt oppressed, barely able to hold a dreadful fear at bay. Did all the Nimmies feel that too? *"Our communicators are intercepting Ninnie messages,"* he said.

"So have ours," Mohammed Raschad replied. *"But I am not certain they are Ninnie messages."*

"What could they be but that?"

"I do not know, Speaker." Through the com-net came a bone-chilling scream of animal anger.

"In Allah's name, Raschad, what was that?"

"An animal. The syndics appear to keep pets."

"Pets?" The idea was alien to a Nimmie. In Nimrudite society all animals save for man were food sources.

"Cats, I believe, Speaker. Brought from Earth. They are written about in the old books."

"What purpose do they serve?"

"When I encounter a Starman, Speaker, I will ask."

The pilot below interrupted. *"Speaker, you must decide. If we do not leave this deck soon we will not be able to leave it at all."*

Ballator's heart thudded. He studied the camera images. Long perspectives of sloping deck and towering spars. Spun webs of monofilament, stays and braces. And the steadily expanding spread of mirror-bright skylar.

And nowhere—nowhere a man.

His inner fear bent him to compromise, to retreat. In politics there was always another way, an alternative.

"All right, Pilot. Let us stand off this deck. We must safeguard the ship."

"Do we re-call the landing force?"

Ballator glared down with his most official face. "The safety of the *Khomeini* is paramount, Pilot. Get us off this deck at once." In politics there was always another day, as well as another way.

The configuration of the sky in the images was changing. Red Nimrud was no longer directly overhead. It was disappearing below the gunwales of the long deck. The stars shone brilliantly through the web of the rig. The sight of the distant suns filled Ballator with unspeakable dread. He did not know why. When he contemplated the stars, his *orgotish* quite failed him.

He said in a faint voice, "We will stand off a few kilometers to show the syndics we cannot be intimidated."

*

Tiny feathers of vaporizing fuel formed around the *Khomeini*'s main engine nozzles. High above the Nimrudite ship a long spar pivoted into position. Chains were released and the spar began a nightmarish, slow-motion fall. After what seemed an eternity, it struck the warship's hull with deceptive gentleness.

Even in near-null-gravity the mizzentop spar was massive. It struck, bent and deformed the *Khomeini*'s atmospheric maneuvering surfaces and pinned the craft to the deck.

Ballator and the men aboard were frozen in shock. Any deformation of the ship's outer configuration could be a death sentence on re-entry. But neither the Speaker nor the pilots were granted any opportunity to respond to the falling spar.

At the moment when their fear rose to its highest intensity, a manic explosion of blue light bathed the *Khomeini* and scintillated through the Goldenwing's rig. Ballator felt a spearing agony, a brutal entry of a psychic sword parting him into halves.

The First Pilot below stared upward, openmouthed. The gimballed chair glowed with white heat. There was a short, shrill scream from the thing—no longer a man—the chair contained. Blood, cooked to a dark viscosity, spattered the deck, the consoles and the terrified men below.

The first unexpected casualty of a war yet to come was Hussein Ballator, Speaker of the Collective of Nimrud.

There were other casualties among the crewmen of the *Khomeini* when the spar struck, but Andrey Volkov and two of his troopers escaped immediate injury. Andrey, Maida Ulanova and Trooper Komorovskiy were close enough to the control consoles to see what happened to the Nimrudite Speaker in the chair above the bridge-deck.

Before their horrified eyes Ballator changed from a living human being to a charred grotesque seared to the gimballed chair in which he had been sitting. Flakes of his incinerated body fell like brown snow to the deck.

For what seemed long moments there was a stunned silence in the compartment. The *Khomeini* normally flew with a complement of a dozen watch-keeping officers on the bridge, but other duties had reduced this number to five. The troopers remaining on *Glory*'s deck to guard the *Khomeini* had seen the pyrotechnic display of forces lighting the spars and rigging over their heads, but they were unaware that some incredibly destructive and malevolent force had penetrated their ship and killed their commander. They still crouched in a perimeter around the *Khomeini,* weapons pointed outward to a vast and empty expanse of deck.

Their fear invited attack and it was immediate in coming. Bolts of energy exploded from seemingly empty space. With an almost delicate precision the terrified Nimrudite soldiers were flashed into vapor. Where they had been, tiny constellations of white-hot matter drifted away into the rig.

In the *Khomeini*'s control room, air was escaping down the open hatch to the empty troop compartment. A watch officer who had witnessed both the death of Ballator and the swift slaughter on the Goldenwing's deck fled from his post in a panic. The panic spread, and outside a swirling, seeking nebulosity formed once more.

The Ninevite hostages were the first to regain command of themselves. Andrey Volkov covered the ten meters between himself and the officer of the deck in a flying, low-gravity leap.

The *Khomeini* could not be flown, but it was vital to close off the ruptured troop compartment and to take control of the vessel before the Nimmie commandos who had vanished into *Glory*'s inner spaces returned to repossess their ship.

The Nimmie officer pulled at his lazegun, but could not clear it from the holster before Andrey struck him with a *savate* that sent him spinning against the outer bulkhead. The nebulosity outside approached the Nimrudite craft once more. Andrey had a momentary impression of light seeping through the hull as though the metal had become permeable. A lazegun bolt from the communications officer burned the air under Andrey's chin and coruscated against the vanadium steel of the outer hull. The light that had invaded the ship blazed, dazzling Andrey. A bolt found the Nimrudite officer with the lazegun and exploded him into charred flakes. Andrey Volkov gagged at the sight. He had the horrid impression that the light, whatever it was, was now seeking *him*.

Komorovskiy, the Territorial from Petersburg, and Timoshenko, the horsebreaker, were late in reaching the Nimmie at the engineering console. But Timoshenko managed to wrap his formidable arms about the engineer's helmeted head and pull him from his seat to the deck. Komorovskiy used his strength to strangle the man, crushing his armor against his throat.

Andrey, pressed against the inner hull, saw a blazing something consume Komorovskiy and Timoshenko and then move like a laze bolt to the Nimrudites of the crew. For a moment the destroyer hesitated as though it were seeking, evaluating, then it retreated down the open hatch to the troop compartment and out of the ship into space.

Andrey and Maida Ulanova stumbled to the open hatch and dogged it shut. Andrey knew that a closed hatch would not prevent another attack, but air had to be conserved. *"Ullah preserve us,"* Maida whispered. *"We have seen the devil."*

Andrey looked around him. Only Maida and he remained alive aboard the *Khomeini*.

28

A WELL-DEVELOPED TASTE FOR WAR

"I am Ekaterina Volkova. What shall I call you, Your Honor?"

Duncan Kr regarded the Ninevite woman with interest. She was tall, good-looking by any terrestrial standard, and obviously in command of this substantial force.

"My given name is Duncan," he said. "Call me that if you like."

"It is not too familiar?"

Duncan managed an ironic smile. He was surrounded by space-armored warriors with energy weapons. "No," he said. "Under the circumstances it seems right."

The female face that showed above the chin-protector of the battle gear was pale. The Ross sun, cooler than Earth's, did not darken skin. The eyes were widely spaced, intelligent and very blue. Duncan wondered if she would be surprised to know that that particular blue closely matched the skies of the homeworld.

"I am Ekaterina Volkova. Of the Territorial forces of Ararat on Nineveh." She paused, waiting for some response. "We do not do this out of malice," she said.

"I see," Duncan said. "It is necessity that forces you to come aboard my ship by deceit and fill her with armed people."

She had the good grace to look uncomfortable. Around her, her people were exploring the branching plena. Duncan guessed that they were learning very little. *Glory*'s terabytes of subroutines were infinitely variable, and the computer contained great libraries of programs written to protect the ship's integrity.

Mira was nearby. Duncan could sense her proximity. The cat was reacting to the changes *Glory* was making in the interior environment. Mira and her brood loved routine and disliked changes. Passageways were being closed and opened, plena rerouted. These activities, combined with the supernormal forces outside the ship, created a feral distress in the cats.

But seven syndics could not defend the ship against armed boarders. *Glory* must fend for herself. *Had* Glory *the ability to learn enough?* Duncan wondered. *Or was she to be the first Golden-wing ever penetrated by hostile forces?*

Duncan floated in the plenum in the familiar nullgrav slouch, as did the silent, ever-watchful Dietr Krieg. He noted that the invaders were handicapped and made clumsy by the mass of the battle armor they wore.

"Are you expecting to fight a battle inside my ship?" he asked.

"If we must."

"You could destroy her."

"Then may Ullah forgive us."

"I doubt that He will, Colonel," Duncan said.

"You know my rank," Kat said. "What else do you know about us?"

"The most significant thing I know is that you cannot be trusted."

His Russian was archaic, but his statement was heard and understood by all of the Ninevites nearby. Their looks darkened.

"I truly regret that, Captain," Kat said. "We thought we were coming to a peace meeting."

"Did you really," Duncan said. "Do you always bring so many troops to a peace meeting?"

"We are a docile people," Kat said with deep feeling. "We are men and women of the soil, not warriors."

Duncan studied her evenly. "I would have said that the people of both of the Twin Planets have a well-developed taste for war."

"That's unfair. You would not say it if you knew us better."

"I have come to know all of you better since you reached my ship," Duncan said.

"We learned that the government of the Accursed Twin was sending a large force. What else could we do?"

"What, indeed? Your opponents were planning mischief. You are here in force only to prevent it."

"It is so," Kat said stiffly. There was nothing Ekaterina Volkova disliked more than to be knowingly and absolutely in the wrong. And unable to correct the situation. "You know nothing about us," she said.

"Worlds who value peace do not train their women for war, Colonel."

"We have done only what we must," Kat said angrily. "You were bringing cargo to our enemies. How dare you judge us? What gave you the right?"

Peter Mornay appeared. His complexion grew pale when he approached the Starmen, but he was steadfast. *Perhaps,* Kat thought, *that was why the Volkova had sent him on this mission: to stand by Kat's side at need.*

A trooper presented herself to Kat. "The passageway ahead is closed off. There is a branch only to the left. We are getting lost, Polkovnik."

"Send a scout, Yelena. Tell him to stay two hundred meters ahead and to stay in contact by com."

"Sah, Polkovnik."

Kat turned back to Duncan and Dietr Krieg. "Where are the Nimrudites now?"

"Tell them nothing," Dietr growled.

Duncan was about to speak when he felt a sickening surge of rage and terror sweep through the plenum. The colonial soldiers were staggered by the force of it. Duncan snatched at Dietr's shoulder. "Do you feel it? Do you recognize it?"

Everyone in the plenum was reacting. Dietr Krieg looked ill. The Ninevite woman was gray-faced, her eyes wide, pupils dilated. Some of her soldiers floated unconscious in the null gravity, like logs in a stagnant stream.

———

Duncan reacted to an invasive, burning anger—not his own. An alien fury that sought to consume him from within. He gasped, *"It is here. Here in the ship."*

Ekaterina Volkova's armored hand closed on Duncan's arm. "What is it? Is it a weapon? What have you done?"

Duncan flung the woman off against the fabric bulkhead. He drew air into his lungs with a burning effort.

"No weapon," he said faintly. "A *being*."

Mira materialized in a panic from the darkness to cling to Duncan's skinsuit with extended claws. The pain the cat inflicted helped Duncan focus his mind. He was filled with animal thoughts, feline images. The cat's emotional overload was so near and so powerful that there was almost no room for the Other.

He realized what had just happened even if he could not see the event. A human being had been killed—horribly. Then others had died fighting. And the Other raged around the *Glory*, hungering for more conflict, more fear, more fury.

"What is it?" the Ninevite woman gasped.

"You can't fight it, Colonel," Duncan said. "None of us can. Not yet. Maybe not for years. The best we can do is refuse to give it pleasure."

"That is—" Kat Volkova groped for a word. "Absurd. . . ."

"Is it? What did you feel just now?"

"Terror. Panic. And a burning. As though I were being consumed by fire."

"That is as good a description as any I can offer," Duncan said. "Someone, somewhere in this ship has died by fire. We have felt it seeking before, but never so near. We never felt it kill before. It has discovered us. We are—prey. I think. We draw *It*—or *Them*. When we are afraid. Or angry. They live outside our space, our time, I think. I believe they can look into our space, *reach* into it. And they can kill here. They just did."

"Devils," whispered Peter Mornay.

"There are no devils, Peter," Kat Volkova said.

"It rather depends on what you mean when you use the word," Duncan said.

"No," Kat said. "We are rational men and women—"

Duncan tried to sooth the agitated Mira. "So tell me if you can, what is your rational explanation?"

"The Universe is large, Captain. Who should know that better than you? In the real universe nothing is irrational. Everything can be explained by human beings."

The emotional flux was ebbing. *But the Ninevite woman was right,* Duncan thought. No matter how mystical and how terrifying the incursion was, it was real and it came from *somewhere.* And that somewhere was within *instant* reach of any location, any place in Einsteinian space-time—the Universe humans perceived.

That *was the prize,* Duncan thought suddenly. No matter what the danger, no matter the cost or the horror, the prize— the glittering prize—that those Others owned was the ability to do what ten thousand years of human science claimed was impossible: *move at a speed infinitely faster than sluggish light.*

Duncan closed his eyes and for a moment imagined what that ability would mean to the universe of men and women. The vista it opened up was stunning, terrifying, glorious.

A soldier bearing cumbersome communications gear presented himself to Ekaterina Volkova. "Polkovnik, we have located the Nimmie bastards. They have reached a place called Hold 3100."

Kat turned to Duncan. "Guide us there," she commanded.

Duncan yearned to Wire, to connect with *Glory.* But there would be time. He knew that now. He moved to the head of the jostling column. Though he had not been there for years, he knew that Hold 3100 was the last and only hold on board *Glory* still unchanged from the days of the Exodus. "Follow me, Colonel," he said.

Mira rode on Duncan's shoulder as he pressed ahead through the narrow fabric plenum. Followed by Ekaterina Volkova, Dietr, and the Ninevite soldiers, Duncan fulfilled his function as Master and Commander of Goldenwing *Glory,* leading the way deep into the bowels of the ship.

29

THE CAVE OF THE WINDS

The plenum leading to Hold 3100 was far narrower than Duncan remembered it being. As he led the way into *Glory's* inner depths he held at bay the fear of the thing raging about outside the ship. To do otherwise would be to invite it within, as someone elsewhere in the Goldenwing had done at terrible cost.

Dietr Krieg, the least empathic of the Wired Starmen aboard *Glory,* was making this journey, Duncan knew, strictly on faith. Duncan could sense the Neurocybersurgeon nearby, separated from him by a pair of burly Ninevite soldiers. At Duncan's elbow, struggling in the confined quarters and null gravity, came the female troop commander. *She certainly didn't lack courage,* Duncan thought. And though she hadn't the faith expressed by the one she called Mornay—a Sharia cleric, Duncan supposed—she was totally committed to her duty as she understood it to be. That was admirable. *In another place and time,* Duncan thought, *Ekaterina Volkova might have been found by a Searching team of syndics.* She might have spent her life between the stars. But that hypothetical woman had never been. In her stead was a warrior, the product of a society that had been at war for centuries. *A great pity,* Duncan thought.

"What is this place they seek?" Ekaterina Volkova asked.

"A hold. Like four thousand others aboard this ship. Larger than most," Duncan replied, not slowing his pace. Traveling in near-zero gravity through the fabric plena of the Goldenwing came so naturally to him that he might easily have slipped away and outdistanced the others had he wished to do so.

———

Mira still rode his shoulder emitting a lexicon of growls and purrs that Duncan would have given much to understand exactly. What he did receive from the cat was confirmation and approval. The assurance came not from Mira, but through her. Duncan was aware that the cat was performing as a drogue. The interface between man, animal and *Glory* was imperfect but very powerful.

"Why would the Accursed Ones choose such a place?" the woman asked.

Duncan said coldly, "They may have had no choice."

"How do you know that?"

How, indeed? Duncan Kr wondered. Was it a choice *Glory* had made for them?

"A supposition, Colonel Volkova. Nothing more," he said.

The woman remained silent for a time as the party moved along through the long plenum. Presently she said, "You despise us, Starman."

"We don't make judgments," Duncan said. It was not in the Starman's canon to be critics of colonial societies, but it was not possible to be *un*critical. Earth's wars, most recently the Jihad, had driven men to the Near Stars. *The right effect,* Duncan thought, *brought about for the wrong reasons.*

"We have been at war, off and on, for nearly five hundred years," Kat Volkova said.

"I know that," Duncan said. "We very nearly refused to come to the Ross system because of it."

"The war is not our doing." For the first time, Duncan became aware that she was tired, frightened, uncertain. But that was the nature of war, wasn't it? Or so the history programs taught.

How much of what he knew about life on the Twin Planets was accurate? Duncan wondered. Who wrote the history books and programs if not the victors? One could quote Pontius Pilate and ask: "What is truth?" The long history of Earth made any answer a dubious proposition.

"You know about the Second Aliyah, then," Kat said. She

wanted this lean, dour man's good opinion. He made her feel immature—childish.

"The people of the Second Aliyah came expecting rewards they had not earned," she said. That was the received wisdom about the Second Aliyah. There was no other in Ararat.

Duncan paused and looked back at the armored woman. "They were castaways."

"Thanks to the crew of incompetent syndics they hired and the ship they flew," she replied angrily.

Duncan replied, "We know about Goldenwing *Resolution*—some of your history has reached us. And I suggest that you study it again, Colonel Volkova. Those 'incompetent syndics' died, every one of them. But not before every colonist was landed safely on Beta. It was later the people began to starve and die while the First Aliyah, safe and comfortable on Alpha, watched."

"You are too isolated from life to understand us," Kat Volkova said.

"I may be," Duncan said. "But your beloved war will not last another five hundred years," he said. "It may not last five hundred days." He turned back and led on through the shadowy fabric plenum toward Hold 3100.

"Where are they now?" Anya Amaya was still un-Wired. The psychic jolt of the invasion of the spacecraft on *Glory*'s deck had so unnerved her that she was terrified to re-socket one of the spare drogues on the bridge. But she could not delay longer. Her skill as Sailing Master was needed and the responsibility of taking *Glory* out of low orbit around Ross 248 Beta was inescapably hers.

She repeatedly asked Damon to locate Duncan—partially out of personal concern for Duncan, but equally out of dread of having to face again the psychic rape she had experienced when the *thing* outside penetrated the Nimrudite craft.

Damon responded to her commands, but his eyes showed the wide stare of the Wired empath under stress. He was having great trouble communicating with Amaya. He spoke aloud with difficulty, grimacing with the effort it demanded. *Glory*'s syndics almost never communicated audibly when they were Wired to *Glory*. Verbal communication was shallow and incomplete, lacking the instant comprehension that was part of the Wired experience. Damon wished desperately for Anya's Wired presence.

"*Glory* is sending them to Hold 3100," Damon said. "She doesn't say why."

Amaya strove to control her trembling. Her body ached from the convulsed emotional explosion she had experienced. "No one's been in that part of the ship for years."

Damon said pleadingly, "Please take a drogue, Sailing Master. I can't handle *Glory* alone."

"Where are the people from the ship on the weather deck?"

"*Glory* doesn't tell me. Please, Anya. This is beyond my capability."

Amaya resisted reaching for a drogue. "Where are Broni and Buele?" she asked.

"Buele Wired in for a moment at junction 30-15. Broni was with him then," Damon said. He tried to devote his entire mind to the infinitely fine and demanding work of unfurling square kilometers of skylar and getting *Glory* under way because that was the last direct order coming from Duncan, down in the belly of the ship.

Anya, reclining warily on the surface of the gel in her pod, searched the flat images flowing onto the screens from the cameras in the rig. The large shuttle from Beta was inert. Only the expanding spreads of skylar moved in the airless dark. *Glory*'s orbit had carried her into night on her broadening swing around Nimrud. The planet partially occluded Nineveh's bright crescent. *Glory*'s sails reflected myriad points of starlight. The colored console screens showed foreign ship, skylar, sky and planets. Nothing living was visible. Amaya shuddered. *Are you there?* she wondered.

She looked again at the damaged Nimrudite spacecraft. How had that happened? Duncan would instantly understand that *Glory* had deliberately dropped the mizzenspar on the intruder for reasons of her own. That might be so. Anya Amaya was more willing than most to accept Duncan's mystic views.

———

Was there still life aboard the ugly vessel? The Nimrudites had moved out and down into an open hatchway abaft the mainmast before the Outsider's assault. Did they have any idea of what had happened? There had been dozens of them. Anya had watched them leave their ship just before the raging horror struck.

What do we call it? Anya wondered. *We are groping for the right words. It. Outsider. Thing.* She felt a dreadful certainty that they—*Glory* and her syndics—would learn to name it long before they began to understand its nature.

And the people from Nimrud—had *Glory* offered them an open hatch to save them from *It?* They had plunged into *Glory* like lemmings. Was their destination also Hold 3100?

Amaya sat up in her open pod and reached for a drogue. She held it for a moment—drew a shivering breath, and seated it in its socket.

"Welcome home, Sailing Master," Glory said. *"There is work to do."*

The hold in which Raschad's Nimrudite force found itself enclosed a larger space than any building any of them had ever encountered. A faint light came from strands of luminescence woven into the fabric of the deck and bulkheads. Tall empty honeycombs of thin metal stood in serried rows for as far as the eye could see in the uncertain illumination.

Mohammad Raschad, accustomed either to the duststorm-ridden surface of Nimrud or to the black expanses of the Rings, was daunted by the emptiness and by the whispering sounds of air flowing through unseen ventilators.

Very nearly every human society had somewhere found a cave of the winds. Raschad recalled with a chill that the New K'uran described such a place as the antechamber to hell.

He called a halt when all of his people had passed the valve that had admitted them into this vast chamber. "Form a defensive line around the valve," he ordered, more mindful than he would ordinarily be of the need to have a clear line of retreat.

This was not what he had been seeking or expecting. The

enormity of the space left him shaken. It was difficult to believe that they were within a great ship, even though Raschad had seen the size of the Goldenwing from space.

But then the ship had stood against the dark, starry sky and the ruddy disk of Nimrud. Size required scale to judge, and against the sky any of man's works was puny, even a shining starship with wings of golden skylar.

This, now, was a different matter. Here the scale was the height of a man against a ceiling that arched up, and up into the distance until it was lost in a faint pattern of golden light like lace against another sort of dark.

The sergeant-colonel glumly stood by his side, armor faceplate hanging open. The old imam thought, *This scale, this grandeur made familiar scenes seem pointless.*

This idea could not be allowed to stand and spread among the people, Raschad thought—even as it spread in his own breast. He studied the sergeant-colonel carefully. The man was a thirty-year veteran of the regular forces. He was in every way the perfect soldier of the Collective, dedicated, brutishly brave, undoubting. Raschad tried to think of the man's name and was shocked at his inability to recall it. But men like the sergeant-colonel needed no names. His profession, title and rank defined him.

It was he who ran the labor camps, trained the military, skirmished in the Rings, mistreated recruits and civilians, and eventually died in the service of Nimrud. In some years he died for the Collective, in others he died for Marx, in still others for the K'uran.

Old Raschad looked at the sergeant-colonel and recognized himself in the other man's face. He sucked in a deep breath of very cold air. In a lifetime of service to Allah and the Council of Four, Mohammad Ali Raschad had never experienced such a powerful epiphany.

"What is it, Imam?"

Raschad composed himself. "Do you know what this place is?"

"No, Imam. I do not. It is damned cold, though," the sergeant-colonel said.

Raschad shut his eyes momentarily. It was best not to explain anything to the sergeant-colonel. He was unaccustomed to being consulted, accustomed to following orders. *We have reduced our society to the simplest common denominator,* the imam thought, *to the perfect Nimrudite man.*

But the perfect Nimrudite was uneasy. He betrayed his feeling in his posture, in his demeanor. *He needs reassurance,* Raschad thought. *They all do. We all do. We require to know that Allah is with us, that He guards us.*

The old warrior looked about with a steadily growing unease. *Am I sure? Can I be certain?*

It was growing colder and the sound of the winds was growing stronger. Where was the cave of the winds on Nimrud? He tried to remember. Traveling was not common on Nimrud. The land was too harsh, the weather too violent. But there was a cave. He remembered it from his childhood, many years before. Perhaps it was only imagination, brought on by the strangeness of this cavern that had once held thousands upon thousands of men and women in the sleep of near death.

The honeycombs dominated the vast spaces. Once there must have been machines and hoists to access the higher honeycombs, but there were none now. Only space and the sound of air moving, lamenting.

"Imam!" One of the flank guards he had ordered out came struggling toward them in free-fall. Armor was difficult without at least a token gravity. "There's movement out there—" He gestured. "There, there! Ninnie troops. Hundreds of them!"

"That's shit, trooper," the sergeant-colonel snapped. "There are no more than a dozen Ninnies on board this ship!"

Raschad was grateful for the sergeant-colonel's stolidity. He was wrong, of course; there were more than a dozen enemies on board, but that didn't matter now. They had found that for which they had come searching. He gave the order to form a skirmish line and begin the advance.

The Krasny was still fighting against the nausea of nullgrav syndrome. He allowed himself to be wedged between two troopers. It was a way of maintaining his balance and position in this insane world of free-fall.

His red-rimmed eyes never left the bulky figure of the sergeant-colonel as he went about his duties of shaping the crowd of armored men and women into a line of soldiers prepared to kill Ninnies.

The Krasny's throat closed with the effort of containing his hatred of the sergeant-colonel. The order came to close face-plates and activate body armament. He responded automatically. The sergeant-colonel had almost succeeded in making a regular soldier of Nimrud of the man called the Krasny.

Almost, but not quite.

As the Ninevites and their hostages approached the entrance to Hold 3100, Duncan looked over his shoulder at Dietr. The Cybersurgeon was genuinely frightened, but his face gave little hint of it. *Anya and Broni and the others can do without me,* Duncan thought, *but Dietr is essential to the safety and health of the crew, irreplaceable.* Mira purred reassuringly. He hoped her faith in *Glory* was well founded.

He led the way through the forward valve. As he entered the hold he glanced longingly at the closed safety compartment in the plenum. He dare not touch it. Instead, he moved through the valve into the hold and stood for a moment looking at the cavernous interior. Even for a syndic, it was difficult to believe that this place was but one—albeit the last—of *Glory*'s stasis holds. There were more than a dozen valves opening into Hold 3100. Not one of them had been open in years.

How many years? Duncan wondered. *For me, not since I was an apprentice, newly Wired, fresh from Chalkmeer, on the gray sea-world of Thalassa.* He had come to this hold alone, testing his courage kilometers from the bridge where the other syndics lay conning the ship through the Hubble Cluster near Procyon, twenty light-years from Earth in exactly the opposite direction from the Ross stars.

Had the air sounded like wind then? *Surely not,* he thought, *or I would have fled to the company of my elders.*

———

"You are smiling, Your Honor," Ekaterina Volkova said at his side. "It is comforting to know you are able."

"I was remembering," Duncan said.

"You have not been here for a long while?"

"Years."

The Ninevite troopers were deploying themselves in some sort of fighting alignment. Was this what *Glory* intended? Did it make any sense at all to ask such a question?

The cat on his shoulder corrected him as if he were her kitten.

Yes, Mira. She is the-great-queen-who-is-not-alive—

Remarkable, Duncan thought. Communication. Man and cat in communion. Induced mental symbiosis. *Glory*'s doing.

The cat purred and pushed her head against his.

"It seems fond of you, Captain," the Ninevite woman said.

"Her name is Mira," Duncan said, caressing the cat. "Her people were gods in Egypt."

Kat removed a glove and extended a hand. Mira sniffed at it suspiciously.

"They don't give trust easily," Kat said ruefully, and redonned her armored glove. "What is that sound? Like wind."

"It is wind. Of a sort. The ventilators. The nearest is up there." Duncan signalled the light-laced heights.

"Far from here?"

"Three kilometers to the center overhead."

Ekaterina looked with interest at the tiers upon tiers of honeycombs. "I had no idea," she said.

"These combs were once filled with religious refugees for Planet Aldrin," Duncan said. "It was *Glory*'s only colonial voyage. She left Earth in 2198." He smiled wearily. "Downtime," he finished.

"Of course," she said with an answering smile. For an instant they were almost friends. "I had forgotten that Starmen live forever."

30

A SHORT BATTLE IN A LONG WAR

The scout who had reported to the imam had spread his news through the entire Nimrudite force. Within minutes every man and woman knew that the enemy was somewhere on the hectares of deck that lay ahead. There was no information on his strength or deployment, but a dark anger seemed to have penetrated into the marrow of the Nimmie contingent. The only heavy weapon they had brought from the surface was irretrievably lost together with its crew, but the expedition bristled with lazeguns and stun grenades. The depression that had settled over the force while moving with such difficulty through the narrow fabric tubes within the accursed Goldenwing appeared to be—if not actually lifting—then changing into a resolve and discipline that was more in keeping with soldiers of the Collective.

The conditions within the echoing cavern of the hold troubled Mohammad Raschad. This was not the battlefield he had imagined it would be. At the back of his mind, hidden there among his less military and self-disciplined thoughts, the old man always carried a particular image into battle.

In the legends of the Second Aliyah there lived a tale of a fountain in Paradise, a fountain that ran red with the blood of martyrs. It was said that in this fountain dead heroes would bathe, and they would be renewed as young warriors ready again to partake of that holiest of vocations, the Jihad.

Raschad knew that his thought was a dream and that dream a fantasy. There was no Fountain of the Martyrs. There would never be the renewing warmth of the blood of heroes. But to know something intellectually was one thing. To believe it with the heart was something else. So each journey into battle began with a refurbishing of the imam's secret wish.

Yet this time—this *time,* he thought—*might be different.* Raschad wished that he could unfurl the green battle flag of the Prophet, but these were degenerate times. Recurrences were fought on different terms nowadays, and without banners or glory.

The force of Nimrudites could now float free of the deck and use the thrusters in their armor to advance. Through the dimness and flowing between the tall, empty honeycombs, the force advanced into the center of the vast hold.

The Krasny looked about him with amazement. The deck over which they were advancing was as big as a grassland. *How much area did it actually cover?* he wondered. More than a hundred hectares, perhaps much more. Once, lifetimes ago, colonists more dead than alive in their cold-sleep were stacked in this place like cordwood. Now there was only emptiness and the soughing of the wind.

For weeks the Krasny had been the butt of the sergeant-colonel's tyranny. He had a feeling that would end soon now.

He looked ahead, past the ranks of armored figures lumbering foward on their thrusters. He knew what would happen. When the enemy was sighted, the first suicidal duty would become the task of the Krasny. Soldiers saw redemption in that sort of sacrifice. But there was no fear left in the Krasny. Beginning with the horrible exercises, leaping into space from a shuttle, snatching at a narrow deck or a bit of wreckage salvaged from some ruin of a spacecraft, the sergeant-colonel had systematically crushed and squeezed the fear from the Krasny. He remembered the day of his meeting with Yuri Vukasin in Nostromograd. He had killed a dozen civilians with explosives that day and he had been proud and exhilarated by his success. He wondered if Simon Egonov were still alive and leading a bombers' cell of Gammah. It all seemed so very long ago. He, himself, had lost a wife to the secret police of Nineveh, but that event, too, was misty—as though it had happened a lifetime ago.

Somewhere on this monster starship there was a Ninnie shuttle and aboard that was probably a full pod of Ninevite politicians. Yuri Vukasin, to be sure.

Would he even recognize his fellow plotter of only a few months ago? *Everything had changed,* the Krasny thought. *Everything had changed because of a crude bull of a soldier who needed badly to be killed.*

Buele reached the drogue storage nearest a high valve to Hold 3100. He held up his hand to arrest Broni and opened the compartment. It seemed to him that he could hear—no, *sense*—the near presence of Mira, and through her, Duncan. Was that possible? *Yes,* he thought as he uncoiled the drogue, *it was not only possible, it was what was happening.*

"Mira is close by, Sister Broni," he said softly.

"Is Duncan?"

"Yes, I think he is. Wait." He connected the drogue to the socket concealed in his hair. Instantly, the Sailing Master spoke to him: *"Buele, where have you been? No, never mind that. Are you at Hold 3100?"*

"Yes, Sister Anya. I can hear Sister Mira nearby. She is with Duncan."

"Where is Broni?"

"Here, Sister Anya. Here beside me."

"Is there another drogue?"

"No, Sister Anya. Do you want me to give this one to Broni?"

"No. But keep her by you. You will need her help when we try to revive Duncan and the doctor."

"Try, Anya?"

"The systems have not been used for years, Buele. Are there masks in the compartment?"

"Yes, Anya. Old ones."

"They will have to do. Explain to Broni."

"There's no other way?"

"No. We are too few. Stay where you are until I give you instructions."

Buele disconnected from the drogue and took masks from the compartment. The masks had been intended for the original syndics should it have become necessary to enter the colonists' hold. The packaging crackled with age, but the masks seemed intact. Buele connected the re-breathers and handed a mask to Broni.

"Try it, Sister Broni," the boy said. "It had better work."

On the bridge, Anya sent an instruction through the computer: *"Begin now, Damon. We can't tell how long it will take."*

"Anya—"

"The drogue, Damon. And do as I tell you now."

Damon thought he caught a mental glimpse of Mira, and through her Duncan and Dietr. But he could not be sure. His empathic talent lacked definition.

Not a religious young man, Damon still prayed to the tree-god of his forested home planet.

The Krasny heard the first alarm through the com-net. A flank guard had seen a shadow and the shadow had been a Ninevite Territorial in armor.

A laze bolt burned a streak in the semidarkness, struck the edge of a honeycomb and exploded into a shower of sparks and molten metal.

There was a tang of ozone coming through the filters of the Krasny's armor. The smell of it had a curiously tranquilizing effect on him. He filled his lungs and reeled dizzily through space, his suit out of control. It was a thing that should have filled him with terror—to be out of control while armored and in battle was, he had been told a thousand times in the last months, the worst thing that could befall.

It was the Ninevites, he thought wildly. After all this they had an advantage, a weapon. All around him he could see soldiers drifting limply, spinning helplessly in the currents of wind from the invisible ventilators.

His fear and suppressed anger spilled over. This could not be the end of it. He had suffered too much and too often. He rolled upright and unlimbered his lazegun. While he was still able, he would burn these decks and bulkheads to molten droplets. He would become a cancer in the gut of this monster ship that had devoured them all—

"You! Krasny! Move forward, you sucking coward—"

Though he was staggering from the effects of the Ninnie weapon, the sergeant-colonel still managed to torment the former terrorist.

Nullgrav syndrome knotted the Krasny's diaphragm and he vomited the remnants of his last meal. The horrid droplets moved languidly through the odd-smelling air, spattered on the sergeant-colonel's open facemask. The burly soldier uttered a curse and struck the Krasny across the face.

The Krasny was suddenly consumed with a red, raging hatred for the sergeant-colonel. Around him his companions were doubling up with unaccountable spasms. The Krasny leveled his lazegun and slashed the red beam across the sergeant-colonel's throat. Blood spewed from severed arteries, head and helmet spun away to rebound from a nearby honeycomb. And the Krasny felt a consuming fire burn through his belly and chest, his groin and legs. He exploded into charred fragments of flesh and melted metal.

Around him men and women screamed. The hold was filled with an overwhelming presence of terror. Brilliant swirls of light quested through the chilling air. As though struck by an unseen fist, armored soldiers recoiled and were sent spinning in the null gravity.

Mira leaped from Duncan's shoulder onto a towering honeycomb and stood there, spraddled-legged, fur risen, tail erect and stiff as a bottle brush. She bared her tiny fangs and shrieked defiance. A shimmering bolt sought her, surrounded her, but checked and fled from her. Mira screamed with feral angry victory.

Duncan, like all the others, was stunned by the onslaught. He was touched by needles of fire seeking the core of his life. The temperature in the hold plunged, the winds blew more powerfully, laden with chemicals.

———

No, Duncan thought, *by all that's holy, no!* To surrender consciousness now would be to succumb to the questing power, whatever it might be.

But awareness was slipping away. *Cold-sleep,* Duncan thought, *Glory is killing us with cold-sleep.* . . .

The wildly searching force seemed suddenly less powerful. It was familiar now, as though it were gradually slipping away into— What? To where?

Mira reappeared on his shoulder. He could feel her heartbeat, but she was no longer snarling. Her fur felt warm against his neck, and still the temperature dropped. Ekaterina Volkova hung in the air near him. She had closed the face-plate of her armor, but it had not kept the air of the Cave of the Winds from her.

Duncan felt awareness slipping away. *Will we awaken, Mira?* he asked. *And if we do, where will we be? And* when *will we be?* The small queen murmured reassuringly and anchored firmly to his skinsuit, closed her eyes and slept.

Broni and Buele, in the plenum immediately outside of Hold 3100, had seen the energy flowing through the fabric of the plenum. *If terror has a color,* Broni thought, *we have seen it.* Neither she nor Buele had been Wired. Had the attack caught *Glory* by surprise?

But what stunned the girl was the sudden appearance of a half dozen of Mira's pride. They had almost materialized out of nowhere, their hair-thin drogues bobbing, their coats on end, their ears flattened as if for battle.

Three cats fastened themselves to the girl's skinsuit, three to Buele. Instantly Broni felt the presence of *Glory.* The contact was different from the material-electronic interface she had grown accustomed to using. Now it was a warm, animal contact that brought with it a myriad impressions: *the taste of strong food, the comfort of sleeping next to Mira, the joy of leaping through nullgrav space, the pleasure of savage sex.*

And commands from the-great-queen-who-is-not-alive— Urgency.

The people in the hold could not be allowed to sink into total cold-sleep. Conditions were not right. They might never awake.

But the calm—

The calm was needed—

The balm of sleep kept the terror at bay—

One of the young males was very explicit. She felt his hunger to hunt the terror—

"Can you *understand them, Broni?*" Part of the message was audible, part was transmitted through their feline interfaces.

"Yes, Buele, I understand—"

Buele handed her one of the masks he had removed from the old compartment near the valve. *"Put it on. No matter what you see, be still, be at peace—"*

One by one the cats detached themselves and vanished.

"Why?" Broni called out.

Buele looked at her through the ancient, dimmed plastic of the mask over his face and she understood him. Even in this situation the wonder of it stunned her. Empathy had become telepathy. Buele was *that* Talented. *They are too angry,* he thought. For a moment she allowed herself envy, but Buele stopped her. *"Be careful. You can bring it back, too,"* he sent.

They slipped through the valve into the hold and closed it behind them. Ninevite soldiers lay everywhere, drifting.

"Oh, God!" Broni said. "Are they dead?"

"Some of them are, but not all. Find Duncan and Mira."

Broni fought to control her emotions. Whatever *it* was, strong emotion attracted it, fed it.

"Look at them—"

"Never mind how they look, Broni," Buele said, his voice muffled by the ancient mask he wore. "Find our people."

"Dietr! There's Dietr."

"Help me with him," Buele commanded.

The Voertrekker girl and Buele bent over the Cybersurgeon, administering stimulants from the ancient cache in the plenum. "We have to get them out quickly."

"I don't care if these others ever get out," Broni said. All about them Ninevite bodies floated, encased in armor. Some dead. Most alive.

Buele said, "He's reviving. Help me move him into the plenum."

They left Dietr anchored to the deck and suddenly surrounded by returned cats.

Back inside the hold, the boy and girl searched among the still bodies.

"Here, Buele! I've found Duncan."

Tears formed in her eyes behind the mask. On Duncan's chest an unconscious Mira still held him with her foreclaws.

When they had moved man and cat back through the valve, Buele found the drogue in the emergency compartment and Wired himself to *Glory*.

For Broni's benefit, he spoke to the syndics on the bridge aloud. "We have them, Sailing Master. All three. *Glory* has won her first battle."

31

ICE

There was no sun shining through the overcast, not even a slight ruddiness. Broni's calculations had predicted that the sky over this land of rock and ice would not be clear before the vernal equinox—if then.

On the ice where two of *Glory*'s shuttles rested, still steaming from the heat of entry, the temperature stood at minus twenty degrees Celsius. By nightfall it would be twenty degrees colder. Ninevites and Nimrudites stood in two formations, weaponless and supplied with Centaurian arctic gear a hundred years out of date but still serviceable.

The former soldiers stamped their feet and breathed out clouds of steam as they regarded their surroundings with sullen distaste. Duncan stood by the flank of one of the blind shuttles, Dietr at his side. He regarded the new colonists with interest.

"We have landed the nuclear generators we carried for Nimrud," he said. "You will not lack for power or heat."

One of the troopers from Nimrud said angrily, "You do intend to maroon us then."

"I do," said Duncan.

Ekaterina Volkova, standing with her disarmed soldiers, regarded Duncan intently. "What right have you?" she demanded.

"In time you will discover it," Duncan said. "Or not. That will be up to you."

"Where are we?" The question came from Yuri Vukasin, bulky in his cast-off Centaurian polar wear.

"You will find yourselves when—and if—the sky clears." Since awakening the cold-sleepers Duncan had taken a dislike to Vukasin. He hoped the "colony" would not suffer for having him among the people. *But I didn't aim at perfection,* Duncan thought. *Only survival.*

There was no use avoiding the subject. It was the most important topic these men and women must ever learn about. It was swift life and death to them.

"When you fought in the Cave of the Winds," he said, "one of yours"—he indicated the stoic figure of Mohammad Ali Raschad and his shivering troopers—"chose to attack and kill one of his own officers." He raised his hands to forestall any protest or comment. This was no time to defend military pride. "Why he chose to do such a thing I neither know nor care. What I do know and care about was that the act of killing summoned a power—" He shook his head. "No, not supernatural. So far we can only guess at its nature. But it thrives on anger and fear. On strong emotions. I once thought it—or they, whatever they are—followed us, followed *Glory.* I am not sure of that now, but we shall see. I think *It* is drawn to this region of space because of *you.*"

The assembled soldiers of both Nineveh and Nimrud protested angrily.

Duncan stared them down. "Centuries of war. Never-ending anger. This is a feeding ground for *It,* I think. Or possibly a place where it hunts." He looked from one to another. "For sport. It may be a matter of *orgotish,*" he said ironically.

His voice hardened. "Maybe I think this because you—all of you—have done the worst possible thing human colonists could do. You have forgotten your mutual human ancestry and you have fought wars against one another. And now you have involved *us.* This is unforgivable." When he spoke he looked directly at Ekaterina, at Yuri Vukasin, at Mohammad Ali Raschad. "For this as much as for any other crime, you must be punished, and so you will be."

"What gives you the right—" Yuri Vukasin began.

"My kind brought you into space," Duncan said. "My kind can move you on."

"That is not righteous," the Imam Raschad said forcefully. "The Holy K'uran says—"

"Your holy books say many things," Duncan said. "When you learn to live by them then quote me scripture."

The politician Vukasin glared at Duncan Kr. "What is this place? When will you return us to our homes? We have battles to fight, a Recurrence to win."

Duncan raised his eyes to the low, ice-laden clouds. In the south they touched the glaciers. In the north, the ice-blue horizon. *There is no better place than here for these people,* Duncan thought.

He said, "This place is what you make it. We have given you the means to shelter yourselves, the power to run machines and feed yourselves. Now there is one thing more. The thing that killed so many is still up there, beyond those clouds. Distance has no meaning to it. You would do well to remember what it can do."

The assembly muttered angrily. Duncan continued relentlessly. "Live together, work together, and—when the time comes—if it comes—*fight* together."

Explosive anger swept the assembled soldiers. There were shouts and name-calling. Duncan looked at Ekaterina Volkova. She was regarding him with a curious calm.

Duncan referred to a roster *Glory* had prepared. "Massoud Bokhara," he said, "you are the senior member of the Ninevites. Mohammad Ali Raschad, you lead the Nimrudites. On Earth, many centuries ago, people with names very like yours had a chance to become one people. They chose otherwise and men have been dying ever since. You may try or not—as you choose."

Ekaterina Volkova said quietly. "You judge us."

"Yes. There is no one else here to do it."

"Must it be done?"

"You were in the Cave of the Winds," Duncan said. "Only the cold-sleep saved us. There is a message there, I think." He turned back to address the two elders. "You consider yourselves men of god. I think it may even be the same god. That is for you to decide. You can separate your people as the people of Earth did long ago, or you can join forces. The choice belongs to you all. But remember what happened in the *Khomeini* and in the Cave of the Winds and why it happened.''

Vukasin stepped forward again. It was remarkable how swiftly men such as he adjusted to the situation. God help these people if they choose him to lead this ragtag company.

''Where are our spacecraft?'' Vukasin asked. ''We are not primitive people.''

''We might argue that point, Ephor,'' Duncan said. ''But your craft are in high orbit. One day you might possibly cooperate to reclaim them. That is not up to me. My duty is to give all of you a chance to survive. I have done that.'' *And the decision was not one easily come by,* he thought. *I am not a saint, after all.*

He looked into a sea of troubled faces. Ekaterina Volkova moved closer to the cleric Mornay. *Was that a foreordained couple?* Duncan wondered. It seemed so. Better the cleric than the politician.

This was a difficult group, Duncan thought. Ethnically similar, they were separated by wide schisms of religion and belief. *Wherever we go,* Duncan told himself, *we repeat the history of the mother planet.* For a moment he considered asking himself by what right he played god with these people. But there was no Prime Directive, no injunction from on high not to interfere with colonial societies. *We do our best,* Duncan thought. *That is all that can be expected of us.*

Wasn't the Sharia once the Law of Islam on Earth? Time and distance changed and shifted men's beliefs, but no matter how similar, no matter that they sprang from the same soil, men could find cause to fight. *Perhaps,* Duncan thought, *we were always destined by our very nature to meet the Terror.*

Another of the Ninevites, a young survivor of the carnage in the warship from Nimrud, had joined Ekaterina Volkova. The resemblance between them identified him as the quondam colonel's brother.

This one had seen the Terror at very close range. He had

cooperated willingly with Dietr. Together with the girl taken with him, he had gone into cold-sleep to join his countrymen and had awakened here on what the castaways were beginning to call "Ice."

Duncan signalled for Damon to prepare the shuttles for a return to *Glory*. A hot plasma began to form around the shuttle engines. Ice melted and puddled under the spacecraft.

Volkova stood near Duncan and said quietly, "You have no right to do this. But I thank you for it."

She knows, Duncan thought. *She knows exactly where she is and how long she must remain here. She* is their true hope. He was reminded of Broni's mother on faraway Voerster. There were similarities between the two women.

"Perhaps we may meet again," Ekaterina Volkova said.

"Perhaps." It was the Starman's lie, spoken again and again across the sky. If ever *Glory* returned here, it would be centuries hence. The Einsteinian paradox ruled the Goldenwings.

But one day, *some*day, if and when the Terror is tamed—?

Duncan mounted the ceramic-coated, scarred nose of the shuttle and entered the flight compartment. He raised his hand in salute and sealed the hatch.

The castaways, resentful to the last, backed away unwillingly. The slaved shuttle, empty now, moved forward and took flight, leaving a deep track in the snow and ice. When it had vanished into the dark overcast, the shuttle containing the Starmen repeated the process. Ninevite and Nimrudite watched it go with sullen anger.

For the first time since taking aboard the unwilling pilgrims, Duncan opened the forward ports of the shuttle. At the moment the craft was slashing through the icy, south polar cloud cap. At 200,000 meters both shuttles burst from the darkness and into a cobalt-blue tropopause. Below lay the blue, pelagic planet of Nineveh. Save for the thick cloud cap over the south continent, the sky was brilliant and free of disturbances.

Glory's shuttles, in line astern now, reached Mach 1 and sent sonic booms rolling and crashing along the surface of a huge tidal bulge. In the rapidly darkening sky of space the planet's twin companion began to eclipse the ruddy sun.

"What will happen to them, Duncan?" asked Damon.

"They will have a season to learn to live together and teach it to their people, or they won't and they will die. It is not a joy to play god, Damon," Duncan said.

Duncan looked at the planet below. A green island continent was rising above the distant horizon. Grasslands and mountains, rivers and high plains. Ararat.

He remembered that seeing it for the first time it had reminded him of his homeworld, gray Thalassa. But far, far more favored by nature. Perhaps that will make the difference, he thought.

He picked up a microphone and spoke into it as *Glory*'s first captain must have done twelve hundred years ago after delivering their colonists to Aldrin.

"*Glory*, this is the Master and Commander. Stand by to take us aboard."